All in all, there are about sixty races whose Confinement Mazes—the routes that lead from their home system to nearby planets—are known and mapped. Put all these together, and you get one big Maze, strewn out over several spiral arms. But there is more to discover. Every once in a while, a new race drops into this neck of the woods and stops to be sociable. More information is then acquired, but the process is slow.

"Tell me. Where does the Skyway end?" I asked.

"At the beginning of the universe."

I drained the last of my sickly sweet drink. "Is there a good motel there?"

Jerry laughed. "Jake, you know how these whoppers get started. Alien booze in human stomachs. Accidental chemically induced insanity."

STARRIGGER

JOHN DeCHANCIE

STARRIGGER

An Ace Science Fiction Book/published by arrangement with the author

PRINTING HISTORY
Ace Original/December 1983

Cover art by James Gurney

ISBN: 0-441-78304-X

Ace Science Fiction Books are published by The Berkley Publishing Group, 200 Madison Avenue, New York, New York 10016.
PRINTED IN THE UNITED STATES OF AMERICA

For Holly,
who stood by me
through the Seven Lean Years

For assistance and encouragement,
special thanks to John Alfred Taylor,
il miglior fabbro.

1

I FIRST PICKED her up on Tau Ceti II. At least I'm fairly sure that was the first time. Depends on how you look at it.

She was last in the usual line of starhikers thumbing near the Skyway on-ramp to the Epsilon Eridani aperture. Tall, with short dark hair, wearing a silver Allclyme survival suit that tried to hide her figure but ultimately failed, she was demurely holding her UV parasol up against Tau's eye-narrowing glare, her thumb cocked downroad in that timeless gesture. She was smiling irresistibly, confidently, knowing damn well she'd get scooped up by the first male driver whose endocrine system was on line that day. Mine was, and she knew that too.

"What d'you think?" I asked Sam. He usually had opinions on these matters. "A skyhooker?"

He scanned her for a microsecond or two. "Nah. Too pretty."

"You have some old-fashioned ideas. But then, you always did."

"Going to pick her up?"

I braked and started to answer, but as we passed, the smile

faded a little and her eyebrows lowered questioningly, as if she thought she recognized me. The expression was only half-completed before we flew past. That made it definite. I braked hard, eased the rig onto the shoulder, pulled to a stop, and waited, watching her through the side-view parabolic as she hoofed it up to us.

"Something?" Sam asked.

"Uh . . . don't know. Do you recognize her?"

"Nope."

I rubbed the stubble on my chin. I seem never to be clean-shaven when it counts. "You figure she's trouble?"

"A woman that good-looking is always trouble. And if you think that's an outdated notion, wipe off the backs of your ears and wise up."

I took a deep breath, equalized the cab pressure and popped the passenger-side hatch. Out in the desert it was quiet, and her approaching footsteps were muffled in the thin air. She was a good distance back, since I usually roar by starhikers to intimidate them. Some tend to get aggressive, pulling cute stunts like stepping right out in front of you and flagging you down. A while back, I smeared one such enterprising gentleman over a half-klick of road. The Colonial cops took my report, told me I was a bad boy, and warned me not to do it again, or at least not on their beat.

I heard her puff up to the cab and mount the ladder up the side. Her head popped up above the seat, and a fetching head it was. Dark blue eyes, clear fair skin, high cheekbones, and general fashion-model symmetry. A face you don't see every day, one I'd thought didn't exist except in the electron-brushed fantasies of glamour photographers. Her makeup was light, but expertly effective. I was sure I'd never seen her before, but what she said was, "I *thought* it was you!" She took off her clear plastic assist mask and shook her head wonderingly. "My God, I never expected . . ." She trailed off and shrugged. "Well, come to think of it, I guess it was inevitable as long as I stayed on the Skyway." She smiled.

I smiled back. "You like this atmosphere?"

"Huh? Oh, sorry." She climbed in and closed the hatch. "It is kind of thin and ozoney." She folded up the parasol the rest of the way, struggled out of her combo backpack-respirator and put it between her knees on the deck, then opened it and stashed the brolly inside. "You should try to stand out there for a couple of hours bareheaded. Trouble is"—she pulled up the hood on her suit—"if you wear this, nobody knows what you look like."

Indeed. I gunned the engine and pulled onto the ramp. We rode along in silence until we swung out onto the Skyway. I goosed the plasma flow and soon the rig was clipping along at 100 meters/sec or so. Ahead, the Skyway was a black ribbon racing across ocher sand straight toward its vanishing point on the horizon. It would be about an hour's drive to the next set of tollbooths. The sky was violet and clear, as it usually was on TC-II. I had a pretty woman riding shotgun, and I felt reasonably good about things, even though Sam and I expected trouble on this run. Except for the present puzzle of why she was acting as if we knew each other, when I was sure we didn't, everything was cruising along just fine. The way she was looking at me made me a little self-conscious, though, but I waited for her to take the lead. I was playing this one strictly by ear.

Finally she said, "I expected a couple of possible reactions, but silence wasn't one of them."

I checked the bow scanners, then gave the conn to Sam. He took over the controls and acknowledged.

She turned to Sam's eye on the dash and waved. "Hi, Sam," she said. "Long time no see, and all that."

"How's it going?" he answered. "Nice to see you again." Sam knew the tune.

I eased the captain chair back, and turned sideways on the seat. "What *did* you expect?" I asked her.

"Well, first maybe pleasant conversation, then a little acrimony seeping out. From your end, of course."

"Acrimony? From me?" I frowned. "Why?"

She was puzzled. "I guess I really don't know." She turned her head slowly and looked out the port, watching the desert roll by. I studied the back of her head. Presently, without looking back, she said, "Weren't you at all . . . put out when I disappeared on you like that?"

I thought I detected a note of disappointment, but wasn't sure. Letting about 1000 meters go by before answering, I said carefully, "I was, but I got over it. I knew you were a free being." I hoped it sounded good.

Another good stretch of Skyway scooted under us and I got this out of her: "I missed you. I really did. But I had my reasons for just upping and leaving. I'm sorry if it seemed inconsiderate." She bit her lip and looked at me tentatively, trying to gauge my mood. She didn't get much of a clue, and gave it up. "I'm sorry," she said with a little self-deprecating laugh. "I guess 'inconsiderate' doesn't quite cover it. Callous is more like it."

"You never seemed the callous sort," I improvised. "I'm sure your reasons were valid." I put it a bit more archly than I had intended.

"Still, I probably should have written you." She turned her head quickly to me and chuckled. "Except you have no address."

"There's always the Guild office."

"Last time I saw your desk it was a six-meter-high pile of unanswered mail with legs."

"I've never been a clean-desk man. Congenital aversion to paperwork."

"Well, still. . . ." She seemed at a loss as to how to proceed with the conversation from that point. I didn't have the vaguest idea how to help her, so I got up and said I was going to put on some coffee. She declined the offer.

I went into the aft cabin, got the brewer working, then sat at the tiny breakfast nook and thought about it for a good while.

"Seems like we done did us a Timer, son," Sam whispered in my ear over the hush circuit. *"Or I should say, we're going to do one."*

"Yeah," I mumbled. I was still thinking. A paradox presents you with few options—or an infinity of them if you look at it another way. Any way I looked at it, I didn't like it. I spent a good while back in the cabin doing that, not liking it. In fact, I didn't realize how long until Sam's voice came over the cabin speaker. "Tollbooths coming up."

I went back to the cab and buckled myself into the driver's seat. The woman was curled up in one of the rear seats with her eyes closed, but she opened them as I was strapping in. I told her to do the same. She came forward to the shotgun seat and obeyed.

"Got it, Sam," I said. "Give me a closing speed."

"One-one-two-point-six-niner-three meters per second."

"Check. Let's get some round numbers on the readout and make it easy."

"Can do," Sam said cheerily. "Coming up on one one five . . . now! Nope. Little more . . . steady. Okay, locked in. One one five, steady!"

"Right." I could see the tollbooths now—"Kerr-Tipler objects" is what they're formally called, though there are many names for them—titanic dark cylinders thrust up against the sky like an array of impossibly huge grain silos lying along the road, some almost five kilometers high.

"Six kilometers and closing," Sam said. "On track."

"Check." Signs were coming up. I signaled for English.

APPROACHING EINSTEIN-ROSEN BRIDGE APERTURE

PORTAL #564 INTERSTELLAR ROUTE 80 to EPSILON ERIDANI I

DANGER! EXTREME TIDAL FORCES!

MAP AHEAD—STOP IF UNCERTAIN

The map—a big oblong of blue-painted metal sticking out of the sand—looked new and obtrusive, as did the roadsigns, so obviously not an artifact of the ancient race that built the Skyway. The Roadbuilders didn't believe in signs . . . or maps. We rolled on toward the aperture. I looked over to check if our passenger had strapped herself in correctly. She had. A veteran of the road. Sam kept reading out our speed as I kept the rig trimmed for entry. Another series of signs came up.

WARNING—APPROACHING COMMIT POINT

MAINTAIN CONSTANT SPEED

EXTREME DANGER! DO NOT STOP BEYOND COMMIT POINT

"Right in the slot," Sam said. "Everything's green for entry."

"Check." The flashing red commit markers shot past and we were in the middle of a gravitational tug-of-war between the spinning cylinders of collapsed matter which created the E-R bridge. They heaved past, towering black monoliths spaced at various intervals alongside the road, their bases hovering a few centimeters off the crushed earth, all different sizes, invisibly spinning at unimaginable speeds. The trick was to keep your velocity constant so that the cylinders could balance out the conflicting tidal stresses they generated. If you slowed or speeded up, you were in danger of getting a head bounced off the roof or a port. Worse, you could overturn, or lose control and go off the road altogether. In either case, there'd be nothing left of you to send back to the folks but some squashed nucleons and a puff of degenerate electron gas, and it's hard to find the right size box for those.

At the end of the line of cylinders there was a patch of fuzzy blackness, a kind of nothing-space. We dove into it.

And got through. The desert was gone and we were flying over road that cut through dense green jungle under a low and leaden sky. We had a 500-kilometer stretch until we hit Mach City, where I had planned to stop for a sleeper. Sam took over and I settled back.

"By the way," Sam whispered, *her name's Darla. Talked to her a bit while you were brooding aft. Told her I'd been flushed and reprogrammed, didn't have her name in my banks anymore."*

I nodded. "So," I said, turning to her, "how's life been treating you, Darla?"

She smiled warmly, and those perfect white teeth brightened up the cab. "Jake," she said, "dear Jake. You're going to think I'm getting even with you for clamming up all that time back there . . . but I'm beat to hell. Would you mind awfully if I went back and tried to catch up on sleep?"

"Hell, no. Be my guest." That was that.

"You stopping at Mach City? We'll talk over dinner. OK?"

"Sure."

She batted long eyelashes at me for a second, flashing her supernova-bright grin, but I could see a shadow of uncertainty behind it all, as if she were entertaining doubts about who I was. She was obviously at a loss to explain my strange behavior. It's almost impossible to fake knowing someone when you don't, or more often, when you've met someone and don't remember. Awkward situations at cocktail parties. But in this case I definitely knew I had never seen her before. But the doubts were momentary. She blew me a kiss in one hell of an ingratiating way and went aft.

And left me to watch the scenery and ruminate.

"Well, buddy—?" Sam meant for me to fill in the blank.

"I don't know. Just don't know, Sam."

"She could be a plant."

I considered it. "No. Wilkes is subtle enough to concoct a yarn like that, but he wouldn't go to all that bother."

"Still . . ." Sam wasn't sure.

"She's giving a very convincing performance if she is." I yawned. "I'm going to wink out, too." I eased back the chair and closed my eyes.

I didn't sleep, just thought about times past and time future, about life on the Skyway. I may have dozed off for a few minutes now and then, but there was too much to chew over. Most of what went through my head isn't worth repeating; just the usual roadbuzz. Anyway, it killed about an hour. Then the sign for Mach City whizzed by, and I took back the controls.

2

SONNY'S MOTEL AND Restaurant is just off the road to the Groombridge 34 portal. It's rather luxurious, in an upholstered-sewerish kind of way, but the rates are relatively cheap, and the food is good. I pulled into the lot and scrammed the engine. It looked like it was early morning, local time. I woke Darla up and told Sam to mind the store while we tried to get something to eat. The lot was crammed and I anticipated a long wait for a table. Along with the usual assortment of rigs, there were private ground vehicles in the lot, all makes and models, mostly alien-built. On Skyway, the transportation market had been cornered long ago by a handful of races, at least in this part of the galaxy, and competition was stiff for human outfits trying to wedge in.

I paused to look Sam over. We had pulled in next to a rig of Ryxxian make, a spanking new one with an aerodynamic cowling garishly decaled in gilt filigree. A custom job, a little too showy for my taste, but it made Sam look sick, bedecked as he was in road grime, impact microcraters, a botched original emulsicoat that was coming off in flakes around his stabilizer foils, and a few dents here and there. His left-front roller sported crystallization patches all over, its variable-traction capacity just about shot. I'd been collecting spot-inspection tags on it for a good while, had a charming nosegay of them by now, courtesy of the Colonial Militia, with the promise of more lovelies yet to come. They do brighten up a glovebox.

We went into the restaurant, and sure enough, there was a god-awful long wait. Darla and I didn't have much to say while we waited; too many people about. I was almost ready to leave when the robo-hostess came for us and showed us to a booth by the window, my favorite spot in any beanery.

Things were looking up until I spotted Wilkes with a few of his "assistants" in a far corner. They had an alien with them, a Reticulan—a Snatchganger, if I knew my Reticulans. Rikkitikkis like humans especially. We have such sensitive nerve endings, you know, and scream most satisfactorily. If he had been alone (I knew it was a male, because his pheromones reached across the room, hitting my nose as a faint whiff of turpentine and almonds), he wouldn't have lasted two minutes here or anywhere on any human world. They are free to travel the Skyway, as is any race. But they are not welcome off-road in the Terran Maze, nor are they loved in many other regions of the galaxy.

But he was with Corey Wilkes, undoubtedly on business, which afforded him some immunity. Nobody was looking at them but me and Darla. Wilkes caught sight of me, smiled, and waved as if we were at a church picnic. I gave him my best toothflash and stuck my nose in the menu.

"What are you having, Darla? It's on me."

"Let me buy you dinner once. I've been working lately."

"This is breakfast." After a moment, I took the opportunity to ask, "What have you been doing?"

"For the last month, waitressing to keep body and soul together. Before that, singing, as usual. Saloons, nightclubs. I had a really good group behind me, lots of gigs, but they threw me over for a new chanteuse. Kept my arrangements and left me with the motel tab on Xi Boo III."

"Nice." The waiter came and we ordered.

There were a few other aliens in the place. A Beta Hydran was slurping something viscous in the next booth with a human companion. Most restaurants on Skyway cater to alien trade, and that includes alien road facilities with regard to human customers. But the air of resentment against the Reticulan was palpable.

I looked around for familiar faces. Besides Wilkes, I spied Red Shaunnessey over in the corner with his partner, Pavel Korolenko. Shaunnessey winked at me. Red was vice-president of TATOO once, but came over to us when he had had enough of Wilkes. Some Guild members still distrusted him, but he had been a big help in the early days of the Guild's struggle. The fight wasn't over yet. We were still trying to wean drivers away from Wilkes when it was easier—and safer—for them to keep their mouths glued to TATOO's bloated tit. I also saw Gil Tomasso and Su-Gin Chang, but they weren't looking in my direction. They were well off their usual route. A special run. Looking around again, I thought I saw a familiar face at a table near Wilkes and company, a tall, thin, patrician gentleman with a mane of white hair, but I couldn't place him. I had the feeling I knew his face from the news feeds. Probably a middle-to-upper-level Authority bureaucrat on an inspection junket.

By the time the food came, the edge had come off my appetite. If I had had any sense, I would have walked out at the first sight of Wilkes, and no one would have blamed me. But there's a primal territoriality in us all. Why should I leave? Why not him?

Red got up and came over. I introduced him to Darla, and I thought I caught a speck of recognition in his eyes. He declined a cup of sourbean, a native brew that tastes nothing like coffee and faintly like a mixture of cinnamon and iodine. He lit one of his nasty-looking cigars.

"Trouble, Jake," he said. "Trouble all over the starslab."

I picked at my eggs Eridani. "This I know. Anything new?"

"Marty DiFlippo."

"What about her?"

"Just came over the skyband. She hit the tollbooths on Barnard's II."

That hurt. I had known Marty well—a good woman, good driver. She could pilot a rig better than most, always on schedule, always with a smile. She had been one of the handful of charter members the Starriggers Guild could claim. I looked out the window for a moment. I had a flashing fantasy of getting lost in the riotous vegetation out there, rooting somewhere in the moist jungle earth. No more joy or sorrow, just light and water and peace. I looked back at Red. "What are the cops saying? Any witnesses?" There is no other evidence available when the cylinders swallow a person. In fact, the question was stupid, as there is no other way to prove that it happened at all. Every year, travelers set off on Skyway and are never seen again, hundreds of them.

"There was a rig behind her when it happened," Red told me. "Said her left rear roller went out of sync on her just as she hit the commit marker. She couldn't straighten up in time, and . . . that was that."

"Who reported it?"

"Didn't get his name. A TATOO driver, for sure, but not one of Wilkes' torpedoes. Just an average guy. Probably had nothing to do with it." Red took a long pull of his cigar. "It could have been an accident."

"Hell of an inconvenient time for a sync loss," I said, putting down my fork. There was no chance of my eating. Darla, however, was digging in, seemingly oblivious to our conversation. "Or very convenient, depending on your point of view." I considered a possibility, then said, "We've never had witnesses before. Disappearances, no clues. How's this? A small, smokeless charge set on the traction-sync delegate—the box is easily accessible, if you've ever looked—detonated by remote control or by a gravitational-stress-sensitive fuse."

"Sounds plausible," Red said. "I'd go for the fuse idea, though I've never heard of one like that. The driver was treated for flash burns and gammashine exposure."

"So? Verisimilitude."

"Yeah. I see what you mean about the delegate switcher. I'd never have thought of doing it that way. Seems to me, if you wanted to send a rig out of control on cue, you'd booby-trap the pulse transformer, or something even more basic."

"Sure, but the hardware's harder to get to. Besides, all you'd be doing would be to send the rollers to their frictional base states, and they become like superslippery bald tires. Pretty hairy when you're taking a sharp curve, but on a straightaway it's really no problem. But knocking out the delegate switcher on a portal approach could be fatal. The rollers would go independent for a fraction of a second as they each go through their friction curves from base state to maximum traction until the backups cut in. I've heard of it happening. The rig goes into a dangerous fishtail, which in normal circumstances can be corrected by a good driver. But on a portal approach . . ."

Red nodded. "I see."

"That's why the driver thought it was the left rear. The rig probably swung its ass-end to the right. But in fact, it was all the front drive rollers coming to the peak of their grab-factor curves before the back ones did. The wind probably determined the direction of the spin, or some other factor."

Red shrugged deferentially. "You make a good case, Jake. But we'll never know."

"*I* know. I've been with Marty, seen her navigate a portal approach with three bad rollers in an eighty-klick-per-hour crosswind. There wasn't much that she couldn't handle, except what I suggested." Red nodded.

Now that I had won my case, I wished someone would argue me out of it. But both Red and I knew I was right. Accidents among Guild drivers were increasing, as was vandalism. Nobody was getting beaten up; that wasn't Wilkes' style.

"You got to remember, Jake," Red said to break the depressed mood, "we're still behind you. I don't know of anybody who wants to pack it in and go back to Wilkes. But if anything were to happen to you . . . well, *merte*." He spat out a flake of precious earth-grown tobacco. (Those stogies of his must have cost fifty UTCs apiece.) "The Guild would be finished, that's all there is to it. At least it would be as a workable alternative for the average independent starrigger." He leaned back and shot out an acrid plume of smoke. "Tell me, Jake. Why are you still on the road? With your salary as president, why, you could—"

"Salary? I've heard of the notion. I think I've cashed two paychecks so far. The third's still in the glovebox, where it goes bouncy, bouncy, bouncy."

Red was surprised. "Really? I didn't know."

"Besides, there's Sam. I couldn't very well sell my own father, could I?"

Red didn't comment, just looked at his cigar.

Something thin with watery blue eyes was tapping me on the shoulder. One of Wilkes' gunsels.

"Mr. Wilkes would like to see you, if you please, sir."

Red coughed once and looked at his watch. "Jake, I'd stay, but we gotta roll. I don't think he'll give you any trouble here."

"Sure, Red. Sure. See you around."

Wilkes' table was over against the far wall. Besides him, and the Rikkitikki, there were three gunsels, including the one who'd fetched me. I didn't like the odds, but it was unlikely that Wilkes would start anything in a crowded restaurant—or so I thought. I tend to think too much.

He was playing with the last few crumbs of an omelette, smiling at me, those curious gray teeth sliding around behind thin lips—he had a way of working his mouth constantly, a tic, I believed. He wasn't an unattractive man. Long blond hair, broad features, eyes of cold green fire, all mounted on a powerful frame. A natty dresser, as well. His kelly-green velvet jerkin was tailored and was in fact very tasteful, going especially well with the white puffed-sleeve blouse.

"Jacob, Jacob, Jacob," he sang wistfully, still smiling. "Good to see you, Jake. Have a seat. Get him a seat, Brucie."

"No, thanks, Corey," I told him. Brucie had made no move. "I'll stand. What's on your mind?"

"Why, *nothing*." Surprised innocence. He was good at it, but he overplayed it a bit. Was he nervous? "Nothing at all. Just enjoying a good meal in a good restaurant—a little *disappointed* when you and your lady friend didn't join us, that's all. You really should observe more of the social amenities, Jake. Oh, I realize your diamond-in-the-rough sort of charm goes a long way, especially with women, but when you see a *friend* across the *room* when you're dining out—well . . ." He was gracious in dismissing the matter. "But I don't take offense easily. You're probably in a hurry, right? Behind schedule?"

"I don't like looking at vomit when I eat, that's all."

It didn't ruffle him. He grinned through the rather indelicate hiatus in the conversation, then said, implacably, "You have a certain directness of expression that I admire, Jake, but that remark was a bit *too* blunt. Don't you think? But . . . then, I should know better than to try and stroke you."

"Was that what you were doing?"

"Oh, twitting you a little, I'll be honest. But I really do want to talk, Jake. I think we should, finally."

"Why, whatever about?" It was my turn to be catty.

"Shoes and ships, Jacob." He waved to the far reaches of the universe. "Things. Things in general."

"Uh huh. But out of the totality of existence, there must be something specific."

"Absolutely right." The constant smile turned extraordinarily benevolent. "Sure you won't sit, Jake?"

"Forget it."

"Fine." He lit a small, thin cigarette wrapped in paper of bright pink, blew smoke toward me. The aroma was sweet, perfumelike. "What say we merge our respective outfits? That's right. Don't drop your jaw too low, Jake, the busboys will use it as a dustpan. Starriggers Guild and Transcolonial Association of Truck Owner-Operators. Together. Hyphenate 'em, or come up with a new name, I don't care. Why continue the war any longer? It's *unprofitable,* destructively competitive . . . and frankly, I'm rather tired of it." The smile was gone, replaced by Honest Concern. "A marriage is what I'm proposing."

"Why, Corey. This is so sudden."

His face split again. "You know, you're not as rough around the edges as you let on, Jacob. Whenever we get together, I kind of *enjoy* the repartee. The parry, the riposte, the barbs lovingly honed—" He blinked. "But I'm serious."

I stood there, debating whether I should just spit and walk away, or go through the motions with him. I couldn't figure out why he was doing this.

"Excuse me, Misterrr Jake," the Reticulan trilled through his mandibles. "I wonderrr if I could inquirrre as to the identity of the female perrrson with whom you are associating?"

"What's it to you, Ant Face?"

I find it difficult, if not impossible, to read an alien visage for emotions. Apparently the insult had had no effect, but I couldn't be sure. I had never before dealt with Rikkis. The mandibles kept clicking in and out in that unnerving sewing-machine motion. Reticulans don't really look like ants, don't even have bug-eyes—you would swear that they wore glasses shaped like a set of zoom camera lenses, and you'd be right, except that they can't take them off—but Rikkis do appear insectoid at first glance, being exoskeletal.

Who knows? Maybe all Reticulans aren't bad. To be fair, it doesn't help that their appearance happens to resonate with images of chitinous horror that scrabble around in the basement of our racial unconscious. The question, however, was: Why was Wilkes presenting me, if indeed he was, with this . . . being? To threaten me? Did he actually think I'd be scared? Give in? Why now, after all this time?

"Now, now," Wilkes said gently. "We don't want an interplanetary incident. I'm sure Twrrrll's question was all in innocence. Did you recognize her, Twrrrll?"

"Prrrecisely. I did not mean to imply an interest in the female perrrson. If I have brrroken some . . . taboo, is this correct? If I have violated some taboo by inquirrring, I am verrry sorrry."

Did everyone know the waif but me?

The alien knew exactly what he was doing.

"Okay, okay," I said testily. "About this merger—"

"There, you see? *Paranoia,* Jake. Paranoia. It kills us all in the end. We *think* ourselves into an early grave. Worry, fear—the etiological root of all disease."

Two beats, then again. "About this merger."

"What would it hurt to consider it? Think it over. Stubborn as you are, you've finally got to admit to yourself that the Guild is on borrowed time. More and more drivers are coming back over to us."

A lie. Everyone with a notion to break and run had done so long before. But he was right in the sense that there were damn few of us left.

"They've added up the pros and cons, come to final tally," Wilkes went on. "TATOO's better for them all around. A dozen new signatories to the Revised Basic Contract this month, with more to come. Oh, sure, the terms of the Guild's Basic are a little better, in some areas. I'll grant you that. But it doesn't mean very much when you can count the Guild's signatories on six fingers."

"Five," I corrected him. "Combined Hydran Industries reneged and went over to you last week."

Wilkes rested his case with a casual motion of the hand. "Need I say more?"

I certainly had no need to say more. I was watching the faces of the three stooges, looking for clues. The one who had come for me looked antsy, darting eyes around the room. From that I got the hint that something could be up. It still seemed unlikely.

Wilkes had been waiting for me to respond, gave it up and said, "Oh, come *on,* Jake. The Guild is nothing more than a shell, if it was ever anything more. Can't you see? It's served its purpose. You've shown me the reservoir of discontent among the membership, and we're re*spond*ing, believe me. Have you read the Revised Basic? I mean, have you *really* sat down and gone over it, clause by clause?"

"I don't have much time for light reading, I'm afraid."

A point scored, an acknowledgment via an upward curl of one end of his mouth. "You really should," he said quietly.

"What's in it for me?" I asked, sailing with the wind just for the hell of it.

It genuinely surprised him. "Well," he said with an expansive shrug, "uh . . . Interlocal Business Agent? For life? Name the salary." It was a hasty improvisation, and he waited for my reaction. "Hell, Jake, I don't know. What do you want?"

"For you to bloody well leave us alone! It's that simple." I erased that with a swipe of my hand. "Pardon me, it's not that simple anymore. You're going to answer for Marty DiFlippo, Wilkes. If I have to scrape myself off the side of a cylinder and come back to do it, I will. *But I will make you answer for her*. And for the others." Conversations lulled at nearby tables.

"Okay, Jake. Okay." His voice was colorless, small.

I backstepped twice, but stopped. "One more thing. If the Guild is doomed anyway, why are you so hot to mate with us?" I wanted an answer. "Why, Corey?"

"Because it annoys me." I suspect it was his first ingenuous remark of the whole exchange. Amused by the novelty, he continued, "Your recent attempts at retaliation annoy me, too."

"What?" This was news.

"You're denying it? Don't insult my intelligence, Jake. I've had loads lifted, rigs sabotaged, deals queered. Nothing major, you understand. But it irks me."

I had heard about the recent increase in hijackings and the like. I attributed it to free-lance skywaymen, as did the media. We had no muscle to bring to bear on him. The injustice of the charge seared the back of my throat.

"Jake, you're a strange man," Wilkes went on, resuming his usual inflected, lyrical style. "There's a kind of . . . a certain Heisenbergian uncertainty about you. An elusiveness. Hard to pin you down. We've been having trouble keeping track of your movements recently. I get a report that you're somewhere, then get another that says you were somewhere else entirely at the very same time. A slippery electron, Jake. Difficult to determine both its position and momentum at once. One or the other, but not both. And the *stories*."

"Stories?"

"The strange tales I've been hearing about you. Fascinating, if they're true. Especially the one about the—"

"Look, Corey," I said, cutting him off, "it's been nice. Really nice. But I'd like to go salvage a meal. Thanks for the offer."

And at my back I heard, "You'll never get out of Mach City, Jake."

I stopped, turned, and delivered an obscenity.

He laughed. "In fact, what makes you think I couldn't take you out right now?"

The three gunsels were eye-riveting me.

"Don't think you're safe in a public place," Wilkes warned, eyes narrowed to slits. "By the way, I own this dump. Silent partner. The help would back me up. Witnesses."

"And the customers?"

"Are you kidding? They'll stampede as soon as you go down."

The restaurant was awfully quiet. Wilkes could have been blustering, but I was worried. They had me, if they wanted me.

"Corey, I wouldn't put it past you, but it'd be just a bit too messy for your taste. Hearings, depositions. Not your style."

I decided to call his bluff, which was the only thing I could do. I turned, but let my peripheral vision sweep behind me, and in doing so caught movement. The pale-eyed slug was reaching under the table.

I spun, but the boy was fast. He had probably had the gun in his lap the whole time. It was leveled at me, and he was grinning, but he didn't fire. My squib was halfway out from under the cuff of my jacket. I dropped, but there was no cover near.

Perhaps three quarters of a second had elapsed when the boy's hand and the gun in it went up in a blue-white ball of flame. The shot had come from across the room.

The alien and the other two had delayed reacting, for the sake of form, I supposed. It would have looked better in the report if only two combatants had been involved—besides, their buddy had had me beaten. Now they pushed the table over and ducked down behind. Everyone in the place thought it an excellent idea. The restaurant exploded as chairs, food, dishes, tables went everywhere.

My squib was finally out, having gotten snagged in a fold of my shirt, and I drew a bead on Wilkes' forehead.

"Hold it!" "Drop 'em!" Two voices off to the right.

I couldn't see who it was. Wilkes suddenly threw up his hands. He still sat there, as if a spectator. "All right! All right!" he yelled.

The pale-eyed one was sitting there too, eyes popped with horror as he watched a gob of melting flesh slither from the charred claw that had been his hand. He started to scream, the whimpering, surprised scream that comes from a sadist unused to the business-end of pain.

I got up. The place was silent, save for the gunsel's warblings. The alien and the other two rose, the humans with their hands in the air, the Reticulan with his forelimbs crossed in front of him, sign of submission.

I chanced a look to the right. Tomasso and Chang were down behind chairs, guns drawn and aimed at Wilkes. I backed away toward them.

"Nice shooting," I said to Chang.

"It wasn't me." He inclined his head to our rear. I looked back and was astonished to see Darla crouched down, holding a monster of a Walther 20kw on the proceedings.

"All right, people."

I looked around the room. About four other people had guns drawn. The man who had spoken was immediately to my left. I knew none of them.

"You," the man said to me. "You leave. We'll entertain this group while you're doing it. We'll give you five minutes. Then we'll let 'em go. The humans, that is. The bug we might fry for lunch."

"Thanks."

We all backpedaled our way out after Tomasso had poked his head out the front door and yelled that it was clear. In the interim, I got out my key and buzzed Sam, told him to pick us up on the road about a block away.

Out in the lot, I thanked Tomasso and Chang, told them their dues were taken care of for the rest of the year.

"Hell, we're paid up!" Tomasso complained.

"Next year!"

Darla and I ducked into the brush bordering the lot. The undergrowth was tangled, but we made it with a little help from Darla's blunderbuss. When we reached the road, Sam was there, and we piled in.

3

"NEVER FIGURED WILKES to make a grandstand play like that," Sam said as we searched the hinterlands of Mach City for an out-of-the-way motel. "Would've made a martyr out of you."

"Just call me Venerable Jake, and take my cause to the Pope. I don't really think he meant to. His boy got too excited."

"Probably. They would have had the exits covered for a genuine ambuscade. Howsoever—"

"There being only one way off this tropical paradise, and that being the Skyway—"

"It's safe to say they have the exits covered now," Sam said.

"A good bet. Anybody still following us?" I asked.

"Not a soul."

We passed plantations, a power plant, a few lonely residences off the road. There was not much to see besides jungle.

"What's this up ahead?"

I squinted. Off in the mass of overhanging greenery were

little houses nestled in the treetops. It looked like a movie set. A sign by the road.

"'Greystoke Groves—Treecabins, Free Total Vid, Whirlpool Jungle Lagoon, Guided Safari Tour, Reasonable Rates—VACANCY.' Charming. Just the thing for a cozy getaway weekend. What say, Sam?"

"All the same to me. I live in a truck."

"Heck, you'll miss the safari. Pity."

"Wouldn't miss it for the world. Hang on."

There was a large parking lot, which Sam traversed. Without stopping, he plunged the rig into the wall of undergrowth that bordered same. Branches thumped against the bulkhead, creaked, and shattered. Sam kept going, cutting a swath through the jungle.

Brightly colored flying critters took wing in our path, screeching their panic. We hit a hidden ditch and slammed down. The engine whined, groaned, and we were out of it, crashing forward again through a cataract of vinery.

"Sam, large tree."

"I know. Damn! Let me back up."

The rollers crackled to maximum grab, and spun.

"Double diddley damn. This stuff is wet."

"They don't call it a rain forest for nothing."

We backed up and whanged against something.

"Ouch. Hold on."

After some uncomfortable maneuverings, we battered our way onward. A centipedelike animal found itself clinging to our forward viewport, much to its chagrin. It extended two sets of antennae, fore and aft, and elongated itself vertically, each end checking out a possible escape route. It (they?) decided on up, and crawled out of sight.

Finally, we came to a crunching halt near the base of a stout treetrunk. Sam cut the engine, and we sat for a while surrounded by chirping, twittering jungle.

Presently, Sam asked, "One of those treehuts near here?"

"I think. Can't really see a thing."

"Well, find the nearest one and see if it's vacant."

"Wait a minute. Is this a clearing up ahead? Go forward a few meters."

Sam started the engine, eased ahead.

We poked through the edge of a paved footpath.

"C'mon, Darla," I said. "Take your pack. Let's look like tourists."

* * *

The woman in the office was a short, dark-haired woman who spoke incomprehensible English, but her Intersystem was as bad as mine. The accent was Spanish, the eyes Oriental, and I took her for a recently arrived Filipina.

"Twenty UTC, please. You have ID?"

"Yes." I showed her my Alonzo Q. Snerd persona, the duly authorized plasticard of which I keep for the times when I feel like Alonzo Q. Snerd. "This is my lifecompanion," I said, indicating Darla.

"Mistah-Missa Snerd? Happy you be here. You got bags?"

"Yes, thank you. By the way, we want that particular cabin," I told her, pointing to the layout on the wall. "We took a walk back there. We hope it's available."

"Number Seventeen. Nice! No one there now. FRONT!"

The bellhop came in from a back room. It was a squat but powerfully thewed, very hairy, anthropoid creature, a native. The species is regarded as borderline-sentient by most authorities. It had two large wide-set eyes that were owl-like, a wet, dark-lipped mouth splitting a short snout, and floppy long ears. Its feet were splay-toed, hairless, pink, and looked prehensile. Its three-fingered hands had what looked like opposable thumbs on either side. The creature had no tail.

"This Cheetah. She take you."

Cheetah grabbed our bags, took the key from the woman, and scurried off through a vine-covered archway that led into a tunnel. We followed her.

At the end of the tunnel was an elevator door. It looked conventional, but the shaft, as it turned out, was nonexistent. Instead, we found an open-air car faked up to look like logs and sticks. It more than likely had a metal frame. We got on and it rose into the trees.

From the upper platform we debarked into a maze of sturdy rope bridges with plank walkways leading from tree to tree, cabin to cabin. Ours was bigger than it had appeared from the footpath, but still quite cozy, resting in the crook of three huge structural boughs. Inside, the decor was consistent with the rest of the place, early-RKO Pictures; floors, walls, furniture, and everything else were made of the native equivalents of wicker, rattan, and bamboo.

I slumped in the peacock Empire chair and sighed. The Eridani creature darted about, opening shutters, flicking on lights, turning down beds, and plumping pillows, all very briskly, and with far more dexterity than a Terran ape could muster. It was surprising, in a way. More surprisingly, the creature turned to me and spoke.

"Huh?" was all I could reply.

"That all, sir? That all?"

"Uhhh . . . Darla?"

Darla smiled at the creature. "Is there a gift shop or store here? I need some tissue paper."

"I go get some! You need, I get!"

Darla offered her a credit note. Cheetah refused.

"No, no! Fwee! Soap, towel, keenex, fwee. No money!"

Cheetah left and closed the door quietly.

"Call me Bwana," I said, not feeling particularly witty.

"She's cute. I've seen them before, at carnivals and things. They're really very intelligent."

"Hmmm. And honest. She could have snagged that tenner."

Darla laughed, scoffing. "Do you actually think she needs money?"

"Why is she working here?"

That stumped her.

I got out Sam's key and buzzed him. "Sam, we've set up housekeeping."

"How is it?"

I turned on the microcam and panned the room for him. "As you can see, charming. How're you?"

"I think I'm taking root. Seriously, I might need a little more camouflage around my back end. Can you see me from up there?"

I went to the window. Behind the shutters it was glazed with nonglare material. The cabin was completely sealed from the outside, and many degrees cooler.

"I can't see anything but vegetables."

"How's this? I have my hi-intensities on."

I saw a glimmer. "There you are. Fine."

"Maybe I'll be all right if I'm that hard to spot."

"What about the hole you left in the scenery back in the parking lot? Suspicious, no? And it leads right to you."

"I was watching the rear view. The stuff seemed to bound back up after we passed. Right now I can't tell the view ahead from the one behind. This jungle is alive, believe me."

"Bit of luck. Okay. Now, what about our situation? I'm having second thoughts. Should we have made a break for it on the Skyway?"

"Negative, son. Much, much too easy to follow."

"Right, just thought I'd ask. What next?"

"Well, we know they picked up our trail from the restaurant pretty quickly. I expected that. Not too hard to tail a rig. And we're pretty sure we lost them downtown."

"How sure?"

"Reasonably sure."

"Sam, how did you know about that dirt road that followed the edge of the marsh? I didn't think you knew Mach City that well."

"Used to spend a lot of time here. There were these two women I knew, mother and daughter, and I . . . well, that's neither here nor there. Anyway, the city council's been squabbling about draining that swamp for years. I knew the idiots hadn't gotten around to it yet."

"Another piece of luck. However, we are stuck here."

"For the moment. But if we can sneak over to Ali's Garage, we've got a chance. He's an old friend of mine. We hole up at his place, I get that new emulsicoat you've been promising me, plus some other cosmetic changes. Then, with luck, we slip out."

"Risky. We could be spotted going there."

"Sure, but I can't see another way. Would've gone directly there, except we would have had to double-back through town to do it. They would've picked us up again easily."

"So we sit here . . . for how long?"

"Until they get tired of looking, or until they're convinced we got through their net. Four Eri days."

"That's also risky."

"Sure. Wilkes is connected here. Hell, he might even own this place. But, have any better ideas?"

"Not at the moment."

Cheetah returned then with Darla's tissue paper. Darla struck up a conversation with her, and they sat down on one of the double beds to chat.

"Well," I said, "I'll let you know if I get a brainstorm."

"Right. Leave the key open."

"Really, Dad."

"Huh? Oh, sorry. Forgot about Darla."

I hadn't.

Despite my disinclination to believe in such things, the possibility of a real paradox here loomed large; in fact, if Darla wasn't faking, the paradox was a fact as cold and adamantine as the roadmetal that had caused it. Will have caused it. But it was hard for me to swallow. On the Skyway, you hear wild stories every day. I've met people who will swear—on any amount of Holy Writ you'd care to put in front of them—that one day, out on some lonely stretch of road, they saw themselves coming the other way . . . or that they were vouchsafed the paradoxical apparition of a relative who'd passed on the year before . . . or that the skywayman who held up the Stop-N-Shop off Interstellar 95 last week was in fact their time-tripping doppelgänger, not them. Sometimes, reports such as these make the news feeds—as silly-season fillers. Up till now, I had thought this was all the credence they deserved. But now I was confronted with the possible reality of a situation which, according to the commonly accepted version of The Way Things Are Supposed to Work, was an out-and-out impossibility. My choices were either to accept it as a fact, or to try resolving the contradiction with every measure of rationality at my disposal. But there were problems with the latter option. Aside from waiting until I could catch Darla in a lie, there was little I could do to assure myself she was telling the truth. What were the alternatives? Chinese water-torture? Tickle her mercilessly until she 'fessed up? And just how does one go about tripping up a liar when one has no facts to throw in her path?

It seemed I really had but one choice: to accept the paradox as real . . . until proven otherwise. I was hearing a reprise of a love theme that should have been very familiar. But it was strange and new. Bassackwards is not the way I like to do things, but Paradox does not grant dispensation from its crazy laws. Nor does Skyway. If you ply her paths, you take the risk. You pay the toll. The Roadbuilders, whoever or whatever they were, must have realized the consequences of a hyper-spatial highway that spans enormous distances instantaneously. They were excellent physicists, consummate engineers, but whether they could have avoided the "pathological" aspects (interesting, the way scientists choose their words) of such a device is a matter for conjecture, since our knowledge of these matters needs jacking up a quantum or two before we could begin to understand.

My task, then, was to find a causal lever to move objects around to my liking in a deterministic system. Estimated chances of accomplishing objective: those of fart in monsoon.

But volition is a delusion we sorely need, a habit we can't break. I had to act. It was necessary for me to lose Darla now in order to gain her "later," lest two Darlas appear where one had gone before. Or something like that. Deadly possibilities loomed. A knock at the door.

My squib was out more quickly this time, even though Wilkes would not bother to knock.

It was a small Oriental man who wore a crisp straw planter's hat and a loosely fitting vanilla tropical suit. He didn't look friendly, but acted it.

"Excuse me, sir. Have you seen . . . ? *Ai,* there you are! What are you doing here, Cheetah? Guests! Guests! Excuse me, sir. She is lazy, always going off somewhere."

Cheetah got off the bed and scampered toward us, slowed and slunk past her master, then broke across the small balcony to the rope bridge.

"Pardon me, sir. She is harmless, but she will take advantage."

"No problem, Mister . . . ?"

"Perez."

"Perez. She just got back from an errand for my LC."

"Ah. Enjoy your stay. Sir, Madam."

A tip of the hat, and he was gone. I went to the window and watched him cross the bridge. He yelled for Cheetah, cursed her in Spanish. She did not look back, disappearing into the foliage.

Darla was behind me, watching over my shoulder. "What did you two talk about?" I asked.

"Quite a lot. Your question about why she worked here intrigued me. So I asked her."

"And?"

"She stays here because she doesn't have a home. Read 'space,' 'territory,' or what you will. From what I could get out of her, her home was destroyed. There's a jungle-clearing project near here, it seems, and what was once her home is now bare earth."

"She couldn't move? Find a new spot? There are millions of square kilometers of jungle left. Most of the planet is virgin still."

"No, she couldn't move, nor could her clan, tribe, or whatever. Once such a group, an extended family sort of thing, loses its stamping grounds, it has no life. Extreme territoriality, attachment to one traditional area, probably passed down for generations. Most of the displaced cheetahs work in the city. Not for long, though. They die off very quickly."

"You got all this from her?"

"No, she was very reticent. I've heard about the problem. The Colonials are very touchy about it." She walked back toward the bed, sat down. "Funny thing. She's very sensitive—receptive. She asked me if the people who were chasing us were near."

"What?" The notion that the animal could have known gave me an odd feeling. I sat down on the Empire chair. "How?"

"She said she could smell the fear on us."

Odder still was to realize that Cheetah had been right. At the root of all actions taken for the sake of survival lies fear unvarnished, the basic component of the mechanism. "Did *she* think they were near?"

"She said no, not now."

"Reassuring."

"I'm tired. I think I'll go freshen up." She got up, took her pack and walked toward the bathroom.

Before she got to the door, I said, "By the way, I didn't get a chance to thank you . . . for a well-timed, beautifully placed shot. Where the hell were you hiding that cannon?"

"I'll never tell," she said craftily, over her shoulder. "I did it for old times' sake." She went in and closed the door.

I buzzed Sam.

"Yeah?"

"Something Wilkes said. He said a lot of strange things. But there was something about stories. Stories about me, and I guess about you, circulating around."

"Stories?"

"Rumors. I don't know. How does it strike you?"

"Leaves me cold."

"We need information."

"That we do. But how? Dare we risk the skyband?"

"I'm going to take a stroll down to the lounge, see if anyone's there."

"Be careful. By the way, any way of getting down here from that birdhouse?"

"Yes. There's a rope ladder rolled up on the porch. Fire escape, I guess. Wouldn't have taken the place if there had been no way down."

I knocked on the bathroom door and told Darla where I was going.

"I still have Brown Bess," she said.

And she could use it. It was a risk to separate, but I thought I had spotted a familiar rig in the parking lot.

Outside, a patch of sky peeking through the jungle canopy was turning silver, spraying beams of sunlight downward. The air was thick, moist, gravid with a million scents. Something chittered in the branches above me as I crossed the first bridge, scolding, warning me.

Before I got to the lounge it occurred to me that I should ask about the clearing project—where, how near—thinking of it as a possible means of escape. There were usually logging roads around such an endeavor.

No one was at the desk. I waited for a few minutes, then went around behind to a door. I opened it.

Perez had his back to me, holding a long, thin wooden rod raised toward Cheetah, who cowered pitifully in a corner of the office. Perez's head snapped around. He turned quickly and held the rod behind his back.

"Yes?"

"Excuse me. My lifecompanion wishes another errand run. Could you send someone up?"

"Yes. Yes, right away."

"She's taken a particular liking to Cheetah here. Loves animals, you know. Could Cheetah go?"

Perez was reluctant. "Yes, of course." He motioned to her without taking his eyes from me.

When she had left, I said, "Unless you desire a totally new look and a fresh approach to life, you'll not abuse that creature while I am a guest here."

Perez bristled. "Mr. Snerd, is it? This is none of your affair. I must ask you to—" I closed the door.

The lounge was very big, with shaman fright-masks looming from the walls, shrunken heads dangling from the open-beam ceiling, potted fronds growing everywhere, a striped native animal hide nailed above the bar. It was a crazy concatenation of Micronesian, African, and native motifs. Memories of Terra grow more blurred with the years. There were few customers, but Jerry Spacks was in a corner booth with an attractive young woman. I ordered an elaborate, improbable drink that was all fruit and little paper umbrellas, and walked over to them sipping noisily.

"Jake? Jesus."

"Hi, Jerry."

"Uh . . . Andromeda, this is Jake McGraw. Friend of mine."

"Hello."

"Hello. Jerry, could I speak with you for a moment?"

Jerry hesitated, looked away. "Yeah, sure."

The girl made a good excuse and left. I sat down.

"Goddamn, Jake, you show up at the most—"

"Sorry. This won't take but a minute. By the way, are you still a Guild member? Haven't seen the lists recently."

"You know damn well my dues are a year behind. But that's moot—I own three rigs now. Pretty soon I won't have to drive at all."

"Moving up to employer status, eh? Good for you." I let him puff and preen for a while, then said, "Jerry, this question may sound strange . . . but what have you heard about me recently?"

Jerry laughed. "Who hasn't heard about the shoot-out at Sonny's? It's all over the skyband. What're you still doing here?"

"That's not what I meant. What have you heard in the way of strange stories about me?"

Apparently he knew what I meant. He settled back, lit a cigarette, looked at me, and said frankly, "Jake, I don't believe ninety percent of the road yarns I hear. Who does? Someone claims to've sighted a Roadbuilder vehicle, you hear someone's stumbled onto a backtime route and winds up being his own grandfather, that sort of thing. I've also heard some things about you, just as wild."

"Such as."

He was skeptical. "Oh well, it seems you and Sam found a way out of the Expanded Confinement Maze and followed the Skyway all the way out to the end."

It was crazy. You could go only so far on the Skyway before the known routes were exhausted. Of course, you could take a chance and go through one of the many unexplored portals . . . and end up anywhere in the universe. If the planet on the other side had a double-back portal—like the one leading from here back to Tau Ceti—you were in luck. If not, you'd be stuck with the option of shooting the next aperture, which could lead anywhere. The reason why all of the above is fairly certain is that no one has ever made a convincing case for having come back from a "potluck portal."

I popped a chunk of sour fruit into my mouth. "I can tell you for a fact that we've done no such thing."

"Hell, I know that. But I've also heard that you're *going* to do it. I've heard the tale both ways."

"Going to?" I mulled that over. "How are we supposed to accomplish this amazing feat?"

I chanced to turn my head. Perez was looking into the room, and our eyes met. He quickly ducked back. A little too quickly.

"With a roadmap."

I turned back to Jerry. "Roadmap?"

"Yeah. A genuine Roadbuilder artifact. How you managed to get hold of one is covered in the next episode, I guess."

What was remarkable to me was how the Skyway breeds these tall tales. The Skyway is half legend, half reality itself. Nevertheless, evidence abounds that the Skyway extends to other regions of the galaxy. Alien vehicles are seen every day on the road, coming from parts unknown, going to—only the occupants know where. Most don't stop. Every once in a while, one does, and we meet a new race: Zeta Reticulans, Beta Hydrans, Gliese 59ers; races like the Ryxx, the Kwaa'jheen, and the beings who call themselves The People of the Iron Sun, whose home stars can't be found on any Terran catalogues; many, many more. All in all, there are about sixty races whose Confinement Mazes, the routes that lead from their home system to nearby colonizable planets, are known and mapped. Put all these known areas together, and you get one big Confinement Maze, little sections of which are strewn out over a sizable portion of several spiral arms. But there certainly is more to discover. Every once in a while, a new race drops into this neck of the woods and stops to be sociable. More information is then acquired—but the process is slow.

"Tell me. Where does the Skyway end?" I asked.

"At the beginning of the universe."

I drained the last of my sickly sweet drink. "Is there a good motel there?"

Jerry laughed. "Jake, you know how these whoppers get started. Alien booze in human stomachs. Accidental chemically induced insanity."

We talked for a while longer, about five more minutes. Jerry told me what he knew about the jungle-clearing project. All the while something nagged at me from the back of my mind: the way Perez had eyeballed me.

"Jerry, thanks a lot. Good luck in your new business."

"Okay, Jake. Let me know what it's like at the Big Bang."

"I'll write."

I went out into the lobby.

Perez was behind the desk, smiling at me strangely, and three sleek roadsters were pulling into the lot.

I dashed for the elevator, and while waiting for the accursed sluggish thing, buzzed Sam.

"Sam, old man, condition puce. Get ready to roll."

"Where to, for God's sake?"

"Look for two roads and a yellow wood that we can diverge into. Otherwise, it's all over."

There was a house intercom by the elevator. I punched our cabin number.

"Yes?"

"Darla, pack up. Now. Drop that ladder and get down to Sam. Make it fast, and use Bess on the rope bridge. Burn it!"

"Right!"

Three men, one of Wilkes' gunsels and two unknowns, were approaching the transparent entrance doors. I looked around and saw double doors that probably led to a kitchen.

I was right, and three cooks, one of them alien, a Thoth, looked up from their dirty work. I didn't stop, and banged out a rear door. It opened onto a hallway that led into the restaurant. A separate entrance provided access from the parking lot. The room was dark and empty. From behind a partition by the waiters' station came the clattering of dishes. I crossed the floor quietly, crouched against the front wall, and looked out a window.

Five more men were running toward the restaurant door. I dived under the nearest table and froze just in time to hear the door thump open and feet pound across the floor. The heavy tablecloth prevented me from seeing. I waited until they left, then got up and risked another look. Three more men waited in the lot, standing by the side of one vehicle, hands thrust under their tropical shirts.

Trapped like a rodentoid.

I needed to get out the door and to the right, toward the end of the parking lot where the footpath came out of the woods; but as I watched, two men came out of the front entrance and ran past my vantage point, no doubt going to cover that very route. The alternative now was to somehow make it across the lot in the other direction and duck into the woods using Sam's swath as an entry point. The three lookouts were still there.

Something was moving in the lot; by the sound, a rig. Then I saw it as it backed up between me and the gunsels. It was Jerry, clearing out in a hurry. Wherever I was, he didn't care to be.

When the gunsels' view of the side door was completely blocked, I sprinted out, mounted the rig's running board, and knocked on the side port about three inches from Jerry's head. He jumped.

He slid back the port. "Hey, Jake. Don't *do* that!"

"Sorry, Jerry. Hello, Andromeda. Can you give me a lift to the far end of the lot?"

"Jake, those *guys* there . . . Never mind."

Resigned, Jerry eased the rig forward. I watched as we passed the main entrance. Nobody showed.

"Far enough?" Jerry hoped.

"Yeah. Stay here until I can get into the woods, okay?"

"Sure."

Sam was right. The undergrowth had rebounded to the point where I could barely distinguish Sam's trail. It was horrendous going. Bent grasses snared my feet, thorny tendrils leeched at my clothing. I stumbled into hidden holes, tripped over submerged rocks, doing it for about two minutes and getting nowhere.

It got worse. I wasn't sure if I had lost the trace. It appeared as if I had.

"Sam! Come in!"

"Where the hell are you?"

"I don't know. Somewhere behind you. Is Darla—?"

"Fine mess. Yes, she's here. I'm going to start the engine. Follow the sound."

"Fine. No, wait!" I smelled smoke—the rope bridge. Now, if I could only follow my nose. But I couldn't see a damn thing. "Forget it. Start up."

Sam did so, and the muffled whine came from my right. I thrashed my way toward it.

"Can you come back toward the lot?"

"Trying to. For some reason, it's harder getting out than getting in."

"Yeah, well see if you can—" Something was on my leg, something warm, wet, and rubbery. I looked down.

A hairless, many-legged beastie with a central body about as big as a grapefruit was hugging my calf. I let out a yell, smashed the thing with a fist, grabbed it with both hands, and pulled. A sharp pain lanced through my leg. I yanked, managed to pull one slippery leg free, and it coiled about my hand, throbbing. I pulled. The tentacle stretched like taffy, then grew resilient and tugged back. I fell, tumbled in the springy brush, writhing, while the pain crescendoed. I beat and tore and cursed at the thing, but it wouldn't give me up. Great scarlet waves of pain coursed up my leg, pulsed in my side. For a frozen eternity there was only the pain and a separate universe to kick and scream in, little else.

The next thing I knew I somehow had a stick in my hand and I was whacking the animal as hard as I could, oblivious to the damage I was doing to my leg. Finally, the thing squealed—the sound of chalk against a blackboard—let go, and burrowed back into the grass.

I lay there for a moment. Presently, I got to my feet. The leg was numb and loath to obey my commands, but I could walk. I paused to look around for the key, which I had dropped, but it was nowhere around.

Movement behind me, the sound of thrashing. I regretted having yelled, but when it comes to creepy-crawlies I immediately lose my gonads, become all hoopskirts and fluster. Definitely phobic reaction.

No time to search for the key.

Sam sounded nearer, at least, but now I had no way of communicating. I groped through the eternal green miasma, flailing at my leafy tormentors, suddenly getting a wild, desperate notion to go back to the main building, ask Mr. Perez for his machete, and pay the rooted bastards back in kind. They did not relent. I hacked at them with what I had, stiffened forearms, my good leg, hate. Tiny insects hummed about me in a swirling cloud, lit on my face and swam on the surface of my cornea, and had pity enough not to bite.

I heard the crackling of a gun. Someone was burning a path off to my left.

Crashing came from directly ahead. Sam. I lurched forward and fell, squelched a curse, and struggled onward again. Sam was near, but I still couldn't see him. My ankle turned in a depression, and for an agonizing few seconds I sucked air and screamed inwardly as bolts of white heat shot through me. But soon I was plunging ahead, throwing my body against the foliage, ramming myself through toward what I took to be the rig's engine sounds. Progress came in bits of eternity.

Finally, I gave up. The throbbing had returned in my leg, neatly phasing with pulses of fire from my ankle. I collapsed backward from the heat, the exertion, the pain. I dug out my squib and waited, letting wriggly wet things lave my face. I didn't care, just lay there, defocusing my eyes on an over-arching canopy of dark green. Sam was getting nearer, nearer. I tried to sit up, found that I could, then looked around.

Something whooshed out of the jungle directly behind me. I turned around and found myself sitting beside Sam's left front roller. It had stopped on the exact spot where my head had been. The engine whined again, the roller moved, and I pounded frantically against the ground-effect vane with all my strength.

"Jake?" Sam's voice on the external speaker.

"Yo!"

The hatch popped open, and I painfully hauled myself up and in.

I fell to the deck behind the shotgun seat.

"Oh, my God," I heard Darla say.

I rolled over and saw her face, one of the most deftly executed of God's pastel drawings. "Hello."

"Where the hell you been, boy?" Sam chastised.

"Out weeding the garden. Let me get . . . *ahhhh!*"

"Careful," Darla said. "Oh, your leg. . . ."

With a little help, I got up and slumped into the seat. Sam was turning to the left, steamrollering through the green-capped swells.

"There's a stream around here. Yeah, the ground's dipping. Should be—"

We didn't see the man, one of our pursuers, until we were on top of him. He had time to turn his head and register the beginnings of alarm before we ran straight over him. He didn't have time to scream. Darla gave a tiny squeak and put her hand over her mouth.

After an interlude, Sam said, "Here we go."

We clunked over an embankment, slid, and splashed into a shallow running brook strewn with polished stones. Sam eased the back end down. I heard the forward accordian-joint between cab and trailer go *scrunch* as it bent to its limits. Sam turned hard left and trundled down the stream bed bumpingly, jarring our teeth and bones to jelly.

"We'll make time this way," Sam said.

"Where are we going?"

"This stream parallels a dirt road farther down. The road should take us down to the clearing project, where we'll pick up another trail that'll get us to the Skyway. We hope."

"How do you know all this?"

"Just following Cheetah's directions. Ask her yourself."

I looked around. In a pile of soft dark hair huddled in a corner of the rear seat, two big wet eyes awaited my approval.

4

THE STREAM MEANDERED through cathedrals of jungle, its banks overhung with weeping vinery. We strapped in and let the rig jostle us as Sam sent it banging over rocks and slamming down over half-meter-high cataracts. It was rough going, but not as difficult as barging through rain forest. The gradual downgrade soon leveled off and the stream got deeper. Then it got very deep.

As the water level gurgled up to my viewport, I said, "I knew those optional snorkels on the vents would come in handy someday."

"I think this is about as deep as it gets," Sam said.

He was right. Ahead was white water. Sam stopped for a moment to decide on his approach, then gunned it for a place where the drop was lowest. We rolled over smooth rocks and splashed into the hydraulics below, like some great, lumbering water beast beached in the shallows.

Anyway, the rig was getting a long-needed washing. The

stream widened out farther down, and Sam stopped long enough for Darla to clean the triple-puncture wound on my leg and bandage it up. I suddenly felt very weird.

"You're in luck," she said. "Cheetah says the *weegah,* which is what bit you, isn't poisonous to humans. Unfortunately, the chemical of the venom resembles chlorpromazine, a tranquilizer, if I remember correctly. You should be winking out soon. You probably got a good dose."

"I feel very calm, but kind of strange. How did you know all that?"

"Oh, passing interest in xenobiology, especially exotic zoology."

"If I die, I want you to do something for me. Go to my flat and kill every houseplant in it."

"Sounds so petty."

But my ire grew abstract as a nirvanalike mood descended. The pain in my leg and ankle subsided to alternating twinges, and I sat back to enjoy the ride as Sam resumed driving.

About half an hour later we picked up the dirt road, but we almost hung ourselves up getting out of the water. We scraped bottom with the sickening sound of abused metal, then gained the rutted road, which bore us away from the stream and slightly uphill.

I grew terribly sleepy. I told Darla to fetch a stimtab from the medicine kit, but she advised against it, contending that the interaction of the drug and the venom was unpredictable, owing to the *weegah*'s alien chemistry. I acquiesced. Now she was a doctor.

Another hour went by, and we came to the clearing. It was a shock. Over at least a dozen square kilometers the jungle had been ripped away like so many weeds. In its place lay chewed earth, shards of pulp, and row after endless row of neatly wrapped bales, bundles of vegetation sorted into homogeneous groups—bark, logs, leaves, chips, pods, fruit, and vegetable mash (these in big metal canisters), all products useful as-is or ready for further processing. The thing that had done the deed was off in the distance, a Landscraper. The machine was a metal platform almost a kilometer long, moving on gargantuan tracks, biting off great chunks of forest at its leading edge, sorting, processing, digesting masses of material in its guts, and dropping the fecal result off behind. Eventually, farms, houses, and factories would follow in its wake. Cleared land was a premium on Demeter (the proper name for the planet and one everybody ignored; most people called it Hothouse).

Cheetah eyed the scene dolefully, and I couldn't help feeling sorry. She looked upon the ruins of her only home.

The road skirted the edge of the clearing for about a klick or so before it swung back into the jungle. At this point we were on the lookout for airborne vehicles, but none appeared.

The new section of trail was heavily overgrown in spots, and wound its way around marsh and hollow until it dead-ended into another road.

"That way!" Cheetah instructed.

Sam turned left, and beneath the feeling of utter tranquility and well-being, I recognized the absurdity of having to be led by the nose out of danger by an individual supposedly without a measurable IQ. But we usually take all the help we can get.

I fell asleep, kept popping awake when Cheetah yelled out a new direction, but eventually there were no more decisions to make and the road before us twined endlessly.

Night fell, as it does very early on Hothouse, with its sixteen-hour rotation, and we ghosted down leafy corridors with the headbeams playing among the trees. Pairs of tiny eyes glowed in the shadows like sparks in a dying fire, watching. Now and again came sounds of rustling in the bushes, nocturnal cries echoing out in the blackness beyond. I dozed, awoke, drifted sleepward, awoke, and the vista before me was the same, dream and reality indistinguishable. I don't know how long we traveled. The trail turned into a green Moebius way, endlessly twisting back on itself, like the Skyway laid out in a galaxy of verdure. . . .

Skyway. Paradox. Causality reversed . . . living lives, loving loves, dying deaths out of natural sequence. . . . We are born, follow our useless paths to the grave, but the paths are two-way . . . cut and splice a lifeline and you get death before life, disappointment before expectation, fulfillment before desire, effect before cause. . . .

The road was long and I drove it, taking the Backtime Extension . . . back to Terra, a lost, blue-white speck against the blackness, an exhausted little planet of fifteen billion souls—despite the constant exodus of surplus population out to the web of worlds linked by the Skyway . . . back to a boyhood in a dying rural town in Northeast Industry, née Pennsylvania,

Federated Democracies of North America . . . a little mining town called Braddock's Creek, whose pits had given up their last flakes of bituminous at around the end of the fourth decade of the century, shortly after I was born . . . a demi-ghost town of boarded-up tract houses long foreclosed upon and abandoned to house-strippers and weather, a depopulated community in this age of overcrowding, victim of Climate Shift . . . short hot summers, long face-numbing winters, with no growing season to speak of. . . . A toddler spending the warm months barefoot playing on shale piles near the mines, mounds of blue-black rubble forever smoking with spontaneous combustion, cooking themselves into mountains of "red dog," gravel good for laying on dirt roads . . . a boy swimming in strip-mine holes brimming with acid-spiked runoff water. . . . We never went hungry in those days, with Father working when he could, coaxing fruits and vegetables out of our chemical garden when he was laid off; and when neither activity paid the bills, doing mysterious things, staying out late at night while I waited for him, sleeping in the big double bed with Mother, lying awake, listening to dogs bark out in the windy night, waiting, wondering when he would get in, wondering what he was doing, and where; Mother never saying anything about it, never acknowledging the fact that her husband spent whole nights away; waiting, until I fell asleep, to wake up next morning in my sleeping bag on the old mattress in the front room, dimly remembering Father carrying me there, kissing me and tucking me in. . . . Dim years spent in boredom and restlessness and missed school because of fuel shortfalls and lack of funding, meatless days, wheatless days, proud happy days when the sun was out and things warmed up and I could run and raise hell and play and not think about or not care about a world where millions, no, billions starved and the incessant brushfire wars raged on, or appreciate the profound implications of the fact that men lived on the moon and in lazily turning metal wheels in space. . . . I remember my father telling me about his remembering when the first portal of the Skyway was discovered on Pluto by a robot probe, and I thought, Why did they put it so far away out there at the edge of the solar system? . . . Watching viddy programs about it and hearing the commentators say what a mystery it all was—who had built it? when? why?—years that melted away too soon, because for all the privation, it was a childhood no worse than most, better than some. . . . And one day Father telling us that we would move, that he had applied for emigration and that we had been accepted, and that somehow he had come up with the 500,000 New Dollar emigration fee charged to all North American residents because economically the region was still better off by far when compared with other parts of the world. . . . The trip by hydroskiff to India, the unbelievable masses of people there, bodies in the streets, dead bodies and some that were not quite dead, stacked like cordwood and sprinkled with white powdery chemicals making them look like woodpiles in a first snow. . . . The shuttle port near Kendrapara on the Bay of Bengal, surrounded by tent cities of stranded emigrees. . . . The thundering shuttle ride and my first space-sickness and the view of a dazzling Terra wheeling below. . . . Being aboard the *Maxim Gorky,* a Longboost ship that made Pluto in eighteen months, most of the time spent with its passengers in Semidoze, an electrically induced twilight of semiconsciousness which made the interminable trip bearable. . . . Spending about an hour on Pluto before boarding the bus which took us by Skyway to Barnard's Star, thence to 61 Cygni-A II, thence to Struve 2398, thence to Sigma Draconis IV, called Vishnu, where I spent the remainder of my childhood on a farm in a valley made green with water cracked from rocks, working as I never worked before or since; where I grew, finally became a man—too soon, when my mother died giving birth to my brother Donald, stillborn. . . .

. . . Until a bump woke me up and I saw that the road had debouched from the jungle onto the ten-meter-wide strip on either side of the highway where no plants can grow save low grasses.

Sam waited for traffic to pass. An impossibly low reaction-drive vehicle with some kind of frictionless underside roared by, its headbeams almost dim compared to its brilliant array of running lights. Sam checked the scanners and pulled out onto the road, the smooth, smooth road of Skyway. It felt good. Acceleration sat in my lap as Sam pinched the magnetic confinement, and soon we were wafting through patches of ground-hugging fog that smelled of dank things in a dank earth, a jungle smell, wet and fetid, a smell that I didn't want to have flushed through my nostrils for some time to come. I closed the vents and pressurized the cab. We would be making a many-light-year jump to Groombridge 34-B, where there was an interchange on the airless moon of a gas giant.

"Hey, look who's awake. Feeling better?" Sam spoke softly.

"More or less. How long did we spend touring those damn botanical gardens?"

"Almost all night. We should miss the dawn, though. I think we're about a hundred klicks from the portal."

"Great. The sooner we get off this salad bowl, the better." I looked back and saw Darla and Cheetah huddled together in the backseat, winked out like three-year-olds. I felt even less mature and sank into oblivion again. Dreamlessly.

The portal warning buzzer woke me up. I felt even better, but my mouth was stuffed with fuzz and I ached all over.

"Better tell those two to strap in," Sam said.

I yelled back and they woke up, rubbed eyes, and did so. Warning signs shot by, and then suddenly we were in fog that shrouded the approach. The safe corridor, a lane marked by two parallel white lines, spooled out at us from the mist.

"You on instruments?" I asked.

"Nah. Using the guide markers."

The fog got thicker, and the lines faded—then, instantaneously, the fog was gone as we passed the flashing red commit markers and penetrated the portal's force-field shell. The shells keep out atmosphere but allow solid matter to go through. It's always struck me as pertinent to ask what would happen if the machinery generating the shell faded. As far as anyone knows, it's never happened, and no one seems to worry about it but me. Nor is much sleep lost fretting over the possibility that a portal could completely fail and drop its cylinders, which has never happened either, at least not in the known mazes.

We felt the fleeting tug of an unseen force, work of the grasping gravitational fingers around us. "Watch it, Sam."

"This has always been a rough portal. Needs recalibrating."

Whump!

The rig dropped, slamming onto the Groombridge Skyway. The jungle was gone, and around us stretched the bleak rolling terrain of the satellite, bathed in the dull red glow of Groombridge 34-B's dwarf primary, overhung by a black starry canopy. The gas giant loomed off to our right and was in gibbous phase, taking up more than 45 degrees of sky.

"Remind me to file a complaint at the nearest Skyway maintenance office," Sam kidded, knowing full well that the recalibration would be done in time by the portal itself. Like the Skyway roadbed, the portals were self-repairing. "One of these days, we're going to materialize *under* the roadway," he said, repeating a bugbear that was part of the lore of the road. "Really, I wonder what the hell would happen. Explosion?"

"Sam, you know damn well it can't happen." I had rung the changes on this argument a hundred times in a hundred different beerhalls. A portal transition is a question of geometry, not of matter transmission. The spaces on either side are contiguous, not congruent. We had just experienced a misalignment in which the ingress side was higher than the egress side. If the situation were reversed, and the difference were a few centimeters, it'd be like going over a bump. No problem. However, if the misalignment were larger, say a meter or more, you'd run smack up against a cross section of roadmetal delimited by the aperture, in which case you'd stay on the cylinder side of the portal and get smeared. But no explosion per se. For the *n*th time, I explained this all patiently to Sam, and he laughed.

"Just ribbing you, son. I like to see your hackles rise when you argue with dumb truckdrivers. But tell me, why don't we hear of accidents like that?"

"For the same reason that all portal accidents are hard to verify. But who knows? Maybe there's some safety mechanism, or maybe there's something about the nature of warped space-time that precludes it. I don't know. It's a wonder they can make the alignments with *any* degree of accuracy over dozens of light-years. There are lots of things about the Skyway we don't know. One of the biggest mysteries is why there's a road at all."

"Well," Sam said, "my guess has always been that they were used to haul heavy equipment from the entrance point to the next cylinder site during construction."

"A technology that controls gravity so well makes vehicle roads seem unnecessary. Doesn't it?"

"You have me there. Hell, maybe there was surplus money in the budget and the bureaucrats couldn't bring themselves to hand back the cash. Had to spend it, bureaucrats being what they are all over the universe."

"I take it you're joking."

"Not entirely. Compared to the staggering engineering feat of building the portals themselves, laying down a self-maintaining road between them would have been a breeze. An afterthought."

"I never looked at it that way," I said, scratching my head. "But, damn it, why did they plunk the cylinders down on the surface of planets? Why not in space?"

"Too many questions, Jake, and we don't have many answers."

The conversation had jogged my memory. "Which reminds me, I had a very interesting talk with Jerry Spacks back at the motel."

I related what had been said. Sam didn't comment for a while, then said, "Sounds like roadapples to me, Jake."

"My sentiments exactly." I looked back at Darla, who had been following the exchange with interest. "What do you think?"

"About what? The Skyway, or the stories about you?"

"Either. Both."

"I believe it. The story about you, I mean. If anyone could discover a backtime route, it would be you guys."

"Thanks." I looked up at the gas giant. It was awesome and majestic, painted with pastel parallel bands, dotted with the black beauty mark of another moon in transit. Below, the powdery regolith of the moon's surface was molded into sensuous low mounds, pocked here and there by blur-edged craters.

I turned back to Darla. "By the way, the question never came up before, but where were you going when we picked you up on TC-II?"

"Mach City," she answered without hesitation. "I've spent time there before, singing. But I was looking for a job as a nighclub manager. Had a line on a job in the city."

"Uh huh." What I didn't know about this woman would overload a rig or two. "Well, folks, what do we do now? Any suggestions? The floor is open, even to Cheetah here."

"We have three choices," Sam informed us, "since there are three portals on this planet. One, we can go back the way we came. Shall we put the matter in the form of a motion?"

A pair of strangled screams from me and Darla, mine being louder.

"The motion has not been carried. Two, we continue our original itinerary and deliver our load of scientific equipment to Chandrasekhar Deep Space Observatory on Uraniborg, and take our chances. Nix on that, too, since Wilkes doubtless knows we're bound for there. That leaves portal number three."

"Which goes to the boondocks of Terran Maze," I put in.

"Well, we could go to Uraniborg and not stop," Darla suggested. "We could stay on Route Twelve and go through to Thoth Maze."

"Hm. The Thoth are friendly enough," I ruminated. "But what would we do there?" No answer. "Hell, we have no choice, really."

"The ayes have it," Sam pronounced, "but the point is moot, because something's coming up fast on our tail. And I mean fast."

I unbuckled from the shotgun seat and almost cracked my head against the roof getting into the driver's seat, forgetting the reduced gravity. I checked the scanners.

"I see what you mean. Too fast for a civilian vehicle, not a rig. Either alien or a Colonial cruiser."

"It's a cruiser all right," Sam confirmed, "and why do I get the funny feeling he's going to pull us over?"

"I'm getting it, too. There's not much we can do, though."

"But we can match him gun for gun."

"No, Sam. We've already got Wilkes on our case. I don't want to tangle with the Colonial Authority."

"Yep, he's got his sye-reen a-blarin'. I'm getting it on all frequencies. *Merte!*"

"Well . . ." I sighed and resigned myself to the depressing inevitable, braked, and started pulling over. Just for the hell of it, I decelerated as fast as I could, and sure enough, the cops overshot us, hotrodding it as they were in their Mach-one-capable reaction-drive interceptor.

Sam laughed. "Look at 'em, the assholes."

The road ahead lit up blue-white with their retrofire, and the poor darlings found themselves about half a klick downroad from us. They had to back on the shoulder, which would probably put them in a good mood right off the bat.

"Getting pretty cheeky, aren't they?" Sam wondered. "I mean, pulling us over like this."

"It's not the first time," I said, "and it won't be the last. Cops just have to do cop things every once in a while. It's traditional. They hate not being able to make an arrest on the road."

The com speaker went *splup!*

"Jacob Paul McGraw?" The voice was female.

I put on a headset. "Yes?"

"Hi, Jake? How're things?"

"Oh, God, not Mona," Sam groaned.

"Just fine," I answered. "How's things with you?"

"Great," Constable Mona Barrows told me in her cheery bird-song voice. "Jake, I'm afraid I have bad news for you."

"Mona, you made my whole day by showing me your pretty back end. Nothing can throw me now. I meant the cruiser, of course."

"Jake, you're all talk, always were. Still, I think this'll smother your fusion-fire. There's a warrant for your arrest back on Hothouse."

Notice how she put that. *She* didn't have the warrant, nor was she arresting me. She couldn't—at least not here, on the Skyway.

"Really? What's the charge? Have they finally called in all my back citations?" But somehow I knew.

"A bad one this time, Jake. Homicide with a Powered Vehicle."

Of course.

"There are other charges. Leaving the Scene of an Accident, Assault with a Deadly Weapon, and a bunch of minor ones."

"Gee whiz, let's hear 'em all."

"Oh, Illegal Off-Road Driving, Failure to . . . Jake, do we really have to do this?"

The cab was quiet. I, for one, could see no way out. I sat there and tried to predict what Mona would do if we tried to make a run for it. It wasn't difficult, since they rarely came tougher than Mona. "Am I to understand that this is an arrest, Constable?"

"Why, whatever gave you that idea? I am, however, officially notifying you that charges have been brought against you within my jurisdiction. My suggestion is that you turn yourself in."

The word "suggestion" was heavily stressed. "Then, why have you pulled us over, may I ask?"

"Oh, Jake, don't go Skyway-lawyer on me. I can't drive and talk at the same time. Besides, you were coming up on the turnoff to Eta Cassiopeiae and I didn't want to drag you all the way back. I've got things to do, and I'm in a hurry. Now, you know you'll have to turn yourself in sometime, Jake. Why not do it now and save us all a lot of bother? Okay?"

"Love to oblige, Mona, but I'd hate myself in the morning."

"Now, Jake," she warned, "don't get any funny ideas. If I have to, I'll follow you until you *have* to come out of that rig to take a pee."

"I keep an empty fifth of Old Singularity behind the seat for that purpose, dear. I usually offer a snort to officers who're kind enough to pull me over to chat."

"Don't get cute. You know what I mean. You'll be pulling over for food or fuel sooner or later."

She wouldn't wait that long. Contrary to Sam's bravado, she could probably outshoot us. Disabling us in this airless environment would, of course, necessitate a "rescue."

"And if I leave Terran Maze?"

"That's your privilege. But you will have to stay out permanently. Not very good for your business, is it?"

"I must agree with you on that point."

"So, what do you say?"

I squelched the circuit. "What's the game, Sam?"

"String her along. We'll figure out something by the time we get back to Hothouse. Maybe Cheetah can find us more of those back jungle roads."

The very thought of such an eventuality made me say, "No chance, Mona. Mona honey, I don't know how you can sleep nights. You know the charges are trumped-up, and I think you know exactly what happened back at Greystoke Groves, and at Sonny's."

"Just doing my job, sweetie. It was Wilkes who reported the fatality and pressed the assault charge. I'm only following orders. True, I know Wilkes wants your blood in a crystal decanter . . . but I have nothing on him! You'd have to press counter-charges for me to help you. But it seems to me he's getting the worst of it. He has one boy dead and another in the iso-clinic growing a new trigger finger."

"In other words, if I turn up dead eventually, the moral weight of the issue will be on my side."

"I'm sorry, Jake. But, as I said, I have orders."

I looked back at Darla. "Darla, it's up to you. She didn't mention anything about a woman suspect. Say the word, we'll go back, and you're out of it completely."

"I'm for making a break for that third portal," she said, those ionospheric blue eyes glowing strangely.

"Jake, are you listening? I want to assure you that you will get all the protection you need, from Wilkes or anybody. I'll personally guarantee that you . . . wait just a sec."

The radio sputtered as she stopped transmitting.

"What is it, Sam?"

"Something coming in ahead. And I think I know what it is."

I looked at the forward view, switched it telescopic, and punched it on the main screen. A large vehicle was decelerating from a terrific rate of speed. I looked at the tracking readouts.

"Mach two point three and decelerating at fifteen Gs," I observed. "And it's not a reaction-drive buggy." I looked up to eyeball it. "There's only one thing it could be."

"Mona's in a truckload of trouble," Sam said, an edge of troubled concern to his voice.

The vehicle, as it appeared on the video hookup, was almost featureless, a low, lengthwise half a watermelon on rollers, gleaming bright silver. As it closed with frightening speed, it looked like a minimal-art representation of a mammoth beetle, or the overgrown pull-toy of a giant child. It was at once comic and deadly.

Mona was obviously thinking of making a run for it, but the thing was coming up too fast. She pulled away about a hundred meters or so, an effort, I suppose, to appear innocent.

Moments later, the "Skyway Patrol" car swooped in soundlessly, pulled off onto the shoulder between the cruiser and us.

The speaker boomed. The voice spoke in Intersystem. "STATE THE REASON FOR THIS INTERRUPTION OF TRAFFIC."

Imagine the most nonhuman voice possible, add all sorts of skin-crawling overtones from the extreme ends of the aural spectrum, then boost the signal till it breaks your ears. I turned down the gain on the amplifier.

"We are rendering assistance," Mona stated firmly, covering her nervousness. There was no question whom the Patrol car was addressing.

"STATE THE PROBLEM."

"The vehicle behind you was experiencing mechanical difficulty."

A pause. Then: "WE DETECT NONE."

"The problem has been corrected."

"DESCRIBE THE NATURE OF THE PROBLEM."

Mona was resentful. "Why don't you ask them?"

"OCCUPANTS OF COMMERCIAL TRANSPORT VEHICLE: CAN YOU VERIFY THESE CONTENTIONS?"

"Yes, we can. We had a loss of magnetic confinement due to a defective electronic component. The component has been replaced."

"FALSE." The voice was emotionless. "WE DETECTED THE ARRIVAL OF TWO NEUTRINO EMISSION SOURCES WHILE PATROLLING THIS SECTION. NO LOSS OF FU-

SION REACTION WAS OBSERVED FROM EITHER SOURCE."

It was over. "Sorry, Mona. I did my best." I did not transmit that.

"OCCUPANT OF LAW-ENFORCEMENT VEHICLE: YOU ARE AWARE THAT HALTING TRAFFIC ON THIS ROAD IS NOT TOLERATED."

It was not a question.

"EXCEPT FOR EMERGENCY PURPOSES OR MECHANICAL FAILURE, THERE ARE NO EXCEPTIONS. YOU ARE AWARE OF THE PENALTY. PREPARE TO END YOUR EXISTENCE. TIME WILL BE AFFORDED FOR RELIGIOUS CEREMONY OR CUSTOM. UPON THE FIFTIETH SOUNDING OF THE TONE, YOU WILL BE TERMINATED."

There began a bonging.

Mona was dead and she knew it, but her ass-end exploded in plasma flame and she took off. Instead of heading downroad, she swung sharply out over the dust-coated surface of the planetoid, trailing a spectacular plume of reddish-gray soil. She was trying to make it to the far side of a nearby rise for cover in the blind hope that the Patrol vehicle couldn't follow. Nobody knew enough about the "Roadbugs" to say one way or the other; none had ever been observed off-road. It was the only chance Mona had, and she took it.

But her engines went dead before she got two hundred meters away. The long, black interceptor sank into the dust. There followed a horrible silence, save for the lugubrious gonging.

Presently, Mona transmitted. "Jake, tell them. Tell them I was helping you. *Please!*"

"Mona, I'm sorry." There was nothing, absolutely nothing I could do.

"I don't want to die like this," she said, her voice cracking. "Killed by one of those bugs. Oh, God."

Almost without thinking, I fired the explosive bolts on the missile rack above the cab, activated one, and let it check out its target. When the green light blinked on the control board, I fired. An invisible arm snatched the thing and flung it aside. It exploded harmlessly out in the moonscape.

. . . bong . . . bong . . . bong . . . bong . . .

"Jake?" She seemed composed now, strangely calm.

"Yes, Mona?"

"We . . . we had some pretty good times, didn't we?"

"We did. Yes, we did, Mona."

One sob broke through the repose, but was quickly covered by a voice turned bitter. "It wouldn't even let me get a shot off, the bastard."

. . . bong . . . bong . . . bong . . . BONG!

"Goodbye, Jake."

"Goodbye."

The flash seared my retinas, left purple spots chasing each other in front of me. When I could see again, the interceptor was gone. A blackened pit lay where it had been.

The Roadbug was already pulling away.

"OCCUPANTS OF COMMERCIAL TRANSPORT VEHICLE: YOU ARE FREE TO GO."

It left us sitting under a tiny red sun and a world of unspeakable beauty.

5

"YOU HAVE NO cause to feel bad," Sam comforted me as we raced toward the tollbooths. "You did what you could. You tried. I was a little worried about how the Roadbug would react to that missile."

"I know. So was I," I said. "I shouldn't have done it. It was useless, and I knew it. I didn't have the right to risk Darla's and Cheetah's lives."

"I would have done the same," Darla said quietly.

"Thanks, Darla. Still . . ."

"Oh, c'mon, son. Mona knew the risk. She knew there's only one rule of this road: 'Thou shalt not close the road, nor interrupt traffic on any section thereof!' And she knew the Roadbugs enforce it to the letter."

"What right do they have to enforce anything?" I countered angrily. "Who the hell are they, anyway?"

Sam didn't answer, because there was no answer. Chalk up another mystery. Two theories were currently in vogue. The Roadbugs were either machines created by the Roadbuilders themselves, or they were vehicles whose unseen drivers wanted to keep the roads clear for their own purposes. Personally, I was for the latter theory. All indications were that the Skyway was millions of years old, and machines—no matter how advanced—just don't function that long . . . or so it seemed to me. But if there were flesh-and-blood beings inside those bug cars, they hadn't shown themselves yet, and I doubted they ever would.

The cylinders were all around, and we felt their persistent grabbing. The aperture swallowed us.

The next planet was a big one, a high-G world, as the sign before the tollbooths had warned, but going in an instant from .3 to 1.45 G was more than a little rough. The planet's acceleration sucked us down into our seats. I groaned and tried to straighten my spine, now turned rubber.

"Whuff!" Darla slumped in her seat. Cheetah bore up stoically.

"Jesus, even I can feel it," Sam said. "Somehow."

We arrived on a vast savannah of dry grass and bare patches of dust rolling out endlessly. Stunted trees dotted the plain. To our right and far away, a herd of bulky animals loped behind shimmering curtains of heat. The sun was low to our left, but bore down arduously. The sky was blue, slapped with watery brushstrokes of bright haze. Migration trails intersected the road. At one point, a dry-wash had undercut the highway itself, leaving exposed and suspended the five-meter-thick slab of metal roadbed. The gap was not great, and the road had no need to drop a supporting stanchion, as it could do when necessary. How it did such things was but another puzzle.

Great black birds, if birds they were, wheeled in the bald-white sky near the sun, searching. No prey or carrion was evident. Here and there along the side of the road were high mounds of powdery earth—warrens? hives? There were no signs of human habitation, though the planet was on the lists for colonization. The place did not look inviting. To settle such a world would be to resign oneself to the sorry fact that doing *anything* would require half again as much effort as on a 1G world: lifting a load of firewood, hefting an axe, mounting a flight of stairs. But humans had adapted to harsher conditions on many worlds. I imagined what future generations of this world would look like—short, swarthy, powerfully muscled, fond of khaki, glued into their wide-brimmed bush hats, opinionated, sure of themselves, proud. Perhaps. Diversity was sure to be the rule as human beings spread among the stars, and the differences might one day become more than cultural. Organisms are products of their environment, and when environments diverge . . .

The road shot ahead, unswerving, pointing to a low black band that rimmed the horizon. Mountains.

"What's the name of this place?" I asked. "What do the maps say?"

"Goliath," Sam said.

"Ah."

We drove for a while, until I realized how ravenously hungry I was.

"Anyone for eats?"

"Me!" piped Darla.

"Soup's on!"

We went back to the galley and fixed a quick brunch: ham-salad sandwiches, giant kosher deli pickles from New Zion ("Ham salad and kosher pickles?" Darla wondered. "We'll be struck dead." "Eat fast!" I said), potato salad, cherry yogurt, all fresh from the cooler. I had stocked up back on TC-I, shortly before hitting the road. We ate heartily.

I stopped in the middle of a mouthful of pickle. "How boorish of me. I forgot about Cheetah."

"Don't worry, she's okay—and that's not her real name."

"Huh? Darla, she can't *eat* human food. The polypeptides are all wrong."

"She brought her own. Go look."

I went forward, and sure enough there was Cheetah, munching wombat salad, or whatever it was, little green shoots with pink pulpy heads. I went back.

"When did she have time to—?"

"I never did get around to explaining why she's here, did I? And you never asked, either. That's what I like about you, Jake; you never question, never complain. You go along with the flow, except when you're pushed. Anyway, when you called I was talking to her, and she said that her 'time' was drawing near. I took it to mean the end of her life, but she wouldn't elaborate. I could sense that she was unhappy. Desperately so."

"She certainly wasn't being treated well at the motel," I said. "As a matter of fact, the pustulant little bedsore who ran the place was—"

"I know. I knew by the way he talked to her." She took a

bite of sandwich and chewed thoughtfully. "Cheetah had told me that none of her people had ever left the planet—'pass through the great trees at the edge of the sky' is the way they think of the portals—and that one day, before the end of her time, she would like to be the first."

"Seems to me I've seen her kind off-world."

"Right, but she doesn't realize that." Darla turned the notion over in her mind. "No, on second thought, she meant her clan, not her species. I told you how attached they are to their families."

"Got you."

"So, when I got the call, I asked her to come with us. That simply. I've had second thoughts about it since, of course. I really don't have the foggiest notion what to do with her. I was thinking vaguely of finding a home for her—but, practical brain that you are, you pointed out the problem of biochemical incompatibility."

"It's not insurmountable," I said. "Her new family, whoever they might be, would have to invest in a biomolecular synthesizer and program it to produce suitable protein material for her. We all know it's a bother to eat the glop, especially when it's not textured and flavor-rendered properly—any human traveling outside Terran space knows it—but she might survive, with a little love, and a lot of Hothouse-brand ketchup."

Darla showed concern. "I hope you're right. I've already gotten attached to her. She's so warm, open. . . . By the way, you're high in her pantheon of Great Beings. You saved her from a beating, and she's eternally grateful."

I polished my fingernails on my shirt. "Well, all in a hero's day, you know. Rescuing fair maidens, screaming like a banshee upon being bitten by a nasty ol' bug, fainting, almost getting my ass shot off because I had to play it proud instead of safe. I should have backed away from Wilkes' table."

"That's you, Jake. Dumb, but proud!"

"I thank you. But you were telling me about Cheetah and how she got here."

"Didn't I finish? Oh, yes. I told her she was welcome to come along with us, and while I was packing she disappeared. By the time I finished, she returned with an armful of fruit and such. I stowed the stuff in my bag, and . . ."

"She knows biochemistry?"

"Huh? No, certainly not. Maybe she's taken journeys before. Perhaps her tribe migrated now and then. I don't know."

"I thought they stuck pretty much to their home turf."

"Then, I don't know how she knew to bring food. But I'll ask her."

I drained the last of my coffee. It was of a good bean, grown on Nuova Colombia. "You also mentioned something about Cheetah's real name. How did she get tagged with the handle of a fictional Terran chimpanzee?"

"That's what the motel people called her." She raised an ironical eyebrow. "Cute, what? Fit in with the theme, I guess. You know, it's amazing how popular those Burroughs books still are after—what is it, going on two hundred years? Anyway, her proper moniker is *Winwah-hah-wee-wahwee*. She told me it means Soft-Green-is-the-Place-Where-She-Sleeps. At least, that's my rendition of it. Her translation was a bit garbled."

"Okay, then, 'Winnie' it is, now and forevermore."

I got up and stretched. The kinks were gradually working out.

"There's one more thing," Darla said.

"About Chee—I mean, about Winnie?"

"Yes. It was something about you and Sam. She said she was confused at first about Sam, about exactly what he was, until she realized that he was . . . well, that his spirit permeated the rig, if you follow me. Then she said she sensed something about you. Something she didn't like."

I shrugged. "Oh, well. A man who's hated by children and cute furry animals can't be all bad."

"Don't be silly. She *loves* you—I told you that. No, it's something concerning you. Something about what happened to you or what will happen. . . . I can't say for sure."

"Premonition?"

She chewed on her lip. "No." She shook her head. "No, forget about the 'happen' stuff. She didn't use those words. It wasn't a prediction, a precognitive intuition or anything. It was just something 'around' you. That's how she put it. The only thing coherent I could get out of her was that she didn't like your jacket because it smelled bad."

I sniffed my underarms. "Well, I guess if your friends can't tell you, who can?"

She rolled her eyes. "Jake."

"Sorry. But it's all a little vague, isn't it?"

"Yes, I suppose. But she seemed so sure."

"What she probably sensed was the lingering aura of my

life of libertinage and debauchery."

Darla giggled. "You mean your life of fantasizing. I happen to know that you're just this side of a monk in such matters. You haven't even tried to kiss me."

"I haven't? Well . . ." I took her shoulders and pulled her toward me, planted on those full pouting lips an unmonkish kiss of journeyman quality. She kissed back after the first fraction of a second. (I think I surprised her.) We continued in this fashion for some time.

When things had gone as far as they could under present circumstances, we parted. Darla commenced a straightening-up ritual: smoothed her hair, adjusted her clothing, checked the state of her lip gloss in the warped reflection of a shiny sugar canister. Her face was perenially made-up, perfectly, even at the worst of times. There was a certain composure about her, a kind of coolness—which attracted me, I must admit. Note: cool, not cold. Self-possessed. Well, there was no nonsense about her (not to say no sense of humor), no wasted motions, no false moves, no hesitations. I felt her incapable of uttering something even remotely insipid. The controlling factor was not intellectual, but was more in the way of being worldly, knowing, aware, *hip*, if you will, to use an archaic term. She was a veteran of the Skyway, but there wasn't a rollermark on her. I couldn't guess how old she was; anywhere from nineteen to thirty. But a special native wisdom sparkled in eyes that had seen more than they told. To use another hoary Terran colloquialism: she had been around. Yes, she had.

"I hate to break up anything momentous, kids," Sam discreetly announced over the aft-cabin speaker, "but there's something up ahead."

I went forward. We were continuing our race for the mountain range, which now hove over the horizon as a brown-gray mass with an intermittent edge of white. Snow-tipped peaks. They looked like mounds of day-old pudding, whipped-cream toppings gone stale and dried.

A vehicle, an old bus, was pulled off the road ahead, and it seemed to be experiencing mechanical problems. A group of people were gathered near the off-road side.

As we drew up I braked instinctively, as I usually do when I spot a breakdown; however, recent events had spooked me to the point where I considered passing them by. But no. One of the stranded passengers waved pleadingly—a bearded black man who wore a loose robe that smacked of the sacerdotal—

and I pulled completely off the pavement at a prudent distance downroad, across one of those spontaneous bridges that spanned a deep dry-wash.

"Well, let's get a whiff of the stuff they call air here," I said reluctantly. "It's supposed to be rated EN-1B, which is as close as you can get. Sam, were those people wearing respirators or anything?"

"No, but take a nasal inhaler of CO_2. You could hyperventilate under extreme exertion. There are a few in the glove box, I think."

The pumps sucked the good air out and let the bad come in. Mark you, Earth people: there is nothing like the first breath of alien atmosphere, no matter how near to Terran normal it is. The weird odors are most unsettling. Strange trace gases never meant for human olfactory systems tiptoe across your nasal membranes in spiked shoes. At best, you gag and choke and cough. At worst, you swoon and wake up with an assist mask slapped over your face, if you're lucky. But the atmosphere of Goliath wasn't all that bad. It carried a whiff of iodine on a stench of decayed fruit, a strange combination to say the least, but the fruity smell masked the medicinal one enough to make it bearable. There wasn't a fruit tree in sight. On the bad side, there was a trace of a nose-tickling element, an irritant of some sort that kitchy-kooed the sinuses maddeningly close to the sneeze-point without getting them over the hump. But . . . I guess you get used to anything. In fact, the longer I breathed the stuff, the less I noticed its noxious qualities. There was good oxygen here to be sure, though at pressure a bit too high. Maybe—mind you, just maybe—a person could get to like running this sort of soup through his lungs.

The air I could live with; the heat was another matter. I wasn't ready for it, even after Hothouse. I sprang the hatch, and it was like opening an oven door. Talk about dry heat versus humid heat, and the misery indices of both didn't apply here. It was punking HOT and that's all there was to it. The heat smothered me, the planet strained my arches, and the sun began to pan-fry my skin in a sauce of sudden sweat.

"Darla! Throw me your brolly, please. Hurry!"

She did, and I popped it open and put it up against the smoldering sky.

I walked slowly across the bridge, stopping momentarily to inspect one of the piers the roadbed had dropped down into the gully to carry its weight over. I didn't risk bending over very far, feeling stiff and top-heavy. I got no clue as to how the trick had been done, and continued on across the bridge.

I was met by the black man. He was on the light-skinned side, tall, round-shouldered, very thin. A big, long-fingered hand enveloped mine.

"Hello! Decent of you to stop. Didn't think you would. I'm John Sukuma-Tayler." His accent was British, his manner amiable. After I told him my first name only, he said, "Awful place to have broken down. The heat's about done us in. Reminds me a bit too much of Africa. I lived in Europe most of my life, and liked it."

"Why did you leave?" I said, a little too bluntly. I was hot!

He took it as humor. "Sometimes I wonder!" He chuckled.

"Sorry. I didn't mean it the way it sounded."

"Don't fret about it. Some of our people are on the verge of biting each other's heads off. The heat's getting to all of us. We're in quite a pickle. Do you think we could prevail upon you to lend a hand?"

"Sure. What's up."

We began walking back to the bus, which was up on its service jacks, precariously so. The bus was an old clunker, but in its day it had been built for speed and taking sharp curves, and had a ground-effect flange all the way around it, which made it difficult to get underneath. The built-in jacks were barely adequate, especially in this gravity. Anyone crawling under would be taking a chance of having several tons of low-slung vehicle squat on his chest. To preclude this eventuality, several of the passengers were shoring up the edges of the flange near the jacks with plastic bags filled with earth. The dirt was being shoveled from a nearby conical mound, one of many that punctuated the plain. No large rocks were handy for the job. The work was progressing slowly.

"All I can tell you," Sukuma-Tayler said with a helpless spread of his arms, "is that it quit, just like that. Powered down and stopped, here in the middle of nowhere. A few of our people have some mechanical aptitude, but no one's really got a look yet. We tore out some seats and tried to get to the engine from the inside, but the bolts holding the shielding wouldn't budge, and we have no power tools."

"Too bad. That's how you get to the guts of this thing. Going underneath might not do you any good. But, it depends on what's ailing it."

"Thought as much. The engine monitoring readouts are still

operative, but they don't say much. To me, that is."

"Let me take a look," I said. "While I'm at it, I'd suggest you get those sandbags out from under the GE flange and put them under the frame bracings. If she goes down, that flange will just crinkle."

The big man furrowed his brow. "You know, you're absolutely right." He shook his head wearily. "Ignorance is so handicapping! Especially with machines."

"Can be deadly, too." I dragged myself toward the hatch.

The verniers told me nothing, being little better than idiot lights. Nothing in the way of plasma diagnostic systems, even though the vehicle had been a commercial carrier.

Sukuma-Tayler eased his lanky frame inside and sat next to me.

"Anything?" he asked hopefully.

"No, not much. It looks like you have full power going through the radio-frequency breakdown stage, but other than that, I can't tell anything from these readouts. Does she turn over?"

"Yes, but the engine just won't catch."

"Uh-huh. Well, that could be anything. If it's loss of plasma confinement, that could be pretty hairy. I couldn't do anything here."

"I was afraid of that," Sukuma-Tayler said ruefully.

"You're lucky in one sense. These old vans are among the few Earth-built buggies still on Skyway. My rig's alien-manufactured, but built to Terran specifications and design, so I'm fairly familiar with this kind of hardware. However, I'm really not a mechanic. It takes an expert."

"Anything you can do, Jake, would be appreciated."

"Well, I'll give it a try." I mopped my brow with an already damp sleeve. "I can't remember, though, whether these old buses use an occluded-gas ion source. If so, you need a pinch of titanium in with the fuel. Otherwise, you get neutral particles flying all over the place between pulses. I forget whether they do or not. What kind of fuel are you using?"

"High-test. Deuterium-tritium."

"Yeah, I thought so. My rig runs on double deuce. Newer design."

"Ah."

"When did you fill up last?"

The Afro scratched his beard. "You know, I really can't remember. These things run forever, it seems."

Continuing my train of thought, I got out my circuit-test gauge. "Got a screwdriver?"

Sukuma-Tayler yelled for a screwdriver, and one of the passengers, a young Oriental man, brought him one. I took it and unbolted the instrument panel, slid it out, and looked for the fuel readout leads. I found them and tested them. Of course.

"I found your problem," I said, pushing the panel back. Naturally, it didn't want to fit back the way it had been. I shoved, got nowhere.

"You did?" He was shocked and relieved.

"Yeah. You're out of fuel."

"What! You're joking."

"No. The fuel-level readout was shorted."

The big man slapped his forehead. "I'll be damned. After all that mucking about—" He leaned out the hatch and yelled, "People! Stop what you're doing. Our friend here has exposed us as the fools that we are." He turned back to me. "So sorry to have troubled you, old man. What classic boneheadedness!"

"It can . . . uhhh! . . . happen to anybody. Gimme a hand with this, will you?"

We shoved the panel back in. The screwholes, contrary negative entities that they are, did not line up. I handed him the screws, and he looked at them blankly.

"I was meaning to ask," I said offhandedly. "Are you some sort of religious group?"

He beamed. "Yes! We're Teleologists. Church of Teleological Pantheism. You've heard of us?"

A man with pride in his faith is to be admired. "No."

"Uh. Well, that's what we are, and we're supposed to be settling this planet. We were en route to Maxwellville."

We stepped outside. There were about seven people in the party besides the Afro, whom I presumed to be the leader. Four of them were women, and all were of various races. I took one man for an Australian Abo. "Not many of you for a colony, are you?"

"We're an advance party. More will be following shortly. We're branching off from a community on Khadija, and eventually we hope to siphon everybody there to Goliath. Our presence on Khadija is . . . well, resented."

"I see. You plan to homestead?"

"We hope to," Sukuma-Tayler told me as we watched his people unstack the sandbags and empty them. "Actually, we have a land grant from the—"

Yelling from the direction of the conical mound interrupted him. We turned and looked. One man who had been shoveling dirt was down on the ground not far from the mound. He was struggling with something that apparently had gotten hold of him. His partner was beating whatever it was with a shovel. We rushed—I gimped—over to them.

The thing was a half-meter-long segmented animal with what looked like a shiny metallic carapace. It had crablike claws, but there were more than two pincers on each. The three elements were positioned for grasping. The beastie had the screaming man's ankle in a tight grip. Even more startling was the sight of the animal hefting a shiny, sharp blade in the other claw, using it to jab its victim's calf with rapid, vicious up-and-down strokes. The man with the shovel gave up whacking the thing with the flat of the spade and used the edge like a chopper. After several strokes, he cut the creature in two. The front half fought on. Several people had run up, and we all made a grab for it at once. We tore the thing apart like a boiled lobster. I saw another man, the Abo, come away with the blade-wielding forelimb, at the price of an oozing crimson slash across his palm.

I came up with a smaller side appendage, and examined it. What looked like small pieces of hammered, copper-colored metal were draped over the animal's soft, rubbery skin. Miniature armor. As a matter of fact, the metal looked very much like copper, perhaps with a slight leavening of tin. Bronze. The armor was attached with a sticky black gum, which was revealed when I pried the plates away from the leg. The skin was dun-colored and soft. I stood there scrutinizing it, absorbed.

"More of them!"

I looked up. More creatures had emerged from the mound while we were wrestling with the first. They were popping out of the top of the mound like blobs of lava from a volcano, wriggling down the steep sides, some of them running madly in circles, others getting a fix on us and charging, blades flashing in the sun. In an instant, there were hundreds of them all over the place.

We backed away toward the bus. I burned one who came toward us in a banzai charge, weapon whirling, pure hate in those black pin-dot eyes. That left two charges in the squib. More of them came at us. I shot two of them and stamped a third into the dirt, but not before he knifed me in the ankle and nicked my left shin with an armored pincer. I picked up his weapon. It was a sword—no other word for it—irregular in shape and crudely wrought, like the armor, but it held an edge to be reckoned with. The ankle wound began to pang.

The creatures were fast. They had already cut off our escape route to the bus and uproad to the bridge. We could only retreat parallel to the highway.

"We seemed to have disturbed their nest," Sukuma-Tayler observed dryly.

"You mean their barracks, don't you?"

We ran. Individual attacks broke off for the moment. They kept pace with us as we drew away, but when I looked back I was amazed to see them mustering into ranks for what looked like an organized pursuit.

Something whizzed past me.

I heard a scream and looked back. A black woman was down, clutching the back of her head. We doubled back, and I bent over her. The projectile had left a bloody indentation in her scalp. I saw something shiny nearby and picked it up; it was a grape-size lump of copper. At closer range the girl would have been seriously injured. As it was, she was knocked silly. I looked out over the sea of crawling metal for the source of the barrage. From what I could make out, they were firing at us by means of a slingshot device operated by three creatures. Two took either end of a long elastic band of black material, probably a variant of the armor adhesive, while a third stretched the middle back about three meters. The release velocity was enough to make it a potent weapon.

Another ball buzzed by my ear. The artillery was advancing, leapfrogging forward after each shot. I helped carry the semi-conscious girl back and away. There was no cover except for other nest-cones. The heat was beyond sapping me now; it was draining away my strength. The others looked to be on the verge of collapse, none of them sweating now, all body fluids leached through pores and evaporated. They had been out too long. I still had sweat in me, but the tap was full open. A floating sense of unreality came over me. I was hyperventilating.

Sam was just now turning around.

The infantry charged. They overtook us easily, hobbled as we were with the girl. By the time we brought her around and got her shakily to her feet, they were on us. The girl went down again.

No one had a working firearm, but we made do with what we had: both spades, a jack crank, a wrench, and an assortment of odd tools. I whacked at them with the parasol until it flew to pieces, then used my size-eleven Colonial Militia fatigue boots on them, wishing I'd worn my high boots that day. None of us fared very well. A man to my right went down, then another woman. I saw Sukuma-Tayler kick at the things until one grabbed him by the shoe and began hacking at his leg. He yelled, turned, and ran with the creature hanging on to him. He tried to kick it off, then went down and wrestled with it.

The creatures were swarming over the first injured woman. She was screaming hideously, but nobody could get to her. I tried to move forward, kicking at them, sending dozens of the bastards flying, but I couldn't make headway. One crawled up my leg from behind and I felt a searing pain in my thigh. I tore the animal off and threw it. I stumbled back over a partially buried length of metal, probably a tent pole. Not taking time to wonder who had had the misfortune to pitch camp in this crawling hell, I pulled it up and started to swing at them with it, with little effect except to keep them at a distance or knock weapons from their claws. I backed and swung, backed and swung, not having time to look up to see where Sam was. I heard him coming.

Finally, the offensive broke off on my section of front and I looked up. Sam was coming across the bridge, crunching and popping his way over a seething carpet of armor. It sounded as if he were running over a pile of eggs and scrap metal.

Something slithered through my legs. It was a mound-creature, but it had come from behind me. I whirled around. To our rear lay another army. Something about them looked slightly different, and I hoped they were from another hive, with any luck a hostile neighbor. It looked as though they were, because our attackers broke off completely and retreated a short distance, waiting for the first wave of shock troops from the other side to pass us by and reach them. We stood there in the middle of everything, watching the suicide squad from the challengers throw themselves at the front lines. They were quickly dispatched—torn apart and left to jerk their lives out in the sand. Theses token charges seemed to be overtures to a major offensive. Heroic? Stupid? Maybe they had a purpose.

There were five of us left. Three bodies lay out in the writhing mass of armor.

"Everybody!" I yelled. "Stand still!"

As soon as I said it, the eastern army attacked. We stood there like log piers in a rushing river. A few stopped to sniff at my legs before charging ahead.

Sam was advancing toward us, passing through the battle line. Darla popped the hatch and aimed her gun at the ground.

"Hold it!" I shouted. "Friendly troops!" I motioned for the survivors to follow me as I picked my way gingerly through the flow of advancing soldiers. I finally reached the cab and climbed in, assisted by Darla. I slid the driver's seat back and helped the others inside. Sukuma-Tayler was the last, and I was surprised to see him alive. I shoved the seat forward, fell into it, and sealed the cab.

Sam was driving. We wheeled around and made for the road. My head lolled up against the viewport.

I saw a severed human leg being dragged away.

One of the women got hysterical, but Darla soon had her under control with a shot of something suitable from the tickler. The woman slumped over and groaned.

The hyperventilation subsided and my head was clear once more, but I closed my eyes and couldn't open them again.

6

WHEN I CAME to, Darla was passing from casualty to casualty, doing what she could with the paraphenalia in the medicine kit. Most of us had moderate-to-severe lacerations. One man, a thin, ascetic blond fellow, had sustained a deep gash that had nearly taken off his foot at the ankle. He also had puncture wounds to the chest. For the leg, Darla improvised a tourniquet out of cloth and a screwdriver. The Afro and I had gotten off easiest, me with slash and puncture wounds to the lower extremities, he with the same plus stab wounds in the arm. We were a sorry lot. Blood ran in bright rivulets over the deck. Darla got to me last.

"Things that attack you all have leg fetishes," she said.

"Well, I'm a liberal in such matters," I said.

"We're short on everything. How long till we make Maxwellville?"

"About two hours," Sam answered, "But that's on straight road. Those mountains look treacherous. The map says the grade reaches forty-five degrees on some slopes. Also, there's one hell of a shitstorm brewing antisunward."

I looked. Thunderheads were stacking up on a grim-looking horizon. Masses of heated air had risen all day to an icy altitude, and now were returning with a vengeance, reincarnated as rain-swollen clouds, black with fury.

"Looks nasty, all right. Could be twisters in there. Which way is it moving?"

"I've been scanning for the last ten minutes. It's heading toward us on a slant from left to right as we look at it. If we can get to those hills in time, we should miss most of it."

"That's good news. Switch on the afterburners."

"Show me where the switch is. I'll do my best, though. I just hope she holds together."

"Why? Problems?"

"You're not going to ask why I took my time getting down to you back there?"

I heaved a sigh. "No, Sam, I wasn't. I figure you had a damn good reason. Of course, if you didn't, I will take a flex-torque wrench to you with exquisite artistry."

"I had trouble starting up, and I stalled out twice on the bridge."

"That doesn't sound good. In fact, I don't like that at all." I still felt sort of giddy. "I'm not going to think about that today. I am going to sit here quietly and have the nervous breakdown that's owed me. Thank you. Good-bye." I closed my eyes.

"Just wanted to tell you," came a voice at my ear. I turned my head. It was Sukuma-Tayler, squatting by my seat. His face was strained, his lower lip quivering. "Awfully sorry . . . damned shame to have involved you in all this. My fault. . . ." Abruptly, he broke down and sobbed. When he had composed himself somewhat, he blubbered, "I'm responsible for their deaths."

"No. You've fallen into the same trap many have—not being totally prepared for alien unknowns. The sameness of the Skyway can lull you into a false sense of security. Many have perished because of it."

"The Guidebook," he said, voice tightened with regret, "I . . . I should have known! I had it, I read it." He shook his head helplessly. "But on the other side of these mountains, where the settlements are, the ecology is radically different. I covered those sections very thoroughly! I simply neglected the other aspects of the planet."

"As I said, a common fault. We didn't bother to check the planet banks at all before we barged in here. But, we all learn, and with a little luck, we live."

"My friends weren't so lucky."

"They won't be the last you'll lose to a new planet. It's a dangerous universe, John."

"Yes, I know. We have lost others, before." He was silent for a moment, then went back to find a place to sit in the crowded cab.

We rode along in silence until the sky grew dark and the first drops of rain spattered on the forward viewport. It wasn't long before it came whipping down in force, driven by a gale-force wind coming from two points off the starboard bow. We were doing around 150 meters per second, and the rig buffeted and shook and kept yawing to the left as Sam fought to keep it on course. Pink sheets of lightning ripped through the gathering gloom above.

The lower parts of my legs were on fire, as was a large area of my left thigh. I had thought that I could handle the pain for a while, but exactly whom was I kidding? I told Darla to load up the tickler with an upper-downer cocktail: a 1 mg solution of hydromorphone with 5 mg of amphetamine sulfate thrown in to keep me alert.

"And no pharmacology lectures, please."

"I'll do it if you can keep this rig on the road."

"Sam, give me the wheel."

I took the control bars in hand.

Outside, thunder walked across the plain in big, earth-shivering steps. The forward port was a solid film of wind-flattened water, distorting the view ahead. The gale grew stronger; the light kept fading until visibility dropped close to zero. I flicked on the headbeams, then focused the spotlight on the road. For good measure, the yellow fogcutters went on too. The lights helped, but visibility was still marginal. It was not blackness out there as much as it was murk, a ghastly greenish drizzle that glowed with a strange diffused light. I looked up and saw it was coming from the sky. It was a twister sky.

Shortly thereafter, Sam confirmed my suspicions.

"Jake, I've got something pretty scary on the scanners."

"Twister?"

"Well, if it is, it's the grandpappy of them all. The electrostatic potential is in the gigavolt region. It's a monster."

"Jesus, Sam, where is it?"

"Oh, it's paralleling us about a klick off starboard."

"Oh."

"You'd better hurry, son."

"Yes, sir."

I floored the son of a bitch.

"Everybody hang on!" Sam yelled.

The warning didn't come in time, for right then I lost the roadway and we hit dirt with a bang, vibrated through a staccato series of bumps, then whumped into something big that splattered the viewport with mud. Whatever it was didn't stop us, but it took several seconds for the washers to clear the view.

"Sam! Find the road for me!"

A final volley of bumps and we were back on the road. I straightened the rig out and eased off on the throttle.

"There you are," Sam said calmly. "Now, do you want to use the thermal-imaging glasses, or do you want to keep us entertained?"

"Okay, okay. Damn things give me headaches." I brought the contraption down and shoved my face into it. A fuzzy 3-D scan of the view ahead in pretty, dappled colors showed the road in deep purple, with ambiguous edges. Also muddying the picture were false echoes from the rain itself—but it was an improvement.

"What did we hit back there?" Sam asked.

"One of those miserable land-crab mounds, probably. And I hope the bank turns down their loan to build a new one. Any more data on the twister?"

"Time for your shot, Mr. McGraw." It was Darla whispering in my ear.

I started to roll up my sleeve. She shook her head.

"Uh-uh."

"What? Woman, do you expect me to drop my pants in the middle of a howling tempest?"

"Now, Mr. McGraw, you know how we deal with uncooperative patients. Drop 'em or it's the rubber room."

"Sam, take over."

He did, and I did, and she did.

"Ow. Damn it. Whoever named that thing a tickler?"

"About the twister," Sam went on. "Jake, I don't know what this thing is, but it looks like we can outrun it. Its periphery is moving at about half our speed."

"That's pretty fast for a twister."

"It's more than a twister. It's a funnel cloud of some kind, but it analyzes as something qualitatively different from a garden-variety Kansas tornado."

"Aunty Em! Aunty Em!" I screamed in my best falsetto.

"You always were a strange boy."

We skirted the storm for a few dozen more kilometers before we reached the foothills. The wind subsided, but the rain still fell in torrents. It was dusk now, and the sky was a hell of red-orange clouds. Visibility improved. The road bore steadily upward, snaking through the steep foothills, but it did so in a very curious and inefficient manner. On this section of the Skyway, the road lay across the mounting terrain like a carelessly dropped ribbon, twisting painfully into complicated figures, doubling back on itself, following a route laid out by a surveyor under the influence of hallucinogenic drugs. The roadway climbed grades that were much too steep, banked crazily on slopes that it should have cut into, arced over dizzying peaks it should have tunneled through. It was a civil engineer's nightmare. There were only two explanations. Either the Roadbuilders had scrupulously avoided disturbing the contour of the land, perhaps out of conservationist convictions, to the detriment of the highway's viability as a passable route . . . or the road had been built so long ago that the mountains had sprung up under it. This latter theory involved the notion that the road had the ability to adjust, to conform, to make a way for itself as slow but persistent geological forces changed the lay of the land over eons—to *grow,* in effect, for it would need to lengthen itself to wend its way through these erupting crags. Since it was apparent by phenomena like spontaneous bridge-building that the Skyway was not an inert slab of material but some sort of ongoing process, it wasn't hard to imagine the roadway having some astonishing capacity to feel its way over a changing terrain and nestle itself in as comfortably as it could. In this case, it didn't look very comfortable at all. It could span a crevice or a sharp dip, but it could not excavate, nor could it tunnel.

Darkness fell and the rain continued. I was on the lookout for flash flooding. Sheets of water sluiced over the roadway as we splashed our way through and upward, climbing slowly, following a torturous path into the steepest part of the range. The grade neared forty degrees on some stretches, and the rollers were polarized to maximum grab. It was barely enough. The slip-factor was approaching *pi* radians on some of the drive rollers. Translation: they were going round and round and we weren't getting anywhere.

Everyone tried to catch some sleep, found places to wedge into so as not to be thrown around. Darla got the most seriously wounded man bedded down in the bunk, and shot him up with analgesics. I asked her how he was doing, and she told me the sooner we got to Maxwellville, the better. I could have guessed; he had lost a lot of blood. Privately, I didn't think he'd make it.

Sukuma-Tayler came up to sit in the shotgun seat, declaring he couldn't find room enough to stretch out. Besides, he wasn't sleepy. Winnie was huddled underneath the dash on his side. He accidentally poked her, and she jumped. The Afro apologized.

"Sorry! Sorry!" Winnie answered, apologizing for being in the way, I guess. If she were representative of her race, how could such an unaggressive species survive for long? I thought of the jungle-clearing project. Indeed, they were not surviving.

"Uh . . . we were never properly introduced," Sukuma-Tayler said. "I didn't realize he could talk. She? Oh. Eridani, isn't she?"

"Yes. Winnie, meet John."

"Hello!"

"How do you do, Winnie."

She curled up and went back to sleep.

The grade steepened, curled to the left in a hairpin turn. A temporary river greeted us. The drive rollers spun, then dug into roadway.

"Makes one wonder, doesn't it . . . about the Skyway," John said.

"Concerning?"

"Well, for one thing, why most people bother to travel the road between apertures, instead of flying."

"Couple of reasons," I told him. "One, no one's been able to make air travel cheaper than ground transportation, even after all these years. It'll always be that way, I think. It's a matter of physics. Two, an aircraft has to be designed with certain factors in mind, like a planet's air pressure, gravity, etcetera. Going from planet to planet poses some problems. I've seen some variable airfoil designs, but they're all clumsy and impractical. And useless when you hit an airless stretch. Of course, you could taxi through those, but that strikes me as silly. Then, of course, there's antigravity."

"Hm. Which is one with the perpetual motion machine, eh?"

"As far as anybody knows. Nobody's cracked the problem to any appreciable degree. Oh, you always hear that some race, somewhere, has developed true antigravity. But I've never seen such a vehicle on any part of Skyway. Even the Roadbugs run on rollers."

"You'd think that somebody would have done it by now."

"Yes, it does seem inevitable, somehow. But there must be monumental problems in the way."

"But there *are* air routes between planets. Correct?"

"Yeah, we riggers have some competition, but the routes are limited." I chuckled derisively. "I'd like to see a flyboy get through a place like Wind Tunnel."

"A planet?"

"Alpha Mansae II. Gales up to two hundred meters per second, dust storms that blanket the planet."

The big man was impressed. "Sounds dangerous, even in one of these juggernauts."

"It is."

The slope-meter was tilting to fifty degrees. I couldn't believe it myself, and I'd seen everything.

"Good God," the Afro breathed as we looked straight up into a bottomless pit of black sky.

The rollers spun frantically, then finally grabbed onto something, and we went over the crest and onto a relatively level area.

"Then again," I said, breathing easier, "there might be something to be said for flying."

"Another point," Sukuma-Tayler went on. It was obvious this gabbing made him feel better. "Granted that with high-speed ground vehicles it's only a matter of an hour or two between arrival point and the next jump—on every planet but this one, it seems. But my question is, why didn't they place the ingress points and egress apertures—I mean the ones that take you to the next planet—closer together? You could put the double-back portal far enough away to prevent any knotting-up of space-time, which is, I take it, why the portals must have so much distance between them. That way, you could nip from planet to planet without much driving at all. You'd only have to go some distance to use the double-back portal."

"I can't explain to you," I answered, "why you need big chunks of normal space-time between ingress points and portals, as well as between portals, even though an ingress point is just a piece of empty road that you materialize on—but I can tell you that the reason is a bunch of Greek symbols and lots of numbers. And it's all very theoretical. Hold on!"

Another monstrous grade loomed ahead. We started to climb.

Suddenly, warning lights flashed behind us, and a horn sounded. An old-fashioned, *ancient* automobile horn. I hugged the shoulder, and the little bugger passed us, shooting up the hill as quick as you please. It was a very strange vehicle, to match the sound of the horn. The horn went:

And the vehicle, from what I could discern out in the liquid darkness, was a mid-twentieth-century American automobile, which in its day had been powered by an internal combustion engine, fueled by either alcohol or a fractional distillate of petroleum, I forget which. The color was a deep red and the finish was glossy.

"An apparition," Sukuma-Tayler said.

"I hope that thing stops in Maxwellville. Those *look* like pneumatic rollers . . . tires, really, but I just can't believe that they are. Anyway, you were saying?"

"Hm? Oh, nothing. Nothing."

We rode in silence for a time, inching up the hill.

Abruptly he said, "Jake McGraw!" It was an epiphany of some sort.

"That's me," I said, perplexed.

"It just came to me. I've heard of you! Yes, I remember the name." He smiled. "You must forgive me, old man. Blurting out like that. But you must know you're something of a legend on the Skyway."

"I am, eh?"

"You are *the* Jake McGraw, aren't you?"

"I'm the only one I know of."

"Of course. Yes. But . . . meeting you like this . . . well, it simply isn't . . . I mean, one thinks of Odysseus, Jason, Aeneas, heroic figures. And you seem . . ." He winced. "Oh, my. I didn't put that quite the way I wanted to."

"And I seem like such an ordinary asswipe. Is that what you're telling me, John?"

He laughed. "Not quite. But the tales told about you are remarkable." He leaned over to me, mock-secretively. "I take it they're all—how do Americans put it?—'tall tales'?"

"Depends on what tales you mean," I said in deadpan. "Now, the one about the sixteen women on Albion, that's purest truth. They all gave birth within the space of six days."

"That *is* one I'd like to hear." He looked at me slyly. "I assume you're joking, but maybe I'd better not assume." He laughed again, but sobered up quickly, the death of three friends choking off anything resembling good cheer.

Presently, he said, "It was your computer that started the association process. Then when I heard your . . . friend, there, say your name—anyway, I noticed that the computer was extraordinarily human-sounding. Exactly how did he get that way? Terran machines can come close to mimicking a human personality, but yours is a different kettle of fish entirely."

"Sam is more than a computer," I said. "His core-logic contains a Vlathusian Entelechy Matrix. It's a component the size of your thumb."

"I've heard of them. The Vlathu keep the process a dark secret, don't they? Who was the impression taken from?"

"My father."

"I see."

It strikes most people as ghoulish. I think I know why, but I don't think of it.

"He died in an accident on Kappa Fornacis V. I brought his body to the Vlathu home planet, which, like Terra, isn't directly connected to the Skyway, and left it with their technicians. They kept it for almost a year. When I got it back, there were no incisions in the scalp, and the brain was intact. Then he was buried on Vishnu, on our farm."

Sam broke in. "You're talking about me like I wasn't here. Damned uncomfortable."

"Oh, I do beg your pardon," Sukuma-Tayler said. "Jake, do you mind if I ask him—? There I go again. *Sam*. Would you mind answering some questions?"

"Go ahead," Sam said.

"How do you see yourself? By that I mean, what is your

self-image in terms of a physical presence? Do you follow me?"

"I think I do. Well, it depends. Sometimes I think of myself as part of the rig, sometimes it seems as if I'm just riding in it. Most of the time I get a distinct impression of sitting right where you are, in the shotgun seat. No, don't get up. The feeling persists whether the seat's occupied or not."

Sukuma-Taylor put a finger to his chin. "That's very interesting. There's another question, but I really don't know how to—"

"You want to know what it feels like to die. Is that it?"

The Afro nodded.

"Damned if I know. I don't remember anything about the crash. I have been told since that the son of a bitch who hit me head-on was drunk and that he came through it alive. I don't think the Vlathu erased the memory, but I don't have it."

Sam's response plunged the Afro into deep thought.

Meanwhile, we had gained the top of the rise, and the rain was subsiding. Dark walls of rock lined the road; the Skyway had lucked into a natural pass. Just then, the headbeams dimmed, then came back to full voltage. The engine began complaining in a low, gravelly murmur.

"Jake, we have plasma instability," Sam announced.

"Not a moment too soon." I sighed. "I think it's all downhill from here. What are you reading?"

"Everything I'm getting says we have a kink-instability developing. Temperature dropping. Yeah, the longitudinal current in the plasma is 'way over the Kruskal limit. Wait, the backup coils are cutting in. Back to normal now . . . hold on. Just a minute. Hell, there it goes again. Shut her down, Jake."

"How much power in the accumulators?"

"We're full up. We can get by on the auxiliary motor, as long as we've climbed our last hill."

7

WE MADE IT.

We coasted down the other side of the range. Beyond the headbeams the land looked very different, rocky and wild. Short, wide-trunked trees hung in dark foliage bordered the road. We drove across wide plateaus, hugged the rim of gaping dark areas that seemed to be canyons. The rain stopped, and the outside temperature plunged. Stars appeared, and the spectacular frozen explosion of a gas nebula was painted across a broad arc of sky. There were no recognizable constellations, for we were eight hundred light-years or so down from Terra on the Orion arm, antispinward. Goliath's primary was not even a catalog number.

These were the boonies, all right.

We even lost the Skyway. It ended abruptly under a massive rockslide, but not before we were warned off by flashing road barriers and shunted onto a crisp, new Colonial Transportation Department highway. The road took us into Maxwellville in half an hour.

The hospital was surprisingly well-equipped. The seriously injured man was semicomatose and in shock, but they shoved enough tubes into his body to wake a corpse, and brought his blood count up with plasma and iso-PRBCs. They even managed to save his foot. The rest of us they treated and released, after re-dressing and spot-welding our wounds and shooting us full of broad-spectrum antixenobiotics. To be extra sure, we all spent time under a "password" beam, which fried any foreign organism in our bodies that couldn't produce genetic identification proving Terran origin.

Then we got the bill. I swallowed hard and pulled out my Guild Hospitalization Plan card, which had lapsed. They took the agreement number, but didn't like it. Sukuma-Tayler insisted that he take care of it. So I let him, telling him I would pay him back.

I went back to the cab.

"John's asked us to come out to their ranch," I told Sam. "What do you think?"

"Fine for you. I'll be in the garage."

I scowled. "I forgot. I hate to be so far away from you. But motels are out. And when the mail rig gets into town, the local constable might be looking for us."

"Better find out when the next mail is due."

"Right." I took a deep breath. "Sam, we keep piling up questions with no answers."

"For instance?"

I went back to get a few things in the aft cabin. I packed my duffel and zipped it up. "Well, for instance, what was that hoo-hah at Sonny's all about, anyway? If Wilkes wants me dead, why doesn't he make his move? Why all that mummery about a merger? What does the Rikkitikki have to do with all this, if anything?" I grabbed Darla's pack, went forward, and sat in the driver's seat. "And why in God's name, if they wanted to surprise us at the motel, did they drive up like Colonial Militia on a drug raid? They've never heard of sneaking? They could have had us easily. But no, they bust in there with rollers crackling and guns drawn. And how did they know we were there?"

"The manager could have been on Wilkes' payroll. The word may have been out for us."

"Yeah, maybe. But it still doesn't make any sense. None of it does, including the wild stories—which everybody but us seems to have heard." I shook my head wearily. "What a weird couple of days." I remembered the lost key, and took the spare out of the box. I loaded up the squib with fresh charges. I undraped my leather jacket from the seat and put it on. The night was cool, but sunrise was not far off. We had spent most of the night in the hospital. I slipped the spare key into my jacket pocket.

"Where is everybody?" Sam asked.

"Waiting in the hospital lobby. I'll go tell John we're coming with him, after we bring you to the doctor."

Dawn came and Maxwellville came alive.

We drove to a nearby vehicle dealership, where Sukuma-Tayler rented a Gadabout, hydrogen-burning, for the trip to the ranch which was supposed to be about fifty kilometers south of town. He and his troupe followed us as we drove around looking for a garage. We found one, and the name of the place had a familiar ring to it.

The garage was a pop-up dome with an adjacent trailer serving as both home and office. No one was home (the place was a mess). The dome was deserted, or so I thought. A lone roadster was up on jacks near the far end. As I drew closer, a pair of boots came out from under it, then legs, then the rest of Stinky Gonzales.

"Jake?" He squinted at me. "Jake! What the punk are you doin' here? How the punk are you, anyway?"

Stinky spoke Intersystem better than anyone I knew; in fact, he was the only person I knew who could speak it idiomatically. His use of the billingsgate was nothing less than masterly. He had been born and raised on a world where Intersystem was the lingua franca as well as the official tongue. There are a few of those. The last time I'd seen him, though, had been on Oberon, an *Inglo*-speaking world.

"What the punk are *you* doing here?" I answered in English, though keeping to his favorite vocabulary. "You finally get run off Oberon?"

He laughed. "You son of a punkin' bitch. What the punk do you think I'm doin' here? Tryin' to earn a punkin' living! Hey, how you been, anyway? You gettin' any?"

"My share, and no more. Busy?"

He gestured around expansively at the empty garage. "Oh, yeah, I'm so punkin' busy I ain't got time to wank it. They're piled up like stack-cats around here." The reference was to a multi-gendered animal native to his home planet; the species is noted for its acrobatic mating rituals. "What the hell you talking about? I just got set up here not two weeks ago. Gotta give it some time to—" He suddenly looked at me, his eyes narrowed. "Hey . . . what's all this crazy *merte* I been hearin' about you?"

"What crazy *merte* is that, Stinky?"

"I don't know. All this punkin' roadbuzz about you havin' a Roadmap or somethin'. Goofy stuff."

"That's exactly what it is." I slapped him on the shoulder. "Got some business for you. Sam's ailing."

"Well, let's throw him against the wall and see if he sticks. Bring him in."

I went outside and told John to take everybody to breakfast. There was a little diner not two blocks away. Then I eased Sam into the garage. It was a tight fit.

Twenty minutes later Sam was in pieces all over the dome. The engine was stripped of shielding and laid bare to the torus. During the process, I discovered to my nasal discomfort that Stinky was still worthy of the nickname only his friends could call him with impunity.

Stinky tapped the engine with his flex-torque wrench, a clinical scowl clouding his features. "I don't know, Jake. This punkin' thing might have to go."

"The torus?" I yelped. "Christ, you're talking big money, Stinky."

"Hey, do you want me to tell you punkin' fairy tales or do you want the truth? The punkin' confinement tubing is hotter than a *[reference here to the sexual habits of the human inhabitants of a planet called Free]* during Ecstasy Week." He crossed his arms and looked the rig over distastefully. "Hey, Jake. How come you don't get an alien rig? This thing's a piece of *merte*." He shook his head. "What do you want with this punkin' Terran *merte* anyway? Look at this thing." He reached and tapped a cylindrical component. "An ohmic preheater." He snorted. "I mean, that's a punkin' *joke*. Nobody uses them anymore, even on Terran models." He crossed his arms and clucked disapprovingly. "I don't know how you get around in this pile of scrap." He looked at me, then hastened to add, "Hey, I don't mean no offense to Sam."

I was impatient. "Right. What do you think's wrong with it?"

He threw up his arms. "How the punk should I know? I gotta hook up the sensors and look at the thing. Okay, so you got a kink-instability. That's only a symptom. What if it's this preheater? They don't make parts like that any more. I'll have to rig up something. Or it could be the vacuum pump. Or the current pickup, or the RF breakdown transformer. Punkin' hell, it could be anything." He shrugged, giving in. "Oh, hell, Jake, I'll do my best. Should be able to do something with it. After I get her fixed, I'll degauss it for you."

I thumped his back. "Knew I could count on you, Stinky."

"I know, I'm such a punkin' genius." He glanced at the exposure tab on his filthy shirt front. "Hey! I better get my rad-suit on and you better get outta here before we both get our *sferos* cooked off."

"Okay. Sam'll keep in touch with me. Let him know, okay?"

"Okay, Jake."

I turned to go.

"Jake!" Stinky called after me.

"What?"

"You're walkin' kind of funny. You all right?"

"We met up with some bugs out on the plains. Things about this long, with—"

"Oh, hoplite crabs. I don't know why they call 'em that, but that's what they call 'em."

"Right, hoplite crabs. They told us at the hospital."

"You gotta watch out for those things."

"Uh, we . . . Yeah. See you."

The gang was waiting for me outside in the Gadabout. I climbed in, and in doing so, I got the itchy, antsy feeling that something was crawling on me. I gave myself the once-over, but found nothing. Too many small, nasty things lately. Nerves.

After running some errands in town, mainly to pick up groceries and sundries, we drove out of town. The mail question was settled when we drove by the Maxwellville post office and saw the mail rig unloading at a side dock. Doubtless it contained a communiqué about us.

Also before leaving, we dropped off two of the group, the Abo man and a Hindu woman, at a motel. They'd been having a low-key argument with Sukuma-Tayler. The two did not care for the way things had been going. They wanted time to think things over—"get in touch with the Plan," is the way they put it. The implied meaning of the phrase struck me as rather diffuse. Sukuma-Tayler didn't say good-bye to them, but he didn't appear to be overly distressed at their leaving.

A short stretch of Colonial highway ended in a dirt road that conveyed us bouncingly along for what seemed like hours, winding around high buttes and towering sheer cliffs, until it split into a Y.

Sukuma-Tayler stopped the Gaddy and threw up his hands. "As usual," he said sardonically, "directions given barely approximate directions taken. Anybody care to guess which way we should go?" He turned to the Oriental man in the front seat. "Roland?"

Roland poked his head out the window, trying to find the sun. "Hard to get your bearings on a new planet . . . especially when you don't know the axial inclination. Do you have the Guidebook, John?"

"The what inclination?"

"Let's see," Roland said, shielding his eyes, "the sun's *there*. So, that means . . . uh—" He scratched his head.

"Well," I put in, "Maxwellville's in the opposite direction of where we want to go, and so is the Skyway." Without knowing why, I turned to Winnie. "Where's the Skyway, honey?"

"That way!" she piped, pointing to our right.

Eyes turned rearward. After a moment's hesitation, John started the Gaddy forward again, and took the left fork.

By now we had a depopulated crew: me, Darla, Winnie, the Oriental, and a Caucasian woman, to whom we were introduced for the first time—Roland Yee and Susan D'Archangelo—plus our Afro leader. The man in the hospital, we learned, was named Sten Hansen.

Susan was light-haired, thin, had hazel eyes and a pixie nose that crinkled when she smiled—a young face, but I put her on the downhill side of thirty, probably having forgone her first series of antigeronic treatments for financial, religious, or ethical reasons. I still had only a shell of an idea as to what Teleological Pantheism might mean or contain. Yee was younger, had short, straight black hair that stuck out in spikes toward the top of his head. He was very easygoing and pleasant, as they all were.

Winnie was right, and eventually we got to the "ranch," which Sukuma-Tayler recognized from pictures. There was only one structure, the house, plopped in the middle of a wide expanse of tableland landscaped in low brush and some very odd-looking trees. The place was partially completed, a free-form Duraform shell with only half the windows in, and those on the leeward side. A lot of weather had claimed squatters rights inside, along with local fauna. Floors and ceilings were etched with watermarks; dust dunes graced the corners; animal droppings added that homey touch. (If you are taking notes, dung is bright yellow on Goliath.) People had been here too. A hole chopped into the apex of the dome in the main living area had drawn smoke from campfires on the floor below, where blackened rocks ringed a pile of ash. Empty food cartons lay all over.

There was a kitchen, or rather a space for one, but no appliances had ever been installed.

"The people who owned the place ran out of construction funds," Sukuma-Tayler told me. "Victims of the last credit drought, about two Standards ago. SystemBank foreclosed, and, well, the price was right, to coin a phrase."

"What kind of temperatures do you get at night around here?"

"A little under ten degrees. Rarely gets below freezing."

"Still, not exactly balmy."

"I agree. Interested in leading a firewood-gathering squad?"

"No, but I'll do it."

The local version of burnable stuff was a reasonable facsimile of wood obtained from what I dubbed a "Wurlitzer tree." Nobody got the joke, since no one had ever heard the name of the most famous make of theater organs of the early twentieth century. From my childhood, I remembered that an eccentric neighbor of ours had reconstructed an ancient Wurlitzer in his basement. The tree looked like the diapason array of that old thing, vertically bunched hollow pipes of different lengths and diameters, from tiny piccolos to big roof-shaking pedal notes, all shooting up from a horseshoe-shaped trunk that reminded me of the keyboard console. There were hundreds of them out in the mesa. The smaller pipes made good kindling, and the big ones, split in half, made passable logs.

We spent the rest of the day cleaning out the house and making it more or less habitable. We even found an old push-broom in a closet, which proved to be indispensable. The Teleologists had lost all their gear, and what they had bought in town didn't go very far. They had replaced some personal effects, self-inflating sleeping eggs and such, but were short of useful implements. The place needed a lot of work, and they were nowhere near tooled-up for the job. But for now, all anyone was interested in was making things tolerable enough to bed down for the night.

I was cleaning out a small back bedroom when I heard someone squeal. I went out to the living area and found Susan standing over something on the floor, prodding it cautiously with the broom. It looked like something between a snake and a caterpillar, decorated in bright green-and-yellow stripes, about twenty-five centimeters long. Centipedelike pairs of legs ran along its unsegmented body. On the ends of the legs were tiny suckers. There was something strange about the head. Above a very nonreptilian face—the eyes were large and looked intelligent—a small pink bud protruded through an opening in the cranium. It was convoluted and looked like part of the brain. The animal was quivering convulsively, in its death throes. Part of its body was squashed just behind the head.

"Yik," Susan gagged, poking the thing with morbid fascination.

"Where'd it come from?" I asked.

"I don't know. I thought I felt something go squish when I was sweeping over there. I must've stepped on it." She crinkled her face in disgust. "Ooo, its brains are coming out."

"Was it on my jacket?" I said, pointing nearby to where it had apparently fallen from a wall hook. There was a footprint across the sleeve.

"Oh, I'm sorry. Yes, I must have done that. But I can't understand why I didn't see the thing when it happened."

The animal stopped quivering, dead.

"Yik," Susan said again.

I picked the thing up with a stick, went outside, and threw it into the brush.

Toward evening, Darla and I took a walk out on the mesa. By then the extra gravity seemed almost normal. We walked among the Wurlitzer trees while Goliath's big yellow sun cranked down to become a dull red semicircle resting atop a low butte far out on the range. The sky turned cobalt blue, cloudless and virginal. No sounds walked with us except the wind that came up at dusk. Soon, a few sparkling stars came out, the thick atmosphere giving their light an added shimmer, and then the nebula made its appearance, grand and majestic as before.

We didn't talk much, both bone-tired from a lost night's

sleep, mind-numb still from our recent escapades. But something was on my mind.

"Darla, something's been puzzling me, among several dozen things. It's about Winnie again."

Darla yawned elaborately, then apologized. "I'm done in," she said. "What's the problem?"

"No problem, really. I was just thinking about how she happened to pick the right direction today—and about how she knew her way through the jungle back on Hothouse."

Darla stifled another yawn. "Inborn sense of direction, I guess." She lost the fight and gave in to another one. Recovered, she said, "Maybe she'd been that way before . . . through the jungle, I mean."

"And today?"

"Lucky guess?" she ventured.

"Simple enough, but again I remind you of what you said about her people's reluctance to leave their territory."

"Again I'm reminded. But that doesn't mean Winnie herself hasn't traveled. After all, she did come with us. Who knows? She may have worked for a jungle-clearing crew before signing on at the motel."

"She helped destroy her home?"

Darla conceded the point with a tilt of her head. "You have me there." She looked at the sky and stopped walking. "You know, your question is valid. We must have covered eighty klicks before we reached the Skyway."

"Which is what led me to ask it."

Darla was about to say something, then keeled over in a mock swoon and rested her head on my shoulder. "I'm so tired, Jake," she said.

I put my arms around her and found a nesting place for my face in her hair. It smelled of hayfields, those I played in as a kid, a memory contained in an odor, like so many. She pressed her body close and put her arms around my neck as the wind reared up a chilly gust, making a sound like a moan over the mesa. We hugged; I kissed her neck, and a little ripple of pleasure went through her. I kissed it again. She raised her head, her eyes heavy-lidded, gave me a sleepy smile of contentment, and kissed me tenderly. Then she kissed me again, this time with a probing intensity. With my fingers I found the deep groove of her spine and followed its course under her jacket down to the beginning of the rift of her buttocks, stopping there teasingly. She answered with a thrust of her hips against mine, and I caressed her behind, came back up by way of the curve of her hip, all the way up to interpose a cupped hand between my chest and hers. Her breasts were small and firm.

But the wind got steadily colder, and it was time to get back to the house. We started walking back.

When we got there we found the Teleologists in the backyard, sitting in a circle on the ground in silent meditation. We stood and watched them. Nobody spoke for a long while, then suddenly Susan did.

"Sometimes I didn't get along with Kirsti." It sounded like part of a conversation, but nobody responded.

After a long interval Roland said, "Zev was a good man. I'll miss him."

Then it was John's turn. "Silvia knew I had to follow my conscience. It was part of my Plan, and she could see that. . . ." He trailed off.

This went on for a time. Eventually John looked up at us. "I suppose you two are hungry. Well, so are we."

They all rose and came toward us. "We were having a Remembrance," John explained. I started to apologize, but John cut me short. "No, no. We were done," he said. "Let's eat."

Supper involved little in the way of preparation, since the main course came out of hotpaks, but Roland had unhinged the useless back door (the front one was missing) and made a dining table out of it by shoring it up with rocks. Places for everyone were set with plates and utensils from a mess kit John had bought. A biolume lantern stood in for a centerpiece, the fire was crackling cheerily, and we settled down to a good meal.

I tore off the top of my hotpak and watched until the contents started to steam and bubble, then dumped the glop onto my plate. The stuff looked more like beef Romanov, after the executions, then beef Stroganoff as advertised, but it tasted surprisingly good.

Conversation was upbeat for a change. The Teleologists talked about Teleologist stuff, but John was kind enough to include us in the chitchat, explaining things as we went along. It turned out that John and his crew were a sect that had splintered off from the main church in Khadija, although terms like "sect" and "church" didn't quite seem to apply. Teleological

Pantheism sounded more and more like a framework within which one engaged in a freewheeling brand of theology rather than a body of dogma, and I gathered that the schism between John's group and the parent body was more personal than doctrinal.

I asked John to give me a definition of Teleological Pantheism in twenty-five words or less, fully granting that such an encapsulation would be grossly oversimplified and unfair.

"Well, I think I can," John answered, "and it wouldn't be too far off the mark." He paused to compose, as if he were about to give birth to a rhyming couplet. "Teleological Pantheists hold as an act of faith, unsupported by reason, that the universe has a purpose, and that there is a Plan to it all. I mean by 'act of faith' that it's a Kierkegaardian sort of *leap,* since there certainly is no empirical evidence to support such a belief."

"Then, why believe it?" I asked. "Sorry. Go on."

"No, the question is valid, but I couldn't answer it in a paragraph, or even fifty. I'll certainly talk about it later, if you like. But anyway, that's the teleological part of it. The theistic part of it involves the notion that the universe is greater than the sum of its parts, that the totality of that which is—reality, if you will—is a manifestation of something beyond the plenum of sensory data we perceive it to be." He stopped to regard the design of his rhetoric, and shook his head. "No, that doesn't *quite* do it. All that does is allude to a fuzzy metaphysics. Shall we say this?" he went on, drumming the table with spidery fingers: "We also accept on faith that there is some Unifying Principle to reality, of which natural laws are only signposts pointing in the direction of the heart of things." He shifted his weight on the hardened foam floor. "That's more or less it, but I think I should point out that the chief difference between us and almost any other religion that involves a deity is that we impose no structure on this Unifying Principle. We don't refer to it as God, or use any identifying tag, and we reject all anthropomorphic notions entirely. We hold that there is little we can know about the nature of this Principle, since it is always in a dynamic state, in a constant process of *becoming,* if you will, as the Universal Plan unfolds. We differ from classical deists in that we can't imagine a state of affairs in which a creator slaps together a clockwork cosmos and then abandons it." He took a sip of coffee. "I think I went over twenty-five words."

"John," Roland said, "you can't fart in less than twenty-five words."

John led the laughter. "I stand accused, and plead guilty, m'lord." And with a furtive smile he added, "But after all, to *air* is human."

Groans.

"You could at least be original, John," Roland chastised him. "That was terrible, and I'd never forgive you, if it weren't for this flat you lent me," he added, indicating the house.

Shudders.

"Besides punning," Susan told us, by way of an apology for the punishment her compatriots were inflicting on us, "Teelies love to talk. A good thing, too, because there's not much else to this religion."

"Susan's right," Roland said. "We don't worship in the conventional sense. We have few ceremonies, nothing approaching a liturgy, and precious little in the way of doctrine. We believe that there must be a flux in these matters as well."

"Thinking is worship," John put in. "So's talking about what you're thinking about. But not everybody thinks alike."

"Yes, exactly," Roland agreed. "We want a religion stripped of every kind of dogmatic rigidity, hidebound orthodoxy, papal bulls, infallible preachings . . . everything."

"We reject revelation as a source of truth," Susan said. "More blood has been spilled over questions of whose holy book is holier than over anything else in history."

"People write books," Roland said pointedly. "Not gods."

"Of course," John said, "there's much more. There are ethical currents flowing from the theological spring. We believe in cooperative living, for example. Granted, that's nothing new—"

"One thing we *don't* do is proselytize," Susan broke in. "We want to convert, if at all, by example or by a kind of osmotic process. Not by handing out pamphlets on street corners."

"Sounds like my kind of religion," I said finally. Actually, to me it sounded like Kant, Schopenhauer, and Hegel run through a protein synthesizer, spiked with a bit of mid-twentieth-century radical theology. "Where do I sign up?"

"Right here," John said, gesturing around us, "and you do it by asking that question."

I eased back against Darla's pack, uncrossed my legs, and put them under the table. "Well, now, I don't think I'd take to communal living too well. I'm nasty in the morning and I raid the cooler at night. Generally, I'm an uncooperative son of a bitch."

John gave me a sugary smile. "But lovable in your own way, I'm sure. However, you don't have to live with other Teelies to be one."

"Just as long as I drop my weekly tithe into the collection plate, eh?"

"No. Add to that list of 'don'ts' the fact that we don't tithe our membership."

"Or take contributions from anybody," Roland said, "or solicit them."

"Who pays the rent?" I asked, shocked. Maybe this was my kind of old-time religion.

"Our support mainly comes from the Schuyler Foundation, set up by an Australian multi-billionaire who was an early convert to TP. He read and was impressed with the writings of its originator, Ariel MacKenzie-Davies." John stretched out on the floor, propping a head up on an elbow. "She's an interesting figure. I'd give you a copy of her seminal work—that is," he said, his voice suddenly going hollow, "if I hadn't been so careless as to leave my kit behind."

That brought it all back, and the conversation died. I tried to resuscitate it.

"Besides," I said, "I'm not one for leaping, faithwise. I mean, I've tried to read Kierkegaard, but I usually wind up Sören logs."

Only Susan, an American, got the joke. Her face brightened enough to register great pain. "Really, Jake," she scolded.

Roland was suspicious. "Did I miss something?"

"Oh, my God," John said. "I just got it. Of course, sawing logs."

Roland was mystified until John explained. Roland shook his head. "Jake, sometimes your cultural allusions and a great deal of your vocabulary are very obscure. To me, at least. You're Nor'merican, of course, but what part?"

"Western Pennsylvania, old US of A. It's pretty isolated, and there's about a one-hundred-year culture-lag. Linguistic atrophy, too. Most of the colloquialisms are out of the mid-twentieth century, even earlier. It was my milk-tongue, and I'll probably never outgrow it."

"But you seem an educated man."

"That was out here, later on."

"I see. Darla, you seem to have an accent I can't place. It sounds . . . well, mid-Colonial, for want of a better term."

"My mother worked for the Colonial Authority for years," Darla said, "and dragged me around from planet to planet. She was Canadian, my father Dutch. So, it was alternately Dutch and English at home, Intersystem in school, and Portuguese, Tagalog, Bengali, Swedish, Afrikaans, Finnish—"

We all laughed. The usual language salad.

"Thank God for Intersystem and English," John said. "Otherwise we'd have Babel out here." His face split into a yawn. "And speaking of sawing logs . . ."

Everyone agreed. We cleaned up the supper mess quickly and made preparations for spending a cold night in a shell of a rundown shack in the middle of East Jesus. (There's one for Roland.)

But before we turned in, a talk with John was necessary.

"John, I should have said something before . . . but there's a price on my head. You and your people could be in danger."

"I thought as much. The Colonial Authority?"

"Yes, them too, but that's the least of it."

"I see."

"How did you know?" I asked wonderingly.

"Those rumors we mentioned. They have it that everyone is after you."

Again, this mysterious shadow following us. I was getting fed up. "Everyone?" I tugged at my lower lip. "Perhaps we should leave."

"I am not about to drive to town at this hour. I'd never find my way back at night."

"We could walk it."

"What? Hike across this wilderness? A strange planet?" He slapped me on the shoulder. "Jake, we owe you our *lives*. Roland will take the first watch. We would have stood watches anyway, you know. Skywaymen about."

"Right. And, John . . ." He turned around. "Thanks."

"It's not often one gets a legend for a house guest." He looked around. "Or shed guest, I should say."

Darla and I watched her sleeping egg inflate. It grew and grew until it looked like a giant, fat green worm. I said so.

"Big enough to eat us both," she said.

We crawled inside. Chemical heat had already made the interior a warm, pillowy green womb, delightfully snug, lit softly by bioluminescence panels. Undressing was a little difficult, though. I felt the cold barrel of Darla's Walther against my back.

"I give up."

"Sorry."

"Darla, keep that thing handy."

"I will," she said.

"What about Winnie?"

"I gave her an extra blanket. She said she's not sleepy."

"Are you?"

"I was, but not now, love. Come here."

Music . . .

Music, not loud . . .

Music, not loud but omnipresent and overpowering, a single towering, shifting chord stacked with notes from the lower end of the keyboard to the top, covering octave after octave. It sounded over the mesa like a choir of lost souls bewailing their damnation, drear and haunting. Violins sang with them, flutes, oboes, bassoons, more strings—lilting violas, threatening double basses . . . a harp, a celeste tinkling contrapuntally. The structure changed, harmonies rearranged, and now it was God playing the church organ of the universe, beatific sonorities flowing from his hands, reverberating from the roof of Creation.

Darla awoke with a start, clutched at me.

"Jake!"

"The Wurlitzer trees," I said. "It's all right, lovely one."

She melted in my arms, sudden fear dissolving like frost before a flame. "I was dreaming . . ." she said in a lost little sleep-voice. The egg was dark. I passed a thumb gently over both her closed eyelids, kissed her warm, moist cheek. She exhaled, all tension flowing out. I drank in her breath, held her close.

Outside, the chord modulated from minor to major, back to minor again, then shifted once more and droned in a modal harmony as the wind passed its airy fingers among the pipes. There were solo passages, virtuoso performances. A concerto. Then the wind blew it all away and left an atonal chaos that resonated with the indeterminacy of existence . . . muddled, mysterious, in the end incomprehensible. . . .

A great sinewy hand poised over the starless dark . . . waiting? Watching? The Hand of the Conductor. Or the Composer.

Both? Neither? The void was formless and embraced all that was to be, would never be . . . infinite possibilities. Skeins of chromatic tones unspooled in the black, the raw stuff of being. Then structures began to build themselves as a diatonic order was imposed. (By what? By whom?) Fugues wove out of the deep, classic symphonies in sonata form drew together. The Hand withdrew, and a ponderous hymn resounded throughout the firmament, praising Oneness, Fullness, Positivity, the Plan, the Organizing Principle. . . .

Strange light, a bundle of softness in my arms, the momentary, odd sensation of not knowing exactly where you are, when you are. The egg was dark, but tissue-thin walls leaked a shifting light.

The Hand . . . the Hand among the waste and void, at the heart of things, the womb of time . . .

"Dawla! Jake!"

There in the secret center, the impenetrable core . . .

"Dawla-Jake! Dawla-Jake!"

. . . of nothingness . . . nothing . . . no thingness . . .

"Jake! Dawla! Up! Up!"

I jerked awake, groped for one of the biolume panels. I wiped one with a palm and saw in its glow a double-thumbed hand in front of my face.

The music had stopped.

I poked Darla.

Her eyes opened wide instantly. "What is it?"

"Winnie, 'sat you?" I whispered hoarsely, widening the birth-canal entrance to the egg. Winnie's face showed alarm.

"Big machines! Big machines! Get up! Get up!"

Darla swiped at the quick-exit seam with two stiffened fingers and the egg cracked us naked into a freezing night.

The fire was a huddle of glowing embers. Roland lay near it, asleep, swaddled in blankets. I went over and kicked him sharply once, then grabbed folds of the other egg and flipped it. There were two bodies in there; good.

"Darla!" I said. "Get out the door, take your pack and gun!"

Moaning and mumbling inside the egg.

"Jake, I'm not going without you."

"Get!" I commanded. "Run that way." I pointed toward the rear of the house. "I'll find you."

Darla grabbed some things, threw me my squib, and ran.

"Get up!" I shouted. "John! Susan!"

Roland was struggling to his feet, bleary-eyed, disoriented. Outside, probing beams of light played over the ground near the house, and the darkness hissed with the exhaust of flitter-jets.

Roland straightened up. "I was just—" He saw the lights, heard the sound of approaching aircraft. "My God! Who is it?"

"Want to stay and find out?"

"Jake?" It was Sukuma-Tayler, head protruding from the end of the egg.

"Trouble, John," I told him.

The egg sprang open and Susan stood up, naked, arms wrapped around her ribcage, grimacing from the sudden cold.

"Everybody out and into the bush. Now! Scatter!"

John got to his feet unsteadily. Susan stooped to find clothes—I rushed at them both, grabbed a blanket and flung it over Susan, and shoved both of them forward. Susan grunted, stumbled, and I caught her.

"Sorry, no time for that, Suzie. Run! Both of you!"

They ran.

On the way to the rear of the house I made a pass at the egg, came up empty, but happened to snag my jacket with a foot. I scooped it up and ran, struggling into it.

I ran into Roland at the back door, shoved him out, and aimed him in a direction ninety degrees off my course. A searchbeam hit the house, throwing stark shadows along the ground.

The brush had been cleared in a ten-meter strip about the house, and I sprinted for the edge. I was just about into it when a disk of light zagged crazily in from my right and swooped over me. I dove for cover behind a Wurlitzer, but knew I'd been spotted. An exciter beam raised flame and smoke from the ground very near. The light wasn't on me, but they knew my approximate position. I waited three heartbeats and dashed to the left, feeling tiny sharp things in the soil prick my soles. I ducked behind another tree and waited, watching the hard circle of light sweep the ground. The breath of the flitter was warm on my skin, conjuring dust devils around me. There was more than one craft. Constellations of red and green running lights plied the night sky, hovering, darting, pouncing. Spotlight beams waved through the brush on all sides of the house.

Another bolt crackled near me, exploding a barrel-shaped

plant into a plume of steaming pulp.

A flickering thought: *They have night-sight equipment. Why the searchlights?*

Sam's key was in my pocket. I took it out and called. I hadn't tried it before because I thought we were well out of range, but it was worth a try.

"Jake? . . . [crackle] *. . . that you?"*

"Sam? Can you copy?"

"[sputter] *. . . Jake? Come in . . .* [pop!]"

"Sam, if you can copy me, I'm about to be nabbed by the Colonial Authority. Colonial Authority. Copy? I'll be at the Militia station in town. Acknowledge, Sam."

The key spat static and not much else.

Another bolt sizzled to my rear. I ran again, this time doubling back toward the house, but as I got into the open a bolt touched down not a meter in front of me. I slid to a stop in the dirt. They had me. Obviously the shots had been deliberate misses. I got to my feet and the searchlight hit me full.

"Jake!" Darla's voice from behind.

"Darla! Stay there!"

"Hey! Over here!" She hadn't heard me over the whoosh of the flitter.

"Darla, stay where you are! They have me covered."

Out in the mesa, shafts of light converged on the others. I could see John waving surrender, Susan huddling near. I looked to my left. Roland, the only one fully clothed, was shuffling back toward the house with his arms raised, spotlighted like a headline act on New Vegas.

A loudspeaker growled. "JACOB McGRAW?"

"Me! Over here!" I waved. "I'm the one you want!"

"COLONIAL MILITIA. YOU'RE UNDER ARREST."

"I gathered as much," I said, addressing the dead shards of Wurlitzer pipe at my feet. The flitter swooped to land. I raised my hands and dropped my gun.

From behind, Darla opened up on the descending craft, the bolt hitting the left front impeller. Sparks rose from the metal and static discharges played over the surface like furious dancing fingers.

Answering fire was swift and accurate. A gout of flame and wispy smoke roiled from the spot where Darla's shot had come from. The Walther did not answer. Sailing flinders of brush fell at my feet.

Frozen in body and spirit, I gaped at the dwindling flames

where Darla's body surely lay, and remembered my dream just then, strangely, fragments of it, wishing the Hand would appear again to take me by the collar and yank me out of this meta-dream I knew as life.

8

COPS ARE THE same everywhere, everywhen.

I stood before the desk at the Militia station, bare-assed and wearing a leather jacket.

Some joker walking by stopped to mock-whisper in my ear: "Did you get a new tailor?"

The cop at the desk showed big yellow horseteeth. He thought it was a scream. The cops who brought me in from the flitter found it the soul of wit.

The joker walked down the hall looking back over his shoulder. "Huh?" he said, milking the gag, smirking. He ducked into an office, not waiting for my reply. Truly, I had one for him.

"Place of residence?" The desk cop is all business, all of a sudden.

"221-B Baker Street, London, England."

"Planet?" It dawns on him. "Look, McGraw," he said, showing me world-weary eyes. "I asked you for your address. When they come back from searching your hideout, I'll get it from your ID. So, let's do it the easy way. All right?" He squared himself at the console. "Now . . . place of residence."

"Emerald City, Land of Oz."

"Name of plan—" Again, he was slow on the uptake. He snarled at me. "Listen, you filthy piece of *merte,* I'm gonna ask you for your punkin' place of residence one more time, then you're in for trouble."

"Punkata teys familos proximos." It was an Intersystem phrase which suggested that he run along now and have sexual intercourse with various members of his immediate family, in so many words.

That got me a hairy back-of-the-hand smartly across the mouth. It was worth it. The rusty taste of blood seeped through my teeth onto my tongue.

A little too late, one of the other cops grabbed his arm. "Don't want him roughed up. We have orders."

The desk cop jerked his arm free savagely. "Don't do that again, Frazer," he warned. "Keep your hands off me."

"Fred, I'm sorry. We got orders. We're to keep him here until the Colonel arrives. I don't even think we should be entering him on the blotter. You better clear that entry."

"What the hell is he standing here for?"

"I don't know. Habit, I guess. They said to—"

"Then get him out of my sight!"

Grumbling, Frazer shoved me over to a chair. The seat was metal and very cold.

There I waited for about ten minutes until somebody very big and very important strode down the hall toward the desk, leaving a wake of underlings snapped to attention *en route*. He was a huge man, all bulk and no bulge, enough fabric in his sky-blue-with-white-piping uniform to shelter tent-cities of refugees. A red mustache thrived in whorls under a ramrod-straight nose. The eyes were caged, iced blue with determination and cold reserve. He marched past me, briefcase in hand, swagger stick tucked smartly under an arm, and the seminude man he passed just wasn't there.

As he went by the desk, three words:

"In ley amenata." Bring him in to me.

After a minute or two, I was led back through a maze of corridors to an office. I was surprised at the size of the station. Goliath was a frontier planet, from what I had seen, sparsely settled. But the planet was smack between two interchange worlds, a strategic location.

The sign on the door read bilingually: *Tenentu-Inspekta* Lieutenant-Inspector Elmo L. Reilly. I had the feeling I was not about to meet a man named Elmo. It was a small, windowless office with a metal desk, metal shelves, a few maps and plaques on the wall, picture of the family on the bookshelf, clean and uncluttered. Chemical light from the overhead fixture softened it a bit, but it was a cold, steely place. The big man sat at the desk, swaggerstick squared to his right, briefcase to his left. He still wore his white hard hat with its visorful of gold scrambled eggs.

"Colonel-Inspector Petrovsky will interrogate you," Frazer told me, and plopped me down in a small metal chair.

"This is not an interrogation," Petrovsky corrected him. Frazer slunk out the door. Petrovsky's Intersystem was weighted with Slavic ponderousness.

"What is it, then?" I asked in the best 'System I could manage.

"That depends. You may or may not be a material witness to a crime. You may or may not be a suspect. That also depends."

"Upon what, may I ask?"

Blue eyes bored through me. "Upon what you tell me and what I take to be truth."

"Then this is an interrogation," I concluded.

"No. An information-sharing meeting." Love those hyphenated monstrosities in the language.

I switched to English. "A euphemism."

"Queros?" He was annoyed. "You speak Intersystem poorly. You place the verb at the beginning or middle of sentences rather than at the end, like all *Inglo*-speakers. Very well, I will speak English."

"Good. I find it hard to carry on an intelligent conversation in Pig Latin."

"'Pig Latin'? This means you disapprove of the official Colonial language?"

"Like most artificial languages, it's a linguistic, cultural, and political compromise. Esperanto or Interlingua are better, inadequate as they are. Lincos is vastly better equipped for communication with aliens. And whatever the philologists say, 'System is still biased toward Indo-European language users."

He grunted. "Interesting academic discussion we are having. However—" He opened the briefcase and pulled out a reader and a case of pipettes. He loaded the reader, stabbed at the keyboard until he got what he wanted.

He looked up sharply. "What do you know of the disappearance of Constable Mona Barrows?"

"What should I know?"

"Do not word-play. Do you know anything?"

"Yes."

"Did she overtake your vehicle on Groombridge Interchange?"

"Yes."

"Then an encounter with a Patrol vehicle occurred?"

"Yes."

"And the Patrol vehicle fired on Constable Barrows' vehicle?"

"Yes. You knew that."

"We did," he said flatly. "The armaments on your truck are not capable of such destruction. We found the remains of the interceptor, or rather the radioactive trace. The telltale readings told us it was a Patrol intervention."

"Then, why ask me?"

"Eyewitnesses, if any, must always be questioned in these matters," Petrovsky stated.

"Better to tell your traffic cops not to do what Barrows did."

"She followed orders. Laws must be enforced. We cannot continue to be dictated to by an outside force, no matter how technologically superior they appear."

"Then again, the Skyway does not belong to us, really," I said.

Petrovsky looked down. Tiny characters danced on the screen. Without glancing up he said, "What can you tell me of the events that took place on Demeter, three standard days ago, at the lodging house called Greystoke Groves?"

"Forgive me if I ask to what events you refer."

"Specifically," he read from the screen, "to the death of a man named Joel Dermot."

"Never heard of him. How did he die?"

"He was the victim of a hit-and-run accident."

"Unfortunate. Must have happened after I left."

"You did not check out of the motel."

"True. I was in a hurry."

"To what were you hurrying?"

"Business."

"Where?"

"Here," I said.

"Goliath? Your destination was Uraniborg."

"Eventually. First here."

"To do what?"

"To discuss business with the people your storm troopers routed out of their beds last night."

"The religious group? Unavoidable. What business?"

"None of which is yours," I told him.

The icy eyes frosted over. "Uncooperativeness will not help you."

"Am I officially under arrest? Am I going to be charged?"

A hesitation. "Officially, technically, you are not under arrest. You are under protective—"

"What!" I was more surprised at the bolt of anger that shot through me. I jumped to my feet, tool-kit swaying in the breeze. "Then I *demand* my immediate release. What's more, you will *without delay* have these mollycuffs removed and my clothes returned to me."

Unruffled, he said, "Mr. McGraw, you are in no position—"

"I am in every position imaginable!" I spat at him. "I have not been shown a warrant, I have not been charged, I have not been booked on a charge. I have not been afforded the opportunity to contact a solicitor. I am in every position to bring civil and criminal charges against you and all participants."

Petrovsky sat back. He was willing to let me rave on.

"Furthermore," I raved on, "you have no evidence or probable cause to use as a basis for taking me into custody."

Petrovsky fingered the russet swirls that covered his lips. "Evidence can be obtained. Tissue specimens from your vehicle."

Which meant they had tried, and failed. Sam would have a tale or two to tell about that. Stinky must have gotten him back in one piece in time, or Petrovsky would have had his evidence. *"Can* be? You arrested me on speculation?" I wasn't going to bring it up, but there had been no mention at all of Wilkes nor of any witnesses. Nor of any charges Wilkes had filed.

"Please sit down, Mr. McGraw. The view from where I sit is not a pleasant one."

"I will also do all that is in my power to initiate an investigation into the death of my friend, Darla—"

A screeching stop. Darla's last name? My, God, I didn't know. The wind spilled out of my sails, and I stood there, blinking.

Petrovsky was suddenly magnanimous. "I will tell you what, Mr. McGraw. You will be unbound and . . . uh, given some clothes, on one condition—that our talk will continue." He turned a rough palm upward. "Perhaps on a more amicable basis. Agreed?"

I was silent. He thumbed the call switch on the com panel.

"You have not been exactly candid with me, Mr. McGraw. But then, I must confess I have not been entirely open with you."

"Indeed?" was all I could say.

Frazer poked his head in the door. "Yes, sir?"

"Remove the mollycuffs," Petrovsky ordered. "And find a pair of trousers for him."

"And shoes," I said.

"And shoes," Petrovsky agreed.

"Yes, sir, Colonel-Inspector." Frazer came over and freed me.

Petrovsky pulled out a pack of cigarettes with a label that crawled with Cyrillic lettering, lit one with an antique wheel-and-flint lighter. He pushed it and the pack across the desk toward me. I needed one and took one. I lit it, and regretted that I had. I squeezed off a cough and sat down.

We looked at each other for a moment, then Petrovsky puffed and eased back, receding through an acrid blue haze. His eyes found something of interest on the ceiling.

A minute went by, then Frazer cracked the door and threw in a pair of gray fatigue pants. "Working on the shoes," he said.

Petrovsky got up and examined a map of Maxwellville. I slipped on the trousers. They were a fairly good fit, if a trifle short at the cuff. I sat down and waited, smoking.

Presently, Frazer returned, and handed me shoes. "These are my own spares," he told me. "When you get your stuff, I want 'em back."

"Thanks."

"Well, it's okay."

The door closed and Petrovsky sat back down. "Now, Mr. McGraw, I will dispense with any preliminary questions and proceed to a matter of some importance."

"Which is?"

"The Roadbuilder artifact."

Rumor, wild stories, tall tales, canards—become adamantine reality with an official pronouncement. It threw me.

"The what?"

"The artifact. The map. The Roadmap."

I shook my head slowly. "I know of no such thing."

Petrovsky caressed the desktop, looking at me, gauging my sincerity. "Then why," he asked evenly, "does everyone think you have one in your possession?"

I saw no ashtray, and dropped the half-smoked cigarette between my feet. "That, my law-enforcement friend, is the punking"—I ground the butt out fiercely—"zillion-credit question. I wish someone would tell *me*." I sat back and crossed my legs. "By the way, who is everybody?"

"Representatives of various races, various concerns, and us. The Colonial Authority, I should say."

"Who else specifically, besides the Authority?"

"I cannot think of one alien race within the Expanded Confinement Maze who would not like to obtain such a map. Specifically, we know the Reticulans want it, and are aiming to get it. Also the Kwaa'jheen, and the Ryxx. They have agents in the field. This we know. Every indication is that there are more."

I took another cigarette. I had quit years ago, but some crises scream for nicotine. "Why? That's *my* question," I said, snapping the lighter closed. "Why is this phantom artifact so bloody important?" I could guess, but I wanted his reasons.

"Just think about it, Mr. McGraw. Think of what it could mean." His tone was more academic than enthusiastic. "Do you have any idea of how far such a find would go toward solving the baffling mysteries of the Skyway? Would it not be the discovery of the ages?" He levered himself to his feet, the extra gravity making his weight more of a burden. "What price would you put on it, Mr. McGraw?" He began to pace, mighty arms folded.

"Okay, so it'd be a fast-moving item." I choked on an inhale. "So what? So you'd find out the Skyway goes all over the galaxy, and you find eighty billion other races living alongside it. The more the merrier. We would've found that out sooner or later."

Petrovsky held a finger up, waved it. "Think. Think what else the map may lead to."

I was totally fed up with it all. I didn't answer. All I could think of was that I had had Darla in my arms one moment, and in the next moment had watched her die. Petrovsky began speaking again, but I didn't hear him.

Darla . . .

"Can you conceive of it? You must admit that the possibilities are staggering."

I shook myself, struggling back to the issue at hand. "I'm sorry. What did you say?"

He stopped and rocked back on his heels, a bit irked at not being paid attention to. "I said that there is the possibility that the map could lead to the Roadbuilders themselves."

I took a long drag, my lungs already scarred enough to take it. "Yeah, and they're running a Stop-N-Shop on Interstellar 84."

"Stop and—?" He walked behind the desk. "A joke, of course. But do you see that even the possibility would make the map invaluable?"

"But the Roadbuilders are long dead, or so rumor has it."

"Ah, but the remains of their civilization? Surely something has survived. The Skyway has. Think of the secrets, Mr. McGraw. The secrets of the most technologically advanced race in the known universe. Perhaps in the entire universe."

Well, now I knew his estimation of the phantom map's value. It was close to mine.

He leaned over the desk, propping himself with arms extended, huge hairy hands splayed over gray metal. He looked at me intently. "Who constructed the portals?" he went on. "Only that race which had mastery over the basic forces of the universe. Consider the cylinders. Masses more dense than these could not exist, except for black holes. Yet the cylinders are clearly artifacts. How were they constructed? Why do they not destroy the planets upon which they rest? What titanic forces keep them hovering centimeters off the surface? Questions, Mr. McGraw. Mysteries. Have you never wondered?"

"Yes," I said. "But I have another question—for you. Why in the name of all that's holy does everyone think I have the answers? Why do you?"

Petrovsky lowered himself into the squeaky swivel chair, took another cigarette and lit it. "I, for one," he said between furious puffs, "do not."

"You don't?" I did a triple take. "Huh?"

"But that is my personal opinion, you understand." He shot pale smoke about four meters across the room. "I put the Roadmap in the same category as . . . say, Solomon's mines, Montezuma's gold, the philosophers' stone, and so forth. What is the phrase in English? Fairy tales. No, there is another."

"'Objects of wild-goose chases' will do. I understand, but you didn't answer my question. Why *me?* Why do you think I have it?"

"You may have something. Or, more probably, you may want people to believe that you have something. A convincing forgery—although I cannot imagine what that could be—could fetch a high price. As to your question, I can only speak for the Colonial Authority. We are concerned with you on the basis of the rumors."

"What? I can't believe it."

Petrovsky plucked the fat cigarette from its nesting-place in his mustache, blew smoke at me. "Perhaps I have misled you. I may have given the impression that all available forces of the Authority are marshaled against you. No. I lead a special intelligence section within the Militia. Our chief function is to investigate all matters pertaining to the mystery of the Skyway. I have an office staff of five, and a few field agents. My rank obtains for me the cooperation I need to conduct operations such as the one you witnessed early this morning." He took off his helmet and tossed it on top of the briefcase. His short hair was the color of fresh carrots. "This is one of many investigations. Many. We have looked into many reports of strange sightings, phenomena . . . rumors. None have proved to be anything other than wild-goose chases, as you so colorfully put it." He dropped the butt, still lengthy, and stamped on it once. I think he was getting sick of them too. "I will be more than frank with you, sir. I do not like my job, but it is my duty. As for the Roadmap, I do not really have an opinion as to its reality or lack of it. When I see it with my own eyes, I will believe it. Do you understand?" His eyes thawed the tiniest bit, just for a moment.

"Yes."

"So." He slapped the desk. Back to the reader.

"Tell me," I said, trying to draw him out on other matters, "Why the raid? Why couldn't you have simply come to the house with a warrant? Or without one?"

"I was about to speak of that," he said. "As I have told you, we are not alone in our interest in you, nor in our surveillance. We also follow those who follow you. The Reticulans particularly intrigue us. We follow them, and they lead us right to you. Always. Most uncanny. But who can understand aliens?" He smiled, the first time. It was genuine, but fleeting. "As I was saying, we traced the Reticulans here, ergo you. They did not go to Uraniborg, as we did. We lost their trace in Maxwellville. However, a constable on a routine patrol found them stopped on the Skyway east of the city. Naturally, he could do nothing. He asked if they were having mechanical trouble. They said no, but he reported them anyway. The vehicle they drove was capable of carrying a smaller off-road buggy. At about the same time, we succeeded in tracing you to the Teleologists' farm. It was not difficult, but took time. But it was apparent what the aliens planned to do. They were stopped on the Skyway at a point about seventy kilometers from the farm by an overland route. I immediately ordered the 'raid,' as you termed it." He smiled again. "Do you see, Mr. McGraw? The raid was to protect you. We fully expected the Reticulans to have already captured you. Fortunately, we were in time."

"I see." Somehow, it was hard to argue with him. What with Roland having fallen asleep, and all of us dead-tired, we might not have stood a chance against the Rikkis. But there was the matter of Darla. "Where are my friends now?" I asked.

"I don't know. They were questioned. We have no interest in them."

"Did you warn them about the Reticulans?"

"Not in so many words. We told them to expect intruders. I assume they left and came into town."

Again, conspicuous in its absence was any mention of Wilkes in all of this. But Wilkes had friends in high places. Doubtless Petrovsky knew he was involved in this Roadmap affair, but it was not clear to me how Wilkes was involved with the Reticulans.

Characters danced on the reader screen. Petrovsky squinted at it, steel jaw muscles tensing. He punched the keyboard with a sausagelike index finger, and the pipette began to rewind. He looked at me.

"I think, sir, that our interview is at an end."

"Uh-huh. Then, I can go?"

He didn't answer. The reader went *ka-chunk,* and he picked it up, put his hard hat back on, cracked the briefcase open, and threw the reader into it. He leaned far back in the chair and clasped his hands over his belly. "I am afraid . . . not just yet." The chair groaned as if the metal were about to fatigue and snap. "I do not have the facilities here to continue my investigation. You will have to accompany me to Einstein, where this affair may be concluded."

"Then you mean to run a Delphi series on me?"

"If necessary."

The twisted logic had my brain in knots. "Look," I said, trying to keep an edge of exasperation in my voice from cutting through, "you've as much as said that you don't believe I have the Roadmap. Yet you want to run a Delphi on me to find out if I do or not."

"I must follow procedure, despite my personal feelings. If you know anything, we will know. If the Roadmap is indeed real, we will know that. If the whole affair is simply a hoax, or a political ploy, we will know that as well."

The word had sounded an odd note, with intriguing overtones. "Political? How could it be?"

"All possibilities must be covered," he said, his gaze deflecting a bit, as if he regretted having mentioned it.

"Anyway," I said, thinking just then that now would be as good a time as any to make a break, "a Delphi would be quite illegal."

"Without proper authorization, yes. But I have that authorization." The hands unclasped and went out at wide angles to his midsection, flopped together again. "The technique is not permanently damaging. You know that."

Was Frazer just outside the door? Likely was. "Yes, but I'd be disabled for quite a while. Lobotomized."

"An exaggeration."

"I thought the Colonial Assembly recently passed a law against the Delphi process."

"Ah, but exceptions were provided for. The language of the bill was quite clear."

And who cared what the Assembly did? Rubber stamps just bounce. "Still," I went on, "you have nothing on which to hold me." How many outside the door? One? Probably two. Frazer and another.

"You are wrong," Petrovsky told me. "We have the deposition of the manager of the motel."

"Perez? What could he tell you?"

"From him we pieced together what transpired."

"I have the feeling," I guessed, "that Perez did not actually witness an accident."

Petrovsky tilted his head to one side. "True." I had to admit, the man was scrupulously straightforward in some matters.

"However, his testimony gives us the 'probable cause' you brought up earlier. Besides—" He gave a helpless, resigned shrug. "There is a dead body to be explained. You must understand."

"Oh, yes."

Petrovsky was honest, but he was hoarding most of the cards.

"Of course," he went on, thumbs back to twiddling in the general area of his solar plexus, "if you *have* some information for me, and would be willing to volunteer it, the Delphi series would be unnecessary."

"That's a fine specimen of medieval logic."

Petrovsky frowned. "I don't understand."

"I think you do. By the way, have a chair."

I brought it up from between my legs and threw it over the desk right at him. A powerful arm went out to ward it off, a little late. The back of the chair caught the bridge of his nose and sent him leaning back precariously, hands over his nose, until he toppled over and crashed into a tier of metal bookshelves capped with cups and trophies. The shelves tumbled over on him thunderously. By that time I was scrunched up against the wall by the door. It burst open and Frazer rushed in, hand on his holster. I let him go, but neck-chopped his partner, who followed close behind. The cop went limp in my arms and I propped him up with one arm and grabbed his gun. Frazer was by the desk, turning around, still fumbling at his holster. "Hey!" was all he could get out before his partner came lurching toward him, propelled by one of Frazer's spare boots applied at the small of the back. They embraced and fell over the desk. I checked out the corridor, went out, and slammed the door.

I was halfway down the hall to the left when I heard someone about to come around the corner of an intersecting corridor. I squeezed off a few dozen rounds into the wall by the corner, sending splinters of Durafoam into Old Fred's face just as he made the turn. He staggered back with his hands up around his eyes. I doubled back down the hall, covering my rear with a burst every three steps, and while *en route,* met poor Frazer again as he rushed out of the office with his pistol finally drawn. I body-checked him and added an elbow to the chin into the bargain, sending him tottering back into the office and the gun skittering down the hall floor. I turned right at the corner and found this corridor empty. I ducked into a dark office to wait and listen, thinking to let forces pass me by as they converged on the starting point of the disturbance.

I checked the gun. It was a standard issue Gorbatov 4mm pellet-sprayer. The clip held 800 rounds and was nearly full, but the charge on the thruster was down. I pulled out the metal stock a bit more to fit snugly in the crook of my arm, then poked my nose out the door. I heard pounding footsteps, shouts. Which way was out, though? I had lost my bearings. Down this hall and to the right—but no, that led toward the desk and front entrance. A back door should lead to a parking lot and squad cars. But where?

Two men tore around the corner to my right, and I eased the door closed and waited until they passed. I waited five more heartbeats, then slipped out and tiptoed in the direction they had come from, hoping to find the way to a rear entrance. I gave a look behind as I ran and saw a shadow leak across the floor. I whirled, hit the floor and fired, the Gorby buzzing like an angry hornet. The man behind the corner got out, "Drop—!" before the gun flew out of his hand, followed by a few fingers. The rest of him was shielded by wall except for his right leg to the knee. His trouser leg flew into tatters of bloody cloth and the hardened foam of the wall smoked into powder as the Gorby vomited its fifty rounds per second. I stopped firing and rolled to the other side of the hall, huddling against the wall. I heard a groan and a thud.

I didn't like where I was. I looked down the hall behind me, but nobody seemed to be approaching.

Hushed voices, arguing. Then, a hoarse whisper: "I don't want him killed!" Petrovsky.

I took advantage of the hesitation to get up and run, spraying the corridor behind me with superdense, hypervelocity BB-shot. I ran through the next intersection and surprised two cops who had been sneaking up for a rear attack. I continued firing behind as I ran, cut to the right, ran past shelves of cartons and equipment, ducked left this time past stacks of empty packing crates, down past a row of lockers, and then found a set of double doors. I backpedaled, crouched, and carefully nudged one door open. It was a garage, with a few squad cars up on jacks and no mechanics around, but no vehicles that appeared operable. The large garage doors were closed, but there was a smaller door, and I sprinted across to it, knowing full well that I had lost time, expecting all exits to be covered by now. I hugged the wall and gripped the doorhandle, threw the door open. Automatic fire riddled the air where I would have stood if I had wanted to commit suicide. A coherent-energy beam sizzled through and started a small fire among the shelves of boxed parts along the far wall—one good reason why such weapons were impractical for indoor use. They were throwing everything at me. High-density slugs thumped into the foam, ricocheting lead and steel sang all over the garage.

One of the doors was swinging; someone had come through. I looked around for cover, but I was ten paces away from anything suitable.

"All right, *kamrada*. It's over, so drop the gun."

It was Old Fred again, pointing a sniper rifle at me across the top of the clear bubble of a squad car. He was grinning evilly, and something told me it didn't matter whether I dropped it or not. But I had no choice, and let the machine pistol clatter to the floor. Fred raised the sights up to eye level, taking his time, drawing a deep breath as if he were in the finals of a Militia sharpshooter tourney, doing it all by the book, eyes on another platinum-iridium trophy for the collection on the mantelpiece, and all it took was one neatly placed shot dead center, nice as you please, one expert squeeze, all coming down to that, one constriction of a flexor muscle, and it was off to a watering hole with the boys and girls for soybeer and snappers. . . .

Petrovsky came barreling through the doors and slammed into him, sending Old Fred cartwheeling over the floor to crash into a stack of tool boxes. When the clanking and tinkling stopped, Fred was on his back under a pile of metal, out cold. Long before that I had made a fraction of a move to go for the dropped gun, but Petrovsky had already drawn a bead on me with his pistol. I was astonished at how quick he was, both on his feet and with his hands.

"So, Mr. McGraw," he said, "there will be no more quibbling over a reason to hold you. Correct?" No triumph in his voice, just finality.

"I'm glad it's all settled," I told him. I really was.

A snatch of conversation came to me from out in the cell block just as the transparent door to my accommodations slid shut and cut it off.

"Colonel-Inspector, I realize that your rank and your special authorization from Central command our complete cooperation, but I must point out to you—"

The speaker wore lieutenant's pips and had accompanied the procession bringing me here. He had looked like an Elmo. I sprawled across the bunk. Petrovsky had his problems, I had mine, but I didn't care about either right then. I was content to lie there and let the filtered air from the overhead vent wash over me, listening to the dull throb of machinery conduct through the walls to temper the silence of the cell. The mattress was lumpy and reeked of mildew and urine, but I didn't mind that so much either. I let my brain idle for a while, allowed it to perk along and mark off the seconds, the ineluctable increments by which my allotted time was measured, one for each beat of the heart, for each millimeter of bloodflow, for each regret, each sorrow. And then one thought came to me: you can easily recognize the good parts of your life because they are starkly outlined in crap. The good things are mostly negative quantities: the absence of pain, the lack of grief, no trouble. Love, the absence of hate; satisfaction, a dearth of deprivation.

And I told myself: *To hell with all that.*

I decided to attempt active thinking again, there being a number of things to try it out on, such as the Paradox—if there really were one. The Paradox seemed to be saying, *You will get out of this, you will see Darla again, only to lose her once more*. And that would be the final time. I didn't like it, but there it was, for what it was worth. As I thought it through, I came to regard the notion as another specimen of crap. There was so little hard information to go on. Did I really have a doppelgänger out there, a future self who had found a backtime route? Did my paradoxical self really have a Roadmap? Questions. More of them: Who had told Tomasso and Chang to be at Sonny's that day, light-years off their usual route? Did anybody? Oh, there were more mysteries, by the score, by the truckload. Wilkes, the Reticulans, the Authority, the chimera of the Roadmap—*who? where? what? why?* And what did politics have to do with any of this?

Petrovsky's slip had been the most significant part of the interview. Of course, the Roadmap would be a great boon to whoever had the luck to snare it. But the Colonial Authority was the only power in Terran Maze, with only a weak Assembly passing rhetorical wind to the contrary. There were dissident elements within the Assembly, true, but they had been bugged, compromised, infiltrated, double-agented, and neutralized long ago, or so the roadbuzz had it. Oh, everybody talked of one glorious day when the colonies would achieve some measure of independence from the mother planet, but what was not spoken about so much was the glum fact that the Authority had already gained a sort of de facto independence and continued to rule all of T-Maze as if *it* were the Cradle of Mankind, and not merely Terra's proxy among the stars. The CA was a self-perpetuating, bloated bureaucracy, a chip off the old monolithic Soviet system that had spawned it, and it was entrenched on planets closest to the home system by the Skyway, with its grip gradually loosening the further out you got.

But I knew very little of what had been happening lately, having sworn off listening to news feeds long ago. T-Maze is big, thank God, and the Authority's chubby fingers could not reach everywhere, nor could they control the Skyway, which has a life all its own. There were undercurrents of rebellion out here, to be sure, at the grassroots level, but this Roadmap affair spoke of vastly larger dimensions. Some sort of struggle for ownership of the map was going on, both inter- and intra-Maze. It was a hunt, and many were riding to hounds. Call me Reynard.

And then there was Darla to think about. . . .

There was a mirror above the wash basin. It was flush with the wall and rung hollow when knocked upon. Doubtless it hadn't been put there with the prisoner's cosmetic needs at heart. I was staring into the blind side of a one-way observation window, but that didn't bother me. What did was the sight of my reflection, a thirty-five-year-old face on a chronologically fifty-three-year-old body that was gradually winning its war of attrition against antigeronic drugs. The face had aged some. People say I look perennially boyish, but the child was sire to the old gent I looked at now, wrinkle lines at the corners of the eyes, black curly hair gone dry and a tad thinner, jowls going slack and pendulous, skin a little more leathery, splotched, beardline more definite, its shadowy stubble more intractable.

Then again, I thought, I might just need a shave and a hot shower. I angled my face to get a profile shot. "Good profile," Mom always told me. "Strong." But what was that puffy area under there—the beginnings of a double chin?

Enough. I lay back down. Self-absorption is not my usual brand of neurosis; besides, I felt a sudden headache coming on.

I wondered if I could afford the luxury of regretting the escape attempt. The cop I had shot would probably pull through okay if they had gotten him to a hospital in time. But an escape/

assault charge was going to be hard to beat. The only thing I had going for me was the illegality of my detention, but I had the feeling it wouldn't go very far. Then there was the hit-and-run charge. True, I hadn't been driving, but drivers are responsible for their automatic systems. . . .

Damn, that headache was in a hurry. I heard a curious buzzing sound coming from behind my head, and it stayed there no matter which way I turned. It quickly grew louder and louder. I sat up, feeling suddenly nauseous and dizzy. I put my head between my knees, but that only made it worse. The buzzing became deafening, as if someone were tearing through sheet metal with a vibrosaw directly behind my neck. Blood pounded in my head and I could see the pulse in my field of vision.

Well, this is it. Heart attack or stroke. Antigeronic treatments or not, the body has ways of extracting its dues from you. I hoped somebody was watching through the window. Petrovsky seemed to want me alive. Maybe he'd convince Elmo I was worth bothering to cart off to the hospital.

I slumped back against the wall.

. . . keep me alive, Petrovsky being the dedicated professional that he was, but going around with one of those isohearts; well, I didn't know about that. . . . They still hadn't perfected them—tendency to go into fibrillation without warning; they didn't know exactly what the problem was, probably a mismatched enzyme that hadn't replicated true. . . .

I was awake, wide-awake. The cell door was open.

I shot to my feet. Someone had just been in here, doing something to me. What? There was a tingling on my upper arm, calling card of a tickler. It doesn't leave a mark, but my jacket had been pulled down off my left shoulder. I still had no shirt. I hadn't been out cold—the state had been like Semidoze, but very unpleasant at first, then a vapid nirvana. I had the distinct recollection of someone bending over me while I was sitting there, and I hadn't even given him a glance, as if it hadn't been important enough to trouble myself. But I had seen, out of the corner of my eye or with some part of my perceptive gear, a familiar face. Very much so, but the face had been a blank, a hole in the cognitive field, a missing datum. I tried to fill in that blank, but I couldn't. The recognition signal was blocked somehow, lodged in the preconscious. I knew, damn it. I *knew* who it was, but I couldn't *say* it.

But there was no time now. I walked out of the cell.

The turnkey was on duty at his desk, with one side of his face down in a plate of stew, eyes open, staring. Quietly, I lifted his master key, went over to the door and waved it at the code plate, and let myself out of the cell block.

Everyone in the station was out but me. Wide-eyed bodies littered the corridors, office workers were slumped over consoles. Cops sat against walls, leaned on doorjambs with their guns drawn, looking at them stupidly, transfixed. In one office a printer had been left on and was spewing out reams of hard copy in a continuous roll, piling up on the floor. From the size of the pile I guessed that everyone had been out for ten minutes at least.

I was looking for Petrovsky's office, or failing that, trying to find where they stored prisoners' valuables, or where they kept evidence. I needed Sam's key. Nobody showed signs of coming to yet, but I hurried, running through the maze of white aseptic hallways, glancing into rooms and dashing off again. Reilly's office was empty, and no sign of Petrovsky anywhere.

I tried a half dozen more offices, stumbled onto an employees' lounge with two cops draped over a table awash with spilled beverage, found a communications room, a storage room filled with filing cabinets, a library, but nothing like a lock-and-key affair where evidence would be stashed. Maybe Petrovsky had been going through my stuff when the blackout hit—if I could find him. . . .

I found him in another office sitting upright at the desk, eyes glazed, deep in a trance that made him look like a red-headed Buddha, helmet in his right hand, white handkerchief in his left, both arms extended over the desk top as if in supplication. His head lolled to one side, gaze on infinity.

And on the floor in front of the desk lay Darla.

9

SHE WAS FACE-DOWN with her head resting on her right forearm. I turned her over to find unfocused eyes looking through me. She had changed clothes and was now in a dark green, ersatz-velvet jumpsuit, with black knee-high boots. She looked very different. I got her to sit up and she responded somewhat, moving as if underwater, limbs like taffy on a warm day, but when I got her to her feet she couldn't walk, couldn't draw it all together to perform all the motions in proper sequence. I leaned her against me, reached over the desk, and pushed Petrovsky back in his chair. I opened the top desk drawer and searched through it for Sam's key, but found only Darla's Walther. I took it, then reached inside Petrovsky's jacket for his pistol. I stooped, put my shoulder to Darla's midsection, and she went up and over into a fireman's carry like a sack of wheat. Her pack was near the overturned chair, and I threw her gun into it and grabbed it.

As I carried her through the station, I wondered how much

time I had. I was getting the feeling that everyone would be coming around soon enough. I didn't bother to guess what had caused the phenomenon, since several methods were likely candidates, but the extent and completeness of the effect were impressive. Nor did I waste time wondering who had done it. Later—if there was a later—I'd write a thank-you note on nice stationery and think about whom to send it to.

I reached the garage, went on through to the man-size door, thinking it strange that no one had come in from outside, unaffected and wondering what the hell had happened—cops returning from driving their beats, coming back from lunch, etc. I cracked the door and looked out into the lot. Two stalwart constables were slouched in their car parked near the door, stupefied grins beamed at no one in particular. I was really impressed now; even more so when further outside I found another cop who had been pulling into the lot when the effect hit—either that or he was in the habit of wrapping his vehicle around a heat-pump unit when he parked. His face was squashed up against the front of the bubble.

Which brought up our immediate transportation needs. Steal a squad car? No chance. No time to hot-chip the thumbprint-lock or deactivate the tracing beacons. Besides, they'd know what I was driving, down to the serial number. Then I forgot the problem momentarily, staggered by the fact that pedestrians on the near side of the street had been hit too. Three people lay face down on the sidewalk. Good trick, that. I cut down an alleyway going parallel to the street behind the station.

Darla couldn't have massed over sixty kg at one-G, but she was a burden on Goliath. Her pack was no bagatelle either. I found a walkway between two outbuildings, put her down, and propped her up against a wall. I firmly swatted her cheeks a few times, crossing carefully over the pain threshold, then shook her as hard as I could. Her cheeks blushed the color of winter dawn, her eyes fluttered, and she sighed, but she was still out on her feet. Well, time to get moving again. I levered her up on my shoulder, hoisted the pack, and stood there debating where I should go. Then I sensed movement behind me. I whirled around, almost toppling over.

Two Ryxx stood in the alley, gawking at us, scrawny bird-legs thrust out at oblique angles to the pavement, shoring up their fat ostrichlike bodies against at least twice the Ryxx homeworld's gravity. Clear assist masks covered their faces,

faces that did not belong on bird bodies, sour old faces like those of Terran camels, but the eyes were much bigger, and there were four of them, two above the snout in the usual configuration, two at the base of the long slender neck. They liked to look where they put those taloned avian feet. They were dressed in the usual manner, in skintight body suits of brightly colored material with embroidered gilt designs around the lower eyeholes. Their huge bony hands—hands that once were framework for wing membrane—were folded up with spindly arms in a very complicated manner at the sides.

I clucked the appropriate greeting, all I knew of their language, which, written out, comes out to: *"R-r-ryxx-ryxx* (click) *r-r-ryxx,"* with each morpheme at a slightly different pitch. With my language ability, I had probably asked them to pass the salt.

The one on the right returned the greeting, and added in 'System, "And hello to you, Roadbrother."

"And to you, Roadbrothers," I said, "many thanks, if I am indebted to you for my freedom."

I turned and walked away after I decided they were not going to respond or change facial expressions to give me some sort of clue. I didn't look back, knowing they were following at a discreet distance.

I went out to the street on which the Militia station fronted further down. This was risky, but I had walked away from the Ryxx automatically, even though they made no move to obstruct me. I stood at the mouth of the alley next to a Stop-N-Shop. Colonists passed by, looked at me and the lithe young girl slung across my shoulder, frowned, and walked on. But I didn't look at them.

There it was. The antique automobile, parked on the street in front of the store. The motor was running.

It had a key! Not an electronic signaller/beacon/radio like Sam's key, but a *key*, for God's sake, a piece of metal that fit into a mechanical lock. I marveled at the interior, the metal grillwork of the dash, the blue fur of the seats, the pink shaggy carpeting of the floor, the pair of fuzzy dice hanging from the rearview mirror . . . and the wheel, the *steering* wheel. Sweet Mother, a *wheel* with a shiny knob stuck to it. What was this? A gear shift, angling out from the salient hump on the floor that bisected the interior, a big old gearshift tipped with a bulbous handle with an H engraved on it, like so:

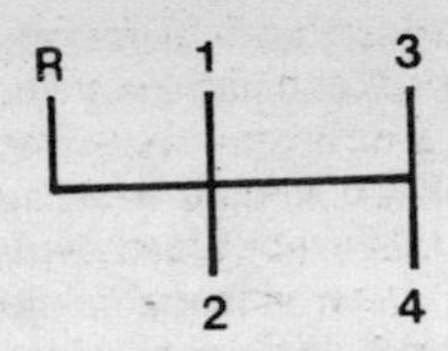

Gears? Steering wheel? Manually operated windows that appeared to be made of glass? This was no Skyway-worthy vehicle. Wait a minute. Oh, here they were, under the dash, the readouts. Not the funny oil pressure and water-temperature gauges, the real ones hidden away: plasma temp, current delta, everything. This was a fusion-powered roadster. A mock-up, not the real thing. But still, what the hell was this? A clutch! Just like in the books. It couldn't be, but I saw no other way of operating the thing.

Let's see now, if I remember correctly . . . depress clutch pedal—letting *out* the clutch—and it should be in neutral. Where was the N? No N. Okay, the line connecting the two uprights on the H. Neutral. Now, shift into 1. First gear. Right, now . . .

The car lurched forward, and I felt the motor dying on me. I floored the pedal again and the car stopped, but something had been straining to hold it back. What was this, this handle over here? Ah, a mechanical brake. I guessed. Sure. I fiddled with it until the shaft popped back into its hidey-hole under the dash. The car rolled forward slowly, coasting down the gentle incline of the street. I finally got the car in gear, and we started moving. Darla was lying faceup on the seat next to me, showing signs of waking up. She moaned softly and moved her head from side to side.

As we pulled away, a tall young man with an odd haircut came running out of the store, yelling.

"Hey! Where the hell do you—? HEY! COME BACK HERE!"

I depressed the accelerator pedal and the car shot forward with alarming speed, the sound of the engine rising to a high-pitched whine.

"You lousy bastards!" the kid yelled as we roared down the street.

Lousy? I hadn't heard the word in years. It was distinctly American and archaic.

The engine howled in protest, demanding to be shifted. I let out the clutch, and the engine raced wildly until I decided it would be a good idea to lift my foot from the accelerator. I wrestled with the gearshift until it found a notch to rest in, then tentatively eased up on the clutch pedal. The car gave a little shake and jumped forward in second gear. The owner had given up running after us and stood arms akimbo in the middle of the street. I waved.

The car had amazing power. More remarkable was how the guts of the machine had been altered to perform as if it were really an internal-combustion-driven vehicle with a mechanical transmission. I turned a corner to the left.

"Jake!" It was Darla, snapping awake. She sat up with a jerk, braced herself with one hand on the dash, one on the seat back, looking around at me and the car, her face frozen in wonder.

Finally, she gasped, "Jake, *what happened?*"

"Good morning. I don't know, but we're out of one pickle and into another."

"Where did you—?" The strangeness of the vehicle hit her. "What *is* this thing?"

"Somebody's idea of history on wheels. I stole it, if you must know. But first, tell me how you avoided getting burnt to a crisp back at the ranch."

"Huh?" She screwed up her face, rubbed her eyes, and leaned back into the seat. "Sorry, I'm still feeling a little strange. How did I . . . ? Oh, yeah." She turned her head sharply to me. "They didn't tell you? You mean, you thought I was dead?"

"Thought you were scorched meat."

"Oh, Jake, I'm so sorry."

"Never mind. Well, how did you manage it? That bolt was dead on target." I clucked disapprovingly. "Little foolhardy to take potshots at a Militia flitter, don't you think? Silly girl."

She grinned sheepishly. "Dumb but proud, I guess." Her expression changed. "Damn it, Jake, I didn't want them to take you. I aimed for the impeller, thinking to send them out of control for a second so you could duck out of the light."

I turned into a side street, getting off the main boulevard. The tires squealed. They didn't crackle—squealed like a puppy getting a paw nipped underfoot. "Wouldn't have made any difference. With their night-sight gear it was broad daylight to them. The searchlights were for our benefit. The human prey instinctively thinks darkness hides him."

"I never thought of it." She bit her lip and frowned, then shrugged it off. "Anyway," she went on, "the impeller had extra shielding, so the point's academic. I fired, then immediately hit the ground and rolled. Even so, I barely made it." She pulled down the wide collar of the jumpsuit to reveal a soft bare shoulder seared with angry red burns. "I had them treated. It's not too bad, really. Second-degree."

"Still," I said, "it was stupid, but I love you for it." I leaned over and kissed her shoulder.

She broke into a big grin and threw her arms around me. "Jake, darling, I'm so *glad!*"

"Whoa! I have to steer this thing." Heedless, she covered my mouth with hers and blocked my view. My arms were pinned by her hug, and the car swerved to the right toward a rig unloading a pop-up dome at a vacant lot.

"Hey!" I yelled when my mouth was finally free, grabbed the shiny knob on the wheel, and shoved it to the right. A woman unloading the rig dodged out of the way, then cussed us out in what sounded like Cape Dutch.

"Whoops! Sorry." Darla climbed down off me. She went through her little straightening-up routine, then looked at me. "Where're we going?" she asked.

"If I knew where Sam was, I'd get out of town fast. I have a feeling that this thing could outrun any Militia vehicle, even an interceptor, maybe. But—"

"My God, I almost forgot," she interrupted, and reached into her right hip pocket, took out Sam's key, and handed it to me. "Petrovsky was trying to persuade me to call Sam in, lure him so they could immobilize him and search the rig. For the map, I guess. I managed to get the key in my pocket before I passed out."

I took the black oblong box and pressed the call tab.

"Jake! Where in the name of Jesus are you?"

"Tooling around Maxwellville, looking for you. Where the hell are you?"

"Out in the bush near the Skyway to the Seven Suns Interchange portal. Looking for that damn ranch, or John, or Darla, or anybody who can . . . [sputter] *. . . what the hell's going on?"*

"Everybody's in town. Can you give me your position more exactly?"

"Not exactly. There's no navigation satellite around Goliath. But I'm about twenty klicks north of the Skyway . . . [crackle] . . ."

The rest of the transmission got swallowed in static.

"Sam, you're fading out. Repeat."

". . . ten klicks above the road . . . use the beacon . . ."

"Sam, I can't read you, but stay put and turn on your beacon. Repeat, stop and turn on your beacon. Acknowledge."

". . . on beacon, rodger. I read you loud and . . ."

"Jake," Darla said. She was looking back through the oval rear window. "A cop car crossed the intersection we just passed through, going to our right. Don't know if he saw us."

"Right. Well, they're up and about. And that kid probably wasted no time reporting his horse-and-buggy stolen."

"I should have given you the key right away, but I was groggy as hell."

"Doesn't matter," I said. "In order to slip out of town, we need a nondescript vehicle. Trouble is, if we steal another . . ."

At that moment we saw John and company in their Gadabout coming from the opposite direction. Winnie was with them. I rolled down the window and yelled to no avail, then remembered the horn. Where? A button? No, right here, the padded knob at the hub of the wheel. The horn tootled its absurd herald, and in the rearview mirror I saw John leaning out the driver's port, looking back. I did a fast U-turn, drew up to them and leaned on the horn. They pulled to the curb beside a vacant lot. Darla got out her gun and I looked around. Maxwellville reminded me of the little Jersey resort towns we used to vacation in when times were good—flat, with low white or pastel buildings, but here there were numerous vacant lots and a great deal of open space. I hoped this wouldn't take long.

Winnie scrambled out of the Gadabout and ran over to us. I got out of the vehicle and she hugged my legs, then jumped in to embrace Darla. I told Darla to keep a lookout, then went over to the Gaddy.

"Jake!" John greeted me cheerily. "You're out!"

"Not for long, if I don't get out of town."

His smile faded. "Oh. Anything we can do?"

"Yeah. Lend me your vehicle."

"Uhhh . . ." His expression froze.

"I know it's a lot to ask," I said, filling up the silence in a hurry. "Tell you what. Why don't you pull into that little diner over there, go in, leave the key in the Gaddy. I'll steal it. Give me about a half hour, then report it. I'll leave the car out on the Skyway, and there'll be no problems."

Susan was in the back seat. She leaned forward and spoke

into John's ear, but not so that I couldn't overhear.

"John, don't do it," she pleaded. "We're in enough trouble. Colonel Petrovsky said—" She broke off and looked at me guiltily. "Sorry, Jake, but we'd like to stay out of this."

"I can understand," I said, wondering if I had the callous gall to yank John out of his seat, shoo Roland and Susan out . . . or just pull a gun on them. But, damn it, you just don't do that sort of thing to friends.

John looked depressed. "I really don't know," he said, shaking his head wearily.

Nothing like the sight of Reticulans to take your mind off a moral quandary. They came ghosting by, four of them, rolling along in their low-slung, bright blue-green roadster. It was a big machine with a trailer tagging along behind, attached by accordian joint. The trailer was easily big enough for an off-road buggy. The vehicle proper was a rhapsody of arcane aerodynamic surfaces, curving sinuously, set about with clear low bubbles, tiny minarets, spikes, and knobs. The aliens weren't looking at me—by that I mean their heads weren't turned—but I knew those camera-eyes were set at extreme wide-angle.

Had they followed from the station? How? I hadn't seen them. *Uncanny,* I heard Petrovsky say. *But who can understand aliens?* And wherever the Reticulans were, the Militia would be close behind.

"Jake, we'd really like to help," John was saying. I don't think any of them noticed the Rikkis.

I turned back to him. "It could mean my life, John."

"—but I . . . Oh, dear." John looked completely lost.

"Let's do it," Roland said forcefully. "We have no choice, morally speaking."

"But the authorities," John wavered. "What exactly is our responsibility . . . ?"

"I think the moral issues are clear," Susan said. "Jake helped us, and last night we helped him. At least we tried to."

"You're doing moral bookkeeping?" Roland chided. "Since when was an ethical issue a matter of debits and credits?"

"I am *not* keeping books," Susan retorted, a little hurt. "I just don't think it wise to get involved any more than we are. We're going to be living on this planet—"

"Jake, as far as I'm concerned," Roland told me, leaning past John to look out the port, "you can have the Gaddy."

"You didn't let me *finish,*" Susan said hotly.

"I suppose it's up to me, then," John lamented, the democratic process weighing heavily on his shoulders.

"Jake, do you really think it's fair," Susan appealed to me, "to ask us to risk being dragged into whatever you're involved in?"

"Huh?" I was looking at the Reticulans. They had turned a corner to the left and had stopped, the rear end of the trailer sticking out from behind the corner of an auxiliary building to a farm-equipment stockyard. I wasn't overly concerned with them at the moment. They were taking a risk cruising around a human city. Darla had her blunderbuss aimed in their general direction. She'd blast first and inquire later if they showed. I kept one eye on the other side of the building. "I'm sorry, what did you say, Susan?"

"Susan has cast her vote," Roland said. "John, what's yours?"

John started to say something when Susan blurted out, "I am really angry with you two!" Her cheeks glowed and she was on the verge of tears. "I'm being totally ignored here and everytime I say something—"

"Nobody's ignoring you," Roland said sharply.

Susan was exasperated. "There you go *again!*"

"People, people . . ." John intoned placatingly.

Darla was looking back at me, as if to say, *What gives?*

A good question. I had my own moral decision to make, and time was running out. I fingered the handle of Petrovsky's pistol inside my pocket.

"We must approach this rationally, as always," John told his congregation. "Now, there's really no big hurry to get back to the ranch. I suggest we go into the diner . . . and *not* leave the key—Jake here being the resourceful sort that he is . . ." He looked at me for support.

"That'd be fine," I said. But it would mean more time wasted, time to hot-chip the antitheft systems. And tools? Where would they come from? "One thing, though," I said, "Do they give you a handikit with one of these things? Tool kit, for emergencies?"

Roland opened the storage drawer under his seat and began to rifle through it.

"That way," John continued, "we could claim we had no intention of helping Jake get away. Aiding and abetting, and all that noise." He turned to Susan hopefully. "Is that acceptable?"

"Lots of debris in here," Roland said, hunting frantically.

"Can't seem to find . . . what's this?" He held up a greasy thingamabob with a stray wire hanging from it.

"Old engine part," I told him.

"No, it's not acceptable, John, and you know it," Susan said huffily. "They'll never believe us. I'm getting out of this car right now."

"Now, wait a minute, please," John said.

Roland looked up. "Oh, she's not going anywhere," he scoffed.

"Watch me," Susan retorted frostily, and started sliding toward the curbside door.

John reached back and grabbed her arm. "Susan, please," he pleaded.

And I grabbed John's arm. "People, I really don't have time for this."

John turned to me, a bit annoyed. "Uh, wait just a moment, will you?" Susan tried yanking her arm free but John held fast. "Roland, talk to her!"

"No tools," Roland said to me.

I grunted. Well, no choice, really. . . .

Susan had the door open and one leg hanging out, trying to pry John's fingers from her arm. "Let me go," she said through clenched teeth.

"Roland, please, talk to her!"

"Quit acting like a child," Roland snapped, glancing up at her while still trying to find something useful in the drawer.

"Go to hell. John, let go!"

"Suzie, please," John said, his voice low and appeasing. "We'll sort this out. Just wait one more minute before you—"

"Oh, let her leave," Roland told him, disgusted. "Where's she going to go?"

"Anywhere! If I can get out of here. I'm warning you, if you don't—"

"Susan, sometimes you're a complete shit. Do you know that?"

She stopped struggling and glared at Roland. "You *bastard*! How dare you say that to me!"

"Well, you tell me how we're going to make a go of this colony when people bugger off at the first sign of trouble."

"The first sign of—?" Susan's rage turned to disbelief. "As if this expedition hasn't been a disaster from the day we left

Khadija! Three of us are *dead,* for God's sake."

"Yes, I know," Roland said, "but we've lost others. A new planet, new dangers—"

"Ever hear of trying to prepare for those things? First that silly breakdown . . . and whose idea was it to disturb those nests of whatever the hell they were? Isn't the first rule you should follow on an unknown planet—?"

"Yes, the first rule is 'never assume,'" John said, "and I broke it. I take complete responsibility."

"And that makes it all right?"

"No, it doesn't."

"Let her go." Roland was fed up. John sighed.

Susan took advantage of the slack and jerked her arm free. Roland immediately reached back and gripped her wrist.

Darla was saying with her eyes: *What are the morons doing now?* I shrugged helplessly.

"Look, damn it, I want everyone to stop grabbing me . . . this instant!" Susan slapped at Roland's fist.

This was getting out of hand. On top of it, I was coming down with the creepy itches again. I brushed off both shoulders. What was it? Nerves? Bugs?

"Susan, please, please calm down," John was saying.

"Let go of me."

"Roland, let her go."

"Where exactly do you think you're going?" Roland asked her.

"To the motel where Roger and Shari are staying."

"We'll drive you there. All right?"

"No, thank you. I prefer to walk."

"Susan, be reasonable. Let her go, Roland."

"Don't be stupid," Roland told her.

"Take your bloody hands off me."

"No, I won't take my hands off you until you listen to reason for one goddamn minute."

"I said *take your hands off me*!"

"JAKE!" It was Darla, standing beside the car with the door open, pointing with urgency to something behind me. I whirled and saw the front end of a squad car peeking from behind a pile of junk in the vacant lot across the street.

"Everybody down!" I dove over the engine housing of the Gaddy, glided over the slippery finish, went end over end to hit ground with a turned shoulder, and rolled to a crouch. The Teelies looked at me as if I were insane. I crawled over, opened

Roland's door. "Get down! DOWN!" Roland got the idea first, grabbed the collar of John's funny-looking gray cassock and pulled him over down to the seat. I was reaching for Susan when the first salvo hit. The aeroglass windscreen of the Gaddy erupted into crushed ice. Susan still sat there—miraculously unhurt—shaking her head, baffled.

"Why . . . why are they shooting at us? We're not—"

I yanked her out of the car and down to the pavement just as the next salvo slammed into the Gaddy. The air was alive with high-density slugs, their hypersonic cracking louder than the report that sent them on their way. The Gaddy shook like green jello as slugs chunked into it from at least three directions. John and Roland tumbled out of the front door in a pile.

"Stay low!" I told them. Looking around, I saw no cover. The lot on this side had nothing to offer but dry scrub brush and a few Wurlitzer trees.

I heard Darla gun the automobile's engine. The tires wailed as she popped the clutch pedal and jumped the curb. She came toward us swerving crazily. A steering wheel's hard to get used to. She crossed the paved sidewalk and ran the car into the loose sandy soil of the lot, sideswiped a Wurlitzer, then straightened out and came at us, the tires shooting streamers of dirt behind. She pulled up alongside the Gaddy and slid to a halt, racing the engine noisily. Then she accidentally let up on the clutch while in gear and nearly stalled the engine, but managed to keep it going. As she opened the driver's door an HD slug whanged off the Chevy, screaming away in ricochet. I didn't have time to be surprised at that. The door now effectively blocked the cops' angle of fire from one vantage point. I helped John get past me, then Roland.

"Everybody in!" I said. "Stay low!" I shoved Susan through the door, Darla helping inside. The antique vehicle was now attracting most of the fire, but it was partially blocked by the Gaddy, which was flying apart in frayed pieces. Roland crawled through, then John hauled his lean frame up and over the seat. Right then another shot hit the door, spanging off as well, but the impact nearly knocked me aside. I pushed and shoved John's skinny butt up and into what I now knew to be an HD-proof vehicle, miracle of miracles. A high-density slug is hard to stop.

The front seat was a tangle of bodies. I pulled myself in, wedging myself into position, trying to force my foot through a snake pit of arms and legs to the accelerator pedal. I got to it and pressed down. The engine howled, but the buggy didn't move. I had to shift into first but couldn't reach the clutch pedal. My left foot was lodged between the door and the front seat. I bent over and ducked my head under the wheel, painfully contorting myself down to where I could push the pedals with my hands. Someone drove an elbow into my ear.

"Darla, shift! Put the thing to number one!"

I felt the shaft move against my neck. I let the clutch pedal slide out from my hand and flattened the accelerator with my forearm. The motor howled and the G-force pinned my neck against the gearshift. We were moving.

"Steer!" I shouted. Out of the corner of my eye I saw her leaning over the back of the seat with her hands on the wheel.

A sudden flash and an explosion. They had brought up exciter cannon. The Gaddy was no more. It also meant we didn't have a chance. Seconds later a white-hot cloud of brilliance enveloped us—and just as quickly we were out of it. An exciter bolt had hit us dead center and we were unharmed.

The vehicle shook with impact after impact, shots bouncing off like stones from steel plate. Darla wheeled to the left and we hit something, but it didn't stop us. The engine was shouting for second gear, but I didn't want to chance it.

Then I suddenly realized we had time. We had taken the worst they could throw at us. "Everybody off!" I hollered, stupidly, because I was the one on top. I let up on the accelerator and untangled myself.

"Ouch!" came Roland's voice. A hand clawed at my face.

Darla took her hands from the wheel and helped pull me off the pile of Teelies. Susan got free and crawled into the back seat, leaving Roland, John, and me to sort ourselves out. We finally did and I came up for air, cracked the door to get my foot free, slammed it closed again. We were coasting through the brush on the other side of the lot. We reached the sidewalk, bounced over the curb, and by that time I had the transmission rammed into second. I floored the pedal and we roared out into the street, the tires yipping like hounds at bay.

"Which way to the highway?" I asked, but didn't get an answer. Two squad cars angled out into the street presented a more pressing question. My answer was straightforward. With all the confidence in the world, I blithely aimed our anachronistic vehicle for the apex of the triangle the blocking cars formed.

"Hang on, people."

Shots caromed off the glass—which wasn't glass at all—and coherent beams played over the curving, glossy hull. Impervious. We hit the squad cars with a loud bang but a mild jolt, shoved them carelessly aside, and raced on down the street. We passed other cop cars, an armored personnel carrier, then broke through the perimeter the Militia had secured. Their second line of defense was negligible: wooden barriers. I made toothpicks of a few of them, screeched around a corner to the right, hung a left, then a right again, then debouched onto a wide boulevard that seemed to lead away from town.

Frightening power throbbed beneath my foot. I'd never driven anything with comparable performance. And it was still in third gear. The "speedometer" read ninety somethings per hour. Miles? Sure. Appropriate to the period.

For the next twenty minutes I drove with nothing in my way but air. Maxwellville thinned to suburbs, then to development tracts, then to nothing but open road with bare land on either side. No roadblocks; they hadn't had time. Everyone sat in dazed silence. The Teelies were stunned, blank faces staring at the mesa rolling by.

Flashing barriers ahead, a new section of Colonial highway, and a sign. TO SKYWAY AND SEVEN SUNS INTERCHANGE—ROUTES 85, 14 AND POINTS SPINWARD. I managed to avoid hitting the barriers. We shot over the entry ramp and out onto new Maklite surface six lanes wide. I called Sam.

"I got a fix on you now, boy."

"That's good," I said. "Where are you?"

"Out in the bush by the starslab. But don't worry, I'll pick you up. What are you driving?"

"You won't believe it, but you'll know it the moment you see it. Old Terran automobile. A replica, of course. But, Sam, I'll need to know where you are. We have to make the switch off the road somewhere, out of sight. Everybody in the galaxy's hot on my trail."

"Really? Hold on." A pause. *"Yeah, I'm painting them now. Too far away, can't tell exactly how many. . . . Hey! What're you trying to do, burn up the road?"*

"That's the general idea."

"What's your speed?"

"Two hundred miles per hour."

"What? Oh, I understand. Wait a minute. If it's a true replica, the speedometer wouldn't read that high."

"The needle buried itself at 100, then came up the other side again, and the numbers changed. This buggy's a replica as far as looks, but under the engine hous—I mean the hood—she's something else again. I'm waiting to get to the Skyway to see what she can do."

"Better step on it now. Something's gaining on you."

"Okay." I thought it was about time for fourth gear. I slid it in smoothly and the car surged ahead, pressing us back into our seats. The numbers on the speedometer now ranged from 200 to 300. I urged the car onward and the needle crept up to 250.

"God, I can't believe this old rattletrap—" I looked at the speedometer again and did a take. "What? Now this thing reads like a machometer!"

"You sure?"

"Yeah. It is a machometer."

"And it's not a reaction-drive vehicle?"

"Negative. I'm at Mach point three five and holding. Sam, how's the Skyway up ahead for high-speed travel?"

"It's all straightaway to the portal, but be careful. You know what they say. No ground vehicle is safe anywhere at over Mach point five."

"Right, but let 'em eat my dust for a while back there."

"They're still gaining."

"They are? Sam, get moving!"

"Say again?"

"Get rolling now. If they're still gaining, it's a Militia interceptor, and I know exactly who's driving it." The ambush hadn't been Petrovsky's doing. That had been Elmo reasserting his authority. But Petrovsky was on his own now, that wide Slavic nose pushed to the scent. "No chance of us meeting anywhere on Goliath. Get moving toward Seven Suns and we'll play it by ear from there."

"Hold on, now, I'm getting more than one blip. There's the fast-moving one, and then there're two behind him, a little slower."

The Reticulans, with a backup vehicle?

"And tailing them at a fairly good clip is another one."

The Ryxx, maybe.

"And behind them . . ."

"More?" Well, hell. "Move it out, Sam. You'll have a lot

more speed on the other side. Vacuum."

"You don't know what Stinky did to me. Feel like a new man. I haven't opened it up yet, but my cruising speed's up by at least thirty percent. Stinky outdid himself this time."

"Good, but get rolling!"

"Okay, okay!"

In no time we reached the old Skyway, pointing straight and true toward a limitless horizon. The machometer crept upward—but what about aerodynamics? The vehicle's shape was rounded, "streamlined" was the word that came to mind, but the surface didn't look capable of slicing an air mass at Mach one. There were no stabilizer foils, no GE flange, nothing. There'd be heavy turbulence ahead if I kept pushing, and possible disaster. But how was the car staying on the road at the speed we were doing now? And in Goliath's soupy air to boot? To say there was more to this vehicle than met the eye was an understatement by several degrees.

"Sam, are you grabbing slab?"

"That I am, son. I'm tracking you at Mach point four Where's the fire?"

"Up my kazoo. By the way, what happened at Stinky's?"

"Well, it's a long story."

"Edit it severely."

"Right. Stinky worked on me all day yesterday, then into evening. He said it was a challenge. It was 'way after dark when he finished, and I insisted he rehook me to the trailer and let me squeeze into the garage. I hadn't heard from you, and I thought it best. He balked at that, but gave in. It was a tight fit. Anyway, about an hour later I hear somebody breaking into the place. So I took off, not bothering to open doors. Stinky's garage is now naturally air-conditioned."

I winced. Stinky would go for the jugular next time he clapped eyes on me. "Got you. Then what?"

"Then nothing. I took off in the general direction John had said his farm was in, but couldn't find anything. I had half a mind to give you a buzz, but it just didn't seem like a good idea."

"You were right. Would've given you away. Besides, I had the beeper turned off. God knows why, but I thought it'd take them a while to trace us to John's place, thought we were safe. But, go on."

"Well, there isn't much more. Wandered all night in the bush. Spotted a couple blips once, powered down and made

like a rock. Airborne bandits, and they passed right overhead. The cops?"

"The same. Sam, you were nearer than you thought. But if that's true, I can't understand why I had trouble reading you."

"Probably because I hid in a deep arroyo. Had a hell of a time getting out of there. What's more, you called on FM."

"Merte. Remind me to have the key redesigned so that the AM and FM select tabs are on opposite sides."

The silence in the car was getting me down. "Anyone for Twenty Questions?" I asked, and felt immediately inappropriate. I glanced around to find Susan glowering at me. "Sorry," I said lamely.

"Now you tell me your life story."

"That is much too long a tale, Sam. Later."

"Damn it, you never tell me anything."

"Okay, a synopsis. The cops nabbed me, then someone sprang me. Don't know who, but I think it was the Ryxx."

"The Ryxx? What the hell do they have to do with this?"

"Don't know that either, exactly, but I have an idea. As I said, later."

Roland surprised me by asking, "Jake, how *did* you get . . . uh, sprung?"

I told him about the neural-scrambler field. "Then someone tickled me with something to bring me around, and I got out."

"Can you describe the symptoms?"

Darla and Winnie began talking in the back seat as I told him.

Roland smacked fist into palm. "Then, I didn't fall asleep on watch!"

"Yeah?"

"I *knew* it! I've never done that, and I've stood watch more than most soldiers."

"You're telling me the same thing hit us last night?"

"No question. I remember sitting there by the fire, feeling a headache coming on. Then a buzzing sound . . . and then there was a strange interlude there. I wasn't asleep. It was like an extended daydream. A reverie. And the next thing I knew you were kicking me and the flitters were on us."

Which meant that it had been the Reticulans who had engineered my escape from the station. One more unfittable piece in an ever-growing puzzle.

Darla leaned over the seat. "Jake, from what Winnie tells

me, Roland's right. She wasn't affected by the field, or the effect, or whatever it was."

"Most likely it was attuned to human neural patterns," I ventured. "I'll buy that. What else did she say?"

"She said she heard someone walk up to the house. She got frightened, tried to wake us, but we were out cold. Then she ran outside and hid in the bush."

"Did she see anything?"

"No, but she says she knows that two humans came into the house, and one nonhuman. She says the nonhuman frightened her a great deal. The smell was bad."

"Does she have any idea what they did?"

Darla asked her. I realized then that, while I couldn't understand Winnie most of the time, Darla never seemed to have any trouble.

"She doesn't know," Darla reported. She looked over my shoulder and then said, "Jake, how fast are we going?"

I looked. The needle had just edged past Mach point five. "Wow," was all I could say.

"Jesus Christ!" John shouted.

I looked up. Sam was ahead. I swerved to the left and we passed him like he was painted on the road.

"Slow down, speed demon!" Sam's voice came from the dashboard under the windscreen, where I had thrown the key. *"Crazy kids! No sense of responsibility."* He chuckled. *"You're right. That buggy is a blast from the past. Look's like a middle-twentieth-century Chevrolet to me. I'm no expert, though, on these things."*

I eased up on the pedal, and the needle fell off to saner speeds. "How's our pursuit doing?"

"He's pacing us now. Knows he can't catch you."

"Yeah, but he can catch you, Sam. Dump the load. Unhook the trailer."

"Not on your life, son. We're paid to deliver goods, not leave 'em strewn over a hundred klicks of road. Besides, he's after you now, not me."

"Sam, I'm not so sure of that. If I had any sort of priceless artifact, especially a map, wouldn't I leave it with you? Why do you think they wanted to search you? Petrovsky might try to disable you and do just that."

"Who the hell's Petrovsky?"

"Sorry. The guy nipping at our tail."

"I can handle any cop who has a notion to breach my road rights."

"Sam, you know you can't. So, cut the crap and dump it."

"Is that any way to talk to your father? Moreover, my disrespectful son, you forget something. I'm still mostly machine—in fact, let's face it—I'm nothing but, or so they tell me. Machines must obey programming. And I can't circumvent your tricky anti-hijack program. Only you can detach the trailer with your thumbprint."

He was right, and I had forgotten completely. "Sorry, Dad."

Alarms blared from somewhere inside the vehicle, startling everybody. We then watched goggle-eyed as strange things began to happen to the instrument panel. Magically, the funny dials and gauges metamorphosed into more conventional-looking readouts, melting and reshaping as if worked by the hand of an unseen sculptor. It took but a few seconds, and the final result was a complete portal-approach display.

"Remarkable," John said beside me, his bony knees sticking up sharply.

"Roland, change places with John. Give me a hand with these readouts." They did. John breathed easier and stretched out, glad to get off the hump that housed the drive train . . . at least I *thought* that was what it was.

I missed the warning signs, a blur beside the road. The cylinders split the sky ahead, towering columns of unknowable energy and substance. As we watched, a phthisic finger of lightning crackled down from a clear sky to touch the lead left cylinder. Branching secondary tendrils snaked from it to link the others in a fiery web, and for a second an eerie bloom of pale blue light grew around the whole portal array, then shrunk back on itself, vanished.

I had only seen it happen once before. You can divide your life into sections marked off by the event of witnessing a portal call down a bolt from the clear blue. Everyone exhaled.

"Seat belts?" I blurted. "Any safety harnesses in here?"

"No," Darla said. "Don't see any, except for this funny hand strap hung between the windows."

Strange. "Well, grab it, or something. Anything." And then I remembered what was on the other side of the portal. "Windows? Are all the windows shut?"

Are all the windows shut? I couldn't believe I was saying it. Could it be that this contraption wasn't vacuum-worthy? But no. Its rightful owner had passed us on the Skyway, and he could only have come from Groombridge, the only portal leading to Goliath. Unless he'd been out on the plains punking around. But there was nothing out there but hoplite crabs and misery. The possibility lingered, but surely the windows weren't glass. . . .

"All shut, Jake," Darla said. "As a matter of fact, the back window on Susan's side was open just a slit, and I happened to catch it closing by itself when the needle went over one hundred. Now my window handle won't budge."

Things were happening too fast, and I was disoriented. The commit marker streaked past, and the guide lane skittered beneath us. We were streaking across a perilously thin edge of safety at a speed that was too fast for reaction, almost. But through the wheel I felt another controlling force, an assisting hand—an automatic system of some sort. The instrument panel was lit up in reassuring green, and things seemed to be going fine.

The cylinders whizzed by in a flickering blur, and we were through the aperture.

We arrived smoothly on a world of mirror-flat ice plains, broken by low outcroppings of dark rock and occasional fracture rills. The road cut straight ahead to a deceptively close horizon. It was dead night, but a million stars gave the ice a sheen by which you could pick out features of the landscape. And almost directly overhead there hung a chandelier of seven bright stars, brighter by far than any seen on most planets. I pressed my face against the window and looked up for a second or two.

There had been no surge of speed when the car had hit vacuum. I checked the machometer. Yes, only a slight increase. The car had some remarkable aerodynamic properties.

I tried calling Sam, but there was no answer. Too early. I had no idea how far behind he had been, and now I was worried.

Alarms sounded again. The sound was different this time. A scanner screen appeared on the panel, showing traffic ahead, and I slowed down. Soon we were down below Mach point three, and decelerating. I didn't want to get too far ahead of Sam. There was now a decision to make: where to go? Seven Suns offered three portals, with three separate ingress points feeding into them: one from Goliath, two from other interstellar routes. One portal led back to the heart of the Terran Maze by a many-light-year jump, another to Ryxx territory. The third was potluck, so there were really only two choices, unless we felt very lucky.

"Sam, come in. Are you okay?"

"I'm fine, Captain. I've got a cop on my tail, though."

I made a decision and braked. "I'm slowing down."

"Negative! Get your butt through that Ryxx portal! Get out of T-Maze. It's your only chance."

"I think I can handle him. This car is some kind of fused-up alien buggy with all kinds of surprises in it. Haven't found the armaments yet, but I've a feeling I may be able to outshoot an interceptor. Whereas you—"

"Son, think a moment. What can this Petrovsky character do to me? If he pulls me over, so what? If he searches, what'll he find? Meanwhile, you can get away."

"He may impound you."

"Again, so what? I'll cool my rollers for a while till you get back."

It did make sense. "Okay. I guess." I didn't like it.

"In fact, I'm kind of hoping he does pull me over. Maybe a Roadbug'll come along and— Hold on."

The key was silent for half a minute. Then I said, "Sam? What's going on?"

"He passed me. I said *he was after you."*

"Yeah." I upped our speed as much as the traffic would allow. I was weaving in and out of lanes now, passing rigs, roadsters, alien conveyances of every sort and description. "One problem about ducking into Ryxx Maze, though. One of those blips you painted was a Ryxx vehicle."

"They sprung you, now they're chasing you. Logical."

"I've learned through the Teelies here that it wasn't the Ryxx who got me out."

"Who did? I'm confused."

"That makes three of us. I'm twice as confused as you. I think it was the Reticulans."

"Oh, well, that explains everything."

"Clear as shit, isn't it?" Something occurred to me. "The thing that really puzzles me is how the Rikkis traced us to the Teelies' farm. The Militia did it by making inquiries in town, but the Rikkis couldn't have done that. And Petrovsky told me that he was following *them*." I realized that Sam was in the dark about all of that. "Sorry, Sam. I'll fill you in when we have time."

"Oh no, go ahead. I'm writing this all down. What about Wilkes?"

"No idea. As far as I know, he's out of this whole mess."

"Well, that's one less fly on the pile." A pause. *"Jake, you'd better see about what guns you can bring to bear on the cop."*

"It'll be hard, on the run like this, but as I said, you wouldn't believe what this buggy's capable of."

The turnoff for the T-Maze portal came up. The Skyway split into one branch that curved gradually to the left and one that continued straight. Most of the traffic veered left, but I kept our bow pointed dead ahead. "Okay, there goes one option. Now it's either Ryxx country or oblivion."

"Are you sure the Ryxx are in on this snipe hunt?"

"I have it on good authority that they are."

"Uh-huh. Beats me what you should do, then. Maybe you should've taken that turnoff."

"Damned if I do, damned if I don't. If I head on through to Theron, it means another high-speed chase and few places to duck off-road, because of the bogs. Next up is Straightaway, which is all salt flats and *no* place to hide, then Doron, where there's another Militia base. If you remember, we were guests there once."

"Oh, yes. I remember. Hm."

"So, I'd rather take my chances with the Ryxx. Besides, you used to have friends there. Maybe Krk-(whistle/click) knows something about this. Wasn't that his name?"

"Approximately. Of course, it's 'she' now. They all turn diploid in later life. But her nest is ten thousand klicks into the Maze. And that was a hell of a long time ago."

Options were indeed dwindling. I half-entertained going off-road over the ice to find the T-Maze road—but I had five innocent lives to consider. I hadn't begun to decide what to do with the Teelies. Maybe turning myself in would be the best thing after all. Finally clear up this mess. Except . . .

Except for the small matter of the Delphi series. But then, maybe it wouldn't be all that bad. Hell. So what if it meant a stint in a psych motel, drooling and finger-painting the walls with my own feces? Couple of months learning all over again to go potty, wave bye-bye. Could do that standing on my head. I'd come out of there a new man.

Um . . . no thanks.

The traffic thinned. The terrain flattened even more, low ridges becoming more scarce. The car became a mite scurrying across a giant billiard ball. Above, the stars were crisp and clear, like clean little holes drilled through black velvet. Around us, in the biggest hockey rink ever, ice glistened in the interstellar night.

A warning tone sounded once again, this time a gonging bell that said, *"Battle stations!"* The instrument panel underwent still another transformation, while the scanner screen tracked a fast-moving blip. Looked like a floater missile.

"Roland, see what you can do with this fire-control board."

Roland scrutinized the panel, tentatively fingered a few controls. "Hard to say what's going on here," he said. "All these systems have funny designations. What's 'Snatch Field Damp' supposed to mean?"

"I can guess," I said, amazed.

"It's closing pretty fast. What's your speed?"

"Point three."

"Well, I'd advise accelerating."

I already was. The car surged forward, pressing us into our seats.

"I think it's at two kilometers, still closing."

"Point three five."

"Still closing."

"Coming up on point four."

"Still closing, but slower." Roland tested a switch or two. "This says 'Arm' but I don't know what it's arming. Some very strange things here."

"Point four."

"Still closing."

I floored the pedal. The engine sent furious vibrations through the wheel and into my hands and arms. A high whine, barely audible, was all that conducted through the hotwall. "Point four five."

"Still closing, I'm afraid. Must have variable thrust. Emergency boosters. Oh, damn. Wait a minute, this must be it. 'Antimissile Zap.' God, this is crazy."

"Point five."

"Closing. Has to run out of fuel sooner or later."

"Don't count on it," I said. "Point five five."

"Still closing. About a kilometer." Roland grunted. "G-force makes it hard to bend forward." He strained to read the panel.

"This must be an automatic system. All right, I've armed it. Now what?"

It struck me that Roland should be having a little more trouble in bending forward. Our acceleration was rapid, should have been something around three Gs. But it didn't feel like that much. "Point six."

"Closing, but slowly."

Another moment. The acceleration seemed to be picking up even more. "Point six five."

"Closing."

"Point seven! God help us."

"Closing. Half a klick."

"Point seven five!"

"Closing! But barely."

Everything was a blur outside. The car swerved murderously with every random movement of my tensed arms. "I don't know how long I can keep this up," I said.

"I'm working on the problem," Roland said calmly. "All right, now, everything seems to be set, but what activates the whole system?"

"Point eight!"

"Um . . . wait a moment. No, that isn't it. 'Antimissle Zap.' Remarkable way of putting it. What's this? I can't understand . . . 'Eyeball' and 'Let George Do It.'" Roland looked at me, baffled. "What could that possibly mean?"

"For Christ's sake, Roland! LET GEORGE DO IT!"

"Huh? Oh, okay." He pressed a glowing tab and something left the rear of the car in a green flash. A few seconds later a brighter flash lit up the road behind us in a soundless concussion.

Roland studied the scanners. "No more missile," he said with satisfaction. He turned to me and grinned. "That was easy." He looked back, then said with concern, "But a bigger blip is gaining on us. The interceptor, I guess. Looks like he's on afterburners."

"I believe," John broke in with a solemn voice, "that we just passed the turnoff to the Ryxx Maze portal."

10

NOBODY SPOKE FOR a while as it sank in. We were heading straight for never-never land with exactly two alternatives: to double back on the road and confront our pursuer, or to swing out over methane-water ice and take our chances with hidden crevices, geothermal sinkholes, and occasional impact craters. I braked automatically, then wondered what I was doing, where I was going. Turn back? Give up? I saw no controls for roller supertraction and doubted that the car could negotiate a surface of metallic methane—pure water ice, maybe, but not water caged in frozen gas. Then again, I had no justification to put limitations on this buggy.

John broke the silence. "Jake? What do we do?"

All eyes were on me—Teelie eyes, that is. Darla and Winnie were talking in hushed tones. I checked the scanner. Petrovsky was gaining on us very quickly now that I had decelerated. I goosed it a little to give me more time. The road was still perfectly straight, the terrain relentlessly flat. I kept my eyes glued ahead. Sudden obstacles would be death at these speeds.

"Jake?" John reminded me softly.

"Yeah." I exhaled, my mind made up. "John, I'm not going to stop. Don't ask me to justify the morality of it. I can't, except to say that I can't possibly give myself up. I'm going to shoot the potluck portal."

Susan gasped. John took it silently. Roland was preoccupied with the instrument panel.

"If you have a gun," I went on, "I'd advise you to pull it on me right now. The portal's coming up."

Outlined in faint zodiacal light at the horizon, the cylinders were rising above the ice like dark angels on Judgment Day.

"Let me say this," I continued. "I wouldn't shoot this portal if I thought it'd be suicide. You can believe me or not. Take it for what it's worth, but I wouldn't do it if I thought there was no chance of getting back."

Roland looked at me. "Of course, Jake. Everybody knows you'll get back—if you believe the road yarns."

"I'm grounding my belief in firmer evidence than beerhall bullshit. Again, take it for what it's worth, but I intend to get back from the other side. In fact, I know I will."

"How do you know?" John asked.

"Can't explain right now. I just know."

John looked at me intently. "Jake, I'm asking you to reconsider."

"Sorry, John. Put a gun to my head and I'll stop. I don't particularly want to shoot a potluck portal, but I will if no one stops me." It sounded crazy even to me.

Susan was quietly sobbing in the back seat.

"Threatening one's driver," Roland said acerbically, "at a little under Mach point seven strikes me as slightly absurd." He turned to John. "Can't you see that Jake's in the Plan?"

I caught quick glimpses of John's face in the lights of the panel as I shifted my eyes fleetingly from the road. Rare to see a man confronted with a literal test of his religious beliefs. John shook his head. "Roland, it isn't simply a matter of—"

"Oh, come on, John," Roland said, impatient with his leader's recent behavior, or so it sounded. "How can you be so myopic? We're in Jake's Plan, he's in ours. You can't deny that there's some kind of linkage here. Can you?"

"Maybe," John said, eyes belying his words. "Possibly." He gave up. "God, I don't know. I really don't know what to do."

"I do," Roland said emphatically. "It's obvious. No matter

what we do, our paths and Jake's seem to cross. I say we let Jake take the lead. It's clear his Plan is informing ours."

Darla was pounding me on the shoulder. "Look out!"

A dark pool lay across the road. I braked hard, but it was useless. In no time we shot across the spontaneous bridge over a geothermal depression and were back on solid ice again.

"Sorry, Jake. False alarm."

"No, keep watching. I need four eyes."

Roland was bent over the scanner again. Suddenly he spun around and peered back through the oval rear window. *"Merte!* I should have been watching. He's back there!"

In the rearview mirror I saw the interceptor's headbeams grow.

"Jake? Are you okay?"

No time to answer. I mashed the accelerator.

"I've got something on the scanner!" Roland stabbed fingers at the fire-control board. Green and red lights flickered. "Come on, George, whoever the hell you are!"

George didn't respond. Something smacked into the rear of the car with a dull thud. I couldn't see the interceptor's lights. A dark mass covered the rear window. I knew what it was, having been on the receiving end of a tackyball before. *Adhezosfero*. Now the sticky mess was crawling all over the back of the vehicle, fusing and bubbling, forming an unbreakable molecular bond with the metal of the hull. Though it was close to absolute zero outside, the thing wouldn't freeze, its chemical reactions providing heat long enough to do the job. Petrovsky was feeding us slack now until the bond formed. Then he'd start reeling us in.

"What happened to the antimissile system?" Roland wanted to know.

"Probably read the approach as a slow projectile," I said. "Tackyball shells are fired from a mortar. Didn't worry George any."

But I was worried. I kept the pedal flattened, hoping to unspool all of Petrovsky's tether line before the bond firmed up, but the boys and girls at Militia R&D had been putting in overtime. This one bonded in a few seconds. A sharp jerk, and that was it. The Russian had us hooked.

"Roland, this thing must have some beam weapons," I said. "Find 'em!"

"I'm looking, Jake. But these designations are in another language."

"The language is archaic American. Read 'em off to me!"

"Okay. Tell me what 'Sic 'im, Fido' means."

"Spell it!" He did, and I stopped him in the middle of it. "Christ Almighty! It must mean attack or fire or something. Hit it!"

Roland did, and nothing happened.

"It has to have a target!" I screamed. "Find the aiming waddyacallit!"

"The what?"

The road behind lit up blue-white with the Russian's retro-fire, and we slid forward in our seats. Roland and John hit the windscreen, and I took the padded steering column in the chest, but I kept my leg stiffened and drove the pedal down, finding new depths of power down there. My foot seemed to sink through the floorboards. The car lurched, then acceleration took us the other way, sending us sprawling back on the cushioned seat. I shot a look in the back. Susan, Darla, and Winnie were a tangle on the floor, Susan's bare foot sticking up comically.

A tug-of-war began, the interceptor's retro engines against the growling power of the Chevy's unfathomable motor. But the Russian had his moves down pat. He paid out line and let me pull, then cut retros and ate the slack up plus more, reeling me in like a deep-sea catch. He was out-maneuvering me and I knew it. And when he had us up close enough, he'd squirt us down with Durafoam under high pressure, spin us into an immobilizing cocoon—one hell of an effective technique against even a vehicle that can outgun you, if you can get close enough. Roadbugs aside, when the cops want to snare you, they get down to business. No Roadbug would save us now.

I only had one countermove. The fish has sharp spines, so be careful where you touch. I considered the consequences for a second or two, then drove the brake pedal against the floor. The move caught the big man up short and he shot past us, dragging the slack length of the graphite whisker line along. It all happened very quickly. The invisible line pulled taut and yanked our ass-end around into a fishtail, but in the process the hardened glob of tackyball slid free from the back of the car. It was too late for Petrovsky. He lacked time or the presence of mind to cut the line free. His headbeams swung around to blind me, then continued the circuit into a wild spin. Something strange was happening at our end: I felt an unseen force fight against the fishtail, some kind of stabilizing inertial field. I was countersteering sharply, but it wouldn't have been enough. We were traveling broadside to the road, but something shoved us back. Petrovsky's vehicle kept spinning, trailing wisps of hot vapor from its rollers, cold gas from its yaw/antispin jets, but it was hopelessly out of control and went whirling off the roadbed, past the shoulder and onto the ice.

In the middle of it all we ghosted through a holo sign. The words were repeated cinematically over kilometers and were projected large enough to straddle the road. The Highway Department wanted no mistake.

WARNING!
UNEXPLORED PORTAL AHEAD!
POSSIBLE INTER-EPOCHAL JOURNEY
PROCEED AT OWN RISK
WARNING!
UNEXPLORED PORTAL . . .

The interceptor began to break up as it spun, wrapping itself in a deadly cat's cradle of the trailing line, the ultrastrong, superthin fiber slicing through hull metal like fine wire through cheese. Pieces flew in all directions, some skittering across the road into our path. I couldn't dodge them, too busy counter-counter-steering against the return fishtail to the left, again being helped by the strange force. We straightened out, then re-rebounded to the right again, not as far this time, the oscillations damping with each cycle. A big chunk of stabilizer foil tumbled across the road, just missing us. I caught sight of the shapeless mass of tackyball bouncing along behind the cop car like a useless anchor dragged over frozen sea, its weight pulling the line into a lethal snarl. As I fought for control I saw the flashing red commit markers ahead. Blind spots, burned in by the cop car's intense headbeams, swam in front of my eyes, and I wasn't sure where road ended and ice field began. The interceptor was pacing us, spinning and sliding over close-to-frictionless surface, heading straight for the portal but wide of the commit markers. I finally regained control and found that we were on the shoulder near Petrovsky's vehicle, with our left rollers on the ice and the right marker dead in our path. I wheeled to the left as sharply as I dared. The interceptor was a rotating pile of junk now, throwing off pieces of itself with abandon. . . . Then it exploded, or seemed to, but I knew it was Petrovsky's ejection seat. He'd never make it, was too near the markers, doomed to be sucked in by the cylinders. Across the glossy hood of the Chevy, sudden highlights flared, reflections of Petrovsky's descent-rockets igniting. We shot past the right commit marker, missing it by a hair.

Now the real race began. We had to beat the wreckage of the interceptor to the cylinders, get through the aperture before the horrendous implosion that would happen as the mass of the wreck was torn atom-from-atom by the portal's tidal claws. The wreck was veering outward now. There was a chance it could move far enough out to miss hitting the right lead cylinder directly, make a wide looping geodesic before it spiraled into the zone of destruction, before it flashed to filaments of plasma falling into the ultracondensed mass of the cylinders. The delay might be only a fraction of a second, but it might be enough.

It was all happening within seconds, but to me the flow of things was gummed up into a languid slow motion. Endlessly, the wreckage wheeled in the icy night, the sweep of its head-beams like some haunted lighthouse on an arctic shore. I looked for the guide lane, the white lines marking the safe corridor through the aperture, but couldn't see them. Red lights blared from the instrument panel.

"Jake? Jake, what's happening?" Sam's voice was faint, far away.

The guide lane was suddenly under me and we weren't dead center. Our left wheels were over the white line. I corrected sharply, thinking this was the end, we've had it, you just don't do this and live, and then felt the car rising on its right wheels as greedy fingers of force closed over us. We were up on two wheels, the car riding diagonally to the roadbed . . . and somehow in those few fractions of a second I reacted unthinkingly, wheeling hard right and tramping on the accelerator. . . .

And then time jarred back to normal flow and it was *wham!* back on four wheels, shooting down the dark corridor of the safe lane, the cylinders black-on-black beside us, and then a brilliant flash that blinded me, followed by an explosion of sound as we hit air and the car's engine shouted in my ears. I saw light, pure and golden and warm; then my pupils contracted and the field of vision split into an upper band of light blue and a lower one of blue-green. Someone was leaning over my shoulder, and I felt hands over my hands on the wheel.

"Jake, slow down!"

Darla was helping me steer. I braked, trying not to panic-stop to avoid skidding. I was half-blind now but could see the road, a strip of black over blue-green. The Skyway was suspended over water and there were no guard rails. A few seconds later and I could see that the elevation was minimal. We were on a causeway crossing shallow water.

But our speed was still fantastic. Land ahead, an island or a reef, coming up fast. The road looked like it ended there, but I wasn't sure. I could see other vehicles parked on the island. I mashed down on the brake and the tires wailed like hellhounds, the back end floating from side to side. We began to drift toward the shoulder and I let up on the brake to straighten out, then started pumping the pedal, but the shore was coming at us fast. I quit pumping and stood on the brake, the sounds of the tires splitting my ears, the sky, sea, and land heaving around us. Darla was no help now—I was fighting her as well as the wheel. I pushed her back and took over, my vision nowhere near normal but adequate in the bright sunlight. We were down to a mere 150 miles per hour, but the shore of the island was upon us. We shot past a wide beach, still on the Skyway, and blurred through a narrow strip of land until we reached the opposite shore and another beach. The road picked up the causeway again and headed out to sea.

Not far from the beach the road began a gradual dip until it sank beneath the deep water beyond the breakers.

My stiffened body was perpendicular to the brake pedal, and I braced myself by pulling backward on the steering wheel. The back end was fishtailing but I didn't countersteer, couldn't, counting on the mysterious force to set us aright. It did, and with a final screaming chorus from the tires we skidded to a stop a few meters from the gentle waves washing across the width of the roadway.

Nobody moved for a long while. I sat there letting warm sunlight soothe my face, not feeling much of anything else. I was numb, my arms like dead things in my lap, my body limp and useless. From outside came the strange croaking cries of seabirds and the sound of water lapping against the sinking road.

Presently, someone moaned. Susan. I made an effort and looked over the back of the seat. Susan was down there somewhere, as was Winnie. Darla was sitting up looking dazed, relieved, glad to be alive, *amazed* to be alive, and totally exhausted, all at once. Our eyes met and a flicker of a smile crossed her lips. Then she closed her eyes and tilted her head back. Roland and John began to pick themselves up from the floor-decking. It took time.

We sat there for a good while longer until I felt a throb of feeling return and a tiny bit of strength begin to trickle back.

Then I put my hands back on the wheel. It took time to get the car into reverse, but I finally figured it out, backed up, turned around, and headed back to land.

No one spoke.

The island was packed with vehicles of every kind, parked and waiting. We reached the end of the beach and I hung a right, going off-road over sand and scrubby rust-colored beach grass, threading through the crowd of parked vehicles. Beings of every sort were represented here, none of which I'd ever seen before. There were humans here too, sitting in their buggies with doors open or standing in groups outside, smoking cigarettes, talking. Others were picnicking on the sand. Somewhere underneath the blanket of fatigue that covered me I was surprised to see them, but didn't dwell on the implications. Everyone seemed to be waiting for something. I could guess what it was, but I didn't give much thought to that either. I kept driving around. The island was narrow but long and crescent-shaped, little more than a sandbar dotted with some suitably odd vegetation, clumps of scraggly brush that looked like land-colonizing seaweed, and a few tall shaggy trees with dull red foliage. There wasn't much else to the place. No other land was in sight.

Near one end of the island, which I arbitrarily designated as north, another spur of the Skyway came in over the causeway from the northwest. It crossed the island diagonally and plunged beneath the waterline as well, its junction with the Goliath spur submerged farther out. Traffic from the ingress point was substantial, backed up along the causeway for half a klick or so. If we had ingressed here, at our speed . . . well, no use to dwell on that either.

Things got congested up there, so I turned around and went back, hugging the western shore until we found a spot that was relatively free of traffic, vehicles, and people, a little knoll above the beach topped with a lone tall tree. Before stopping we passed a middle-aged man in an electric-blue jumpsuit standing by his roadster, smoking, looking at us curiously. As I drove by he tapped his nose with an index finger, signing that the air was okay here. Thank you. I rolled down the window and Goliath's syrupy stuff whooshed out and let in tangy salt air and sea smells, very Earthlike. From long experience I could tell by the sound of the rushing air that there wasn't any pressure differential to worry about. The atmosphere was fairly heavy here too. I've had a touch of the bends once or twice, and I should have checked it out first, if I could have found the readouts. But I was dreaming along, not caring, barely there at all. I stopped the car at the edge of the gentle slope down to the beach, put it in neutral and jerked up on the hand brake. I didn't shut the engine off. Then I opened the door. Took me time to get my legs moving—pure homemade jelly. Then I got out, staggered down the hill to the flat, and sank to my knees. I fell forward and stretched out in the warm sand.

Darla came down and lay on her back beside me. She'd taken off her suit and was down to halter and briefs, golden skin exposed to whatever passed for solar radiation here. Darla could have been a blonde easily. The downy stuff on her arms and body was very light. And on the side of one shoulder, a heart-shaped port-wine mark, tiny one.

I shut my eyes and stopped thinking. Seabirds, or whatever they were, croaked above. I wasn't looking, wasn't thinking of looking. I just listened to their calls, heard combers wash the beach, an occasional engine sound, the distant rumble of the Skyway. My closed eyelids glowed red-orange. Gradually, I started to feel very warm in my leather jacket. I lay there for as long as I could stand it, then sat up and shed the jacket, took off my shoes (I still had no shirt), then turned around to lie down with my head next to Darla's. The sky was hazy, very light blue, hung with streamers of soft gauze. I saw the flying things. They were fish. Looked like fish, anyway, with flat silvery bodies and huge winglike pectoral fins made of thin translucent membrane stretched over a frame of sharp spines. They were soaring, really, not flying. I watched one ride an air current directly above, unmoving with respect to the ground, gliding on the stiff ocean breeze. It hung there for a minute or so, then lost lift and started a dive toward the water. Halfway down it folded its wings and stooped, plunging head first into the depths beyond the breakers. I heard the splash and lifted my head. Not far from where it went in another one launched itself from the water straight into the air, shooting up a good ten meters before it unfolded its wings with the sound of a parasol suddenly opening. It caught a good updraft and began to rise.

Then I noticed the wrecks. Hulks of abandoned vehicles awash in the breakers, all kinds, some with Terran Maze markings. More of them up and down the beach half sunk in the sand, some so covered-over and sprouting with beach grass that I'd mistaken them for dunes. Apparently this planet had been a dead end for some time. Those without flying vehicles had been stranded here, left either to swim for it, bum a ride, or die. Surely there was some way off now. Or was there?

I let my head fall back. Of course there is. What's all this traffic about then? Everybody doomed? Stop thinking.

But I didn't stop thinking, and wondered about Sam. He was an hour behind us, at least. Would he shoot the potluck portal? Did he know I had? We might have been well out of scanner range, but then he must have tracked us to the Ryxx Maze cutoff and seen us go beyond it. I lifted my head again. I could see the ingress causeway from Goliath. We'd wait and see. I lay back again. I had fussed over everything of immediate concern, seen all there was to see, and right then I didn't care about Reticulans or cops or treasure hunts or even Teelies. Not at the moment, because a breeze was carrying cool salt air to lift some of the heat from my baking skin, Darla was beside me, things were quiet, and I didn't give a *merte*.

A shadow fell over my face, and I opened my eyes. It was Darla, looking at me. She smiled, and I smiled. Then she giggled, and I did too.

"Let George do it," she said. It was like repeating the punchline to a very funny joke. We couldn't stop giggling.

"Sic 'im, Fido," I managed to say between waves of mirth.

We broke out laughing, all the tension exploding away in an instant. Darla collapsed over me, helpless as I was, convulsed, two complete idiots on the shore. We were like that for five minutes. It was overreaction, an undertone of hysteria to it, the terror of it all hitting us, tearing out shrieks of laughter.

And when it was all gone it left us spent, breathless, and sober. We looked at each other, and for the first time I saw a hairline crack in that smooth, cool shell, saw vulnerability in Darla's face. Her mouth was half open, her lower lip quivering the slightest bit, eyes widened and searching for something in mine, looking for a cue. *I'm afraid. Is it okay? Will you let me?* I wanted to say, *Yes, love, it's okay, you can let go, don't be afraid to feel fear when it's justified, and, yes, I'll be strong for you, just so that next time you let me have a turn*... but suddenly she was wrapped up safe in my arms and there was nothing more to say.

Very quickly we were naked, her briefs and halter materializing in my hand somehow. Flimsy things they were, scraps of soft cloth, and the next thing I knew we were making love without a thought as to who was around. It was sudden, a little desperate, and more than a physical bonding. We needed to tell each other that we were still alive, still here, still able to feel, to touch, needed proof that we still had bodies all of a piece, warm and pulsing, bodies that lived and moved and tingled and glowed, that could feel pleasure and pain, exhilaration and fatigue. We had to convince ourselves that we weren't bits of lifeless stuff squashed up against some unimaginable object, that we weren't plain dead. And as it is after all brushes with death, there was a sense of the preciousness of every moment, of every sensation, an awareness of the miraculous nature of life. We celebrated that, and celebrated ourselves.

Afterward, there was deep calm. Birdfish croaked their soaring song above. With my head on Darla's breast, I watched little crustacean things scuttle across the sand—didn't look anything like crabs, more like tiny pink mushroom caps up on tripods. Not far from us, an animal with a brightly colored spiral shell popped partway out of the sand, shot a stream of water into the air in a neat arc once—*spritz!*—and screwed itself back into the beach. I noticed for the first time that the white sand under us had sparkling elements in it, millions of little glassy beads. Pure silicon tektites, probably, products of meteor hits long ago. Or maybe not so long ago. Something had altered the geology of this planet since the Roadbuilders had laid their highway here.

I heard a hum and looked up. An alien aircraft, climbing from its takeoff from the northern spur. Lucky bastard. Then I hoped for him that he knew where the egress portal was, and that the road to it was landable. Otherwise, he'd have to double back all the way here and go slumming among the groundsuckers. He probably wouldn't run out of fuel. With fusion, it's a rarity, but you do see some very primitive equipment on the Skyway now and then, belonging to races that you'd have to call overachievers.

After a long while I got up and stood over Darla, looking at her slim golden body. She opened her eyes and smiled. Then I looked up the knoll. The man in the loud blue jumpsuit was looking down at us, standing far enough away so that I couldn't tell if the curl to his lip was a smirk or a friendly grin. I didn't care if he'd been there for the whole performance. Glad to oblige.

"How's the water?" I yelled up at him. "Safe?"

"Yeah, sure!" he shouted back. "Go ahead!"

Darla stood up, unashamed. I took her hand and we ran down to the surf, splashed in on foot a ways, then dove into the first breaker. The water was piss-warm but it was good to wash the sweat and sand off. My first bath in—how long? Darla's too, I supposed, unless she managed to get one while I was . . . but of course she had—at the Teelies' motel. Wait a minute. Had she gone there? She hadn't said. In fact, she hadn't gone into what had happened after she avoided getting fried out in the bush. I had assumed she went into town with the Teelies after the cops left with me, but I didn't know. She would tell me sooner or later, I guess. I ducked my head, came up sputtering, and rubbed myself down briskly, trying to get the jail smell off me. Institutional stink. The water was a buoyant, rich saline solution with a slightly slimy quality. It was like swimming in thin chicken broth. Darla was out beyond me in deeper water, backstroking lazily. Behind her and out a good distance, another birdfish rocketed from the water and took wing.

All right, let's face the question. Exactly how the hell did Darla wind up in the Militia station with Petrovsky? Did they come and get her? Did she come down to try to arrange my release? She said that Petrovsky wanted her for questioning, but Petrovsky said . . .

Something large and dark was moving in the deep water behind Darla. I stood up and peered out. I didn't like it, and Darla was out too far. I called to her and told her to come in. She asked why with a questioning grin.

"*Now,* Darla."

She got the message and shot forward into an Australian crawl, making it to shallow water in no time. Her stroke was very strong. Then a breaker took her straight in to me. I pulled her to her feet and pointed seaward. Just then something broke water out there with a boiling splash. I saw only a huge dark mass and a gaping mouth stuffed with more teeth than could possibly fit. Then the mouth sank, closing on something below the surface. The sea churned with the struggle, fins and flipperlike appendages thrashing up from the water over a wide area. Two very large animals were going at it.

Darla hadn't really been in danger, but had she been out a bit farther . . .

"That bastard!" Darla said bitterly, turning toward the beach. "He said it was—"

I looked. The man was gone.

She turned to me and wrapped her arms around her ribcage, suddenly chilled. "Weird," she muttered with a sour look.

God preserve us from smirking weird bastards.

11

WHEN WE GOT back to the car, John was sitting in the front seat with his legs hanging out the door, grinning at us. Winnie was playing in the sand very near, drawing figures with a piece of shell. I grinned back, welcoming his change of mood.

"Where're your two *kamradas?*" I asked.

He pointed to the nearby tree, in the shade of which Roland and Susan lay wrapped up into a ball.

"They seemed to've patched things up," I said.

"Yes, they have," he said approvingly. There wasn't the least hint of jealousy. "How was the water?"

"Fine, but the sea life is a little too interesting."

"Trouble?"

"No, not really." I sat down on the front seat, wishing I had a cigarette. I tried to forget about it, looked up the beach to the causeway. No traffic as yet. I took the key from the dash and tried calling Sam. No answer. What if he didn't come through? I'd miss him, but we did have a vehicle. But no food . . . hmmm. And no money. What passed for coin-of-the-realm outside the known mazes? No doubt we'd find out. Food. God, was I hungry. How long? Supper last night, nothing since then. I sighed, then slipped the key into my pants pocket.

After a while, Roland and Susan gathered themselves together and walked over.

"Hi," Susan said to me, smiling a little sheepishly.

"Hello, Susan."

She seemed calm, even content. It was quite a change. "Well," she said brightly, "we seem to have . . . to've gone and *done* it, haven't we?"

"Yes, we have. I'm sorry."

She shook her head. "No need. I pretty much understand it all now. Roland is right about you. You're definitely a nexus for us." She laughed and crinkled her nose. "More Teelie talk. What it means is—"

"I think I understand," I said. Then, realizing I'd interrupted her again, I said, "Sorry, you were explaining. Go ahead."

"It doesn't matter. I get interrupted a lot mainly because I talk too damn much. I'll tell you later."

"Okay, but again, I'm sorry."

She drew near me and put her hand behind my neck, bent down, and was about to kiss me, but looked first toward Darla, as if to see if it was okay. Darla was crouching beside Winnie, watching her draw. Then Susan kissed me sweetly.

"You did what you had to do, Jake," she said. "It wasn't your fault. You have a Plan too."

"I do? And here I thought I was improvising so brilliantly."

"No, no. Your task is to discover the Plan first, then go with it, accept it."

"Uh-huh. Karma."

"No, not karma. Karma is another word for fate, predestination. A Plan is just that. A scheme, a plot, something to follow. Plans can be changed, but only if they have linkage with the overall design of things."

"I see. Okay, I'll try." What could I say?

She kissed me again, then went over to see what Winnie and Darla were up to.

"Hmmmm." Roland's voice came from behind me.

I turned on the seat. He was studying the instrument panel again.

He looked at me. "I think I've finally figured out the beam weapon, if that's what this is all about," he said, indicating an area of readouts on the fire-control board. "By the way, did you notice that this whole business disappeared after we got through the portal?"

"No," I said, not oversurprised that Roland had had the presence of mind to notice anything amidst all the excitement.

"Must be automatic. Pops out when the defensive systems detect a threat—that missile, for instance. But the driver can make it come out anytime. Here." He showed me a small button on the steering column. "Don't fret. Everyone was well away from the vehicle when I pushed it. That'll make the board appear when the driver perceives a danger that the car doesn't." He pointed to the beam-weapon controls. "Anyway, *this* thing . . ." He broke off and shook his head. " 'Sic 'im, Fido'," he repeated. He turned to me with a bemused smile. "Isn't that the strangest thing?"

"Well, not really," I said. "The owner obviously wanted to confuse anyone who stole the car. Like us. Me."

"Then why label anything?"

"A good point. Poor memory?" Actually, the fact that the owner clearly had a sense of humor might explain it better, I thought.

"Well, who knows. At any rate, you choose a target simply by doing this." He touched a finger to the scanner screen, covering a blip with his fingertip, then withdrew it. Lines on the screen converged and the blip was centered in a flashing red circle. "That locks the system on target. And the fire switch is here."

"What have you got there?"

"The tree, I think. The thing's probably calibrated to ignore ground clutter, but that tree's a bit tall."

I looked around the immediate area. A few vehicles were parked a good distance behind us. The Weird Bastard's roadster was gone, and everyone in our party was toward the rear of the car. Then I looked at the tree. It was a shaggy, scrubby thing, not what you'd call attractive. The car was angled a little to the left of it.

"I take it the car's orientation doesn't matter."

"Doubt it," Roland said.

"Okay. Well, hold your fire for just a minute."

I got out, went over to the tree and took the grandest pee of my life. I'd been lucky to keep it in so long. Back on the Skyway there had been moments . . .

I walked back to the car and slid behind the wheel again. "Okay, Gunnery Sergeant. Fire when ready."

"Right." He hit the switch.

Something left the right underside of the car, something big and glowing, a writhing shape of swirling red fire, screeching like a hellbeast on the loose. The sound sent a cold twinge down my spine. The shape was vague, but there was something alive in there, a suggestion of a living form, limbs churning, legs moving over the ground, but the shape changed as it moved and parts of the phenomenon spun like a dust devil. It was big, at least three times as high as the car, and moved quickly, catlike, taking only a second or so to cover the distance from the car to its target. Furious flames enveloped the tree, then fiery arms surrounded it and tore it from the ground by the roots, flinging it up into the whirlwind where it was tossed and battered about as it burned. Flaming limbs flew in every direction. And all the while the shape of the cloud was shifting, changing, and the sound was like nothing you'd want to hear ever again. The tree was thrashed and ripped apart, tumbling in a vortex of demonic combustion. It went on for some time.

When there was nothing left, the phenomenon dissipated, fading into the air. All that remained were smoking fragments in the sand. Thin smoke rose from where the tree had been.

I found that I'd been gripping the wheel very tightly. I relaxed and sat back.

After a long silence Roland said, "So that was Fido."

"Yeah." I suppressed a shudder. The thing had really gotten to me. "Any ideas?"

Roland thought about it. "Energy matrix of some kind."

What had gotten to me was the maniacal single-mindedness of the thing. True, its target had been only a tree, but I had the feeling it would have done the same job on anything in the known universe. Anything. And not stop till the job was done. "I take it that by 'matrix' you mean energy molded by some kind of stasis field?"

"Either that, or it was an unimaginable sort of life form."

"Life form? Good God." Right then I admitted to myself that this vehicle was giving me a good case of the leaping creeps.

"Actually," Roland said, "I don't have a clue as to what it might have been."

"Yeah." I had no idea either, and wanted to drop the subject. I got out of the car, a little unsteadily. Up and down the shore as well as inland, people and beings were clambering into their buggies and moving away. I didn't blame them. John, Susan,

Darla, and Winnie were lying prone in the sand, looking up at me with shocked bewilderment, except Winnie, who still had her head tucked under Darla's arm.

"Sorry, folks," I said. "Should have warned you, but we weren't expecting anything like"—I motioned over my shoulder—"whatever the hell that was."

They all began to pick themselves up. I went back to inspect the rear of the car, where the storage compartment was. There's another term for this area, but it eluded me. Black clumps of solidified tackyball still clung to the metal, some to the back window. I hit them with the heel of my hand until they snapped off. It had been a big gamble, but I had banked on the possibility that the hull of this strange vehicle would not admit a permanent bond. I'd won. The stuff had bonded superficially, but wasn't up to taking a sudden shear stress. I wondered if we'd seen the end of the surprises the car had in store.

I went around to the front again, stepping over the drawings Winnie had etched in the sand, now partially erased. From what I could see, the figures were vaguely spiral.

I got in behind the wheel. John was now sitting where Roland had been.

"Well," I said, "I guess we hang around here for a while." Right then I noticed something, cocking my ears. "Hey, isn't the motor running?" The engine idled so quietly it was hard to tell.

"I shut it off," John told me. "When you got out after we stopped, you didn't look like you were . . . I'm sorry, did I do something wrong?" He looked deflated. "Again?" he added dismally.

"No, no, I should have said something. It's just that there should be antitheft devices on this buggy. But I can't understand how the weapons were operating. Oh, I see." The key had a setting marked AUX. John hadn't turned it back all the way. "Hm. Wonder what happens if I try to start it again?" John didn't look as if he understood the implications. Against my better judgment, I turned the key.

The air was full of cats, big cats with fur that stood straight up, crackling with static charges that needled every square inch of my skin. I leaped out of the car, hit beach, and rolled. The effect stopped the instant I was out, but I felt scratchy and raw all over. I looked up to see the car come alive. With two quick, solid bangs, the doors slammed shut by themselves and the windows rolled up. In seconds the vehicle was locked up tight.

Only John and I had been inside. Presently, he came limping around the car, brushing sand from his bare chest. His hair was salted with sand as well, and he stopped to bend over and brush it out. I got slowly to my feet, wondering why I sometimes do the things I do. John came up to me.

"Jake?"

"Yes, John."

"I just want to say . . ." He groped for words. "You're the most *un*boring person I've ever met. I don't know how else to put it." He gimped off.

A left-handed compliment, or a right-fisted insult?

On second thought, I never do a damn thing. It keeps on *happening* to me.

12

I FELT AMBIVALENT about losing the Chevy. On one hand I was almost glad to be rid of the thing and its bottomless bag of unsettling surprises; on the other, I hate to walk, which is what we did. We hoofed it down to where the Goliath spur cut the island almost in two. Farther south the vehicle density was higher, and I figured that whatever was coming to fetch everyone off the island would come in there. I was right; there was a harbor of sorts three quarters of the way down the concave curve of the crescent on the eastern shore. (By now I knew my intuitive orientation had at least a chance of being right—the sun was declining on the other side of the island now, and to me that was west. Strange that most planets do seem to rotate to the east.)

I stood looking westward, back along the stretch of road to the far shore and out along the causeway curving off into the snot-green sea. I thought I could see the causeway end out there, a few hundred meters beyond the ingress point.

"Roland, how far do you think it is from where we ingressed to where we stopped?"

He shaded his eyes against the sun and looked west, then glanced toward the near shore, then back. "Two klicks, maybe less."

"And what do you estimate our speed was when we shot through?"

"Mach point eight, but I wasn't looking."

"Neither was I, but that sounds good. So, we went from around two hundred fifty meters per second to zero in a little under two klicks. What's that work out to in Gs, eyeballs-out? Mind you, I didn't start braking immediately."

I could almost see the electrons flow. I had Roland down as either a natural lightning calculator or a microcalc implantee. At times—just for seconds—his eyes went cold and silicon-ish. He answered quickly. "Too many." He shook his head, puzzled. "It doesn't figure. Can't be right."

"That's what I thought, but it has to be right."

"But we didn't feel that kind of deceleration. Normal panic-stop Gs, yes, but . . ." He thought about it. "Which could only mean that our strange vehicle doesn't feel constrained by ordinary physical laws like conservation of momentum."

"Right, which is impossible, or so I'm told." I remembered something. "One thing—I was in no shape to think about it at the time, but I felt a wave of heat hit me when I first got out of the car. At first I thought it was the sun, but it got cooler as I walked away from the car. Could've been my imagination—"

"No, you're right, the car was radiating heat for a while after we stopped. Very noticeable, but when I touched the hull, it was only slightly warm."

"A superradiator substance, probably, but that's not surprising, given the speeds it can hit in an atmosphere. Tell me this, d'you think the car could have been converting unspent momentum directly into heat?"

He shrugged. "Why not? I'm inclined to believe almost anything at this point."

I scratched my three-day growth of beard. "Yeah. Spooky, though, isn't it?"

"Um . . . spooky. Yes."

The others were waiting for us on the other side of the road. It had been a long trek, and we still had a piece to go until we made the harbor, or so we'd been told.

"Trouble, *ja?*" one elderly woman with a German accent had asked us. "Vehicle break down?"

"Uh, yes. Tell me, is it true that there's no way back to the Terran Maze from here?"

She laughed, showing a gold incisor. The sight of it threw me until I figured out what it was. When had dentists given up *that* peculiar technique? A century ago? Two?

"Oh, *nein, nein, nein, kamrada,* no, no, no." Apparently it was a damn silly question. *"Gott,* no," she said, still laughing. "Impossible. You take wrong portal, *ja?* Make mistake."

"Yeah, I guess we did. Thanks."

"You go down zere," she said, pointing south. "Zey vill haf boat comink, *ja?* Ferryboat."

"Thanks. Are you taking the ferry also?"

"Ja, ve alzo." She anticipated my next question. "Ve stay up here till boat is comink," she went on, waving with disdain toward the lower end of the island. "Too much people. Aliens."

Her lifecompanion smiled at me. He was a little older, bald, and wore eye-lenses . . . glasses, spectacles. We left them chuckling to each other, as if they'd now heard everything. Walking away, I reflected on the fact that there seemed to be a lot of middle-aged and older types around. Antigeronics hard to get here? Gold teeth, spectacles—okay, things were primitive, but what about the vehicles?

"Jake!" It was John, calling to me across the road. "The women want a privy call. Must find some cover, you know."

"Right."

"Someone's coming," Roland said, pointing to the western causeway.

"Sam!"

"No, a roadster . . . two."

I shaded my eyes and looked. Two green dots were heading toward us. Reticulans, right on schedule.

I practically threw Roland across the road. We needed cover fast, but there was nothing in sight but a slight rise a good minute's run down the sand. I yelled for everyone to run like hell, and they did with no questions asked. They were learning.

Flattened in the sand just over the top of the rise, I watched two insect-green roadsters cruise across the island and come to a stop at the edge of the eastern beach. The lead vehicle was the one with the trailer, and the backup was more like a limo, bigger, with an extra rear seat, plus plenty of aft storage. The shadowy figures behind the tinted ports in the rear didn't look like Reticulans, but I couldn't tell if they were humans or not. Both vehicles pulled off the road, probably to talk things over. After a minute or so, they crossed the Skyway and headed north, perhaps following our distinctive tire tracks. Were they? No, that trail skirting the beach was well-traveled. Our trace should have been obscured by then. When they saw the submerged roadway, it was fifty-fifty that they'd head north. Still . . .

When they were out of sight, I got up and brushed the sand from my chest. I was now shirtless *and* jacketless, having left my brown leather second skin in the Chevy, along with Petrovsky's pistol. Force of habit had saved Sam's key for me, since I don't usually leave it lying around. I had whatever gods who were on my side to thank for the presence of mind to have put it in my pants pocket.

I walked down the other side of the hill and had a mild temper tantrum. Darla watched me kick sand, pick up a stick, and beat a poor patch of land-weed into pulp, then fling the stick away.

She walked over to me. "Finally getting to you?"

"Merte!" I said. "Shit! Piss!" I kicked more sand. "Hell and goddamn," I finished, done with it.

She thought it was very amusing. I did too, after a moment. I looked at her. She was in briefs and halter, wearing her knee-high boots, carrying the jumpsuit in a roll under her arm. Roland was carrying her backpack. If my mind had been less occupied, I would have had trouble not staring at her. Roland was staring, not that I blamed him. The briefs were very sheer. Susan was topless and was by any standard an eyeful as well, but she wasn't drawing a glance from him. But then, Susan was a known quantity, so to speak.

"Darla, how are those damn bugs following us?"

"I don't know. It's very strange, but they are a Snatchgang, aren't they?"

The others pricked up their ears. I wished Darla hadn't said it, but now they knew, if they hadn't before. Snatchgangs go after one quarry, and one only, so the Teelies weren't in danger, unless the Rikkis had a mind to use them to get to me—which, when I thought about it, was indeed a possibility.

"Okay, they're a Gang, but how did they trail us through a potluck . . . and *why?*"

"Could they have scanned us?"

"They were behind Sam, and even he might have lost us. And Sam didn't shoot the portal, so they didn't follow him through. No, they're using some exotic tracking technique, known only to Gangers. But what is it?"

Darla considered it. "Chemical trace? Pheromones?"

"Possibly. But can they detect minute quantities of the stuff over hundreds of kilometers of airless void?"

"Some Terran insects can be sensitive to a few molecules in a cubic klick of air, so maybe—"

"Yeah, but Rikkis aren't insects; they're highly evolved life forms. Even bear their young live, like us."

"I was going to say that with the aid of technology, maybe they could do the same through vacuum."

I stroked her shoulder. "Sorry, love. I'm being testy, I know. Your point's well-taken. But . . ." I looked up at the sky and massaged the back of my neck. "God, am I tired." I yawned and got hung up in the middle of it, couldn't stop. "Excuse me," I said, finally recovering. "One thing, though. When did they tag me?"

"At the restaurant? Sonny's?"

I'd been thinking about that for quite a while. "Yeah, the restaurant. But I never got near the Rikki. If they were spraying the stuff at me, it would have landed on other people too. Muddled the trace."

Darla bit her lip, shook her head. "I dunno, but they must've done it somehow, Jake. We know it wasn't Sam they tagged. It was you, your person, somehow."

"What were they doing at the farm, retagging me because the first one didn't take, or wore off?"

"Sounds plausible. Maybe they were just looking for the map. You asked why they followed us through a potluck. It could only be because now they're sure you have the map, or know where you can get it."

"Yeah, everyone must be absolutely convinced of that now. I guess it did look like we deliberately ducked through that portal, with Petrovsky literally trying to drag us back. Okay, so maybe nobody saw that part of it, but we sure didn't hesitate any."

"No, we didn't. And now the Roadmap myth is reality."

I nodded. It was, and I had made it so by trying to debunk it. I sighed. "Let's get moving."

"Good. I'm going to wet my pants if we don't."

Roland came down from the crest of the knoll, where he'd been watching the road. "Another vehicle went by," he reported.

"Ryxx?" I asked.

"No, a human driving, a man. Strange, the buggy looked familiar. I think I saw it back on Goliath, but I don't know where." He scratched his head. "Oh, I remember. It was in the dealership lot. An old piece of *merte*. The dealer tried to dump it on us, cash sale, instead of a rental."

"One man, you say?" Now who the blazes could *that* be?

"Oh, the hell with it," Darla said suddenly, and squatted in the weeds. "I can't wait. Gentlemen, please . . . ?"

I said, "Huh? Oh." I turned to John and Roland. "Okay, troops, eyes front."

"God, men are so lucky," Susan said, taking her station near Darla.

Lucky? Okay, so we can write our names in the sand. It's not exactly an art form.

As we neared the harbor we found more aliens, most of them sealed up inside their vehicles, unable to step out on this planet without technological aid. Through the viewports we saw squidlike things swimming in a watery medium, blobs of gelatin sitting comfortably in a fog of yellow gas, many more forms that we couldn't make out at all. Some beings motioned enigmatically to us as we passed, raising tentacles, claws. Others followed us with conical eyestalks, observing. From most there was no reaction.

The island was a trade-fair of vehicle design. There were objects lying about that didn't look like vehicles at all, odd geometrical shapes and flowing, melted things giving no clue as to how they moved. There were humans here too, waiting patiently like everyone else. And rigs as well, strangely enough. I asked one starrigger when the ferry was due in.

"She'll be in," was all he said, and spat in the sand.

"Thanks." I walked away.

The harbor was large but did not look deep, though the water's clearness may have been distorting. I was puzzled by the fact that there wasn't a dock or pier or anything in sight. Instead, at the apex of the deep indentation that formed the harbor, a graded section of beach angled steeply into the water. The sand looked packed and hard there.

"What do you make of it?" I asked Roland.

"A hydroskiff?"

I rubbed the scratchy stubble of my beard. "Funny, when I heard 'ferryboat' I thought of just that, a water-displacing vessel of some kind. Besides, you'd want flat beach to pull up on."

"Right. Things seem primitive enough here, at least as far as humans are concerned. Maybe it is a boat."

"Well," I yawned, "we'll see eventually." I plopped myself down on the sand.

Winnie was drawing again, and this time I watched her. She made one big spiral figure, smaller ones nearby, and linked them with lines. I was intrigued, and asked Darla if Winnie had explained.

"Something to do with her tribal mythology," Darla told me. "Haven't figured out what it's all about." Her answer gave me the ever-so-slight feeling that she was being evasive in some way. But no, she was just tired and didn't want to be bothered. Still, I wondered. Winnie now was drawing lines within the big spiral. I went over to her, knelt in the sand, and asked her as clearly as I could what she was doing.

"Twee, many twee," she said, indicating the large figure. "But not like twee... like light! Many big twee like light." She pointed to the smaller spirals. "Many light, many light, many light..." I couldn't follow the rest of it, but if she was talking about galaxies and the Skyway linking them, it'd be a remarkable mythology indeed, if it weren't for the fact that it could have been learned by osmosis from contact with humans. That was the most likely explanation. A more sensational interpretation was an old pitfall some anthropologists in the past had spent time at the bottom of. *Many light, many light...* Winnie had passed through the Great Trees at the Edge of the Sky and was now in the realm of the gods, plying the paths through a forest of stars. Or whatever. As I watched her I again felt some share of guilt for what humans had done to her natural habitat, and wondered if there could have been any way to avoid it. Surely there was more jungle on Hothouse than Cheetah homeland. I couldn't imagine the species' total population planet-wide as being anything over a few hundred thousand, if that, but I wasn't sure. Hothouse wasn't all jungle, of course. True, there were millions of square kilometers of rain forest, but the planet had more ocean surface than Terra, plus the usual assortment of climates. It boasted icy polar continents, though small ones, deserts, plains, everything. The problem was that a lot of the tropic regions were parched and uninhabitable, and temperate areas were scarce due to the fact that Hothouse's land masses were bunched up around the equator. Mulling it over, I soon had it figured out: Winnie's people had naturally settled in rich food-gathering areas. These same areas of jungle produced high yields of organic raw materials used for a wide range of products, including antigeronic drugs—definitely the most lucrative cash crop ever. Hothouse was one of the few sources for them.

I looked at the web of lines within the big spiral. She'd executed them meticulously. The lines crisscrossed the entire figure, and I was curious as to how she could be so definite about them if they were mostly imaginary. Well, she'd learned the pattern from somebody, who'd learned it from somebody else, who'd learned it from . . . ? Did the Cheetah who started the tradition have an active imagination . . . or could the pattern be based on fact? More to the point, was it possible that Winnie's people could have had contact with alien cultures long before humans invaded their planet? Yes, not only possible, but probable. And could they have picked up hints of where major Skyway routes led throughout the galaxy? Yes, it was possible all right, and I should have thought of it immediately.

Something dawned on me, and the very thought of it made me laugh out loud. Absurd, no? Winnie's sand drawings . . . the Roadmap? Couldn't be. This was no map, merely a stylized rendering. Fascinating cultural phenomenon, yes—but an accurate map of the most labyrinthine road system in the universe? Not even close. First, you'd want to know what portals to take, and you'd need supplementary planetary maps for that. Make the first right, go *x* number of kilometers, etc. And you'd want to know what stars were on the routes, what part of the galaxy you were in, and all that. There was a limit to how detailed you could get in the medium of sand and stick. No, it seemed to me that a proper Skyway map would be not only three-dimensional, but hyperdimensional as well. Graphically impossible perhaps, but you'd need some sort of mathematical understanding of how the time element worked into the picture. Over long distances you'd want to keep an eye on the curve of the geodesic, since every jump involved some time displacement. Simple relativity. And somewhere along the line, according to legend, the geodesics took weird shortcuts and closed up "timelike loops," causing you to double back on yourself, or do something even more outrageous.

But the more I thought about it, the more the idea grew on me. No, I could never convince myself that this was the vaunted Roadmap, but what if everybody *thought* it was? I tried that on for size. Maybe the Reticulans wanted Winnie—maybe they came to the farm to kidnap her. But how could they have found out about her mapping abilities when I had just learned myself? If they knew about it before me, they could have grabbed Winnie at the motel anytime. Unless . . . unless—ridiculous! It was all nonsense. Well, what else? Let's see, how about this—maybe they're figuring this way. They see me shoot a potluck portal. They know I didn't have the Roadmap on my person, since the Militia didn't get it . . . and they're thinking, wait a minute, what's this guy doing? He must have the map. Sam doesn't have it, because Sam didn't shoot the portal. Hell, maybe they disabled Sam and searched him. So Sam's out, and they think—well, what the hell does he have, since he barely got out of the station with his skin? The Cheetah! It must be her, because why the hell did he bother bringing her along? Yeah, that's it. The Cheetah. Sic 'im, Fido. Get that map.

Oh hell, Sam back there disabled and helpless, and me here on the other side of nowhere. No, think a minute. Wouldn't they have let Sam shoot the portal and then search him? Because if they saw Sam turn around and go back, or hesitate, then they wouldn't bother with him. In that case I'd have to have the map, otherwise I'd be expecting Sam to shoot through. But if all that were true, why didn't Sam shoot the portal? What happened to him?

I gave up, slumped back into the sand, and threw my arm across my face.

"Darla?"

"Yes, Jake?"

"Are you keeping a lookout?"

"Uh-huh."

"Good girl. G'night."

"Sleep tight."

13

IT WAS A ferryboat.

Rather, that's what it looked like when it first appeared above the horizon. Then it started looking strange. There was a boat there all right, or at least the superstructure of one, but close to the waterline something else was going on. Far out, it looked like a ship run aground on a shoal, but as we watched, the shoal moved with the boat—it looked like it was carrying the boat. Other objects appeared, globular translucent things in the water, and as the whole improbable apparition neared shore, they looked like inflated bags bobbing in the water at the edges of the dark line of land. The overall impression I got was one of a shipwrecked vessel plunked down on top of an island. There was even some vegetation growing here and there.

The boat-structure was big enough, and the island was fair-size as islands go, but for something moving in the water it was huge, filling the mouth of the harbor until there was barely room to float a dinghy to either side. The superstructure was just that; there was no hull. There were three huge decks up on pilings smack in the middle of the island, and the design was out of the last century, possibly earlier, all the way back to the late 1900's. It looked new, gleaming white with red and gold trim, proudly thrusting flying bridges to port and starboard, and sporting three, count 'em, *three* smokestacks, two of which belched puffs of white smoke. Why they were doing that was anybody's guess. Crewmen were scurrying all over the decks. Humans mostly, but there were a few aliens. The island proper was also busy, but here there were no humans. Animals—beings—slithered across the ground toward the leading shore, converging on a point that would be closest to the beach. They were seallike creatures, from what we could see, with sleek wet bodies, three sets of flippers, with the front pair looking larger and very prehensile, fingerlike. Their bodies were a dull orange color.

What was very strange was the surface of the island. It was not land. Between clumps of seaweed and barnaclelike growths there lay a base of brownish-gray blubbery material, mottled with whitish scars and creases. There was more to see. Dotting the island were clusters of domed structures made of piled sea vegetation, cemented with mud or congealed sand. The seal-beings lived in these; some were still wriggling out of roof-holes and rushing to join the others.

The shape of the island was more apparent now; it was roughly oblate, a squeezed circle, with six air-bag structures positioned at even intervals around it. The bags were multi-compartmented and looked like gigantic floral arrays of balloons bunched in the water. Whether they contained just air or a lighter gas wasn't apparent, of course, but obviously they supplied flotation. At the leading edge of the island was a high bulge.

The shore slowly came alive. Humans stretched and yawned, mashed out cigarettes, knocked out pipes. Hatches slammed and engines started. Lines began to form starting at the top of the wide, inclined section of beach.

We walked along the curve of the harbor and watched, fascinated.

"Are we to assume," Roland said, "that everybody's supposed to drive up on this thing and park?"

I looked the island over. No guard rails, lots of obstacles, no apparent way to get up to the decking, lots of curving slippery surface. "Can't imagine that," I said, "but I can't imagine the alternative."

"It's a big fish and it swallows everyone," Susan said. We all stopped and looked at her. She giggled. "What else?" she asked.

About fifteen minutes later, we stood on a narrow strip of sand to one side of what we now knew to be the loading ramp. "I'll be damned," John said.

About seventy-five to one hundred seal-creatures were lined up behind a bony ridge that crested the forward bulge like a mammoth brooding brow. The creatures were using their forward flippers to beat rhythmically on the ridge. It all seemed orchestrated. Sections of them would start a rhythm sequence while another slapped out a syncopated beat. Then the first group would stop while the other played on, while still another ensemble joined in. As the percussion concerto continued, the high curving bow of the island inched closer to the end of the loading ramp. It took a while. Finally the two islands met, and the creatures began to beat in unison, smacking out a single rhythm—one . . . two . . . three . . . *one-two-three;* three long, three short, keeping perfect time. The forward bulge began to rise slowly, as if on hydraulic lifts, raising the orchestra of drummers with it.

I think it was Susan who gasped audibly when the gigantic eye rose out of the water. I know it shook me. It's one thing to calmly contemplate a creature of that size. As it was docking, I mulled over the biophysics of the thing. How long would it take a nerve impulse to travel from one end of the critter to the brain (wherever that was) and back again? Thirty seconds—a minute? How about internal heat? Getting rid of it would be a problem. Propulsion also. If the air-bag organs had evolved from fins to flotation aids, how did the creature move? But it was quite another thing to have that eye staring at you, an alien eye to boot. The outer structure was a red polyhedron with hexagonal facets. At the center of each hexagon was a six-sided pupil slowly contracting, and the whole eye was shot through with a riot of purple veins. I forgot about the biophysics and let the wonder wash over me.

And when that subsided, there was the mind-numbing sight of the mouth opening to contend with. The cavity was curved and so big we couldn't see the other side. The immediate interior was lined with a grinding surface composed of pinkish-white slabs of translucent cartilage, hexagonal in shape. Farther back in the mouth the light grew dim, but we could see pale tissue forming the entrance to the throat, and below it, like a floor, a dark area. A tongue. This began to flow forward like a moving carpet. It swept over the tooth surface and came out to kiss the beach. The tongue was purple.

The punch line came when a group of crewmen in white uniforms came walking out of the cavernous interior and stepped onto the sand. They took up stations a few meters apart and began to admit vehicles into the mouth of the beast. We all laughed.

"How biblical," John said.

"Told you!" Susan said triumphantly.

Biophysics my ass. How do they mate?

"Well . . ." I thought of something. "Who's got money?"

The Teelies gave me hopeless looks.

"I have some," Darla said. "The ride's on me." She frowned. "That is, if I have enough for all of us."

"Wonder if they're taking on deckhands."

We made our way through the lines of vehicles moving down the ramp. The men at the entrance were taking fares. I walked up to the nearest of them. He spoke no English, and our exchange in 'System got me nowhere. He gabbled something and motioned impatiently toward the next man. Everybody followed me over.

"Excuse me . . . sailor?"

"Huh?" This one was young, on the chubby side, with stringy blond hair. Fuzz sprouted on his upper lip. His uniform was immaculate, flowing with red and gold embroidery, and he wore a matching white cap with a black shiny visor. "I'm an officer, *kamrada*. Belowdecks Supervisor Krause. Whaddya want?"

"Sorry, Mr. Krause. How do we book passage on this . . . vessel?"

"Don't have tickets?"

"No. Where do we get them?"

"From me. Where's your vehicle?"

"Had a breakdown. How much for just passenger fare?"

He craned his head around and glanced at us, then turned to take another fare. "Uh, that'd be—" He jerked his head around again and noticed Darla. "Yeah. That'd be a hunnert consols."

"Consols?"

"Yeah, consols. Consolidation Gold Certificates. CGCs.

Consols." He took a blue square of plastic from a gloved alien hand. The face of the card bore a stylized picture of a boat mounted on an island-beast.

"You don't take Universal Trade Credits?"

He laughed. "Not on this stretch of road, *kamrada.*"

"Sorry. You see, we just came from—"

"Yeah, I know, you just lucked through. That right?"

"Lucked . . . yes, we did."

"Well, welcome to the Consolidated Outworlds, *kamrada*. Your UTCs won't buy you *merte* out here."

The guy's manners were growing on me like an itchy wart. "What do you take from aliens?"

"Gold, precious metals, gems, anything. Hey, I got fares to take. Okay?"

"Sorry to put you to any trouble, but we're in a pickle."

"Yeah, yeah. One troy ounce of gold'll do it. Apiece, that is."

"Jake." It was Darla, holding out some gold coins to me. I took them. They were very old pieces, South African gold. Amazed, I turned to her and was about to ask where she'd gotten them, but she smiled, sphinxlike, and I knew. That bottomless pack again. I looked at the coins. They were probably worth more as collector's items than as specie—on the black market, of course. The CA handled all gold. I handed them to Krause.

"Jesus Christ." He jingled them, feeling their weight. "Where'd you snag these, a museum?" He bit into one, checked the tiny toothmark. Something about pure gold; you can tell. "Yeah, they'll do. But . . . uh, you're two short, right?"

"I'm afraid that cleans us out. Is it possible that some arrangements could be made? Otherwise we'll be stranded here."

"Sorry, no credit. But . . . well, maybe we can work something out. Know what I mean?"

"Such as?"

He was eyeing Darla. "Like to buy you and your friends a drink. In my cabin, of course. Can't fraternize with the passengers 'cept at the Captain's table, but what the Old Man don't know . . . unnerstand?" He took more tickets. "Yeah, in my cabin, especially your *femamikas* here—" He did a double take, finally noticing Susan's breasts. "Sure would be my pleasure."

"Look, friend—"

"Jake, take it easy." To Krause, Darla said, "I'd love to lift a few with you, sailor, but my friend Susan's a teetotaler. You and I can have a pretty good time, though, just the two of us." She actually winked at him. "Deal?"

He laughed. "I dunno, three heads are better sometimes." He must have noticed my face turning black, and sobered up. "Yeah, sure. Just you and me."

I held out my hand. "Our money, please."

Darla took my arm. "Wait a minute."

"Hand it over, sailor. We'll starhike it."

"Suit yourself," Krause said, reluctantly handing me the coins, "but hikers don't have much luck around here. Limit's four passengers per vehicle, big extra charge for more."

Yeah, sure. "We'll take our chances."

"You're going to be sorry come high tide, *kamrada*."

When we got back to the beach, Darla was ready to kill me. "Starhike it? Who's going to pick up five of us plus an alien anthropoid?"

"We'll go in different vehicles."

"Feel lucky today? I don't." She stamped a boot in the sand. "Damn it, Jake, sometimes I don't understand you. Do you actually think I'd let that cretin get near me? Sure, I'd go to his cabin, even have a few with him. But you'd be surprised what else I have in that pack. Little transparent capsules that make you very sick for a long, long time. And they work fast. Wouldn't kill him, of course. Understand? Besides, even if I had to sleep with him . . ." She didn't finish.

She was right. "Sorry, Darla. I should have finessed it."

"But you have to take every trick, don't you?" She was furious with me—and proud of me, all at once.

"Jake, Roland?" John was standing at the waterline, letting little waves lap over his feet. "Is it my imagination," he asked, "or is the water getting higher?"

"He's right," Roland said. "I've been noticing it. And there's the cause." He pointed to the eastern sky.

The edge of a huge white disk was showing above the horizon. A moon, and a big one, twice Luna's size, I guesstimated. The tides would be fierce, and high tide here could mean complete inundation. Great.

"What should we do?" John asked.

"I'm going back to him," Darla said. "I hope he's still in a mood to deal."

She was so right I wanted to strangle her. "Hold it a minute. There's got to be another way. He could be trouble."

"Not the type. I've met his ilk before, the chubby little fart. You stay here. I can handle him."

"Maybe one of the other men . . ."

She gave me a world-weary look. "Jake."

"Right." I gave it up. Our relationship was about as well-defined as ghosts in a fog. Not only did I not have a leg to stand on, the leg had nothing to stand on.

"What's that noise?" Roland asked.

I tore the beeping key from my pants pocket. "Sam! Sam, is that you?"

"Who the hell were you expecting, the Chairman of the Colonial Politburo? Of all the goddamn stupid things you've done, boy, this has to be the grand prizewinner. There's three things any moron can learn in life without too much trouble, but you can't seem to get 'em straight. Want to know what they are? I'll tell you. Don't spit out the port at Mach one, don't eat blue snow on Beta Hydri IV, and don't ever poke your nose through a potluck portal! Common sense, right—and you'd think any pudknocker'd pick that up real easy, but not you, boy, not by a long shot—"

We laughed and laughed and laughed.

14

"AND ANOTHER THING," Sam was saying when we finally found him, "what the hell's the idea of not telling me where you're going?" He was mad as heck.

"Too busy at the time. Sorry."

"Well, maybe you were, at that," he grumbled.

"I hate to bring it up, but where the hell have *you* been?"

"Rescuing Petrovich, or whatever his name is."

"Petrovsky! I thought he was cylinder-skin. My god, Sam, how? And *why?*"

The others were crowded in the aft cabin, discovering how many bodies could fit into a sauna stall—except for Darla, who was whipping up a quick brunch. They were making a lot of noise. It was good to be back home.

"Well, it was like this," Sam said. "There I am, cutting vacuum like nobody's business. Must've hit Mach point four five there for a stretch—Stinky's a genius, by the way—and I'm calling you and calling you and not getting an answer. Then I see the flash and sure enough it's gammashine, and I'm saying to myself, well, scratch one male offspring, but I think—maybe not, what with that strange buggy you were driving. I figure maybe you're just disabled and can't key for help. So I start scanning on infrared for survivors. What did I know? Last thing I expected was that you'd shot the portal. Anyway, I pick something up out there about three klicks from the commit markers, and I pull off the road onto the ice and go on out. And there's this cop in a vacuum suit lying on his back in the middle of nowhere, no sign of his batmobile, but his ejection sled's in pieces all over the place. He's frozen solid to the ice and there's something funny about his left hand."

"Hand?" I said.

"Yeah, he didn't have one. Instead, there's this big frozen gob of blood on the end of his arm, looking like a cherry ice pop. Damnedest thing you ever saw. But the rest of him was in one piece . . . and he was alive."

"Jesus." And I knew what he'd done too. He'd angled the blast of his descent rockets to push him away from the cylinders' grav field instead of setting him comfortably down, but how he'd survived that desperate gamble was beyond me. The severed hand wasn't hard to explain either. It was a miracle that the tangled line hadn't cut him in two. "How'd you get him into the cabin?"

"First I had to unfreeze him from the ice. I put the exciter gun on wide beam and cooked him a bit until he could move. Then he hauled himself in. There couldn't have been an unbroken bone in his body, but he did it. Then there was the problem of his arm. If I recycled the cab and brought it up to room temperature, he'd bleed to death. If I kept it vacuum, he'd have frozen. The suit had self-sealed but he was half icicle already. So I had to figure out a way to pressurize and keep the temp below zero. They just don't make life-support gear like that—had a hell of a time bypassing the right systems."

"Did he say anything?"

Sam hesitated the barest second. "Not much, just groaned a lot."

I looked back just then and noticed Darla standing at the kitchette, listening intently—eavesdropping. "Go ahead," I said.

"Well, I grabbed slab back to the Ryxx cutoff, but there wasn't any traffic. Had to go all the way back to the T-Maze road. Gave a yell on the skyband, and two riggers picked him up. Incidentally, on the way I saw our Rikki friends."

"I know, they're here. Do you think he pulled through?"

"He was out cold by the time they got to him, so I really don't know. But he's one hell of a survivor type." Sam paused. "What d'you think, did I do wrong?"

"Hell, no, you did the right thing."

"Well, my conscience is clear anyway. And one way or another, he's out of the picture."

Darla came forward and handed me a bowl of beef stew and crackers. I thanked her, then tore into it, finishing it off in record time. I washed it down with a can of Star Cloud Ale. The burp was thunderous. I smiled at Winnie, who was in the shotgun seat, finishing off the remnants of her picnic lunch. She burped and grinned back. Some things are truly universal.

"Shameful the way young women run around these days without wearing so much as a blush," Sam said.

"I heard that, Sam," Darla called out. "Tell me you don't enjoy it."

"I'm getting old. Hell, I *am* old. In fact, I'm dead."

"Sam, cut the *merte,*" I said. "You'll never die, and you know it. Did I ever tell you they had to bury you three times before you'd stay down? You kept popping back up like crabgrass."

"Such talk. Where's your respect for the deceased?" Sam chuckled. "Darla, I was kidding you—back in my day prudes were saying that morals couldn't get any worse. I happen to agree. It was a decadent period, if the term means anything. Spend a weekend with me on New Vegas and I'll tell you all the juicy details."

"Name the date, Sam."

He laughed. "Jake, tell me more about this whale we're going to get swallowed by. Sounds like it's got the iceberg fish back on Albion beat to hell. Did I ever tell you about the exozoological expedition I went with to trace their migration patterns? This was while you were still in school. Must have been twenty-five, no, thirty Standards ago. . . ."

Sam went on with a yarn he'd run into the ground years before, and I wondered what he was doing until I heard his voice over the bone-conduction transducer in my ear.

"Son, brace yourself. Darla's an agent. I think she's working for Petrovsky."

Well, it was out. I would've had a hard time keeping the ugly thing's head submerged any longer. I realized that I'd known for some time.

"That's it, just keep a poker face. No hard evidence, but listen to the playback."

It was Petrovsky, babbling Russian in my ear.

"He was delirious by this time. Listen."

Babble, then a name, then more babble, and again the name, over and over. The name sounded like Dar-ya. It had been a long time since I'd studied Russian, but I didn't think Dar-ya was the Russian equivalent to Darla, if there was one. I turned toward Sam's eye and silently shook my head.

*"No? Christ, I'm sorry, son. I have a hell of a time picking up some words now and then, especially from non-*Inglo *speakers. Thought it was 'Darla,' but it did sound funny."*

But it very well could be Darla, I thought, as I heard Petrovsky now saying, ". . . Darishka, Darishka . . ." And then another name, suddenly: ". . . Mona . . ."

"What d'you make of that?"

I'd heard through the roadbuzz circuit that Mona's current liaison was with a Militia Intelligence officer, and a high-ranking one, so it tracked. Could Petrovsky have fallen madly and instantly in love with Darla? Knowing the man even to the limited extent I did, it didn't make sense.

"Well, it's something to think about, Jake."

Sam's understatement only pointed out to me the need for less thinking and more *facts*. "Sam," I said aloud, "sorry to interrupt your enthralling story, but I want you to do a search for me."

"I was just getting to the exciting part. Okay, what is it?"

"Do you still record news feeds whenever you can?"

"Every chance I get, just like the program says. I even got the six o'clock on Goliath. Why?"

"How long do you keep 'em?"

"Thirty Standard days, then I pitch them."

"Merte. Okay, listen. I want you to fetch anything from your news file with these tag-words. 'Corey Wilkes,' 'intelligence,' 'Colonial Assembly,' 'Reticulan,' 'Militia,' and . . . um, let's see, what else . . ."

"'Roadmap'?"

"That's a long shot, but go ahead."

"Why 'Colonial Assembly'?"

"A hunch."

"Right. Wilkes should turn up like a bad penny. He loves hobnobbing with the great and near-great, makes the feeds all the time. Okay, then, let me go down to that dusty basement where I keep old newspapers. Want me to start now?"

"Yeah," I said, "but hold off reading it out until I tell you. Meanwhile, I'm due for a shower."

Everyone was out of the stall by then, all fresh and scrubbed and settled down to eat. I went to the ordnance locker, got out the liter of Old Singularity, and had a jolt. The tidal forces were terrific. Then it was into the locker-size stall for a steam treatment followed by a fog bath. Standing in the swirling mist, I shut my mind off and the pattern of the last few days emerged crisp and clear. The fine detail was missing, but the overall view was enough. I was beginning to see things, understand things. With a little luck, I'd soon know more. The biggest unknown was still Darla, but even she was slowly taking shape like a wraith in the mist. The fog had parted fleetingly back there on the beach. What had I seen? Could her vulnerability have been grief, her passion the widow's consolation?

After a shave and a change of clothes—and a second shooter of Old Singy—I had evolved up to human form again. I went forward.

We spent another twenty minutes in line before we got down near the row of fare-takers. I was in the wrong line if I wanted to see Krause, the sociable sailor, again, so I jockeyed for position and cut somebody off in the next line over. An alien warning signal buzzed angrily behind me.

"Hi, there!"

Krause was looking down, shuffling tickets in his hands. Glancing up he said, "How's it going, *kamr*—" Then the recognition. "Oh. Thought you . . . uh, had a breakdown."

"Fixed her up real good. Now, about those fares. You were about to tell me about how we can exchange metal for currency aboard ship, weren't you?"

"Yeah. Forgot to mention it. Sorry." He took a red disk out of his pocket, attached it carefully to the front port, and smoothed it over. "Sure, you just drive right in, park, then go up to the purser's office and make the exchange. He'll give you a chit, and you hand that over when you debark. Oh, and the sticker won't come off . . . um, without a special chemical."

"Wouldn't think of trying to remove it. What d'you think the fare'll be for this rig?"

"Uh, wouldn't know offhand, sir."

"Guess."

"About fifty consols." He thought about it. "Maybe less."

"Lots of bodies in here. What about those extra charges you mentioned?"

He looked away. "Not this trip. Only special runs."

"Uh-huh." I pointed to the gaping throat. "Gee, do you mean we're actually supposed to drive in there?"

He chortled, his manner turning suddenly chummy. "Yeah, it's a shocker, isn't it? Naw, we're in our fifth year with this boat and we haven't digested a passenger yet. You'll get used to it."

"Through there?"

He turned and pointed. "Yes, sir, that big opening over—"

I took his hat. "Nice hat," I said.

"Hey."

"Here you go—whoops! Sorry." When he bent over to get it, I grabbed a handful of greasy yellow hair and fetched his face up against the hatch. He kissed it hard.

"Jake, you shouldn't have," Susan said as we moved away.

"I know. I did enjoy it, though."

I drove into the mouth of the beast.

15

THE THROAT WAS a yawning cavity that narrowed into an esophageal tube tunneling downward into the bowels of the island-beast. The walls of the passage were pale and sweaty, heaving with peristaltic motion. It was slippery going, but the rollers handled it fairly well. After a quarter klick or so the tube opened onto a vast dark chamber. There were hundreds of vehicles already parked here, many others in the process, their headbeams moving in the darkness a long way from the entrance. I followed the line of buggies heading toward them.

"I'll be . . ." Sam began. Then he said, "I can't think of anything that fits the occasion. I'm speechless."

We all were. It took a good while to get to the parking area, and we spent it in silence. Finally we could see sailors in white tops with red and white striped bell-bottoms directing traffic, slicing the gloom with powerful torches. I pulled alongside one of them, a skinny, baby-faced kid, and cracked the port. A faint odor of decayed fish came through, plus a whiff of brackish stagnant water, but the overall smell of the place wasn't hard to deal with. It simply smelled like the sea.

"Where to, sailor? Looks like you're running out of room."

"Over against the wall, starrigger!" the sailor yelled, playing the torchbeam against a glistening area of greenish-white tissue.

I eased the rig forward until the front of the engine housing kissed the wall. The tissue quivered and drew back slightly, then slowly came back to meet the rig and began oozing over the housing, then stopped.

"Drive into it!" the kid shouted over the din of engine sounds. "Push it back!"

I did. The wall receded before us, billowing out like a giant curtain. Before long I felt it resist, and I hit the brake.

"Go ahead," the kid told me in a high voice. "It'll stretch a klick before it tears a c-meter. C'mon, move that punkin' pigmobile!"

"Aye, aye, Cap'n!" I gunned it, and the wall shivered and yielded. I rammed the rig forward until I heard "Ho-o-o!"

"Are we the main course, or just the appetizer?" John wanted to know.

"There must be five hundred vehicles in here," Roland said.

"More," I ventured.

Somebody rapped smartly on the hatch. I turned to have a torchbeam stab my retinas. "Hey, swabbie!" I growled. "Want me to show you how that thing doubles as a suppository?"

"Take it easy, truckie." It was the same sailor who'd directed us. She was young, very young—no more than sixteen or so. Antigeronics can't give you that kind of baby-skin. She wore her hair cropped short under a traditional Dixiecup hat, but the hat was gold, not white. And she wasn't all that skinny, either. She was blooming under that deckhand outfit.

"You can't stay here, you know," she said.

Blinking, I looked around. "What about non-oxy breathers?"

"Them we don't care about, but all humans go topside. Insurance regs." She started to leave.

"Wait a minute," I called after her. "Don't get testy, now. Just a few questions."

"Make 'em short. We're way behind schedule."

"Consolidated Outworlds—is that a human-occupied maze?"

"Mostly."

"Hmm. Okay, now, are we actually in the stomach of this thing?"

"No, a predigestive sac. Fiona's got two of these and twelve stomachs, but we don't like to use those unless we have to.

Have to spray 'em down with gastric inhibitors—and they smell bad."

"Fiona? It's a female?"

"Hard to say one way or the other."

"Huh? Oh . . ."

"Is that it?"

"That's it, except to ask if all the deckhands are as good-looking as you."

"Ah, shut up." She turned on her heel and stalked away.

"Hey! One more thing."

"What?" she answered impatiently.

"How do we get topside?"

"Elevator!"

"Elevator?"

Elevator.

And there it was, a circular metal-framed shaft rising through a hole in the roof. The juncture of frame and roof was sealed by a white spongy collar that seemed to be there to protect the surrounding organ-tissue. The elevator car was bullet-shaped and transparent, suspended by thick metal cables.

"Any construction you'd do inside this beastie," Roland said as we boarded the car, "would be more like a surgical procedure."

"Yeah, but the patient's sturdy enough to withstand it," I said, then added *sotto voce,* "Did you plant that transponder?"

"Yes, at the base of the frame."

"You agree it'll shoot Sam's signal up this shaft?"

"Don't see why not. But how do you get it out of the shaft and through the doors?—if there're doors."

"We put another one up top, of course."

The car was filling up, and we got scrunched to the back. A tall, blue, webfooted alien trod on my instep as he backed up, then turned his piscine head and wheezed something that sounded apologetic.

The trip up was a long one. The outer door at the top of the shaft was an ornate gilt folding gate which opened onto what looked like the plush lobby of an ancient Terran hotel. There were red leather settees and armchairs, matching ottomans, coffee tables, freestanding ashtrays, and potted plants. The walls were done up in red and gold fabric. It was a scene out of the past—tastefully done too, nothing like the usual quickie/functional decor you see back in the Maze. It was a big place, packed with sentient flesh.

"Ah, atmosphere," John said.

I turned to Darla. "Spot anybody?"

She took a long look around the place. "No."

"Yeah, but they're here, or will be. Everybody who was chasing us. Maybe even Wilkes."

"He'll be here," she said, as if she knew. Maybe she did.

Another long wait, this time to get a cabin, and that was after standing in line at the purser's office. I gave Darla back her coins and traded about a quarter of my gold stash for consols, paid C-38.5 for the fare, and gave John some cash in partial payment for the hospital bill he'd picked up back on Goliath. When it came time to register for the cabin, I had my fake ID in hand, but the clerk waved it off.

"Don't need your ID, sir, just your name. This is a free society."

I looked at the plasticard, which stated that I was one T. Boggston Fisk, Esq., and I thought, there's a time to run and a time to stop running. Time for the fox to turn and face the dogs, come what may. I put the card away.

"Jake McGraw, and friends."

He bent over the keyboard, then straightened up quickly and looked at me. "Did you say . . . Jake McGraw?"

"That's right."

"Glad to have you aboard the *Laputa,* sir."

"Glad to be anywhere right now. Tell me, when do we get where we're going? And where *are* we going?"

"We should make Seahome by tomorrow afternoon, sir. That's the biggest town here on Splash."

"Splash? That's what the planet's called?"

"Well, it isn't really called anything officially, and every language group seems to have its own name, but in Intersystem it's called Akwaterra."

"Straightforward enough. I take it there are large land masses then?"

"Big enough, but not continent-size."

Welcome to Splash, but don't go near the water.

The *Laputa?*

Carrying my bag only (Darla had opted to keep hers), a steward led us to another elevator. We went up to B Deck, where we followed him through a maze of corridors. Roland lagged behind, planting more transponders at various strategic and inconspicuous locations.

Our adjoining staterooms were lavish, the crappers positively palatial, with sunken tubs made of a gold-veined stone that looked something like marble. There were few modern conveniences, but the charm more than made up for the lack. I tried to think of the last time I'd used a bathtub.

John knocked on the connecting hatch and stepped in. "I haven't seen plumbing like that since I lived in London," he said.

"Really?" I said, distracted. I still wasn't sure whether I liked having the Teelies next door, for their sake more than mine. Time for them to start disassociating themselves from me. I had wanted at least half a ship between us, but Roland had insisted on keeping nearby.

"Don't want to lose you now, Jake. You're our ticket home."

"Home? Where's that?"

He acknowledged the point. "You have me there. But our people are still important to us. We must get back somehow."

"Sorry. I understand." Maybe Roland was right. They'd be more vulnerable away from me.

Susan walked in, looking depressed. She had her shirt back on and was wearing her tan bush pants, but she was barefooted, having left her sandals in the Chevy.

"There are shops on board, Susan," I told her. "You should pick up some footwear. John has money."

"Yes, I will," she answered dully and slumped into a velvet armchair.

John went over to her. "What's wrong, Suzie?" he asked, massaging her shoulders.

"Oh, I was just thinking of Sten back there in the hospital. He's probably worried sick, wondering what happened to us." She looked at me. "We were on the way to the hospital when you . . ." She lowered her head and began crying softly.

It made me feel just great. Darla took her by the hand, led her to the other room, and closed the hatch.

"Does she have these mood swings often?" I asked John.

"Suzie's emotional and changeable, it's true. But you must realize, Jake, this whole affair's been a nasty shock for all of us."

"Sorry, sorry. . . ." It struck me that I'd been apologizing a lot lately. I had to reach down deep into my resources to remind myself that I had done nothing to deserve any of this, nor was any of it my fault. A sense of guilt for unspecified and probably imaginary offenses is a load that gets dumped on you early on. Most people spend a lifetime looking for a place to set it down.

"John, would you excuse me for a moment? I want to talk to Sam."

"Of course." He went to the hatch and opened it, turned to say something, but thought better of it. "We'll talk later," he said, then went out and closed the hatch. He had his own guilt to deal with.

Winnie was on the couch, huddled up with her arms wrapped around her knees, looking at me with wet, questioning eyes. I winked at her, and she gave me a grimace-grin in return. Funny that she responded to a wink. I couldn't remember ever seeing her eyelids close except in sleep; she never blinked them.

"I'm copying you fine," Sam said when I keyed him. *"How'd you do it?"*

"Roland engineered it, but those button transponders did the trick. We have them planted all over the ship. What have you got for me?"

"Well, when I went down to the basement, I got quite a shock. There's tons of stuff from years back. I checked a list-out of that news-recording subroutine. The way it's coded is all goofed up. It tells me to erase all the junk I've kept for the last thirty days, but allows me to keep what I've recorded that day, the day I houseclean. What the subroutine does then is give everything that's left in the workfile a PROTECT tag. Then, when I erase again, all that stuff gets dumped into the reference library. As a result, there's all kinds of random crap down there from years back."

"I'll have to stop buying that cheap off-the-shelf software and do my own coding for a change. You find anything interesting?"

"Yes, very. Like this item in Pravdu *from about three years ago."* Sam snorted. *"Never fails to amuse me that they thought the change of one letter makes a Russian word into an Inter-system one."*

"Makes it easier for them. Go ahead."

"Okay. Quote, Tsiolkovskygrad, Einstein, October 10, 2103. The season premiere of the New Bolshoi was well-attended this year, as it is every year, but last night standing-room-only crowds packed the house to see a daringly innovative staging of, blah blah blah blah, etcetera. Skip six paragraphs. Among the notables attending were Kamrada *Big Cheese,* Kamrada *Head Whatshisname, your mother's Uncle Pasha, and—here it is, get this—Minister of Intercolonial Affairs Dr. Van*

Wyck Vance, daughter Daria Petrovsky-Vance, and some prominent friends of the Authority, including labor leader Kamrada *Corey Wilkes, unquote. I'm multiplexing the 2-D image. Are you getting it?"*

I put one end of the key to my eye and peered through the pinhole lens. The microscreen showed a loge full of bored faces, one of them belonging to Corey Wilkes. He was seated next to—yes, it had to be—the same patrician-looking gentleman I'd seen at Sonny's and thought I recognized. Van Wyck Vance. Next to him was a blond woman with her head turned, talking to the woman behind her. The face was hidden, the hair was longer and probably its natural color, but . . .

"Sam, zoom in on the blonde."

"How? Like this?"

"Little closer, screen right."

. . . But the port-wine mark on her bare right shoulder told me it was Darla.

"Now we know who 'Dar-ya' is."

"More than that, Sam. It's Darla. And I saw her dad at Sonny's."

"How can you—? Oh, you mean the little mark on her shoulder? I missed that, but now I remember. More advantages than you'd think in women running around naked, aside from the obvious ones."

I stretched out on the silky bedspread and put the key on the nightstand, leaving the circuit open. I closed my eyes.

"What's it mean, Jake? From what you've told me, it looks like all along she's been Petrovsky's agent. Now we know she's his LC. But if she's Vance's daughter, and Vance is in cahoots with Wilkes . . . where does that put her?" I didn't answer right away. *"Jake?"*

"I don't know. We need more information."

Sam sighed. *"Damn it, sometimes being a machine is hell."*

I picked the key up and held it close to my mouth. "Sam, everything they've done has been to make us *run*. And we tucked tail and ran. The scuffle at Sonny's was to start things off, and also served the purpose of setting me up to be tracked by a method I haven't figured out. They knew exactly where we were when we hid out at Greystoke Groves. But did they surprise us? No, they flushed us out of there and followed us, dogging our every step, somehow anticipating our every move while staying a planet or two behind. And all for one purpose:

to watch us until we ducked into a potluck. We did. To them that meant we had the Roadmap. And we do. We've had it all along and didn't know it."

"Uh-huh. And what is it?"

"It's a who. It's Winnie."

"What?"

I told him about the sand drawings, then went over my reasoning concerning why the drawings could qualify as the 'convincing forgery' Petrovsky had mentioned.

"Convincing? Who'd be convinced by scratches in the sand?"

"Apparently everybody. That's the only way it figures. Remember, they might not know that Winnie's knowledge is based on myth. And furthermore, *we* don't know it either, for a fact. That line may be real, or they may not be. I haven't had time to find out for sure. I tried back on the beach, but Darla's the only one who seems to understand her."

"How did Wilkes and company find out about Winnie? Through Darla?"

"I don't know. We know she reported to Petrovsky at the station. Wilkes may have a spy in Petrovsky's intelligence unit. Another thing that isn't clear is whether Darla knew about Winnie's abilities when she reported. The drawings didn't show up until we got here, but Darla's been talking to her all along, so she may have reported on the possibility earlier. Left some kind of message, secret radio, something."

"And the Reticulans?"

"A Snatchgang working for Wilkes, but why Rikkis would work for humans, and for what compensation, isn't obvious."

"You can say that again. Okay, okay, but I don't understand two things." He laughed. *"What am I talking about? I'm fuzzy about a lot of things. Put it this way. There are two main confusions. One: How the hell did these stories about us get started in the first place? And how come we never got wind of them until recently?"*

"Sam, how long were we off the road before this run?"

"Christ, I don't know. Couple of months. Why?"

"Couple of months to bring in the harvest back at the farm, right? And to do some necessary business. Before that, where were we?"

"Hydran Maze, pleading with those waterbags not to tear up the Guild Basic and go over to Wilkes."

"How long?"

"Don't remind me. Seemed like years, waiting three weeks at a time for some bureaucrat to get over her estrous cycle so we could get an appointment. How long? Another three months, all told."

"Sam, your antialien prejudice is showing."

"Not at all. I'm just pissed, is all."

"Six months off the road," I said. "Okay, here's Crackpot Theory Number One. Somehow, we get out of this mess. With Winnie's help, we find our way back, but we do a Timer. We luck onto a backtime route and return to T-Maze before we leave . . . about six months before we leave. Word gets around somehow. There's a map; get the map, everybody says. Everybody wants the goddamn thing. And some combination of Wilkes, the Authority, the Reticulans, and the Ryxx is aiming to get it . . . somehow. Our future selves stay low until the heat's off. They know better, leaving us to get chased."

"You'd think they'd have the decency to fill us in."

"They may have their reasons. Anyway, we run, find Winnie, leave the Maze, get into a mess, get out of it, go back in time, etcetera. That's the Paradox. Somehow, it all has to work."

"How many somehows was that? I lost count."

"Too many, but I'm ready for Crackpot Theory Number Two, if you've got it."

"I don't. I've got one more big confusion, though."

"Which is?"

"Why the hell didn't they just grab us back in T-Maze and beat the merte *out of us until we handed it over? We didn't have anything, but they didn't know that."*

"They're smart. They're aware of the Paradox. Wilkes as much as pointed it out to me back at Sonny's. They're reasoning that I got the map at some point along the journey, but they don't know exactly where. So they wait until it looks like we deliberately slip through a hope-to-Jesus hole." I took a deep breath. "Well, what do you think?" I asked, knowing he'd been playing devil's advocate all along.

"Well, I've never knowingly bought a crock of excrement before, but I'll buy yours if you answer one more question. To wit: if we have the map already . . . I mean our future selves, of course . . . if we've already returned six months ago with the thing, or with Winnie or whatever, why in the name of all that's holy are they trying to get it now? It's done, finished. How can they hope to change what's happened?"

"That's a tough one. Would you still buy my crock if I told you I had no idea?"

"Yeah, but I'm gullible."

"Got anything else from the file?"

"Well, under 'Colonial Assembly' I got the usual pile of nonnews, except for one item that cross-referenced with 'intelligence.'"

"Give it to me."

"I'll digest it. It's about two Assemblymen—actually a man and a woman—being suspended by the Authority pending an investigation into their part in activities which've been deemed by the Authority to be outside the bounds of the Assembly's proper sphere of concern. Probably wanted to wipe their asses without having to petition the Authority in writing first."

"How did it cross-reference with 'intelligence'?"

"The information was based on Militia intelligence reports."

"Sounds like a smoke screen—the story, I mean. Got any background on it?"

"A bit. If you remember a while back, there was some roadbuzz about a secret intelligence cell within the Assembly. Undercover operatives, special operations, that sort of thing. The funds for it were supposed to've been disguised as temporary staff salaries for a couple of investigative committees."

"Wow. Who leaked all that?"

"Authority plants in the Assembly, of course. They carry on a loose-lip campaign in cocktail bars and bedrooms; and when the story gets widely circulated, the Authority acts. That way the plants don't blow their cover. For good measure, the Authority may have had a spy right in the cell."

"Double agent?"

"Right."

"Okay." I sat up on the bed. "Sam, you did a good job. We have one more piece of the puzzle. Right now I don't know where it fits, but it's a big one. Talk to you later."

"Report in regularly, will you?"

"Sure." I got up and went to the connecting hatch, put my ear against it. Roland, John, and Darla were talking quietly next door.

I turned to Winnie and said, "Let's you and me go for a little walk, honey."

16

WITHOUT HESITATION, SHE followed me to the hatch. We went out into the hallway after I'd checked it out. I closed the hatch softly. She took my hand, her double-thumbed grip feeling strange but firm and trusting, and we walked along the red-carpeted, gold-papered hallway. I'd never been on a true water-displacing vessel of this size, but it reminded me of pictures of old Terran buildings. There was a feeling of space here, none of the economical crampedness you'd expect, let alone the nightmarish claustrophobia of a deep-space ship. And from what I'd seen of this Outworld maze, the ship seemed out of place in its luxuriousness. As we neared the lobby area I discovered the reason for its affluence. There was a casino. I didn't stop to gawk, but I caught a glimpse of lots of action, chips flowing at dozens of tables where every game in town was being played. There were aliens in there too.

Before going into the still-crowded lobby, I parked Winnie in a small room full of food-dispensing machines, hiding her behind one of them. I told her to wait until I got back. At the desk, I asked the clerk where the crew quarters were. He gave me a puzzled look before he answered me politely, and I wondered briefly if the "fraternization" proscription that Krause had mentioned was really true. But the clerk didn't ask for my reasons. He showed me a deck plan of the boat and indicated the crew's quarters in the stern end of C Deck, the lowest of the three.

"Are you looking for someone in particular, sir?"

"Yeah, a girl. Young, about this high, short blondish hair, on the thin side."

He thought for a moment. "Oh, I think that's Lorelei. Pretty sure that's the one. She's a belowdecks mate, but we should be all squared away down there by now. We're about to put to sea, and she should be off-duty."

"Fine. Thanks." I went back and got Winnie.

It was good to get out of the lobby and into relatively quiet corridors. I felt conspicuous, especially with Winnie, and kept my eyes peeled for a familiar face. None showed. I still felt edgy, but thought I'd risk a tour on deck. I wanted to see how they got the monster out of the harbor.

We went through an undogged hatch out onto a deserted part of the outer forward deck. It was a recreation area, with games painted on the wood decking, canvas chairs stacked by the bulkhead, a few tables under umbrellas. We stood at the railing and watched as the ship-animal retreated from shore backwards, trailing a wake of bubbling water. A smaller complement of beaters was on duty at the bow, but there were still at least fifty of them, slapping out a slow rhythm. It must have been a delicate bit of seamanship; the beats were measured and deliberate. We were halfway out of the harbor, leaving behind a deserted island back-lit by a smoldering orange sun. It looked as if the island were moving away, and not us. Below, I could see most of the upper surface of the beast. Seal-creatures were all over the place, dragging piles of seaweed with their forward flippers, popping in and out of the dome-structures, generally going about their appointed tasks, whatever they were. I could see that the resemblance to Terran seals was superficial. The heads were bigger and the wrinkled faces flatter, with not much of a snout. And the eyes were strange. It was a little too far to tell, but it looked as though they might be structurally similar to the beast-eye we'd seen.

We were on the upper main deck, but above us was a poop

deck where the bridge was. Officers leaned over the rails watching the ship's progress. I wondered how the bridge was relaying orders to the pilot-musicians, or if the bridge was giving orders at all. True, a captain hands the conn over to the pilot when entering or leaving harbor, but what about in open sea?

I felt eyes on me, and looked toward the starboard flying bridge. A stocky, bearded man in a gold uniform was staring at me. The captain. No, not actually staring—appraising, sizing me up, the shiny visor of his cap starred with sunlight. I couldn't see his eyes, but I felt their clinical gaze.

I took Winnie's hand and we went back inside. We took a long trek through the ship, avoiding main areas of activity. We passed near a dining area filling up with hungry patrons, went by a ballroom, a darkened theater, skirted the trade and shopping deck, and then found a narrow stairway that led all the way down to C Deck. Below, we encountered an empty six-bed infirmary looking very underequipped, found lockers, storerooms, and strangely enough, a sign that read TOPSIDE HOLDS 5–10. I had thought that cargo would be shipped belowdecks, but some items were probably too fragile for beast-gizzards.

We finally came to the crew quarters. I looked around, found a maintenance closet full of mops and pails, and told Winnie to wait inside. She looked at me nervously, then crept inside and sat in a corner, her big eyes glowing in the shadows. I whispered to her reassuringly, telling her I'd be right back and not to be afraid. I hoped she understood—but then, my communication problem with her seemed to be one-way, with me having all the trouble.

The crew area was divided up into little cabins of four or five bunks each. Most of the hatches were closed, but I saw a few sailors racked out on their bunks, asleep. It had been a long watch. Luckily, there were name plates listing the occupants of each cabin; perversely, only first initials and surnames were used. Think of asking for her last name? Not you, Jake. I took a stroll through the maze of passages, squinting in the dim light. I found a total of four L. Somebodys. Lorelei Mikhailovich? Not likely, but you never know. Lorelei Souphanouvong? Improbable. That narrowed it to two, L. Finkelhor and L. Peters. Peters it is. I knocked.

A muffled reply. I knocked again. Grumbling and general complaining.

The hatch opened and there was Lorelei looking bleary-eyed in a tattered blue robe. "Yes?" She squinted at me. "Who're you?"

"Is my face that forgettable?"

After a second, it hit her. "Oh, yeah, the truckie." Her eyes grew wary. "What do you want?"

"A favor . . . and a chance to appeal to your conscience."

"Huh?"

"I'm in a spot, and I need your help."

She frowned, puzzled, then shrugged. "Come in, then," she said, widening the hatch.

"First I want to show you something. Or rather someone."

"Who?" she wanted to know. "Hey, where're you going?"

"Want you to meet a friend of mine," I said, walking down the hall. I stopped and beckoned. "Come on."

"I'm not sure I should," she said sourly. "Aren't you the one that was going to stick a torch up my behind?"

I was about to explain that I'd mistaken her for a man, but caught that faux pas by its ugly little tail before it scampered out. "Sorry about that. I was jittery as hell. First time I ever parked inside a sea monster."

This mollified her somewhat. She stepped out into the passageway. "Okay, but any weird stuff and I scream rape. You won't like what happens to you after that."

Probably not. She followed me at a good distance. I got to the closet, opened the door. This made Lorelei stop and eye me all the more distrustingly.

"Okay, Winnie," I called.

When Winnie peeked around the bulkhead, Lorelei came out of her tough-cynical character like a fresh pea from a wrinkled pod, suddenly all girlish smile and looking even younger than I first thought her to be. The smile looked much better on her than her usual sullen pout.

"Oh, isn't she cute!" Lorelei beamed. "It is a she, isn't it? Where'd she come from?"

"Winnie," I said, pointing, "this is Lorelei."

"Hi, Winnie!"

"Hi! Hi!"

"Winnie comes from a planet named Hothouse. Ever hear of it?"

She came forward and stroked Winnie's head, feeling the thick glossy fur. "No. Is that back in T-Maze?"

"Yes. Were you born here? I mean, in the Outworlds?"

"Uh-huh. Look at those ears. Oh, she's darling. Is she yours?"

"Uh . . . Winnie's not a pet. She's a person—but, yes, she's traveling with me and I'm responsible for her. How would you like to look after her for me?"

Lorelei giggled. Winnie seemed to be fascinated with the color and texture of Lorelei's robe, fingering and sniffing the cloth. "Oh, I wouldn't mind. . . . " she began, then bit her lip. "Gee, I don't know. I'm pulling double-duty all this run. We're shorthanded, and I don't know when I'd get the time."

"You won't need much. Winnie's able to take care of herself. Actually, I had something specific in mind."

"What's that?" Then, remembering, she said, "Didn't you say you were in trouble?"

"Winnie's the one who's in trouble."

"She is?"

"Yes. I want you to hide her. You must know every nook and cranny of this ship, places where she could stay without anyone discovering her. Right?"

"Well, yeah, but why?"

"Lorelei, there are people on this boat who want to kidnap Winnie. Maybe worse. She's in great danger."

She was shocked. "Who'd want to hurt *her?* And why, for God's sake?"

"It's difficult to explain, but basically the situation is this. Winnie has some valuable information, and these people want it badly. And to get it, they need to get her."

Lorelei put a protective arm around Winnie's shoulders. "She has information? What could she know that anyone would—?"

"Winnie's a very intelligent creature. Don't let her looks fool you. As I said, she's a person, not an animal."

"Hm." She looked at me skeptically, a little of the cynicism returning. "How do I know you haven't kidnapped her?"

"Ask Winnie."

She screwed up her face to make a snide retort, but thought better of it. She bent over toward Winnie and pointed to me. "Is he your friend, Winnie? That man there. Friend?"

Winnie turned to me and smiled adoringly. "Fwenn!" she said and reached over to clutch my hand. "Jake fwenn!" She nuzzled my arm. "Fwenn fwenn fwenn! Jake-fwenn!" I was only a little embarrassed.

Lorelei grinned sheepishly. "I guess you're not fooling!"

She straightened up and stuck out a smudged hand. "Glad to meet you, Jake."

I took her hand, then heard voices in the adjoining corridor. "Quick, in here," I whispered. We piled into the closet.

When the two sailors had gone I said, "What do you say, Lorelei? Will you help us out?"

"Sure. I know just the place, too. I can bring her food and water when I'm off-duty . . . but she'll have to keep quiet and not fuss."

"Winnie doesn't fuss. She'll behave." I thought of something. "Food's going to be a problem, though. She needs food from her planet, special food, like all aliens. Like us, too." I sighed and leaned against the bulkhead. "No help for it, I guess. Unless . . ." Well, there was a slight possibility. "Lorelei, is there any crewman who might be from Hothouse? He might know of substitute foods, things that are all right for Winnie to eat. Biochemistry is funny that way. Is everyone in the crew a native Outworlder?"

"No, there're plenty who lucked through, but I never heard anyone say they were from Hothouse."

"Hm. How about Demeter? That's the fancy name for the place. No? Anyone ever mention they hailed from Mach City? It's the biggest city."

"No, not that I . . ." In the bands of light coming through the louvered door I saw her massage her forehead with her palm. "Mach City. Wait a minute. Where've I seen that before?"

"You've seen it?"

"Yeah, somewhere, written on something. Damn it, I can't remember where the punk it was." She snapped her fingers. "Oh, yeah! It was marked on a crate we brought up from belowdecks."

"Cargo?"

"Yeah. We put it in a topside hold. Special class stuff. The crate wasn't marked, but some of the boards came off on one of them in the freight elevator. There were big bales of stuff inside, leaves and stuff, wrapped with plastic bands, and on the bands there was a name. Some company . . . don't remember what it was, something about chemicals, but it said Mach City. It was in System, *Polla dey Mach*. I remember 'cause I asked where Match City was, and Larry—he works with me—he says, 'You dummy, it's *Mock* City.'" He's a punkin' moron . . . but he's cute. Anyway, that's how I remember. We brought up a lot of those crates."

Well. Well, well, well. "Lorelei, is there any way we can get at those crates?"

"Sure. The holds are locked, but that's no problem for me. Why?"

"Possibility that Winnie might be able to eat some of that stuff. It's also a good bet that . . ." A good bet? Sucker bet. I knew what the bales contained. "Lorelei, look—"

"Call me Lori."

"Lori. I might not be able to get down here again soon. Could you take Winnie into the hold tonight and open one of those crates? Let Winnie hunt around in there for a while. She may find something to eat. She'll know what she can or can't consume."

"Uh-huh. I can do that."

"Good. Now, can you get her into hiding right away?"

"Yeah, but I'll have to be careful."

"Do you want to wait until tonight? Keep her in your cabin until then?"

"Not really. I have bunkmates, you know."

"Can you trust them?"

"Two I can, but the other one's a blabbermouth."

"Then you'd better take her now. And another thing," I said, wondering if this decision was wise, "don't tell me where you're keeping her."

She was surprised. "Not tell you?"

"I think it best, but it could put you in some danger. Are you still willing?"

"I can take care of myself," she said evenly.

"I think you can. And I really don't think these people will want to mess with a crewmember. It'd make too much trouble for them." I felt for Winnie in the dark. She found my hand and grasped it, and I squatted down and said, "Winnie, I want you to go with Lori here. You go with her, okay? She'll put you in a nice place where you can sleep. You'll be alone, but you won't be afraid. Jake will come get you later." Her grip tightened. "No, I won't forget you, Winnie. But you must be very quiet and be a good girl. Lori will come to visit you and take you to get food. But you mustn't be afraid. Understand? Nothing will happen to you. No one will hurt you. Okay?"

"Kay!"

"You'll be a good girl?"

"G'gowull!"

"Huh? Oh, yeah, good girl." I cracked the hatch and looked out, then closed it. "Almost forgot. We need a way to communicate. I don't trust the room phones. Can you get a written message to me?"

"I think so."

"Good. After you hide her, send this message to stateroom 409-B. Got that? 409-B. Send this: 'Your suit will be ready tomorrow morning.'"

She repeated it.

"Right. That's tonight's message. For emergencies, send . . . um, let's see. Send, 'The galley regrets it can't provide the special wine you ordered.'"

She repeated that and said, "Got it."

"Now, can I leave messages at your cabin?"

"Yeah, just slip it under the door. I'll be there when I'm off-duty. I get so worn out, most of the time I'm sacking anyway."

"Okay. Here." I took her hand and pressed a wad of bills into it.

"No, you don't have to."

"Take it, and no back talk. You're taking a risk and you should be paid. Never be an altruist. It'll kill you in the end."

"What's an altruist?"

"It's what everyone wants the universe to think they are, but the universe knows better. Never mind." I looked out again. "Right. Get going, and don't let anyone see you with Winnie if you can help it."

"Right. C'mon, Winnie."

I watched them tiptoe down the dark passageway, then turn a corner.

17

AND WHO SHOULD I see on my way back up? None other than the Weird Bastard stepping out of his cabin, catching sight of yours truly and slithering back into his hole like a mudsnake. I sprang forward and shouldered the hatch, wedging my boot between it and the frame.

"A word with you, sir."

"Get out of here!"

"We really have to talk."

He threw his weight against me hard and nearly took my foot off, but I shoved back.

After a struggle, he stopped pushing and leaned against the hatch. "I'll call security!" he said.

"You can reach the phone from here?"

He thought it over. No, guess not. "What do you want?"

"As I said, a few words with you."

"Say 'em."

"Actually, I wanted to take you to dinner. Have some friends

I want you to meet. They live in the ocean, you see, and they have big, nasty teeth."

Suddenly his weight was off the hatch. I threw it open and dashed into the room where he was already rifling through a satchel on the bed. I kidney-punched him and maneuvered him into a full nelson, made sure he hadn't gotten to the gun, then threw him against the bulkhead. He hit it with a thud and crumpled. I went through the satchel until I found it. A good little piece, a Smith & Wesson 10kw with a Surje powerpack grip, compact, lightweight, and deadly.

He was on the floor with his back against the bulkhead, groaning but conscious, looking at me worriedly. I went to the hatch, closed and locked it, then walked toward him, twirling the pistol.

"Maybe you'd like to explain that little episode on the beach," I said, "while you still have a working mouth."

"I don't know what you're talking about."

"You'll have to do better than that."

He ran a hand through his unruly salt-and-pepper hair, then spent a good deal of time scraping himself off the floor. I stood well back, watching for the sudden move. He was a big man, but if I was any judge he didn't have any fight in him, just a streak of guile that he was trying to hide now with a *merte*-eating grin. "Oh, yeah. Yeah, I remember now. I did see you on the island. Sure." He shrugged and threw his arms wide. "What's the problem? Must be some kind of misunderstanding here."

"I asked you if the water was safe, and you said yes. It wasn't."

Innocence bloomed on him like mold. "I didn't know! I see people swimming in there all the time!"

"How long do they usually last?"

"Huh?"

He was lying, of course, but right then it occurred to me that I didn't need another enemy on board. He could have other uses. "You didn't know about the danger?"

"No, I swear. Look, *kamrada,* it's just a misunderstanding, believe me."

I didn't bother to ask why he'd run at the sight of me, deciding to live the lie with him. "Well," I said, "if you're telling the truth, it looks like I owe you an apology."

"It's the truth, I swear it." He stepped away from the wall and straightened his clothes. "I don't swim myself, but I have seen people in the water from time to time."

"Uh-huh." I gave him a conciliatory grin. "Well, I guess it's all been a mistake then. Hope you'll accept my apologies."

He was all eager smile, his body sagging in relief. "No problem, no problem," he said. "I can understand. I guess you were hopping mad. Don't blame you, I really don't. These things happen."

"Yeah." I handed him his gun. "No hard feelings, I hope."

"No, no, none at all. Like I said, I don't blame you a bit. Would've felt the same way myself." He slipped the gun into a pocket of his bright-blue jumpsuit. "Tell you what. Let me buy you a drink."

"Sounds great."

I let Paul Hogan buy me a drink. The lounge was crowded, noisy, and the drinks were expensive. We talked pleasantly for a while over mugs of local brew. Turned out he was a slave trader by profession.

"Indentured servitude?" Hogan said. "You could call it that. There's a contract involved and a term of service specified, but the contract can be bought out at any time by the contractee. Slavery?" He shook his head in protest. "No, not at all. It's strictly a business relationship. Lots of people luck through to this maze with nothing but the clothes on their backs, their vehicles, and a pocketful of worthless currency. They need jobs, and I can get 'em. I'm a broker . . . an agent, that's all." He lit a funny-looking, bright-green cigar. "Ever tried these? Give you a real nice buzz." He blew smoke out one side of his mouth. "No, the reason I came over to you on the beach was because of the Cheetah. The Hothouse creature."

"Really?"

"They make great domestics. Not many of 'em in this maze. I was going to ask you if you wanted to sell it."

"Sell Winnie? No, I wouldn't think of it."

"I could offer a good price." He took a long pull of his drink, eyeing me like a specimen on a slide. "Uh, it seemed as if you lucked through traveling pretty light. How's your money situation? Need a loan?"

Ah ha. The Bait. "We're okay for the moment. 'Course, we'll have to do something to earn a living eventually." Nibble, nibble.

"Tell me, how'd you happen to shoot a potluck? I'm just curious. Different people have different reasons."

"Really? In our case it was a mistake. Missed a sign, and

before we knew it the commit markers were on us."

"Uh-huh, uh-huh." He puffed the cigar thoughtfully. "Some people do it on purpose. Did you know that? In fact, we get more and more of those every day. Don't ask me how the word got back to T-Maze that there was something here to luck through to, but something makes 'em come. They want to get out from under the Authority's thumb. Freedom, that's what we got out here. High technology, forget it. Modern medicine, the same. Lots of things are in short supply here—but if you don't mind roughing it, this maze is wide open. We're young and growing. Lots of opportunities." He sat back and crossed his legs. "You're right about having to do something about money eventually. Prices are high around here, believe me. You should give some serious thought to selling the Cheetah. In fact, I'm going to sweeten the deal for you, give you something to think about. I'll pay part of the price in drugs."

"Drugs?"

"Antigeronics." He snorted. "You didn't think you could get 'em here as easy as you can back in T-Maze, did you?"

"I can't imagine anything being under tighter control than anti-g's," I said. "My last treatment was after a four-year wait and a dozen different permits. And it cost a fortune."

"Sometimes you can't get them here at any price, and you'll die waiting. But I have good connections."

"How much are we talking about?" I asked, stringing him along.

"I can give you, say, a quarter-treatment's worth. The full oral series."

In a dark corner of the lounge, a quartet struck up a vaguely Latin American number. The instruments were acoustic—marimba, trap drums, and double bass—except for the lead omniclavier. I listened to the music for a while, looking out through the floor-to-ceiling windows at a night sky aglow with moonlight over a silver-flecked sea.

"Paul, a quarter-treatment's not going to do me any good if I can't get the rest."

"Best I can do, Jake. We're talking big money here."

"If you can swing a full treatment, forget the cash. I'll take just the drugs."

"Can't do it, Jake. Like I said, my connection is good, but the supply is short."

"Who's your source?"

He flashed a smug grin. "My source is *the* source, friend.

None better, but that's the deal. Think about it." He drained his mug and wiped his mouth with two fingers. "Here, let me give you my card."

He gave me his card, which read PAUL HOGAN ASSOCIATES, EMPLOYMENT SPECIALISTS, with an address in Seahome. I finished my beer, made my excuses, and got out of there.

When I got back to the stateroom, nobody was there. I knocked on the connecting hatch and opened it. No one.

I sprawled on one of the double beds and keyed Sam.

"Yo!"

"Keeping busy down there? Anything interesting?"

"Oh, sure, nothing like watching a stomach wall ooze."

"It's oozing?"

"Yeah, but they keep spraying the place down with some kind of stuff. How's it going up there? Any trouble?"

"Things are coming to a head, but I keep getting the feeling I'm the pimple." I filled Sam in about Lori and Winnie, then ran down all the new bits of data I'd picked up, especially what I'd gleaned from Hogan.

"This is all getting very interesting," Sam said, "It's also getting a lot clearer."

"There're still some big murky areas, but I think . . ."

"Yeah, what?"

"Sam, just a thought. I know we're wedged in pretty tight down there, but could you muscle your way out if you had to?"

"No problem. May have to flatten a few buggies to do it, though. Why? Where do we go then?"

"I have an insane idea."

"Oh, God."

I heard the hatch opening. It was Darla, letting herself in with her key. She stopped dead when she saw me. "Jake! Where the hell have you been?"

"Talk to you later, Sam."

"Any time."

"Hi, Darla."

She came over and sat on the bed beside me. "You disappeared."

"Sorry. We went for a walk."

"Where's Winnie?"

"Wanted to talk to you about that. I gave her to somebody."

Her face didn't change expression, but a submerged ripple of surprise crossed it, once, and was gone. "You gave her to somebody? Who?"

"Uh, guy by the name of Paul Hogan. Deals in exotic animals, for zoos and such. I thought it best." I put my hands behind my head nonchalantly. "Had to do something sooner or later. Right?"

"Zoos? They have those here?"

"Apparently. Well, he didn't say zoos exactly. Now that I think of it, it seems improbable. Exotic pets, maybe." She frowned at me. "Darla, I don't like it any better than you, but it had to be done. He said he'd find her a good home."

She didn't like it, but said nothing. She was thinking.

"Where's the gang?"

"Hm? Oh, they're out shopping."

"Did you go with them?"

"No, I was looking for you."

"I should have let you know, but we got to wandering, then we met Hogan, and then . . . well, I wanted to get the matter taken care of. Sorry."

She didn't quite know what to make of it. "Where did you—?"

Voices in the next room interrupted her. A knock came on the connecting hatch.

John poked his head in. "Hello?"

"Come on in," I said.

John stepped in, decked out in a bush outfit. He looked like a khaki beanpole. "What do you think?" he said, turning like a ballerina.

"Nice outfit," I said. "Yours too, Suzie."

Susan's was more conventional, a green all-climate suit with brown knee-high boots. "We got backpacks too," she said, proudly displaying hers. "And some camping equipment, new eggs, everything."

"Yes," John said. "We thought we'd be proper starhikers for a change. Spent a bloody fortune. The prices!"

Roland walked in wearing a match for Susan's outfit. "Jake! Where the punking hell were you?—if you don't mind my asking."

"With Winnie. I found someone to take her."

"Oh, Jake, you didn't!" Susan was shocked.

John, in a sudden reverie, said, "Odd . . . I was wondering where all this stuff comes from. I didn't think to check the labels. They seem good quality."

"I checked them," Roland said. "The labels were all from Terran Maze. Where else?"

John furrowed his brow. "But I was under the impression . . ."

"You get the door prize, Roland," I said. "The Outworlds aren't as far out as you think."

"Lots of things don't make sense here," Roland said.

"You mean goods are being shipped here from back home?" John said.

"Exactly," Roland answered.

"But how are the suppliers getting paid? I mean how . . .?" He was lost in thought.

"I don't know," I said. "But nobody dumps goods through a one-way hole, do they?"

"Not likely," Roland said.

"Then there's a way back?" John said, shocked at his own conclusion. Susan was round-eyed, hope springing to her face.

"Apparently somebody knows a way," I said, "but they may not be telling."

"But if we could find it," John said.

"If this maze is as big as most are," Roland said, "that could take years. A century. And I have a feeling a great deal of this maze is unexplored."

"Well." John sighed and sat down. "Food for thought."

Susan looked crestfallen.

"Speaking of food," Roland said, thumping his stomach. "I suppose they have cabin service."

"I'm for the dining room," I said, drawing a strange look from Darla. "I want good food, civilized conversation, wine, and wit."

A knock at the outer hatch, and everyone froze.

"Come in!" I yelled.

Darla's Walther was in her hand before I could see her move. "Jake! What're you doing?" she gasped.

"Roland, get the hatch, will you? I keep forgetting the thing locks automatically."

Roland gave me a puzzled look, then went to answer it.

"Darla, put that thing away. We have guests."

"Mr. McGraw?"

"No, he's over there."

A ship's officer stepped in. "Mr. McGraw?"

"Yes?"

"Good evening. Jean Le Maitre, Executive Officer."

"Bon soir, Monsieur Le Maitre. Comment ça-vas?"

"Bon, Monsieur. Et vous? Comment allez-vous ce soir?"

"Très bien. Et qu'y a-t-il pour votre service?"

"Le Capitaine présente ses compliments, et il voudrait . . . excuse me. Does everyone speak French here?"

"I've just exhausted my knowledge," I said.

He laughed. "Then I'll speak English. Captain Pendergast presents his compliments, sir, and requests the honor of your company at dinner this evening, at his table."

"Tell the Captain," I said, "that we'd be delighted."

"Would eight bells be convenient for you?"

"That'd be fine."

"Excellent. The Captain will be expecting you. Until eight, then . . . *mesdames et messieurs."* He clicked his heels together, bowed, and left.

"La plume de ma tante est sur le bureau de mon oncle," Susan said dully.

18

I NEEDED A weapon. I had been getting and losing them at a rapid rate lately. Another squib would be just the thing, but I doubted one could be found, as they aren't a popular item. Everybody wants a hand-cannon, for some reason. True, you can't cut through vanadium steel with a squib, but I know of few dangerous beings made of steel. You get few shots with a palm-size weapon, but you only need the one that does the job. There was a hitch, however. From the shootout at Sonny's everyone knew I favored a squib and knew exactly where I kept it hidden, if they didn't know before. All right; I'd get a shooting iron too.

The shopping area was large, divided up into stores that sold anything and everything, with no particular emphasis on any one market. I browsed through one that offered clothing, toiletries, camping equipment, food, and shelves of miscellaneous bric-a-brac. They sold weapons too. A pretty middle-aged woman showed me to a display case. The selection wasn't much; there were half a dozen odd pieces in various models, an S & W like Hogan's among them. I had second thoughts about getting a wall-burner. Maybe the 10kw would be enough. She took it out of the case for me. It was basically the same as the slave trader's, but the powerpack was a different, earlier design and was a good deal bulkier, awkwardly so. I didn't like it, but the alternatives were few. There were two Russian slug-throwers, a Colonial-made beamer, and one antique replica that qualified as a hand-cannon by anyone's lights, if you didn't mind throwing a barely supersonic projectile.

"Let me see that one," I said.

She chuckled. "Are you going to shoot it out with the sheriff?"

"I think you have the wrong period. It's a nice piece, though. What's its rating . . . er, caliber?"

"I wouldn't know, sir," she said.

I looked. "Oh, it says right here. Forty-four magnum. Hm. Have any ammunition?"

"I only have one box of twenty shells. Sorry, but I let someone talk me into taking that thing on a trade. Thought I could get a good price from a collector. No takers."

"It's authentic?"

"Oh, yes. Reconditioned, but it's the genuine article."

I doubted it. In fact, it looked as if it had been doctored up to look the part. She'd gotten stung, all right, and she was trying to off-load it on me. "No kidding?" I said innocently.

"Shoots pretty good, too," she said. "I used it to bang away at some croakers once. Didn't hit anything, of course."

"Uh-huh. I'll take it. How much?"

She'd let me steal it from her for fifty consols. I pilfered it for thirty-five, and I could see by her eyes that she was glad to get that. She even threw in a holster. I put the thing on, then slipped the gun into it. "Nice doing business with you. . . ."

She smiled prettily. "Belle. Belle Shapiro. Hey, you're not going to walk around the ship with that thing, are you?"

"Why not?"

She shrugged. "No rule against it. Most people like to keep their hardware concealed, that's all."

"I'm a straightforward sort of person."

Her grin widened. "I think you are too. That makes two of us. Like to join me in a drink later? I'm about ready to close up shop."

"Love to, Belle, but I'm expected at the Captain's table, and something tells me a heavy evening lies ahead."

"Too bad. Well, some other time."

"You're sure there's no problem about wearing this?" I asked, taking the gun out and loading it with five shells, leaving the hammer over an empty chamber. I'd seen those old *mopix* too.

"No problem, though the Old Man has been threatening to start a policy of having all beam weapons checked at the desk. We've had a rash of fires lately. But it'd take too much time, and no one's been able to come up with a way to scan the luggage. Can't get the equipment."

As she spoke, a wild thought came into my head from parts unknown. "Belle, is there a pharmacy aboard?"

"No, not really. What do you need?"

"I don't know exactly. Something to keep me awake."

"Oh, I have plenty of high-altitude stuff." She went to another part of the store and brought back two big glass jars filled with pills of different colors and sizes. She popped the lid of one jar and began fingering through it. "Let's see . . . I think these little green ones are pretty good. You say you want to stay awake?"

"Yeah, very awake."

"Well, maybe these pink numbers." She bit her lip. "No, those are broad-spectrum antineoplasmics. I think." She looked at me. "Very awake . . . or *extremely* awake?"

"Like this," I said, making my eyes round and crazed.

She snickered. "That much? Wait, I might have something." She opened the other jar and dug her hand into the contents like a kid searching for just the right shade of jelly bean.

"Do you know what's in any of these?"

"Most of them," she said. "I used to keep a list, but I lost it. Here they are." She pulled out one big choker of a horsepill, bright purple in color. "Now, I don't know what's in this one, but it's some kind of antidepressant."

"You don't know the chemistry?"

"No, but it'll cure the blues, that I can tell you. They're a popular item."

"I'll take one. Can you get me a glass of water?"

"Sure, honey."

She brought the water, and I managed to gulp down the pill. Then I got out of there.

I was late for dinner.

19

THE STEWARD ANNOUNCED me. "Mr. McGraw, sir."

I was admitted into the Captain's private dining room.

It made the rest of the ship look like a tramp steamer by comparison. The walls were swaddled in gold fabric with red and white trim, hung with tasteful seascapes. The carpet was red and knee-high to a dwarf. Hanging above the broad expanse of table was an ornate crystal chandelier, throwing lambent light to glint off the silver service and the gold sconces. The china was pale chalk, probably porcelain, the tablecloth satin white and immaculate. I was impressed and stood at the door for a moment.

"Come in, Mr. McGraw." Captain Pendergast wiped his mouth delicately with a gold-colored napkin. "Please," he said, smiling warmly and gesturing to a chair. The other guests looked up at me. Darla, John, and company were there, but I recognized no one else except the redoubtable Mr. Krause. Darla and Susan were the only women.

"Sorry I'm late, Captain." I nodded to the other guests. Krause didn't look up.

"Not at all, Mr. McGraw. Please sit down."

Pendergast's dark blue eyes followed me until I was seated a few places down from him. I unfolded my napkin and laid it on my lap like a proper gentleman, then remembered that I don't like sitting at a table with a cloth draped over my knees, and put it back on the table.

"I suggest you try the seafood dish, Mr. McGraw. I do hope you like seafood."

"I wish you would call me Jake, Captain. Is it local?"

"As you like, Jake." His Intersystem was clipped and Teutonic, but with a Low Dutch broadness around the edges. "Yes, it's local catch. Some people consider it quite a delicacy, although its nutritional value is limited." The corners of his thin-lipped mouth curled upwards. "But we don't always eat to live. Do we?"

"I always enjoy eating," I answered, "and I always hope to live to eat again."

"Yes, it's a perilous universe," he said. "To the natives this particular fish is pure poison. Strange, isn't it? If you don't care for it, we have a choice of entrees."

"I would like the fish," I told the steward standing patiently at my side. He left the room quietly. I turned to Pendergast. "You mentioned the natives. You can communicate with them?"

"With some difficulty, yes."

"What do you call them?"

"The name for their tribe . . . we like to call it a crew . . . is—" He barked twice, then smiled. "As you can see, the language barrier is formidable. Most English speakers call them Arfbarfs."

"Arfbarfs?"

At the other end of the table, Susan giggled into her wine.

"Yes, or Arfies, if you like. Properly speaking, they are Akwaterran Aboriginals, or simply Akwaterrans."

"Are they sentient?"

Pendergast stroked his dark beard. "I'll leave that judgment to the exopologists. Do have some wine, Jake."

A young officer to my left filled a long-stemmed glass. "Tell me, Captain," I said. "What is the proper term for the . . . ?" My Intersystem failed me, and I stumbled about for words.

"Would it be better for you if we spoke your native language, Jake?" Pendergast's English came out even better than his 'System. As usual, other people's language-hopping abilities made me feel sublingual.

"It'd be great," I said. "Thanks, and I'm sorry for the trouble."

"It's nothing. I assume Intersystem isn't spoken on your home planet. Which was . . . ?"

"Vishnu. No, it's either English or Hindustani."

"I see." He gave me a disapproving look. "But Intersystem is so easy to learn." He left it at that, and began eating again.

It made me feel wonderful. I took a long drink of the wine. It was flat and slightly sour.

"This is apropos of nothing," said a portly bald man in a pink formal suit across from me, "but did you know that the 'system' in Intersystem doesn't refer to *solar* systems?"

Eyes drifted toward him. "Really, Dr. Gutman?" said another young officer.

"Yes. Common misconception." Gutman cut with surgical precision into a breast of something vaguely avian. "It really refers to linguistic systems." He slipped a sliver of meat into his mouth and chewed slowly. "Everybody thinks planets," he said, more to himself than to anyone. Slowly, his gaze came around to me. "Don't you find that fascinating?"

"Enthralling," I said, and drained my wine glass.

"Jake, you wanted to know the proper term for something," the Captain said to crank the conversation back up again.

"Yes, the name for what your ship is riding on. The island-animal."

Pendergast had his fork poised above his plate, looking with some concern at his food. "We like to think of both metal and flesh as 'the ship.' STEWARD!"

The steward came through the hatch like a shot. Pendergast held up the plate as if it bore something putrid. "Tell Cookie that if I wanted my fish this well-done, I would have had the gunnery detail use it for target practice. Bring something edible."

"Yes, sir!"

"The Captain was telling us a few things about the ship when you came in, Jake," John said to me. To Pendergast he said, "We were all wondering how the ship is . . . uh, steered. Is that the right word?"

"It's so primitive," the Captain answered, "I'm almost embarrassed to tell you. We have a taut steel cable strung between the bridge and the bow, with the bow end implanted into the megaleviathan's skull. The helmsmen are Arfies who send signals along the cable by beating on it. They are under my direction, of course. However, for maneuvers like docking, we must rely completely on the pilot crew."

"Remarkable," John said. "Megaleviathan? Is that what you call the island-creature?"

"Like everything on Akwaterra," Dr. Gutman said, "or Splash, as most everyone calls it, there is no official name. Scientifically speaking, that is. We don't have the resources to fund science here."

"But we will one day," one of the fresh young officers said enthusiastically. "Right, Captain?"

"Let us hope, Mr. Ponsonby," the Captain said, buttering a roll. He looked in Krause's direction and did a take. "Mr. Krause! What's wrong with your lip? Run into a hatch?"

Everyone looked at Krause's fat purple lip. Krause wanted to run and hide, but mumbled something about an accident.

I thought it behooved me to do the charitable thing and rescue him. "Who's idea was it," I asked the Captain, "to use the beast as a ferryboat?"

"Mine," Pendergast said flatly. "There was a conventional vessel on this run before, and it was lost. Dr. Gutman said we can't underwrite scientific inquiry here. He's wrong in that: We can—if the knowledge gained is practical and useful. I headed the first expedition to study the megaleviathans. It was readily apparent to me that we could make an arrangement with the Arfies and use the beast to ship vehicles and passengers over this very important stretch of submerged Skyway." He took a sip of wine. "It was apparent when we learned that the mega feeds only once a year . . ."

"And just about swallows half an ocean when she does," one of the officers broke in, drawing a dark glance from Pendergast. "Sorry, sir," he said, and coughed quietly into his palm.

"For the rest of the time," the Captain went on, "the animal's digestive system is dormant—by a factor of ninety percent. It took some doing to find the right analogs to Terran histamine H_2 inhibitors, which we use in shutting it down completely."

"Why didn't you just build another conventional vessel?"

Knowing smiles around the table.

"The seas are very dangerous here," Dr. Gutman said.

"Yes," I said. "We found that out when we went swimming back on the island."

Raised eyebrows all around.

"You were very lucky," Gutman said. "More wine, my dear?" he asked Darla.

"Yes, thank you."

"The animal's reproductive cycle must be an amazing thing," Roland said, anticipating my next question.

"It is," Pendergast said, "from what we know of it. But to answer your implied question . . . no, megas don't mate in the conventional sense. They're hermaphroditic, but there the similarity to Terran biology breaks down. Dr. Gutman, you're vastly more qualified to speak on the subject."

Gutman went on at some length, lecturing on the sex life of the megaleviathan. No doubt the lecture was an old routine. All during it, I felt more eyes on me than there were on him, a feeling that had persisted since I sat down.

". . . and at various intervals," Gutman was saying, "quite without any warning that we've been able to discover, the mega gives birth to a relatively small life form that looks somewhat like a Terran dolphin. It's the product of some kind of parthenogenetic process which is also a complete mystery. The animal is born fully developed, and swims away. Sooner or later it comes wandering back and proceeds to swim up the main vaginal orifice of the mega, never to come out again. About a year after that happens, the mega disgorges an egg from the same opening. This sinks to the sea floor and buries itself in the mud. The egg is very large, by the way, about the size of an average house. Six years after that, from what we've observed, a new mega is hatched from the egg."

"Sounds as if the whole process is a closed loop, genetically speaking," Roland commented. "How do new genes find their way into the pool?"

"It's doubtful that a dolphinoid returns to fertilize the mega that birthed it, except by accident," Gutman said. "A simple tagging procedure would clear the matter up, but the little devils are frightfully hard to catch." He smiled wryly. "Besides, that's pure research, isn't it?"

"Well, if it's true, that opens the cycle up," Roland said. "Still, it's fascinating."

"Isn't it, though?"

"To me," Darla interjected, "the Arfbarfs are more interesting. I've been trying to think of a more striking example of interspecies cooperation. I don't think there is one in the known mazes."

"Strange you should say cooperation," Pendergast said. "Most people assume the megas are simply beasts of burden, but their relationship with the Arfies is a classic symbiosis."

"Really?" John said. "How does the mega benefit? It's easy to see that the Arfbarfs—"

Susan convulsed with another bout of giggling. "Sorry," she said, red-faced. "It's that name."

"Akwaterrans, then," John went on. "Living on one of these beasts should be very handy for an amphibious species—but the mega?"

"I'll sum it up in one word," Pendergast said. "Barnacles."

"Barnacles?"

"The native equivalent. Marine crustaceans that attach themselves to the sides and keel of the beast. They're very prolific in these waters. Over a very short time they can weigh a mega down, and if the Akwaterrans didn't clean them off and eat them, the mega would eventually founder and sink."

"I see," John said, and sat back as another steward poured coffee.

My food finally came, just in time for dessert. I tasted the grayish-green mass of stuff on my plate. It was awful.

"That one looks underdone," Pendergast observed.

"It's adequate. But if it's all the same to you, I'm going to bypass the main course and head straight for dessert. Is that cherries jubilee?"

"Yes. Freeze-dried, I'm afraid, and the brandy's domestic."

"I'm patriotic at heart."

All during dinner, Darla had been stealing glances at me, trying to divine my mood. She must have been having a rough time, because I was riding an express elevator to the roof. The Purple Pyrotechnic Pill was kicking in.

Listless conversation went on among the other guests until Roland turned to the Captain and said, "You've explained why the Arfbarfs and megas get along, but how does the ship contribute to the arrangement? Or does it?"

"Let me offer my own one-word explanation," Gutman said, after having polished off his dessert in three gulps. "Food." He handed the empty bowl to the steward for seconds. "Surprised? You'd think that with a sea teeming with life there would be no problem. But there is. Arfie crews are stratified according to a division of labor. There's a crustacean-scraping class, a pilot class, a fishing class—they need fish to supplement their diet—a young-rearing class, various other smaller ones, including an officer class. As a result, relatively few

Arfies gather food for the whole crew, and there is no crossing of class lines. Taboo. When the crew gets sociologically top-heavy, food-gathering becomes a problem. It's hard work scraping barnacles, as any swab can tell you. And as for fishing—"

"One-word explanation?" Pendergast scoffed. "I'll put it more simply, Mr. Yee. We won't scrape the keel for them, but we do help with the fishing, using nets, which the Arfies haven't got the hang of making yet. If you're an early riser, you might want to watch us trawl tomorrow morning."

"Thank you, Captain," Gutman said dryly.

A siren wailed somewhere in the ship, making me jump a little. The elevator was shooting through the roof.

"A little after-dinner entertainment, ladies and gentlemen," Pendergast said. He rose and went over to a set of double hatches on the far bulkhead. He opened them and walked out onto a small lookout deck. We all got up and followed.

Searchlight beams were sweeping the island, lancing out into the sea-sprayed night, but bright moonlight clearly revealed what was happening. The island was being invaded by a writhing mass of red spaghetti. Crimson tentacles were snaking their way from the shore toward a cluster of dome-huts, and hundreds of Arfies were on them like ants, hacking and cutting with sharpened seashells. Even with their numbers the Arfies were having a hard time checking the monster's progress. More clumps of tentacles oozed over the shoreline, separated, and began to flop and wriggle their way inland. More amphibians flung themselves at these, chopping and slashing with abandon. It was a nightmarish scene, overhung with orange clouds glowing spectrally with light from a bloated ruddy moon. It was the first time I heard the Arfies barking. The sound was a three-way cross between a bullfrog, a dog, and a good human burp. Pendergast's imitation had been accurate to a point, though emphasizing the canine element.

"Don't look too long, ladies and gentlemen," Pendergast said. "The gaze of the gorgon squid will turn you to stone." Turning to me he said, "You can see why a conventional ship is vulnerable in these waters, even a hydroskiff. And this is an average-size gorgon."

More tentacles boiled in the water around at least a quarter of the island's perimeter, slithering up on shore and coming inland to join the battle.

"It looks big enough to give the mega trouble," I said.

He shook his head. "They're big, but not big enough to take down a mega. It's after the Arfies."

The Arfies were sustaining casualties. We could see struggling forms wrapped in tentacles being dragged over the edge. I heard a beeping sound and turned to see Pendergast take a small communicator out of his vest pocket.

"Port battery reports ready, sir."

"Very well. Hold your fire." He looked at me, noticing my surprise. "We don't like to intervene unless we have to," he explained. "It's a natural check on their population."

I'm sure the Arfies are all for ecology, I thought, *but*...

We watched for about five minutes. The Arfies fought the gorgon to a standstill for a short period, but slowly the monster gained the upper hand, even though hundreds of severed tentacles lay everywhere, twitching and leaking dark ichor. Finally, a gargantuan head rose from the water a short distance from shore, and then a polyhedral eye surfaced, its facets fired with reflected moonlight. Pendergast lifted the communicator. "Take it out," he said quietly.

"Aye aye, sir!"

An exciter bolt sizzled from the ship, coming from above us and to our left. The eye steamed, then exploded, its liquid humors gushing out and running viscously down the side of the head. A high-pitched gurgling yell split the night. The monster began to withdraw, dragging its mass of limp tentacles away from the horde of defending Arfies. Within a minute, the last of it had retreated into the water.

When it was all over and we were back inside, relaxing over brandy and cigars, I remarked to Pendergast, "I'd say there was no question that the Arfies are sentient. They're tool-users."

"Many species use tools," he said, sounding a little defensive, "even have language abilities—Terran apes, for example, if you remember the old experiments in which they were taught sign language—but no one accuses them of being truly sentient. After all—"

"I wasn't making a political statement, Captain," I said to soothe whatever sore point I had touched. "It's also apparent that the Arfies have a definite niche here which humans can't compete for. No, I merely meant that it's hard to understand why the Skyway goes through here at all. It would seem that the Arfies have at least the potential to evolve into a technologically advanced race. Whoever built the Skyway seemed to want to avoid linking up worlds populated by advanced tool-users. None of the races we know have direct access to the Skyway from their homeworlds. The access portals are usually more than half a solar system away."

"I understand," Pendergast said, sipping brandy from a huge snifter. "But I can't give you a satisfactory answer."

"Which brings up another point," I went on. "To whom does this maze belong?"

Another sensitive area, if the strained expressions around the table were any indication.

"We think it may be a part of the original Terran Maze," Dr. Gutman said. "A lost part. I take it you've noticed we can breathe here unaided."

"So can some aliens. What makes you think it's a lost section of the Terran Maze?"

"What makes you doubt it?" Gutman riposted. "Surely not because it's so far removed from most of the Maze."

"I don't doubt it. I was merely asking." Gutman was right, but why was he being so touchy? It's true that as far as Euclidean space is concerned, mazes ramble all over the place, with some planets as much as a thousand light-years away from the home system.

"There is only one portal on Akwaterra," the Captain intervened. "However, there is another stretch of Skyway, also submerged, that leads to a dead end. No portal. We think it was the proposed site of the double-back portal to Seven Suns. You may be aware that there is an ingress spur on Seven Suns that no one seems to use."

"Could the portal be underwater?" I asked.

"No. It was never installed. Why not, is anyone's guess."

"Ran out of funds, no doubt," Gutman quipped, eyes atwinkle. "The bond issue didn't pass."

"You seem to be all questions tonight, Jake," the Captain observed.

"I have one more, possibly more important." I gestured around the room. "Where does all this come from? You said the brandy is domestic. Does that imply that you can sometimes get imported? Imported from where, and by whom?"

"Congratulations," Pendergast said. "You've asked a question that never occurs to most luck-throughs. They see we have some home industries here, and they assume that all goods must be homemade. Take the titanium this ship is made of, as an example. We have domestic steel here, but we haven't been able to locate any rutile deposits. No doubt they're submerged. We lack many things here. But what we can't make, the Ryxx sell to us."

"The Ryxx?" John gasped. "You mean there's a way back to Ryxx Maze from here?"

"Not by Skyway. But through normal space, yes."

John looked at him blankly. "Normal space?"

I said, "Do you mean that the Ryxx haul goods here by Skyway and return by starship?"

"Yes." Pendergast lit a slender, bright-green cigar. "A remote world of theirs happens to lie only twelve light-years from one of ours, which makes it a hell of a long trip at sublight speeds, but they don't seem to mind." He smiled. "Nobody thinks much of space travel on the Skyway, not when you can get in your vehicle and drive ten parsecs without leaving the ground. But the Ryxx never gave up their development of interstellar travel. Gives them a competitive edge."

"What do they take back?" I asked.

"In the mood for riddles?" he asked with am impish grin. "What's yellow and looks like gold and is worth going a long way for?"

"I see." It made sense. Gold and a few other precious metals are always worth the trouble. "You have gold here, I take it."

Everybody laughed. "Yes," the Captain said, looking around at the lustrous walls. "You'd never know it, would you? Yes, we've plenty of it, but we can't eat it. Perfectly useless substance, which makes it a perfect medium of exchange, even among alien races."

A steward came in and whispered something into the Captain's ear. Pendergast looked at me.

"Seems there's a call for you at the desk, Jake."

20

ON THE WAY to the desk I was worried. Only Lori would be calling, and that possibly meant trouble. I had received her code-note just before leaving to shop. I was worried for other reasons too. I'd come away from the dinner with the vague impression that Pendergast was in on everything. That meant we could be prisoners on this ship. I was concerned for the Teelies especially. I had told them to get lost after dinner, get out into the nightlife, go to the casino, go dancing, anything. Keep to public places. But where were they to go now?

The clerk on duty put a phone in front of me, a boxy affair made of a coarse-grained wood, like the ones in the room. I picked up the receiver.

"Yes?"

"I have your jacket," a male voice said. "Want to come and get it?"

"Who is this?"

"The guy who owns the car you stole."

The pill made my mouth work before I knew what I was saying. "The guy who owns the car I stole. Well, well. No fooling. What can I do for you?"

"You can come up to my cabin and get your jacket, and let me take a poke at you."

"Least I could do. Right? Let me ask you this. How do you know I stole your vehicle, or that I stole anything?"

"A little birdie told me."

It was an expression I hadn't heard in a long while. In fact, something about his accent rang bells all the way back along my lifeline. He had a true American accent, and to me he sounded like what most people accuse me of sounding like—an anachronism. I remembered what he had yelled at us as we had pulled away in his vehicle: *lousy bastards*.

"Your little birdie is full of *merte*."

"Look, Mac. Next time you steal a car, don't leave a jacket with your name on it lying around . . . like on the front seat. Dig?"

Dig? "Okay," I said. "You have me. Now what?"

"Like I said, come on up and get it. I'd like to meet you anyway. It's not everyone who can handle my car and survive." He chuckled. "Don't worry, I won't start swinging at you. It was a hell of a merry chase, but I got my car back. So, no hard feelings. I was going to shoot that potluck anyhow."

"You were? How did you get here? And how did you know I shot the potluck?"

"How did I know? You must be kidding. Half of Maxwellville was on your tail, pal. I just got in line. How did I get here? I bought an old bomb at the used car lot, that's how. Paid top dollar for the goddamn thing. Cleaned me out! On second thought, I ought to punch your lights out just for that."

I was marveling at the grammar, the vocabularly—"bomb" for substandard vehicle, the use of "dollar"—the red-white-and-blue, good-natured gaucherie of expression. It was a voice from the past, my past, eons ago, hundreds of light-years away.

"Well? You gonna come up?"

"What's your cabin number?"

"Three twenty-two, B Deck. Got it?"

"Got it."

"I'll be here." He hung up.

First, I had a call of my own to make. I automatically stabbed a finger at the base of the instrument, then saw there were no touchtabs. I asked the clerk how to put a call through.

"The operator, sir. Just hang up and pick it up again."

I did, and a woman's voice got on the line, asked me for a cabin number. I gave her Paul Hogan's.

"Yes?" He sounded uneasy, his voice hoarse.

"Paul? Jake. Wanted to know if you'd had dinner."

Silence. Then he asked thickly, "Did you send them?"

"Send who?"

"You're lying."

"No, really. What happened?"

His breath came noisily into my ear. "Three men. They wanted your Cheetah. Thought I had it."

"I see. No, I didn't send them. Did you recognize them?"

Another pause. "Yeah."

"Corey Wilkes' boys, right?"

"You son of a bitch!"

"I said it wasn't me, Paul. He's your connection—correct?"

A burst of obscenity, then he hung up.

"Weird Bastard," I muttered into a dead phone.

Darla had done her job well.

I was flying. The Purple Pyrotechnic Pill was shooting off the grand finale as I stood in front of Cabin 322. It took me a while to settle myself down. I knocked, and the door immediately flew open, startling me a little. By that time, seams in the carpet were unsettling me. But my emotional states were changing rapidly, like a flutter of card faces in a shuffled deck.

A young man had opened the door. He was tall, with light close-cropped hair, wearing a white pullover shirt and black trousers, black boots. He looked very young without benefit of anti-g's, maybe twenty or so. When I saw him, I forgot about being startled and felt fine. He looked friendly enough, but then I got edgy again and balked at going in, even when he smiled amiably, stood aside, and gestured me through. Then in another second I was okay again and stepped in.

But as soon as I was astride the open hatch, I got an overpowering urge to shove it away, back against the bulkhead. I did it forcefully, and the hatch hit something, connecting with a body behind it, someone hiding. I drew the .44 and threw my weight up against the hatch and pushed. The kid leaped toward the other end of the room, but I didn't worry about him; he looked as if he was on my side at the moment. He flew over an armchair and surprised another ambusher hiding behind it. Meanwhile, I shouldered the hatch and squashed whoever was back there one more time for good measure, then threw it aside. One of Wilkes' bodyguards stood there against the wall, rocking back on his heels, looking at me abstractedly. Then the whites of his eyes rolled around and he slid to the floor with his back against the bulkhead, squatted for a second, and fell over. I kicked the dropped gun away and turned to see the kid wrestling with another man behind the overturned chair. I went over and whacked the bodyguard's head when he came rolling around, the pill making me misjudge the force of my swing. I hit him very hard. His head crinkled like a hotpak carton under the heavy wood-and-metal grip.

The kid hauled himself off the floor, and I went to check the corridor. I closed the hatch and kept one eye on him as I looked over the first man. This one was merely out cold, but his comrade would need medical attention. The kid picked up a gun and tucked it into his belt, then came toward me.

"Nice move," he said. "How did you know he was behind there?"

"I didn't," I told him. "Any more of them?"

"There was another one, but he left. These two had their guns at my head all during our phone conversation. What's this all about, anyway?"

"Wish I knew exactly," I answered, "but the gist of it is, they want something I have."

"Really? And here I thought they wanted my car."

"The Chevy?"

He was mildly surprised. "You know antique vehicles? Most people don't."

"Not really. But I've been wanting to talk to you about that buggy of yours. Exactly where did you get it?"

He went over to the dry bar and poured himself a drink. "Care for a snort?" he asked.

"No, thanks. Is it an alien-made vehicle?"

"It's a long story," he said. "Some other time." He walked to the bed where a pile of clothes lay heaped and pulled out my leather jacket. "Here," he said, tossing it to me.

I let it drop, still holding my gun at my side.

"Take it easy," he laughed, going back and pouring himself another drink. "If these jokers are out to get you, you have my sympathy. Not necessarily my help, but my sympathy. Aside from the sock in the nose I owe you, we don't have any problems. Put that six-gun away."

I did, and sat down on the bed. "One thing. Did they tell you to call at the desk and have me paged?"

"Yeah. Why?"

"You didn't try my room first?"

"No, but they did mention you were dining with the Captain. That help?"

"Yes, thanks." I picked up the jacket and put it on. It felt strange to get back inside it. "Sorry about your vehicle. It was a case of desperate need."

"So I gathered. And I was stupid enough to leave it at the curb with the motor running. If you'd've tried starting it—"

"We found out what happens then, believe me."

"I figured as much. You have to disarm the antitheft gear before you start. Is that why you ditched it?"

"Ditched? Uh, yeah, that was why."

I watched him pour another bolt of straight liquor from a dark brown bottle, down it, then grimace. "Rotgut," he gagged.

"You said you were going to shoot the potluck on Seven Suns. Why?"

"I'm trying to get back home," he said, as if the statement were self-explanatory. I made no comment.

After a moment, I asked, "When you found your car, did you see anyone lurking around there? Reticulans, maybe?"

"Yeah, as a matter of fact, I did see two Rikki cars, but that was down near . . . what's the matter?"

I was on my feet, ripping off the jacket. I flung it to the floor and stared at it. As soon as I had put it on, I had had a relapse of the itchy creeps, but this time it was stronger, and different. There was something *on* that jacket. Bugs. No. Not bugs. Something else, but I couldn't see what it was. But it was *right there*. A convulsive shudder went through me.

"Hey, are you all right?"

I sat down and tried to get a grip on things. "Do you see something?" I asked, a panicky breathlessness in my voice.

"Your eyes look kind of funny. Are you on something?" He looked around. "Where?"

"Right there," I said, pointing. "The jacket."

"No," he said. "What do you see?"

I tore my eyes from it. "Nothing. Forget it." I sat there while my mind raced in neutral. I felt compelled to get up and run from the room, but couldn't quite come to a decision to make the first move. "Maybe I should have that drink," I said.

"Sure. You seem jumpy as hell. Not that I blame you." He stepped to the bar and poured me a glass. "These two punks are enough . . ." He stopped and laughed to himself. "You know, where I come from, that word doesn't mean what it does here. I have to watch myself sometimes in mixed company."

"Word?" I said emptily, not really listening.

"Punk. The way I learned it, the word has nothing to do with sex, except when one of them tries to put a move on your kid sister."

With difficulty, I plodded back to the conversation. "Where are you from? I mean, on Terra. You weren't born out here."

"I'm from the States. L.A. Santa Monica, really."

"'The States'? Not too many people call it that anymore."

"I guess not." He brought the drink over. "I'll never get used to calling the country I was born in 'New Union of Democratic Republics.'"

I took the glass of whiskey and upended it into my mouth. I tasted nothing at all. "We should leave," I said.

The one by the hatch groaned.

"You're right. What the hell should we do with them, though?"

"Leave them. Pack up and go down to the desk, get another cabin. Say you have some noisy neighbors. If you can't get one, you can move in with us."

"Good idea. Thanks." He dragged out a satchel from under the bed and began to stuff it with the mound of personal effects and rumpled clothes. "Are there more where these came from?" he asked.

"Yes," I answered. "And Rikkis, too."

"Jesus, those mothers give me the willies. I hear once they start chasing you, they don't quit. I've also heard that—" He stopped, straightened up, and wiped his forehead with a sleeve.

"What is it?"

"Goddamn headache," he said, his expression pained. "Jesus! That came on quick. Must've racked my head up against something."

I sprang to my feet and stood there, immobilized. "Let's go," I said. "Now!"

"You're a bundle of nerves, do you know that? Take it easy. Didn't you lock the door?" He knitted his brow, rubbed the back of his neck, then looked around. "Do you hear something?"

"Like what?" I said breathlessly.

"A buzzing sound. What the hell is it?"

21

THE NEXT FEW minutes . . . hours . . . I couldn't tell which, were a dream remembered, then dreamed again. The last thing I recall clearly was watching the kid put his hand to his head and slowly sit down on the bed. I was rooted to the spot. Gradually, I grew aware of people around me, then of hands gripping my arms and leading me down corridors, endless corridors, then finally into another room.

Voices. I was seated in a chair but couldn't move, staring at the ceiling, watching pretty afterimages from the glare of the overhead lights. For the first time, I noticed that they weren't biolume panels, but glowing tubes, fluorescent tubes, recessed into the ceiling.

"Do you think he knows?" somebody whispered.

Another voice: "Careful. He may be coming out of it."

The second voice I recognized. Corey Wilkes.

"Darla-darling," the first voice said, "can you think of anywhere the creature might be?"

"No," Darla answered. "Is Pendergast searching?"

"I assume. Corey?"

"Yes, but the crew's busy as hell," Wilkes said. "Something about another ship out there, following us."

"I think it's imperative we find her before we make Seahome," the first voice said. "She could slip off the ship easily."

"You're absolutely right, Van," Wilkes said. "But one thing worries me. The story he told Darla about Hogan was to throw us off the track, of course, but he may have given her to one of the other passengers after all."

"Then, what the girl told us isn't true?"

"No, she's probably telling the truth, but Jake may have taken her from the hiding place and then given her to someone else, just to further muddle things." Wilkes laughed mirthlessly. "Of course, all of this is predicated on the assumption that the creature *is* the Roadmap, and we only have Darla's word on that. Frankly, I'm still a little skeptical."

"Darla?" Van said. "Can you convince him?"

"She's the Roadmap," Darla said flatly. "But before you get anything useful from Winnie, I want some assurance that you'll let him go."

"That was the agreement, Darla-darling, but . . . Corey, we can't speak for the Reticulans, can we?"

"No," Wilkes said. "He's their sacred quarry. There are ceremonies to be performed, obligations to discharge."

"Then what we agreed—you're backing out?"

"Not us, Darla."

"I assure you," Darla said coolly, "that you'll get no further help from me interpreting for Winnie."

Wilkes was unruffled. "Oh, that may not be *quite* the problem you think it is. Granted, it's your field, and all, but I may be able to find someone else."

"In the Outworlds?"

I could almost hear Wilkes' Cheshire-cat grin. "Don't worry, Darla, we'll let him go. And I'm sure I can persuade the Rikkis to let him loose. They relish the hunt even more than they do the kill. But they will continue to track him down."

"Then it's agreed," Darla said quietly.

A shadow moved in front of me, but I didn't take my eyes from the light.

"I want to hear more about the maps," Wilkes said. "You said you wrote something down."

A rustling of paper. Then Wilkes said, "Well, this looks like the Perseus arm . . . and here's the Orion, I suppose. Uh-huh. Fine. So, it's a simplified map of this part of the galaxy, so far as anyone knows. And these lines are major Skyway routes?"

"Yes."

"What about these Xs all over the place?"

"Open clusters, I think. Winnie calls them 'tangle-many-trees.' Thickets."

"How charming. But there has to be more to it than this. What about this . . . this epic poem you mentioned? Can you recite some of it?"

"I'll try. Winnie's pidgin English is awfully difficult to render into something coherent. But parts of it go like this: 'These are the Paths through the Forest of Lights, and this way you shall go to find Home. In the land of bright water, keep the sun at evening on the right hand and follow the path to the great trees at the edge of the sky. . . .'"

"That's a portal, I take it?"

"Yes. 'Pass through them but do not touch, for they clutch like the'—and here's an untranslatable word, but I think it's the name of a plant that preys on small animals '—and you will come to the land of white rock that is cold to the touch.'"

"Now, that sounds like Snowball to me," Van said.

"Yes." Wilkes wasn't sure. "Go on, Darla."

"'Again, at evening keep the sun, which is small and dim, at the right hand and follow the Path to the great trees which grow here out of the white rock. Pass through them, but do not touch, for they clutch . . .' That stanza keeps repeating. Anyway, it goes on like that, endlessly."

"Not coherent?" Van laughed. "It even scans."

Silence, except for the sound of pacing.

Finally, Wilkes said, "I'm not sure I buy it."

"Corey, Darla's telling the truth."

"I don't doubt her, Van. I simply doubt that this could be the map. Why hasn't anyone got wind of this before? Winnie couldn't be the only member of her race who's privy to this mythology."

"No," Darla said, "but she could be one of an exclusive group of initiates. A secret order. Primitive human tribes have them."

"I see what you mean. But why haven't the exopologists gotten any hint of this?"

"Lack of basic field research," Darla explained. "It's tough to get a permit to study anything on Hothouse."

"And we know why that is," Van said. "The Authority doesn't want any scientific corroboration that the Cheetahs are truly sentient and deserve protection."

More pacing. "But how long will the knowledge stay secret?"

"I'm not worried," Van said. "I doubt that the Authority will ever lift its de facto ban on exopological field studies on Hothouse as long as the planet is a source of drugs. Of course, there's always a chance someone may find out, but it's a calculated risk."

Again, a shadow crossed my field of vision.

"Corey, you may have your doubts about Winnie's map, but I have my own as to whether this is the best way to go about preventing this map, or any map, from getting wide circulation. This Paradox business, I mean."

"Do you still think we can do anything back in T-Maze?"

Van sighed. "No, I suppose not. From what Darla's told us, Grigory wasn't any closer to ferreting it out of the dissident network than we were. That's why he went after Jake. Right, Darla?"

"Grigory was never convinced that the map was more than a myth," Darla said. "But it's true that the map is in the hands of the dissidents. Jake as much as gave it to them when he plunked it down on Assemblywoman Miller's desk."

"And why in the name of God did he do *that?*" Wilkes wondered, more to himself than to anyone. "At any rate, this was after he returned from his . . . quest, heroic journey, back from the future or the past or wherever the hell he went." Wilkes began pacing again. "But Miller is in a psych motel, isn't she?"

"She doesn't have the map, nor does she know where it is," Darla said. "By now it's probably been copied and recopied several times over. No telling how many people have it now."

"Which is why," Wilkes said pointedly, "we're doing it this way. Stop Jake here, intercept him and get the map, and it never gets back to T-Maze. Things go back to the way they were before."

"Or the whole universe disappears, us with it," Van said gloomily.

"In that case, we'll never know what hit us. As painless a death as you could hope for. But that's doubtful. Paradox is built into the Skyway, if you believe legends, and I do. The universe can surely survive a Paradox or two."

"But . . . it already *happened,*" Van persisted, unconvinced. "They have the map. I just don't see how we can change that one immutable fact. And as long as the dissidents have it and the Authority doesn't, everything's fine. Why fiddle with it?"

"How can you think like that, when at least a dozen dissident leaders were arrested not a few days ago? The Authority's closing in, Van."

"Yes, I suppose it is," Van said dejectedly. "I was hoping against hope that somehow we could avoid all this."

"So was I," Wilkes said. "But even if what Darla says is true and the Authority doesn't know about the Roadmap yet, surely Grigory will be able to convince them sooner or later."

"That's what I don't understand. How can he convince them if he isn't convinced himself? Darla?"

"You must understand," Darla explained, "that Grigory had been acting pretty much on his own. He was kicked upstairs to his job, and he resented it, but his professional dedication was unswerving. You know how he is, Van. It's essentially a public-relations job, investigating strange phenomena and manufacturing explanations for public consumption. Not a day goes by when someone doesn't report having a visitation from the Roadbuilders. You've heard the stories. Usually no reliable witnesses, no corroborating evidence. Just wild stories. The Roadbuilders will return someday and make the road free again, abolish all oppressive governments, open up the entire Skyway to every race. That sort of thing. If you believe the stories, the Roadbuilders have handed out hundreds of maps to humans and nonhumans alike, but no authentic artifacts have ever materialized. It was Grigory's job to debunk all the stories, kill the hope that generates them, the hope that people have of someday getting the Authority off their backs. That's why the Authority can't really bring itself to believe in the map unless it has its nose rubbed in it. I agree with Van that Grigory—if he's alive, which I doubt—won't be able to convince the Authority, even if he comes to believe in the map himself, which I also doubt."

Wilkes said, "And this Eridani creature is the key to the whole thing. Is that what you'd have us believe?"

"As far as I can tell, she is."

"Well, I have no problem with that," Van said. "There's certainly something to it. Maybe it's not a complete map, or an accurate one, but it's a *map.*"

"As I said," Darla told them, "I haven't had the time or the opportunity to study Winnie's drawings. You'll have to make the final judgment, based on the evidence."

"If only we had more to go on," Wilkes complained.

"Only Winnie can give us more information," Van said. "But we have to find her first."

"We'll find her," Wilkes said confidently. "Darla, can you be sure that Winnie's journey-poem clearly reveals that there's a way back to T-Maze through Reticulan territory?"

"No. That fragment was all I had time to translate. Lots of distractions, and then Jake spirited her away. But back on the island I specifically asked her if she knew a way home. That's when she started reciting the poem."

"A way home," Wilkes repeated. "Hmm."

"I think he's coming around."

It was like a camera coming into focus, suddenly, and there in front of me was the tall, white-haired man I'd seen at Sonny's, Dr. Van Wyck Vance, wearing a midnight-blue jumpsuit. He was smoking a cigarette wrapped in tan-colored paper, blowing smoke at me. I looked at him. It was just like the last time; I was abruptly awake, aware . . . but this time I could recall clearly what had happened when I was under. The entire preceding conversation settled into my forebrain as if it had been recorded and just now fed in.

Wilkes was seated in an armchair to my right, Darla on the bed across the room. Vance was standing in front of me.

"Hello, Jake," Wilkes said.

I nodded, then turned to Vance.

"I don't think we've been introduced," he said. "I'm Van Wyck Vance."

"I know," I told him. "I've met your daughter, Daria. She speaks highly of you."

They turned to Darla, who shook her head.

"How did you know?" Vance asked.

"A little birdie told me."

Vance took a thoughtful puff on his cigarette, then shrugged. "Well, you said he was resourceful, Corey."

"Yes, he is," Wilkes said.

Darla said, "Jake, Daria is a name I rarely go by. Van always called me Darla."

"Her mother named her," Vance said, sitting down next to his daughter. "I never cared for it. I remember when she used to come home in tears—her schoolmates were teasing her by calling her 'Diarrhea.' Remember, Darla-darling?"

"I'm glad to say I've repressed that."

Vance laughed.

I was sitting in another armchair with nothing binding me, and I thought now would be a good time to get up. I started to.

"Roadmap!" Wilkes said sharply.

I was startled enough to plop back down, then looked around for someone with a gun. Nobody was holding one on me. I felt weak. My head felt like a ball of fuzz sitting on my shoulders.

"You won't be able to get up, Jake," Wilkes informed me. "I planted the posthypnotic suggestion while you were under. Actually, I should say post*hypnogogic*. This thing doesn't induce a standard hypnotic trance." He held up a thin bright-green tube about half a meter long. "Subjects are ten times more suggestible under it. Even consciously being aware of the plant doesn't break the spell."

"The Reticulans are very good at mind-control technology," Vance said.

"Unfortunately," Wilkes said, "they don't know enough about human physiology yet to make this thing really useful. Twrrrll tells me they're working on it, but we're still as much a mystery to them as they are to us. If you were a Rikki, Jake, you'd be my obsequious slave, and would tell me anything I'd want to know, or do anything I'd want you to do. As it is, all the wand does to humans is either knock 'em out or turn them into shambling hulks in a highly suggestible state—and I'm not enough of a psychometrician or a hypnotist to always get the results I need." He brandished the wand at me in the manner of a headmaster reprimanding a wayward pupil. "You're a tough customer, mister, I'm not at all sure I could make you tell me where you've hidden your little alien friend—and even if I could, I have the sneaking suspicion I'm going to need your active cooperation to actually get hold of her. You've got her stashed with somebody on board, somebody—a group, I bet—with whom we can't readily punk around. A gaggle of Buddhist nuns . . . boy scouts . . . the damn Archbishop of Seahome and his acolytes. I wouldn't be surprised. You're *slippery,* Jake. Slippery. No, I'm afraid I'll have to resort to old-fashioned methods of persuasion. Meantime . . ." He stroked the wand lovingly. "This gizmo will keep you right where I want you."

Vance said, "I suppose a truth drug wouldn't do either?"

Wilkes shook his head disdainfully, continuing to caress the wand.

"Ingenious little things," he went on. "Very powerful. The effect can cover a city block. You adjust the field-strength here." He fiddled with one end of the rod, which was ringed with a wide silver band. "This doodad here. The only drawback is that the effect can be thwarted by taking a simple tranquilizer. Of course, if the subject doesn't know that . . ."

"Tranquilizer?"

"Yes. You'd think the opposite would be true, wouldn't you? A high-altitude pill of some kind. An antidepressant. The way I understand it, that does almost no good at all."

"Almost," I said, feeling foolish.

"Why, are you on something? You did seem to be semiaware while you were under. Good try, Jake."

"Seemed like a hell of a good idea at the time."

"I'm curious, though. Did you actually know about the dream wand? Did you happen to be awake that night when we walked in at the commune?"

"Commune?"

"The religious group's place. When a subject's already in normal sleep, there's no awareness of going under."

I looked at Darla briefly. She looked slightly confused, so I thought it would be better not to mention the wand's use at the Militia station.

Wilkes picked up the byplay and looked at Darla, then at me. "Something?" he asked.

"We do have the mystery of Jake's escape from the Militia station to explain," Vance reminded him.

"Oh, yes. Twrrrll was sure he detected another wand in operation there. But that was most likely the Ryxx, don't you think?"

"How did they get hold of a dream wand?"

"Oh, the Ryxx are master traders. They probably paid the right price to a renegade Rikki and got it. Or they may have a similar technique of their own. Besides, we did see two Ryxx nearby."

Vance grunted noncommittally.

"Who knows?" Wilkes conceded. "They may not have done it, but they have just as much reason as we do to keep the map secret. Granted, it's hard to understand why they didn't grab Jake as soon as he came out, or *try* to, anyway. But they didn't.

And I'm not going to waste time wondering why. Someone got him out of there, for whatever reason."

I said, "May I ask a question?"

"Sure," Wilkes said.

"Why did you come to the Teelies' farm that night?"

"You'd have to see to understand. Darla, would you call Twrrrll in here?"

Darla didn't get up. Vance rose and said, "I will." He went to the connecting hatch, opened it, and called the alien's name.

After a moment, Twrrrll came in. It struck me how tall he was, how sickly thin his limbs were, and how they contrasted with his seven-digited, powerful hands, hands that could envelop a human head and squeeze. His feet were huge as well. He wore no clothing except for crisscrossing strips of leatherlike material that wrapped his thorax like a harness.

"May I be of serrrvice?" the alien asked.

"Jake would like to see the *mrrrllowharrr,*" Wilkes said.

"Verrry well."

It was a strange sensation to see him undrape an invisible something from his shoulders and cradle it in his hands. Stranger still to watch him stroke it with two fingers and trill to it softly. As he did so, something even more unsettling was happening to my perceptual apparatus. It wasn't like watching something flicker into existence out of thin air. No, not like that at all; for the thing was there all the time. Everyone has had a similar experience. You look and look for a misplaced object, something you just had a minute ago but inexplicably misplaced, like a pen on a desktop. You search and search and can't find it, until someone points it out for you and it's right under your nose. The thing in the alien's hand existed, was there, but the fact simply had not registered in my brain. All at once the animal materialized, but I knew it had been there all along. I had seen it, but had not recorded it as a datum.

"It still amazes even me, Jake," Wilkes said.

It was a match for the caterpillar-snake thing Susan had accidentally killed at the farm, its pink brain-bud glistening moistly in the overhead light. I felt queasy, desperately hoping my worst fears were unfounded.

"It was with you all the time, Jake. On your jacket, most of the time. Probably right under your collar, tucked away safe and snug."

I felt like throwing up. "How?" I said in a strangled voice.

"Strange survival tactic. Marvelous, really. Not visual camouflage, but *perceptual* camouflage. God knows how it's done, but the animal makes its predators forget it's there. Some extrasensory power, no doubt. Your perception of it gets shunted directly to the preconscious, bypassing the primary perceptual gear. Is that basically the way it works, Twrrrll?"

"Yes. We would use different terrrminology, perhaps. But yes."

"Trouble is, the *mrrrllowharrr* is very sluggish, which makes it vulnerable when it gets underfoot. Isn't that what happened at the farm?"

I took my eyes from it.

"Darla?"

"Yes. One of the Teelies accidentally stepped on it."

"We were hoping that's what happened, and that you hadn't become aware of it somehow. Its hold on the mind isn't absolute. We couldn't locate the carcass, but Twrrrll convinced us to take a chance and plant another one, this one's mate. We put it on your jacket, which you conveniently left outside your sleeping egg."

"Why?" was all I could say.

"It leaves a psychic trace, Jake. The Reticulans can follow it anywhere. Even through a potluck portal."

The alien left and closed the hatch, leaving behind the smell of turpentine and almonds.

"All that nonsense at the restaurant," I said when my stomach had quieted down. "It was only to plant that thing on me?"

"Right, and I nearly ran out of chitchat before that thing finally made it over to you, crawling over the floor."

"Then why the gunplay?"

Wilkes triumphant smile dissolved. *"That . . ."* He grunted. "That was a mistake. Rory—the one who drew on you—is a little dim. Likable, but dim. I mentioned that we wanted to throw a scare into you. To Rory that meant he should wave his gun around. I, uh, had to let him go, of course. Luckily, Darla was there to save the day." He studied my face, as if watching a seed that he had planted take root.

"I didn't know, Jake," Darla said in a low voice. "Not about the *mrrrllowharrr*. I didn't see the thing."

"Corey, really," Vance said deploringly. "Jake's opinion of my daughter must be low enough. Do you have to rub it in?" To me he said, "Darla wasn't working for us then." He turned to her with a thin smile. "And I'm not even sure she's with us now. Are you, Darla-darling?"

"You know where my loyalties lie, Van," Darla said resentfully.

"I do? Maybe you'd like to remind me once again."

"It isn't important. The deal is that I hand over Winnie to you . . . correction. That was the deal before Winnie disappeared. The deal is now that I help you find her in exchange for leaving Jake alone. I go back to T-Maze with you, using your secret route through Rikki country." Darla looked at me. "You were right, Jake. There is a way back from here."

"But we're not letting it get around," Wilkes said to me in a stage whisper.

"I know," I said. "And I know about the antigeronics you're running into the Outworlds. Neat little scheme, and one hell of a big market to have cornered."

"Nothing gets past you, does it?" There was a sort of admiring awe in Wilkes' voice. "Go on, Darla."

"When we get back, I alert the dissidents to destroy all copies of the map. Anyone who has had anything to do with it will have to go underground, take to the road until the crackdown runs its course. The movement will be hurt, but at least the Authority won't get the Roadmap. Meanwhile, the secret will be safe with us."

"And what about Winnie?"

"She can be taken back to Hothouse and left with the movement network there. As far as I know, nobody knows about her yet, not even the dissidents. They may have the map, but they aren't aware of its source. I can't be absolutely sure, but it's a good bet even Grigory never realized her significance. He never mentioned her to me."

"Hmm." Wilkes brought his palms together and touched both index fingers to his lips. "We have some problems here. Namely, you yourself are wanted by the Authority. If you're caught, you'd have a hell of a time explaining how you got back from a potluck portal."

"I won't have to. Nobody saw us shoot it, or knows that we did, except you and your partners."

"And Grigory."

"Grigory's dead."

"Do we know that?"

"I told you what happened on Seven Suns."

"Yes, and you haven't played your role as grieving widow very convincingly."

"You must know I signed a life-companionship contract with

Grigory for other than personal reasons."

Vance said, "When everything is secured back in the Maze, Darla will come back here with me."

Wilkes brooded. "All very well and good, but still . . ."

Somewhere in the room, Sam's key beeped.

"Aren't you going to answer it, Darla?" Vance asked. "Only polite."

Darla took it out of her pocket, then threw it across the room to me. "He should," she said.

I picked it up and looked at Wilkes.

"Is there a camera on that thing, Jake?"

"Yes."

"Set it up on that table, will you please? And point it at me."

I did, and opened the circuit, then sat back down.

"Hello, Corey! Long time no see, and all that merte."

"Hi, Sam. Your son is our guest."

"So I gathered. What's up?"

"We want the Eridani creature."

"Uh-huh. Can't help you, Corey."

"That's too bad."

"Sorry. These sailors down here ought to be able to tell you she hasn't shown up."

"They were posted after we learned about the girl. She could have brought the creature down before that."

"Girl?"

"Yes, the sailor-girl Jake recruited to help him hide the creature. Before we knew about it, we assumed Winnie—is that her name?—we assumed she was still topside with Jake. And then Jake dragged a red herring in our path. Nice touch." He turned to me. "Where in the world did you meet Hogan, of all people?"

"At a literary luncheon," I said.

Wilkes cackled. "Anyway. We still want her, Sam. And we're going to get her, or somebody's going to get hurt."

"Yeah, yeah. Corey, did anyone ever tell you that you were the slimiest piece of merte *ever to get flushed into a plasma torch?"*

Wilkes eyes flared. "Yes, several times, and in even more colorful language. Did anyone ever tell you that I was the one who had you killed?"

"You did? How?"

"Oh, it was beautiful. The people who got the contract

assured me it was foolproof. The man driving the buggy that ran into you did it deliberately. He had special impact padding, all kinds of anticrash gear. An expert. No one even began to suspect it was anything other than an accident."

"Congratulations. So what?"

Wilkes thumped a fist into his chest in mock pain. "Oh, Sam, you strike even from beyond the grave. Here I am, maybe the first murderer ever to have the satisfaction of gloating to his victim after the fact, and I can't get a rise out of you."

"You're talking to a machine, you know."

"Am I? I've heard that an Entelechy Matrix transfers a person's soul to a machine."

"Soul, my ass. Look, let's lose the verbal sparring and get down to cases. Exactly what's going to happen if you don't get Winnie, as if I didn't know?"

"You *don't* know." Wilkes sighed. "Oh, well. Come on, Jake. I want you to see this." He rose and crooked his finger at me, walking over to the connecting door. He opened it and pointed.

I got up and walked over, robotlike. I looked into the room. My eyes were drawn first to the sight of Lori. She was naked, slumped in a chair in a far corner, under the wand's spell. Then my gaze drifted to the four Reticulans, Twrrrll among them. They were regarding me impassively, standing around a strange piece of furniture, made of black wrought iron, which looked like a cross between a table and a bed. The legs were fashioned into alien animal limbs, adorned with ornamental tracery exhibiting runic symbols. An elaborate headboard was executed in the same manner. Across the top of the table lay a network of troughs, not unlike the bottom of a roasting pan, with tributaries branching out to the edge and running off into gutters that would conduct blood, or any kind of body effluent, down to the foot of the bed, there to spill into two large copper pails. The pails were chased with more cryptic markings. To one side stood a much smaller table done in the same style, upon which lay an assortment of strange bladed instruments.

"Roadmap!" Wilkes whispered hoarsely into my ear. The electric tension flowed out of me and I went limp, swaying on my feet. "The Reticulans have always been hunters, Jake. They never lost the impulse, as we did. It's still the driving thrust of their culture. Interesting, don't you think? Long ago they depleted their home planet of 'honorable game,' as they call it. Then they discovered the Skyway. You'd think fifty or sixty new planets would hold them for a while. But the Reticulans are an old race, Jake. One of the oldest on this part of the road. Very recently, a few hundred years ago, they took to hunting outside their maze. They're feared and hated everywhere, as well they should be."

He craned his head around to whisper in my other ear. "Can you imagine what it's like to be vivisected, Jake? That's how the Reticulans will honor you, their sacred quarry. Unless you hand over Winnie, in which case I might persuade them to let you loose for a little while longer. They probably consider it a challenge to track you without the *mrrrllowharrr.*"

He closed the hatch, then shoved me toward the chair. I sat down heavily.

"How much good will it do, Corey," I asked, "to tell you I don't know where she is?"

"None at all, I'm afraid," Wilkes said airily. He got a cigarette from a gold case on the table and lit it, blew smoke at the ceiling. "Your little girl friend says the same thing."

"What did she say?"

"She says she hid Winnie up on the poop deck in an unused radio shack. She went back later and the animal was gone."

"You don't believe her?"

"Yes, I do, but I can't believe both of you don't know."

"Winnie may have got frightened at something and run."

"Fine. Then Pendergast's people will find her eventually, and everything'll be wonderful. But I'm only giving you another hour, Jake. Then—"

"It's a big ship, Corey," Vance said, fiddling with my newly bought revolver. "Maybe we should give it a little more time."

"Okay, two hours." Wilkes threw up his arms. "Hell, I'll wait all night. I'm easy to get along with. But *somebody* knows where she is, and personally I think it's you, Jake. But we'll wait."

22

WE WAITED.

Conversation was desultory. Vance and Darla sat at a table at the other end of the room, drinking coffee brought in by another of Wilkes' bodyguards. At various intervals they all popped pills to keep up their immunity from the wand's effect. Wilkes told me it was still on low power.

At one point, Darla came toward me, bearing a cup and saucer.

"No, Darla," Wilkes told her.

She stopped. "You said he was your guest," she said sarcastically.

"Don't want you slipping him any tranqs."

"Do you think I would?"

"I don't know, and don't care to take the chance. But I don't want to be inhospitable. I'll pour him a cup." He got up and went to the table and did, then fetched it over to me. "Enjoy, Jake."

"Thank you." I sipped it and found that it wasn't coffee but some kind of grain beverage, with a bitter aftertaste.

"Corey," I said, "there's one thing that's been bothering me since the start of this thing."

"What's that?"

"Why didn't you just kill me?"

Wilkes looked over the newssheet he was reading. "Good question. You can't say I haven't had plenty of opportunity." He folded the sheet and put it aside, then went back to tapping on his lips with his fingers. "This damned Paradox thing set me to thinking. If I just up and killed you, it very well could have turned out that nothing would have changed. You'd be dead, and the map would still be in circulation, brought back from the Great Beyond by the 'you' that never died. Paradox. Or maybe there's really no Paradox and somebody else brought the map back—one of your religious friends, for instance. They could be in on the whole thing."

"They're not," Darla said emphatically.

Wilkes shook his head sadly. "Another statement that I can't accept at face value. For all I know, they could be part of your dissident network. Maybe they brought the map back and pumped Jake's image up into a legend. Who knows? No, I came up with a plan of sorts. I had to nab you, and I wanted to wait until you shot a potluck to be certain you had the map. After all, none of the stories about you say exactly *when* you got it."

"So you herded me through a potluck."

"Right, and it wasn't pure luck that you chose the Splash portal. If you think back over all the options you had, you'll find there were few. You could have gone elsewhere, however, which is why the *mrrrllowharrr* was necessary."

"Back at the motel—you sent your crew to flush me out of there?"

"Yes, to keep you running. Knew you'd find a way to escape, and you did. You're *slippery,* Jake." He kept crossing and uncrossing his legs in a compulsive, jerking movement. "Anyway. I had to get that punking map, find out . . . no! *First* I had to find out if it even existed, then find out where it came from." He looked uncomfortable. "And I still don't know."

"I'll tell you where it came from, Corey," I said. "You created it."

"How so?"

"If you'd have let me alone, I never would have hid out in that motel, never would have met Winnie, etcetera, etcetera."

He laughed. "The irony hasn't escaped me. Believe me, I've thought about it. But what was I to do? Talk about having few options. No matter what I did seemed doomed from the start. . . ." He trailed off and looked at the ceiling. "Well, that's neither here nor there," he added offhandedly.

After a pause, Vance said, "I wish you'd finish that, Corey. I'm still in the dark as to how getting the map now will alter reality or in any way change the fact that the dissidents have it." He got up from the table and walked over to Wilkes, stood over him, and said pointedly, "I really wish we could clear that up once and for all."

My head was beginning to congeal a little, but it had taken me the better part of an hour to think through what I said next. "There's nothing to clear up, Van," I blurted out. "Can't you see that your little drug scheme is going right out the port?"

He slowly brought his eyes around to me. "What do you mean?"

"He means to drive a wedge between us, Van," Wilkes said mildly. "Oldest trick in the book. Don't fall for it."

"Suddenly I'm very interested in what he has to say. What exactly did you mean, Jake?"

"First, tell me a few things. How did you get in on this, and why?"

He was annoyed. "Doesn't strike me as pertinent."

"Then we don't play."

He went over and sat on the bed, picked up the revolver and absently fiddled with it, looking at me.

"Thinking of shooting someone?" I asked.

"Huh?" Aware now that he had picked it up, he said, "No. Don't even know how this thing works." He tossed it aside, then glanced at Wilkes and looked back at me. "All right, you win. A little history. Word has been out for a year or two that I'm to be purged. Oh, it's an outdated word, of course. They want to ship me back to Terra for 'evaluation and reassessment.' Fortunately the mills of the Authority grind slowly, and I had some time. But where would I go? Easy. Someplace like the Outworlds. But the cost of living's pretty high here. And strictly cash, no Authority vouchers. I had no gold socked away to speak of. Of course, here you can go up into the hills and pan for it—they actually do that, you know—but I'm not the prospector type. Corey approached me about this drug thing. Sounded good, cornering the market and all that. He needed me, he said, to work out all the details about diverting raw material from Hothouse and secreting it out here." He shrugged. "I had no choice, really. I went along."

"Why the raw stuff?" I asked. "Why not the finished product?"

"Actually," Wilkes said, "that was my original idea. Van talked me out of it."

Vance nodded. "The controls are just too tight. The Authority guards its monopoly well. When you get right down to it, it's the source of their power."

"Okay," I said, "so you got the idea to process the stuff here."

"A big investment on my part," Wilkes reminded him. "You should keep that in mind, Van."

"I will. We have a small factory and lab near Seahome, about ready to become operational."

"And what about the Reticulans? What's their motivation for letting you truck gold back through their territory?"

"Same as anybody's," Wilkes answered. "They need gold as much as any race does for intermaze trade. I know it sounds mundane, but their economy is *royally* screwed up. Their social structure is top-heavy with nonproductive ruling classes who're preoccupied with quaint pastimes like hunting and riding eight-legged beasties around in the woods. They won't stoop to getting their hands dirty. Most technological things are left to slave classes. Beside, Reticulans think it more honorable to *take* by conquest rather than to create. Only the Roadbugs have prevented them from running amuck, taking over every maze in sight. So, they're hard up for cash." He extended a hand deferentially to Vance. "Sorry. You were saying?"

"I was about to say that when we heard the Roadmap rumors, we knew that it was only a matter of time before the Authority would come barging into the Outworlds. Anyway, that was my fear. I'd have no place to hide." He picked up the revolver again and began to twirl it on his finger. "Now. Tell me about how the whole plan is null and void."

I drained my cup and tried to put it on the lamp table next to me, but I misjudged and sent it clattering to the carpet. "Sorry. Could I persuade you to turn that gadget off? I'd rather have a gun leveled at me, or be tied up."

Vance looked at Wilkes tentatively, but Wilkes shook his head. "I'm a little shorthanded, Van. Jake has a habit of *brutalizing* my bodyguards." He gave me a grouchy look.

"No? Okay. Van, it looks to me like you're going to be up

merte creek without a paddle. Wilkes doesn't want to change reality, he just wants the map. Once he has it, he'll sell it to the Authority. Or to the Ryxx, or the Hydrans, or to the highest bidder."

"Beautiful, Jake, beautiful," Wilkes marveled.

Vance lowered his eyelids in deep thought. When he came out of it, he exhaled noisily. "I'm getting the distinct feeling that I've been very, very stupid."

The hatch opened, and Wilkes' bodyguard showed Pendergast in.

"Where the hell is the Peters girl?" the Captain bellowed at Wilkes.

It was the first time I'd seen Wilkes slightly embarrassed. "George, just a moment."

"She's a crewmember, Wilkes. You may be running the drug thing, but I'm still captain of this ship. If you've done anything to—"

Wilkes got up and hastened toward him, extending a placating hand. "In the hall, George, please. . . ."

"Oh, Captain? May I have a word with you?"

Pendergast spun around. "Who the bloody hell was that?"

Even I had forgotten that Sam's key was still sitting on the coffee table.

Wilkes motioned to his bodyguard. "Turn that thing off." To the Captain he said, "It's nothing. An open circuit to McGraw's rig computer."

Pendergast shouldered past him into the room. "What do you want?—wherever you are," he said looking around the room.

"Tell Mr. Wilkes what happens to the gizzard of a whale when it gets perforated by a floater missile. Go on, tell him."

Pendergast's brow furrowed into dark lines. He turned slowly to Wilkes. "You say this is a computer?"

"Entelechy Matrix," Wilkes murmured. "On the table there."

The Captain's eyes finally found it. "Let me tell you what happens," he barked at Sam. "The entire GI tract of the beast goes into convulsions. You wouldn't survive—" He halted, tongue-tied with the absurdity of what he had said. "Son of a bitch," he muttered.

"I might even stop breathing, huh?"

"What do you want?" Pendergast said evenly, walking toward the table.

"First, I want this hold cleared of your crew. Everyone.

And I mean up the elevator and out of scanner range. Second, I want my son and his companions delivered down here safe and sound."

"Your son?"

"McGraw," Wilkes supplied.

"It'll be done," Pendergast said.

Wilkes walked back into the room. "Captain, we can't, not just yet. He's bluffing."

"You know me well enough to know I'm not, Corey."

"I won't take chances with this ship!" Pendergast shouted.

"Sam," Wilkes said. "You'll have them when we have the creature."

"I said I wanted my son and his companions, and I meant all of them."

"You'll have them," Pendergast said, "and you'll have safe conduct to debark this ship. But I guarantee that you'll never make it off Splash."

"We'll take our chances."

"George," Wilkes said soothingly, putting a hand on his shoulder. "You forget that we don't have the creature to give. Another thing—the Reticulan's tracking technique is inoperative at this point. We could lose him for good."

Pendergast's eyes widened, and he turned his head sharply to the connecting hatch. "Is she in there?" he breathed. "With *them?"*

"You don't have to worry, Captain," I broke in, as things began to lose their dreamlike quality. I now realized why the coffee had tasted bitter. "They won't rip her apart. She's not sacred quarry."

Pendergast strode to the connecting hatch and threw it open savagely.

"No, but you are, Jake," Wilkes said darkly.

The Captain lunged at Wilkes, but the bodyguard got in the way. Pendergast elbowed him aside, but the boy brought his gun up menacingly. Pendergast stopped, his face dark with fury. "You think you can threaten me?" he growled at Wilkes.

"George, take it easy. I thought she was hiding something when you talked to her, and she was. Jake paid her a lot of money to hide the creature. I had to question her myself. She was in no danger."

Pendergast put a hand to his forehead, his rage suddenly ebbing. "What's going on?"

"The wand, George. You haven't taken the antidote."

The ship's warning siren keened again.

"What is it, George?"

"The pirate mega," Pendergast said, his voice detached.

"Pirate?"

"Yes. We've been tracking her. We're expecting an attack at dawn." He shook his head to clear it and rubbed his temples. His communicator began beeping inside his pocket, but he ignored it. "I've got to get out of here. I'm needed on the bridge." There was a distant look in his eyes, as if none of us were present. "Winds must have changed," he mumbled, then walked unsteadily out of the room.

"Jimmy, close the door," Wilkes said. He went to the coffee table and picked up Sam's key. "Sorry, Sam. He probably won't remember your threat, not for a while anyway."

"Corey, sometimes I have trouble understanding how you could be the same person who founded TATOO with me."

"We all change, friend."

"It's all unraveling, Corey."

"Not just yet," Wilkes said tightly, and shut the key off. "Tell Twrrrll to release the girl," he told Jimmy. "And the other one, too."

"Is it true, Corey?"

Wilkes turned to face Vance. "Is what true?"

"That you'll sell the map to the highest bidder?"

"No." Wilkes sat in the armchair. "Not to the highest bidder. I'd be a fool to sell it to nonhumans. What do you think homo sap's chances would be in a galaxy dominated by some alien race that got hold of the Roadbuilders' technology? What if, for instance, they"—he pointed toward the adjoining stateroom—"got hold of it? No, I'll give it to the Authority."

"I think your Rikki friends got the idea of going after the map a long time ago," I said.

"No doubt they did," Wilkes conceded.

Vance was struggling to understand. "But . . . you realize that to return with the map you'll have to travel through twelve thousand kilometers of Reticulan maze?"

"I'm not going back that way."

Vance was baffled. "How?"

"I'll go back by Ryxx starship."

"What?"

"Yes, they've got the time dilation down to three years, ship time. A long haul, but they have cold-sleep technology. Surprised? Didn't you know that the Ryxx don't mind taking human passengers? It's *expensive,* and they don't get many takers, but . . ."

"Yes, I knew. But the Ryxx want the map too!"

"Yes, but they don't know I have it—or will have it. They're after Jake, not me. They don't know me from Human One. And as far as I can tell, they don't know about Winnie either. How could they, if what Darla says is true?"

"What makes you think you can sell anything to the Authority?" Vance asked, disbelieving. "The Authority takes, it doesn't buy."

"It'll buy from me. You must know that yours isn't the only friendship I've cultivated in high places. Some of them are your friends, or were before you became an unperson. The transaction has already been arranged. And part of the price will be immunity from prosecution."

Vance paled. "What?"

Wilkes spoke to me. "You may remember that I mentioned something about your queering deals I had set up. I got word that our drug operation had been compromised. I really don't know who was responsible. As Sam said, things tend to unravel. Van, you didn't get wind of it for obvious reasons. But the deal was null and void long before any of this."

"So the Authority does know about the Roadmap," I said.

"Of course they do, and they've given up trying to get it from the dissidents—or rather, they're having a hard time. I told them I could get it for them."

"But you'll be gone for twelve years!" Vance said. "More!"

"Think again. Most people never consider the backward time displacement you undergo when you shoot a portal. But when you go back through normal space, you eat all that time back up. I should get back to T-Maze almost exactly at the same time I left. No Paradox, and it all works out very neatly." Wilkes licked his lips, his eyes focused somewhere in the air. "Or . . ." he went on abstractedly, ". . . or I just might try to find that backtime route. You did, Jake—or will, or shall . . . damn it, these verb tenses give me a headache! Anyway, if you can, I can, once I have the map."

"What about the Reticulans?" I asked.

Wilkes' face split into a gray-toothed grin. "We'll part company in Seahome, where I'll rent a long-distance vehicle and floor it for the planet where the Ryxx launch their ships. You can be sure I'll scour the buggy for *mrrrllowharrr*. I'll fumigate the punking thing."

Silence.

Vance was deeply depressed. Finally, he said, "Pendergast is going to be very interested in hearing this."

"But you won't be telling him, Van." Wilkes took out Darla's gun from under his jerkin. "Sorry, but until your last dose wears off, this will be necessary. Darla? You'd better come over here and sit with your dad."

Darla got up and began to walk over, but stopped when a knock came on the hatch.

"Get it," Wilkes told her.

Just then Jimmy came through the connecting hatch, shoving a sleepwalking Lori before him. He pushed her onto the bed, where she sprawled, naked and still out cold.

Darla threw the door open. It was John.

"Darla! Are you all right? You vanished . . . oh, dear." He saw Lori and stood there gawking.

"Come in!" Wilkes called brightly.

John averted his eyes from Lori, then smiled nervously. "Mr. Wilkes, I presume. I've heard a great deal—"

Jimmy reached out, grabbed him by the collar, and yanked him into the room. He checked the corridor and closed the hatch.

"And you are . . . ?"

"John Sukuma-Tayler. A friend of Jake's."

Wilkes rose. "John, it's a pleasure, but you caught us at a bad time. Won't you join your friends there on the bed? Jimmy, check him over."

Jimmy patted him down and pushed him toward the bed, made sure his boss was covering everybody, then went back into the Rikkis' stateroom. A moment later he returned, herding another zombie. It was the Chevy kid. Jimmy sat him down, and the kid keeled over onto a pillow.

"Couldn't you have *dressed* her?" Wilkes scolded his bodyguard.

"Ever try dressing a corpse?" Jimmy retorted.

"Check out the hall one more time, then go get her clothes, for God's sake."

"Right."

The pills Darla had dissolved in the coffeepot were taking full effect, but I couldn't be sure if I was free of the wand completely. Nevertheless, I was ready to make my move when Jimmy left—but a split second after Jimmy cracked the hatch,

Vance stood up suddenly, pointing the revolver shakily at Wilkes' back.

"Drop the gun, Corey."

"Van, sit down," Wilkes said irritably over his shoulder. "You'll hurt yourself with that old . . . *Van!*"

Wilkes' jaw dropped as Vance's finger jerked against the trigger. Vance clenched his teeth, finding it harder than he had thought to bring the hammer back without cocking it first. His left hand came up to help.

Surprised, Wilkes was slow to bring his pistol around, but Jimmy was quick. His shot sent a bolt scorching through Vance's skull, the mass of white hair exploding into flame. But the hammer came down. A thunderous explosion shook the room, and a weird dance of bodies began. Wilkes was spun around and yanked up and back like a puppet on strings, went lurching back toward the table. Vance's body marched backward like a ghost with a fiery head, hit the wall and rebounded, then teetered over. I was on the floor going for the dropped .44, trying to get furniture between me and Jimmy, but by the time I got to the gun he and Roland—who had come bursting through the hatch—were waltzing arm-in-arm into the room, each holding the other's gun arm, until Darla cut in with a chop to the back of Jimmy's neck, sending him down. Wilkes hit the table and the top part of it flipped up from the base, sending cups and silverware catapulting across the room to crash and ricochet off the walls. I was on my feet, rushing toward him. The gun was still in his hand, but I reached him just as he brought it up, and kicked it away. The fight was over. I picked up Darla's pistol and stood over him. Darla tore the blanket off the bed, sending Lori flopping to the floor, and rushed to Vance. Wilkes looked up at me, his face blank and stunned, a red flower blooming on his pretty white blouse.

"Roland!" I called. "Close the hatch!"

"Wait." He went to it and peeked out, then beckoned to someone. Susan poked her head in, and Roland pulled her through, then shut the hatch. Susan saw that John and everyone she knew was all right, then burst into tears and flung her arms around Roland.

John was picking himself off the floor. I went to the connecting hatch and turned the mechanical lock, then took John's arm and slapped the grip of Darla's pistol into his hand. "Keep an eye on that hatch," I told him. "If you so much as hear something, shoot." He nodded.

I went for the wand, picked it up off the floor. It throbbed faintly in my hand, and I rotated the silver band until it stopped. Lori began screaming, rising to her feet with her arms flailing at phantoms. I ripped the sheet off the bed and covered her, wrapping her in my arms. "It was all a dream, honey, all a dream," I whispered in her ear as I walked her over to the overturned coffee table. I scooped up the key and called Sam.

"Sam, it's Jake."

"Jesus Christ! What's going on up there?"

"Everyone's okay. How's your situation?"

"What the hell's all that caterwauling?"

"We're all okay, never mind. What's happening at your end?"

"Everybody left. Went topside, I guess. Something's going on up there."

Just then I heard shouting come from out in the hall. "Yeah, the ship's being attacked. Exactly by what, I don't know. Can you get free down there like you said you could?"

"Sure."

"Then do it and wait for us. We have to find Winnie, and—"

"Winnie's here."

"What! How in hell did she . . .? Never mind, never mind. Good. Okay, listen." I thought fast. "We'll try to make it down there somehow. Be ready to roll."

"Fine. Where to?"

"We're going to find a place to hide until we can negotiate our way off this tuna hotpak dinner."

"But where?"

"Pack plenty of antacid."

23

THE KID WAS awake now, looking around at everyone and blinking. "Good morning," he said. He got up from the bed. I handed him the still-howling Lori and told him to try and calm her down. I went to Darla. She was on her knees, curled into a ball over the unmoving, blanket-shrouded form of her father. The stench of burning flesh and hair filled the room.

"Van," she was moaning. "Oh, Van."

I gripped her shoulders. "Darla, we have to go. The Rikkis."

She began to weep, great violent sobs shaking her body, but there was no sound.

"Darla. We have to leave." I let her go on for a while, then took her arms and gently pulled her away. Her body became rigid, then slowly relaxed. I pulled her to her feet and turned her around. Her face was a contorted mask of pain. I escorted her to the other side of the room and helped her on with her backpack, which I had found near the table. I told Roland to check the corridor. Susan calmed down and he moved her aside. "It's okay," he said, peering out. Far down the corridor came the sound of screaming and general commotion.

"All right," I announced, "everyone move out!"

Lori was hyperventilating. I helped John sling her over his shoulder and held her while he balanced her precariously. I picked up Jimmy's gun and handed it to the kid, then gave Darla her pistol back. It took a while to get everyone ready, but finally I had them filing out into the hall and to the right, hugging the walls, with Roland taking point. Everyone was armed but John and Susan. I was the last one out. I stood at the door and looked at Wilkes. His eyes pleaded with me.

I was about to say something when a low, rumbling sound shook the floor and the connecting hatch suddenly flew to splinters. A Reticulan came striding through, bearing a strange silver weapon of curving surfaces and a bell-shaped business end. I ducked behind the bulkhead and brought the .44 around and fired. The alien's head exploded into puffs of pink mist, shards of chitin clattering against the walls and floor. The body kept walking toward me. I backed away, turned, and ran down the hall, whirling and backpedaling every few steps until I made it to a corner. I stopped for one last look and saw the headless body topple into the hall, its legs still working. No one else came out. The others were looking back at me. I barked at them to keep going.

A little further ahead, the Teelies stopped to pick up their backpacks, which they had left in the hallway. I grabbed John's and struggled into it while we ran. I rushed to the head of the line and told Roland to bring up the rear.

There was smoke in the corridor, and shouting and crashing sounds came from somewhere up ahead. As we neared the source of the disturbance, the smoke got steadily thicker, until we had a choice of turning back or asphyxiating. I did not want to face the Reticulans, and as far as I knew there was no stairway to the lower decks in that direction, which is what we needed. But there was a side corridor nearby that looked like it led to a way out on deck. I ducked down it and made sure everyone followed me before I went to the head of the line again. I cracked the hatch and found that it opened onto the starboard deck, but I wasn't sure I wanted to go out there.

Beyond the railing and out to sea, a blood-red moon squatted on the horizon. Silhouetted against it was the outline of what I took to be another megaleviathan, minus the ship-structure, slowly closing off the *Laputa*'s starboard beam. Above, the air was filled with flying motes of fire. Giant shapes crossed the glowing disk of the moon, batlike, nightmare shapes, and from all around came the sound of great leathery wings flapping. Dots of flame circled the *Laputa* like swarms of fireflies, some suddenly deorbiting to come arcing down on the ship. I heard a thump and looked to my right. One had hit the deck not far away. It bounced against the bulkhead and came to rest against a stack of deckchairs. It was a melon-size flaming ball of something, a pitchlike substance probably, trailing a length of fireproofed braided lanyard. The fabric-and-wood-frame deckchairs ignited immediately. I craned my head out to get a better view. Spot fires flared everywhere along the upper deck, and fire details rushed everywhere, shouting, trailing firehoses like white wriggling snakes. I didn't want to go out there, but there was no choice. I looked for the nearest stairs for B Deck, saw none, but decided it was best to head aft.

"Put me down, God damn it!"

It was Lori, screaming at John. I closed the hatch and walked back. John was setting her down and apologizing profusely. She took a swing at him, missed, and when I took her arm she sent a haymaker toward me. I caught her wrist.

"Lori, settle down! It's me, Jake! Remember?"

Her eyes focused on me and the hysterical hatred drained from her face. She blinked and looked again. "Who? Oh, yeah. Yeah." She looked around, bewildered. "What happened? Where are we?" Then she noticed the sheet and her lack of clothes. "What the punkin' hell . . .?"

"A pirate mega is attacking the ship," I told her, thinking it better to concentrate on the present problem than on past traumas which she may or may not remember. "We have to get belowdecks."

That brought her around. "Are they firebombing?"

"Yes, and it looks like they're pulling alongside to board."

"Where are we?"

"Top deck, starboard, near the bow."

"This way—and hurry!"

We went out on deck and made our way aft, keeping a lookout for falling fireballs. The bombardment continued, but most of the orbiting lights had fallen. It seemed like a coordinated attack, with the bombardment probably scheduled to cease just prior to the boarding attempt. I saw now that the fireballs were making circular epicycles as they orbited, and when two searchlight beams from the ship converged in the air above us and to our right, I saw what bore them. These weren't merely sailing fish, but giant airborne animals that looked like mythical sea serpents, with long tapering bodies and mighty pinions beating the night air. On their backs rode smaller animals, Arfies, from what I could make out. One Arfie in each flight crew, the bombadier, twirled a fireball around his head before letting it go. The ship's exciter batteries were taking their toll. The beast in the searchlight beams blossomed into an orange ball of fire, momentum carrying flaming remnants into a descending arc ahead. But there were too many of them, and apparently only two operating batteries.

"Look out!"

It was Roland, and I looked back. Something was swooping toward us, coming directly from behind. We all hit the deck, and I felt air swoosh over me as the animal passed. It smacked into the deck further ahead and went crashing into a canopied dining terrace, then stopped. We got up and looked, backing away prudently, but before anyone could make the intelligent decision to turn and run, big shapes flopped toward us from out of the darkness—Arfies, four of them, armed with crude axes and other, stranger implements. I shot at one of them but apparently missed, or it may have been that the animal was very hard to bring down. Roland and Darla started firing. Darla's first shot seared off a forward flipper of one of them, but he kept coming too, barking insanely, picking up his dropped weapon with the other flipper and charging. Roland used half a charge to flame another of them in its tracks, then turned the beam on the one I had missed, with the same result. But the two remaining were fast—and big. Up until then I had only seen Arfies at a distance. They were massive beasts, with blubbery rolls of fat padding their undersides and powerful muscles along the flanks to work the flippers. They looked almost nothing like seals or walruses now—more like amphibian versions of a Brahma bull. We backed as we fired. I got off two more shots with little effect, but Darla finally got her target cut to pieces and it slumped over unmoving. Roland was digging in his pockets for another charge, and Darla was now out. I fired my last round at the remaining Arfie, then threw the gun at it. He kept coming and we all ran, scattering, but the thing chose to follow me. I was wondering what happened to the kid. He was off to my right, hitting his gun with his fist as he ran.

"Won't work!" he yelled.

I yelled for him to throw it over and he did. It was an odd

make with a tricky safety catch, which I knew about from having owned one. I thumbed off the safety, turned, and emptied the powerpak in one steady beam right at the creature's head. It was dead by the time it hit me, but it hit like a runaway rig.

The next thing I knew, I was being helped to my feet. I was shaken up, but more or less in one piece.

"You almost flew off the deck," Roland told me, handing me the dream wand, which I had stuffed in my back pocket.

"Thanks." I took the wand and slipped it into a side pocket of John's backpack. I looked aft and saw that the flying sea serpent was still pinned in the wreckage of the dining terrace, its wings snarled in the canvas canopy and thrashing uselessly. "We can't go that way, unless we want to deal with that thing. Lori, can you get us belowdecks another way?"

"We'll have to go back through the ship."

We found the nearest hatch and went back in. Smoke was hanging thick in the corridors. Shouting came from all directions as passengers clogged the halls in an effort to get to the stairways. It was bedlam. Lori took my arm. We followed her back the way we had come, made a few turns, then ducked into a small room lined with cabinets that held bedding and linen. Near the back wall a ladder descended through a hatchway in the floor. I looked down. The ladder went down a long way. She told us these were quick-access shafts, and that only the crew used them. We started down. It took a good while and a few trod-upon fingers before all of us made it down to C Deck, winding up in a storage room full of crates and miscellaneous equipment.

"Where to now?" I asked Lori, taking off my shirt and handing it to her. She had doffed the sheet before taking the ladder.

"Thanks. You'll have to take the ventilation shafts to get below decks. They'll have the elevators shut down."

"Ventilation shafts?"

"Yeah. Otherwise you couldn't breathe down there, leastwise not very well."

It made sense, but I had a question. "Isn't all that air kind of hard on Fiona's tummy?"

"Sometimes. Every so often she burps and it all empties out. That's why you can't stay down there."

"You mean she can burp up a vehicle or two?"

"Sometimes she does, but we spray the sacs down with

antispasmodics to keep that from happening often."

"Well, let's go."

It was a long trek through the ship to the stern. We passed more storerooms, then the crew's quarters, where Lori stopped to get decent. I got my shirt back. We continued aft, past the infirmary and the topside holds, through the crew's mess, the galley, and some workshops, then through a section of economy-class cabins, and finally into heating and ventilation rooms. The machinery was still running, but if the fires got out of control, it wouldn't be for long.

"What happens when the equipment shuts down?" I asked our guide as we climbed through a thicket of pipes.

"Oh, there's enough air down there to last for a while. But if Fiona gets upset over the attack, she may start burping."

"Oh."

Access to the shaft was through a tiny door in a metal cylinder into which fed a maze of piping. "This is the outtake shaft. The intake one has a bunch of filters. Watch the updraft." She held the door open for me. "There are rungs running down it."

I poked my head through and saw a tubular shaft dropping straight down into darkness. The updraft almost made me bang my head against the door frame. I took my head out and stood up. "What about light?"

"I have a torch in my kit bag," John said. "I can lash it to my epaulets. Roland has one too, I think."

I handed him his pack, then said to Lori, "Are you coming?"

"No, I belong here," she said firmly. "I should report for fire detail."

"Well, okay. I don't think you'll be in any danger now, except to answer to Pendergast for hiding Winnie."

"I can handle him." She frowned, and asked, "What are you going to do down there anyway?"

"Find a place to hide," I said, "until I can convince your captain that we're no threat to him . . . or to the Outworlds."

"But you'll never find your way down there. You could wind up as Fiona *merte*."

"Well, I've been called worse."

"But you might hurt her too!" Conflicting impulses crossed and recrossed her mind. Then something hit her and her mouth hung open. "Oh, my God! *Where's Winnie?*"

"She's safe, down in my rig."

"Huh? How did she get down there? And why did she leave

the radio shack? I told her to—" She slapped her forehead. "The siren! The general quarters alarm is right above the shack. She must have got frightened when it went off during the gorgon attack! God, am I stupid," she groaned.

"Don't think about it. Turned out for the best anyway. Just take care of yourself." I gave her a peck on the cheek. "And thanks."

I stooped toward the hatch, but she caught my arm. "No, wait. I want to see if Winnie's all right. I'll go down first."

The updraft actually made it easier to descend, but the rungs were small and slippery, and the shaft started tilting to an awkward angle. I stopped now and then to look up and check everyone's progress. Darla and the men were doing all right, but Susan was struggling with her heavy backpack. I saw her lose her foothold several times, with Darla boosting her rear end back up. We continued the long descent. The air currents weakened as we got further down, then the odd angle worsened until it became a real problem to hang on, making it necessary to use the rungs as handholds only and fight for purchase with our heels against the smooth wall of the shaft, skidding and scuffing our way down. The angle was steep, but further ahead it began to level out. Before we got that far, the shaft began to move, sometimes lurching violently, banging up against us and making it hard to judge where to grab next. I heard a squeal, and before I could look back, Susan slid past me, disappearing into the darkness. Then the shaft buckled crazily and John was next to go. I reached out for him, but missed. The hand grips were almost directly above now and were impossible to grab if you were sliding. The flexible shaft was dancing like a length of rope in the wind, pitching wildly in every direction, and it was Darla's turn next, but I managed to catch her as she passed—and lost my grip in the process.

It was a quick trip down. Very soon we were off the smooth plastic of the tube and onto a wet, warm sliding-board of organ-tissue. In the total darkness, I braced for a sudden stop, not knowing what we were sliding into, but before long I could see light ahead. Then the slope leveled out and we skidded over flat surface for a dozen meters until we stopped. We were soaking wet. A torch beam hit me and then swung to Darla. It was John, and he walked over, Susan with him.

"Interesting idea for an amusement-park ride," he said.

I got up and helped Darla to her feet. "Where are we?" I asked him.

He played the beam ahead and I saw a few parked vehicles in the distance. "Good," I said, got out Sam's key, and was about to call when something hit the back of my legs and bowled me over. It was the kid. He apologized, then groaned, as anyone would with 90 kilos of truckdriver on his chest. I got off him. John swung his light in the direction of the shaft. Lori and Roland were skating toward us like champions, then broke into a nimble trot over the treacherous surface until they reached us.

"You people were in a hurry," Lori said cheerily.

"What was all that jerking around about?" I asked.

"Oh, that's nothing. We don't bother to spray down empty areas. And the floor's so slippery because we didn't put down rosin here."

"Oh." I keyed Sam.

"Where are you now?"

"Turn on your high beams."

He wasn't more than a minute's walk away.

After me, it was Lori whom Winnie hugged when we all got in, and I was at a loss to explain how Winnie could have gotten any sense of betrayal from Darla, for clearly she had. At first, she barely acknowledged her onetime friend and interpreter. Perhaps she read the guilt in Darla's face, invisible to me, but by now Winnie's empathic powers were a given. I only wondered as to their extent. Whatever that was, I knew that Winnie's second sight was keen enough to see Darla's grief, and perhaps her regret at using Winnie as a pawn, because before long Winnie was hugging Darla too, her capacity for forgiveness and compassion probably greater than anything. It was a moment of revelation for me, because up until then I really didn't have a robust sense of Winnie's personhood, couldn't really accept her as the thinking, feeling being she obviously was. I didn't know what prejudices had gotten in the way; I have my share, but maybe the problem had been a simple lack of attention on my part. Winnie's subtle brand of personality and intelligence were easy to lose amid the gunfire, the frantic chases, the noise, and the intrigue. Her innate shyness and reticence didn't help either. All along I had caught glimmers of the light she was hiding under a bushel of soft, ape-brown hair, but I hadn't had the time nor the opportunity to groom through the shag and see what was glowing. Nor did

I now. We had to get somewhere, and quickly. But where?

"The pyloric tube between this sac and Fiona's starboard stomach-cluster would be best," Lori said.

"Sounds cozy," I said, thinking that it sounded horrible. But before we could get going, we had the kid to contend with. He said he was coming along for the ride, but was adamant about finding his car.

"I don't want my Chevy burped up like a pizza," he told us.

"Where we're going," I said, "it could wind up as whale food."

"Not my car, buddy."

I silently agreed with him. That vehicle could give anyone an ulcer. The kid borrowed John's torch and walked off into the gloom. Lori said that there was something she wanted to look for, and left too. The rest of us took the opportunity to get out of wet clothes. The digestive fluid was beginning to eat through them and irritate the skin. Susan wailed that her new suit was ruined. I told her to shove all our laundry in the Sonikleen right away.

Lori returned first, carrying a piece of gear that consisted of two tanks worn on the back, connected to a length of hose with a spraygun on the end. She explained that one tank contained aluminum hyroxide, the other an antispasmodic chemical.

"It numbs Fiona up so she doesn't get the dry heaves," she said.

About ten minutes later the kid's strange vehicle pulled alongside us in the aisle. Abused vehicles lay all around, the result of Sam's forcing his way out of the pack. I hoped Pendergast's insurance was paid up. I convinced the kid that the best bet would be to drive his car into the trailer. The observatory equipment only made up a quarter-load and was stashed in our special "eggcrate" section for fragile goods. We had plenty of room. Sam slid out the ramp and let him in. I went back to look the trailer over, check for damage. The stargazer stuff seemed in good shape for all the rocking it had taken, but then Sam and I specialize in hauling delicate equipment, especially scientific gear. I improvised some chock-blocks for the Chevy out of spare bracing bars from the eggcrate nook, then looped tether lines through the Chevy's shiny chromium—

"Hey! What d'you call these things?"

"Bumpers."

—bumpers, and tied the lines off as taut as I could. It would have to do.

After Sam sealed up the trailer, we were ready. I started up and pulled away, heading for the part of the sac that was devoid of vehicles. There the floor got slippery again and started a gentle slope downward. Lori warned me to go slowly, and I took heed. The ceiling lowered and the walls got closer, the passage narrowing finally into a tunnel. The walls seeped clear fluid in glistening sheets, rolling and billowing like a flag in a soft breeze. The passage started to wind, then became serpentine. We slithered along until we encountered an obstacle, a white disk of tissue sealing off the passage like a drumhead. It was a valve. Lori told me to ease up to it and give it a nudge, which I did. After some prodding, the valve dilated and we went through. From there we wound our way back along the tube, passing more valves which plugged other passages branching to the side. We continued on the main route for a few more minutes until Lori told me to stop. She got into her spray gear and stepped out. When the door opened, an acrid, vomity stench found its way in. Everyone gagged. The walls here were more active, rippling excitedly in little waves that traversed the tube from rear to front. Lori sprayed the walls down with white goop, and in a minute or two things calmed down. She got back in. There was enough good air in the compressors to get most of the vomit-smell out, but enough lingered to make the wait uncomfortable. But we waited.

"How long should we stay down here?" John asked.

"Until the fight's over, whenever that is," I replied. "But if the ship is seized . . . well, it's anybody's guess."

"We'll win," Lori said confidently. "We always do."

"Why do the pirates want to take over another mega?"

"Theirs is probably getting old. Megas are scarce. Who knows? They may just hate humans."

"Very likely," John said sardonically. "Humans are the beings you love to hate. Suzie, could you move over a bit?"

It was very cramped inside the cab. Everyone shifted positions in the back seat for optimum comfort. Darla and Winnie were in the aft cabin.

John began, "Strange to find pirates on—"

The rig suddenly shivered, then nosed forward and began to slide. I braked, but it did no good. We slid forward for a few meters before the tube leveled again. The walls were heaving inward now, constricting around the rig and squeezing.

"Fiona's spasming," Lori said, looking worried. "The attack must be disturbing her. I'd better spray again."

"Wait," I told her as the tube buckled and whipped around, the contractions squirting us farther forward. We waited for it to stop. "Okay, now."

We watched Lori spray the tunnel around us liberally. The rig got shoved forward again and I had to give Lori a blast on the horn to warn her. She turned, lost her footing and slipped, but crawled out of the way in time. She continued spraying until she ran out of stuff, then mounted the boarding rungs to get back in. Just as she got her head through the hatch, Fiona spasmed again and the rig jerked forward. The edge of the hatchway caught Lori smartly against the side of the head. Roland reached and caught her before she fell out. He hauled her in and the hatch slammed shut by itself. The tube twitched and jittered all around us, the floor dropping out from under again, and we slid along the pyloric tube like the undigested bit of food that we were. This time we didn't stop. I didn't want to reverse the transmission, thinking that the rasp of the rollers would only irritate Fiona more. The walls continued their inexorable urging, closing over the rig like wet folds of cloth, leaving smears of fluid across the ports.

"Hang on, everybody! Get strapped in as best you can. Get Lori strapped into the bunk."

A temporary lull allowed them to get Lori bedded down and secured, then the spasming began again. Roland got thrown forward and whumped up against my seat.

"Hang on to something!" I barked. "I don't want any more casualties." Then I laughed to myself. To be Fiona-*merte* was our destiny right then, and I couldn't see a way out of it.

It was an endless fateful journey. We got bounced, buffeted, and thrown around. The organ walls bore down relentlessly, slobbering over the hull of the rig. We rolled counterclockwise, went over forty-five degrees, then came back to vertical and keeled over the other way all the way to ninety and stayed there.

"Sam!" I yelled. "Anything we can do?"

"I was just thinking that this is probably the most ridiculous situation you've ever gotten yourself into."

"What?"

"I said, I was just thinking to myself—"

"I heard, I heard! You're a godsend, did you know that?"

"What?"

We passed through a valve, and I totally lost my bearings. We could have been upside down for all I knew. Somebody's leg flopped over my shoulder and I chinned it away. Somebody screamed. Visibility was zero, the headbeams reflecting off greenish-white tissue and half-blinding me. I wanted to turn them off but was afraid to take my hands from the control bars, useless as they were. Powerful contractions began, forcing us ahead in a kind of hellish birth process. The pitching and swaying lessened as Fiona settled down to the task of pushing us on to our destiny within the world of her bowels. After a few minutes—it seemed longer—we squirted through another valve and suddenly, mercifully, it was over. We hit water and were totally submerged. The rig bottomed on something soft, cab-first, then the trailer. I heard the antijackknifing servos groan, straightening the trailer out. Then we started moving forward again, more gently this time, carried by an inexorable flow of water.

My passengers sorted themselves out and came up for air. Everyone was okay. John came forward to the shotgun seat and strapped himself in. I tried to keep the rig trimmed out straight, but the current was carrying the trailer around into a jackknife that the servos couldn't handle. Countersteering did no good, so I said to hell with it and hit the antifishtail jets. Through the sideview I could dimly see the gas bubbling away into the water. We were inside another tube, this one bigger, with walls that looked more rigid.

"Where the hell are we?" Sam said.

"Don't know, but it's a good guess we're out of the digestive system," I said.

"How'd we manage that?"

"Fiona must have a way of sorting the stuff she does and doesn't want to digest. We don't rate as food, I guess."

"Not worth *merte*, are we?"

The current grew stronger. We floated from time to time, bounding along, washed forward like flotsam in a rain sewer. I settled back and kept the rig trimmed as best I could, not wanting to broach to and start tumbling. It wasn't easy, but I managed. We went along like that for a bit until the passage narrowed and the water pressure increased. I lost all control then, but the rig kept itself straight by rebounding off the sides of the tube. The tissue-material was darker here, and tougher-looking. The back end slammed against it, then the cab.

Soon, a rushing, rumbling sound grew, along with a low throbbing pulse-sound, and the water churned and grew bubbly. The turbulence shook us, but compared to the gastric action, it was nothing. The rushing sound increased gradually to a dull roar.

"Hull temperature's been increasing steadily," Sam informed me.

"Yeah? Well, now I think I know how Fiona propels herself. She must have a gill system that circulates water through her and shoots it out the back end. The system must carry off waste heat too." I looked out and saw a dark opening ahead.

"Sounds reasonable," Sam said. "Trouble is, this rig is no submarine."

After a final surge and a burst of thunderous sound we left Fiona for calmer waters. The water outside was a blizzard of bubbles, gradually dissipating as we sank nose-first into the depths. I told Sam to keep up readings on the outside pressure, but it proved unnecessary. In the headbeams I could see a muddy sea bottom coming up fast. I groped around frantically for something to do to keep the nose up, but couldn't find anything. Fortunately the floor sloped downward and away, and the front rollers hit neatly. The cab slid forward and let the trailer fall in gently behind. We came to a stop.

"How far down are we, Sam?"

"About eighty meters."

"Well, that's not too bad."

"Sure, we'll just swim."

"Let's see if we can't do a little better than that."

I nursed the engine until the drive rollers were spinning slowly, then twisted the traction-control handles on the bars to maximum grab, and the rollers caught. We moved forward through a lake of sludge. The slope bottomed out into a trough and then the sea floor began to rise again, only to dip once more, continuing into a series of rolling hills.

"How's Lori?" I called back. A moment later Darla came forward.

"She's still out. Definitely a concussion, but her pupils are responding to light. But you can never—" Lori's scream interrupted her, and she rushed back.

"Sam, how did Winnie wind up with you?" I asked.

"I was going to ask the same question. There were a whole bunch of sailors snooping around me, and she must've sneaked through them somehow. I kept hearing a faint knock and I couldn't figure out what it was, and I couldn't locate anything on any of the monitors. So I took a chance and cracked a hatch open. And Winnie crawled through."

"Amazing," I said. Addressing the Teelies I said, "By the way, people, you all did fine—many thanks. But how the hell did you know where to find me?"

"We didn't," John said. "But Darla told us about Wilkes and your predicament. She didn't tell us much, something about a dispute between your truckdriver guild and the other one. Anyway, when Darla vanished on us, we overtipped a few stewards and some of the other help to get some information. We didn't get much, but we did find out Wilkes' cabin number. We assumed the worst."

"Again, many thanks."

"Nothing, really. I only had a mild heart attack."

"Jake, unless I'm badly mistaken," Sam said, "we're going up."

The rolling hills continued for a while, then the sea bottom began to rise, turning from sludge to mud, then to packed sand. We were in a tidal area; no vegetation to speak of.

Lori stopped screaming and began crying. She had remembered the Rikkis. Darla and Susan comforted her.

It was another half hour before we made the beach. I drove through the breakers and up onto dry sand, pulled behind a dune, and parked. I had doused the lights as soon as we had broken water. Then I got out.

About ten kilometers offshore, the *Laputa* was burning, a smeared orange glow on the dark horizon. I sat in the sand and watched it burn.

Presently, a face took shape in my mind, the one that was a blank in my memory of someone bending over me in my cell at the Militia station. It was my face.

Me.

24

It was a brave dawn, the disk-edge of a molten sun just showing above the vanishing point of the Skyway. The land was flat, magnificently flat, the kind of terrain the Roadbuilders had favored. A film of low rust-colored grass covered everything from sky to sky, bisected by the black line of the road. A brave dawn, cloudless and clear.

We were taking a break before going on. We had spent all night finding the road, with Winnie's help, and now she was drawing her figures on some lading sheets with a pen that Roland taught her how to hold. He and the Teelies watched her draw, sitting with her in the grass by the road. The kid was inside the rig watching over Lori, who was less hysterical now. I told him to make sure she didn't fall asleep. It looked as if she would be all right.

It was quiet, no wind at all, and the land was empty all around. Before dawn, we had seen some lights off the road; farmhouses most likely, but they were few. This was virgin land.

I drew Darla aside.

"Make a short story long and tell me, Darla. Who are you? And what are you?"

"My name is Daria Vance," she said, then took a deep breath. "Surviving daughter of the late Dr. Van Wyck Vance."

"And the legal lifecompanion of Grigory Petrovsky. No?"

"Grigory Vasilyevich Petrovsky. Yes. Or his widow."

"Is that grief? Or hope, maybe?"

"Neither," she answered quietly.

"All right, so much for what I know. What I don't know is who has the Roadmap."

"You mean the real one, don't you?"

"I mean the one I brought back. It wasn't Winnie."

"No, it wasn't. That's why I was willing to give her to Wilkes in exchange for your life."

"But aren't Winnie's maps accurate?"

"I don't know that yet. They seem to be. Jake, you don't understand. Winnie was a total surprise to me, and when I made my contact with the dissident network on Goliath, nobody knew about her."

"The contact. That wasn't Petrovsky?"

A grunt of ironic laughter. "No."

"Why did you shoot at the flitter?"

"For the reasons I told you about." She turned to look at the sunrise. "And of course, I didn't want to be Grigory's prisoner."

"His prisoner?"

She looked at me intently, her small nostrils flaring. "At no time was I working for Grigory during this."

I settled myself in the grass. "Darla, why don't you start from the beginning? Tell me the story of your life."

She told me. About three years ago she was a graduate student at the University of Tsiolkovskygrad, and got involved with the dissident movement, peripherally at first, then more deeply. She found that the movement was vastly more organized than she had thought, but, like most revolutionary organizations, was confined to a small cadre of activists, in this case the usual assortment of bohemian hangers-on one finds around universities—*artistes-mangués*, dropouts, perpetual students, oddballs, and other perennial types—along with some genuinely idealistic younger students and seriously committed faculty. From this intellectual hub, the movement radiated out to the colonies to encompass a fair number of people from all walks of life. Politically, the movement was a hodgepodge of ideologies, from the beady-eyed right to the bearded, bomb-throwing left, with most everything in between, including a smidge of religious doctrine. (Wilkes had been halfway justified in suspecting the Teelies, though Darla was fairly sure that they had no formal affiliation with the movement.) Then, at a dinner party her father gave, Darla met Petrovsky, who took an immediate interest in her. The interest was not mutual. However, the dissidents thought it a dandy idea to have a pair of ears in the same bed with a high-ranking Militiaman, especially an intelligence officer. Darla was asked if she were willing to make the supreme sacrifice. She was. It wasn't very long after the signing ceremony that Darla was approached by her lifecompanion's superiors and asked to become an informer—asked, in fact, to inform on friends who were suspected of being subversive. For some reason, possibly because of who and what her father was, it never occurred to them that Darla might be a dissident herself. Why should she turn against her father and her class? (That the bureaucracy was a social class couldn't be doubted, though to speak of it as such a thing was ideological heresy.) And hadn't she married within the Authority?

"In other words, you became something of a double agent."

"Right," she affirmed. "It was exactly what the movement was hoping for. We were then in a position to feed disinformation to the Authority."

"All right," I said. "Now, from what I've gathered, this Roadmap is real enough, and so was my backtime trip. Okay. When did I come back? And who did I give the map to?"

"About eight months ago, you barged into Assemblywoman Marcia Miller's office and dropped it on her desk. I think your exact words were, 'Happy birthday, honey.'"

"That's all I said?"

"No, otherwise she would have taken you for a crank, and the thing would still be on her desk, probably being used as a paperweight. You mentioned my name and the fact that I was a double agent, and that you knew, quote, 'all there was to know about the dissident movement,' unquote—and told her what the object was."

"Wait a minute. Was her office de-bugged?"

"At the time, yes, or so I was told. And since the Authority didn't immediately act to seize her and the map, it probably was."

"Okay. I have more questions about the map, but let me clear up some other things first. How did you get assigned to me? And who assigned you?"

"The network did. Around the same time when you came on the scene, my situation vis-à-vis the Authority became untenable. We learned then that the Authority's infiltration of the movement was very deep, a fact even I hadn't been able to uncover, but you have to remember that I was primarily a conduit for bogus information from the movement to the Authority. And when my disinformation started sticking out like a sore thumb, I was compromised. I had to go underground." She smiled wanly and shook her head. "A misnomer. There is no underground. I took to the Skyway, as everyone does who wants to stay loose." She ran her fingers gently through the grass. "That was when Grigory got kicked upstairs to his dead-end job."

"And when your father became an unperson?"

"No. His trouble goes farther back."

I mulled it all over for a while, then said, "Here's a very big question. When you first got in my rig, why did you act as if we'd met before?"

"I wasn't acting. The first time was about two months after you gave the map to Miller. We had been tailing you. For some reason, it was very easy, and since I've gotten to know you better, I can't help but think that you wanted to be tailed."

"Where did I go?"

"From planet to planet, no particular pattern to it."

"Was I alone?"

"Yes. Just you and Sam."

"And you tried to pump me about maps and things, but got nowhere."

"Exactly. I gave up and ducked out on you, and we dropped most of the surveillance. By that time our technical people had had a chance to examine the object you handed over. It was apparent to them that the thing was a product of an unknown technology."

"But they weren't sure it was a map?"

She nodded. "Oh, yes, they were sure. But the nature of the data was so complex, it was practically indecipherable. I was told to find you and try again to get more information. By that time, it seemed everyone in creation knew about you, about the map, everything. We then got a report that you were seen in Hydran Maze. You were tailed from there to Barnard's, where you picked up a load, the one you're carrying now. We found out you were going to deliver it to Uraniborg. On the way there you picked me up for the second time. The first time."

The Paradox was real.

"How did Wilkes get into all this?"

She lowered her eyes. "Through me. I told my father about the map." She looked up at me defensively. "The Authority was closing in. There have been scores of arrests recently. Nothing about it in the news feeds, only the vaguest hints. The map-object was a hot potato being passed from hand to hand, sometimes minutes before the knock on the door. It looked as if the map would wind up in the Authority's hands after all. That was when I told him. He was going to take me with him—here." A single, gelid tear welled in the corner of her left eye. "I tried to save him. . . . I tried to save the movement . . . both . . . I—" She bent over and wet the grass with bitter tears.

I let her cry as long as she needed to, then took her shoulders and lifted her from the grass, gently pried her hands from her face. "I need to know one thing more, Darla. What is it? The object, I mean. And who has it now?"

A mantle of calm settled over her. She stopped quivering and her breathing slowed. She did her straightening-up ritual, then took a deep breath. She reached for her pack, withdrew an ordinary-looking makeup box and opened the lid. It contained face coloring, the kind some women use for those partial Kabuki masks that are in vogue now, the kind of makeup job a lifecompanion of a high Authority 'crat might wear to the opera. She dug in two fingers and plucked out a black object. She wiped it off with a spare shirt from her pack, then took my hand. She pressed it into my palm. It was a jet-black cube about fifty millimeters on a side.

"You do, Jake. You have it now."

Stunned, I sat and gaped at it. The color was the blackest black I had ever seen. It wouldn't have made a good paperweight; the thing was like air in my hand.

"Touch two leads to it at any point," Darla said, "and you get a flood of binary numbers in a patterned sequence. No one's been able to figure it out, but the best guess is that it's a multidimensional coordinate system. No doubt touching leads to it isn't the proper way of getting the information out."

I rose to my feet shaking my head, confounded beyond words.

"I know," she said. "It's a closed loop. The Paradox. A future self gives you—the past self—something that he got from a future self when *he* was the past. . . . It's a classic contradiction. Where did the thing come from in the first place?" She got up, drew near me, and put a hand on my chest. "No one planned it this way. We gave up trying to make any sense out of the cube. And just a few days ago, when the Authority finally acted on what they got from running a Delphi on Miller, there was no one around to take the relay but me. I couldn't leave the cube behind. When you picked me up the second time, I wasn't sure about the Paradox. It was just rumor then. I thought you were . . . the 'you' who handed the cube over. You weren't."

I walked away from Darla, transfixed, holding the cube as if it were about to explode in my hand. I don't know how long I stared at it. Presently, I was aware of being near Winnie and the others.

Roland came over to me, an excited look on his face.

"Jake, it's fantastic!" he bubbled. "Winnie's map, I mean. There's a beltway, Jake. A beltway that circles the galaxy, spiraling in to the core. And as near as I can tell, about ten thousand light-years from here on the outer arm, there's a junction with a route that connects up the Local Group." He seized my shoulder. "The Local Group! Jake, can you believe it? The damn road goes all the way to Andromeda!" He squinted at the dark cube in my hand. "What the hell's that?"

I didn't answer, and walked away.

The sun was halfway up now, painting the sky with rosy promise, and the black road ran straight into it.